Gutter Punk
City Streets Trilogy, Book Three
By Susanne Perry

GUTTER PUNK

First edition. March 18, 2021.

Written by Susanne Perry.

For Taylor, Shae, and Haley

"And these children that you spit on as they try and change their world, are immune to your consultations; they are well aware of what they're going through."

David Bowie

"The only thing that may save us as a species is seeing how we're not thinking about future generations in the way we live."

Erik Erickson

Chapter One

"A Cold World"

"We need to get out of here, Pooki," whispered Elle. "We've been here for, like, two days."

"Yeah," answered Pooki. "I'm sick of these dudes. I'm sick of their faces, and I'm sick of them beating on us for kicks." Pooki wanted to cry, but she was too tired and in too much pain. And she was angry. Angry, physically hurt, and scared. "I hope they don't hear us talking, Elle. Do you think they can hear us?"

"I don't know. They're pretty sauced. If they keep drinking, maybe they'll pass out," said Elle. She was as exhausted and hurt as her friend. She had bruises on her face, arms, and shoulders. The least the creeps could do was to offer the kids some of their whiskey to take the edge off.

There were two of them. The younger one was a skinny dude. He had offered Pooki food and a place to stay. They met up in the alley behind Mahli's Asian Café where Pooki was searching the dumpster for something to eat. Pooki had asked Elle to come with her because they were safer together. It hadn't mattered this time.

The skinny guy was okay at first, but he turned weird. He got mean and he enjoyed it when things became violent. It crossed Elle's mind that he might be a spotter with the West Coast Track, looking for young bodies to traffic. If he was, Elle knew that she and Pooki were done. Neither of them would be seen or heard from again.

They didn't know the other guy existed until they got to the address. This second guy was older and not too bright. He was a big guy. He liked to hit and he hit hard. It was too late for Elle and Pooki to wonder if they had been overheard. The assholes were coming back from the other room.

"Forget it, you little shit!" hollered the big, old guy. "You're not going anywhere. You still owe me for food. What about the movies you been watching? Who paid for that, huh? We even let you take a shower and clean up your scrawny ass." He grabbed Elle by the hair and started to shake her. It was the guy's version of foreplay. The attacks had been going on since yesterday.

Elle had had enough but the jerk wouldn't leave her alone. "Please, man, I can't take anymore. You gotta give me a break, okay?"

"A break, you freeloading piece of shit?" he shouted at Elle. "Here's all the break you get, now shut your mouth!" He hit Elle so hard on the side of her head that she saw stars.

The old guy went after Elle again. He wasn't taking no for an answer, and his buddy was laughing at the show, enjoying it like staged entertainment. Pooki grabbed the closest thing at hand—a dinner plate. It was heavy, thick, ceramic. She smashed the plate into the guy's head. He went down on his belly, his pants around his knees. He was stunned, but he wasn't knocked out. Elle climbed out from under him, eyes wide.

"You little fuck!" screamed the skinny guy, sticking up for his moron friend. Then Elle and Pooki saw the knife in his hand. He started slashing the blade around in wild arcs, punctuated with stabbing motions. He was fueled by whiskey and outraged that two street kids would dare to defend themselves.

Elle stayed low and scrambled away. Pooki tried to move a safe distance from the swinging knife, but she was right in the path of the blade. Before she could back away, the knife sliced across the side of her abdomen. Blood spurted and Pooki's hand flew to her wound. She sunk down to the floor, wide-eyed.

The skinny asshole couldn't believe what he'd done. He stared at the knife for a moment, and then he tossed it to the floor. Elle didn't think twice—she reached down, grabbed the knife from where it had landed and pointed the bloodied blade at the two creeps.

"Stay the fuck where you are!" Elle screamed. The older one had pulled his pants up by now and started to make a move toward the knife. Elle looked at him and said, "Go ahead you crazy asshole, you think you're faster than me? I owe you some painful shit right about now!" It was a surprise to Elle that the moron stopped. He stared at the blade in her hand. Elle heard his labored breathing. He grunted. Apparently, the sight of blood hadn't sobered him up.

Keeping the knife out in front of her, her eyes peeled on the creeps, Elle reached for a dish towel that had been left on the table. She scooped Pooki up off the floor and pushed the towel into the wound. Pooki moaned with pain. There was a lot of blood, but Elle had to ignore that for now and get them the hell out of there. She put Pooki's arm around her shoulder and they backed out the front door. Elle and Pooki stumbled down the front walk of the crummy place. Elle tossed the knife into a rhododendron bush and they headed down the dark street to find help.

Chapter Two

"The City Council Meeting"

Pomp was the word that came to Liz's mind. Yes, pomp bordering on puffery. She hated it. Liz had no patience for public displays of municipal self-importance. She had witnessed these City Council meetings drone on and on and still accomplish nothing. When called upon to attend, Liz had to restrain a strong inclination to scream, *just get on with it!* Instead, she appreciated pragmatism, that emotion-sparing, matter-of-fact approach to problems that didn't waste precious time. As a cop, Liz valued quick, common sense decisions because time was too valuable and sentiment had no place in law enforcement. Useless fanfare, as she saw it, had no place in her world either, and for this she was glad.

The atmosphere in the council chamber this morning, however, was different. The proceedings were flavored with barely-contained hostility. It was like sitting on the lid of a tea kettle about to boil. Members of the community had interrupted their morning routines to attend. Many had reached the end of their patience and were determined to be heard.

Liz sat with Mike toward the back of the expansive hall. The captain Liz reported to at the precinct had asked her to attend and Mike was there to support a new colleague. Considering their areas of expertise, either of them could be called upon for input. They hoped it wouldn't come to that.

The members of the City Council listened as several speakers aired concerns about the street kids who congregated downtown. The kids sat in doorways and panhandled, they said. They overran the park and took over street corners, said the speakers. Columbia City wasn't as large as Portland, the nearest major city across the river to the south, but neither did it have the resources the larger city could call upon. The pros and cons attributed to urban areas were relative anyway.

A downtown businesswoman was at the speaker's podium. She had given her name, but Liz didn't catch it. Liz thought she recognized the woman as the proprietor of a sandwich shop located near the park.

"I've tried to be decent to the street kids." she stated. "I asked them, as nicely as possible, to please move along. My customers can't even get in the door. They try to be understanding, my customers. I apologize and thank them for their patience, but who wants to meet for lunch at a place where they have to wade through a group of dirty kids to get in the door?"

"If you weren't giving those gutter punks food, maybe they would stay away from the storefronts!" The outburst came from a man sitting behind her in the front row. Many in the crowd nodded at his outburst, murmuring their agreement.

"That's enough! Quiet, please," returned the Council Chair. "Sir, you will have an opportunity to speak, but please respect the time allotted to the current speaker. If you interrupt again, you will be asked to leave."

"But it's true, damn it! Don't you get it?" The man had heard enough and was too irate to control his anger beyond shaking his head and chuckling with disgust. "She complains about the street kids, but they know they'll get a free meal if they hang near her doorway. And when they move up the block, they end up in front of my place. I'm an accountant. I have nothing they want! I can't entice them with anything to get the hell away!"

A few people in the audience responded with their support of the man's plight. A couple of people stood and applauded his remarks.

Liz listened and watched, waiting for the scene to turn ugly. The Chair motioned to the guard at the door. The uniformed officer approached the man who had made the angry outbursts. "You need to come with me, Sir," he said, his deep voice full of authority,

"Fine. I'm leaving," he said, waving his arms in frustration, side-stepping the other attendees seated in the first row. "This was a worthless attempt, trying to talk to you people anyway." He pointed to the Council Chair. "When you arrive at your office in the morning, how often do you have to clean up piss—or worse—from outside your doorway? Huh? That's how I started my day three times in the past month!"

As he and the officer reached the end of the aisle, the man turned around and shouted, "And it does no good to call the police. I've tried! They tell me these punks are breaking no laws!" The officer gripped the man's upper arm with the intent of leading him up the aisle toward the door.

As the man was escorted out, the Chair attempted to regain control of the meeting. "This is a public proceeding," he spoke firmly, temper in check. "We encourage you to exercise your right to speak, but I will insist that our business be conducted with a degree of decorum."

Satisfied that the meeting could continue, the Chair addressed the woman from the sandwich shop. "Are there other points you wish to make before we hear the next speaker?"

"He's probably right," she said, with resignation, referring to the man who had interrupted her. "I give the kids food that would be thrown out anyway. I ask them to take it to the park or somewhere else," she explained. "I never intend for them to bother my neighbors. I apologize, but what they do is out of my control." She shook her head in defeat, picked up her things from the podium, and prepared to return to her seat in the audience.

A young woman near the front of the room stood and asked to be recognized by the Chair. She was tall and from where Liz sat in the back of the chamber, she could see the shock of short, jet-black hair. It was Quinn, Mike's new colleague.

"May I address the comments we've heard?" The Chair directed Quinn to the podium and the young woman stepped up to speak. "My name is Quinn Hadley. I know many of you already, but if we haven't met, I'm the director of the City Youth Center."

"Our goal is to help kids get home, or with extended family or friends, if that's the better option. Too often, we're lucky if kids will accept a meal and a place to clean up or rest safely. Having said that, I understand that the gentleman who interrupted was out of line, but I understand his frustration. He's running a business and he was probably there long before the kids." Many of the people in the audience nodded in agreement.

"The way some of the kids behave can be irritating; sometimes it can be alarming. Please remember that acting like a responsible adult is learned behavior. Too often, kids are on the street before they have acquired those skills. And they have not learned to trust or they've been hurt by trusting the wrong people."

Quinn turned her attention to the audience, indicating the woman who had been speaking. "This woman is trying to help. On the face of it, she's doing the best she can and I won't fault her for that."

"What do you suggest, Ms. Hadley?" asked the Chair. "Many of our citizens need some course of action, at least in the short term."

"First of all, the City must keep the public restrooms in the park open and well lighted. What the gentleman described is disgusting, but it's going to happen when people don't have access to facilities. And it's not just street kids. Our city has a large population of people experiencing homelessness in varying degrees. Some are families dealing with a temporary setback, but others have been on the streets for a long time. Some of these folks are ill, physically or mentally and it's not as if we can force them to receive care. Drug use is rampant. Services aiding people with addictions are overwhelmed."

Quinn paused for a moment and surveyed the faces of council members on the panel, hoping to strike a deal. "As for the street kids, if the city will do its part with facilities, we can offer help to merchants and other businesses downtown.

Call us if you are having a problem with kids near your business. We will talk to them and try to intervene," said Quinn as she handed out business cards. "The gentleman was correct that the police can't do much if the street kids aren't breaking a law. I can't promise results, but our staff can try. We have more time to deal with the kids than the police."

That was certainly the truth, thought Liz. A police lieutenant, she was responsible for a crew of homicide investigators with more to worry about than a few street kids crowding doorways.

Mike leaned over to Liz and whispered, "That could work. At least, it's worth a try." The years in social work had taught Mike Dwyer that the job was all about doing more with less. The previous year, the City Council had asked Mike to manage their emergency housing facilities, otherwise known as the homeless shelters. Mike agreed to do the job for two years. He'd gone from managing one shelter to four, including the Youth Center. That meant that Mike was Quinn Hadley's boss.

Liz heard positive responses to Quinn's offer. People in the audience were at the point of trying anything. They all knew something had to be done about the gutter punks.

Chapter Three

"The Punks"

Checking the time, Liz whispered to Mike, "I need to head to the precinct. Walk me out?"

"Sure," Mike answered. "Things are winding down. I'll wait for Quinn in the lobby."

They were seated only a few steps from the heavy, double entry doors. Liz and Mike made their way into the lobby, which ran the entire breadth of the one-story building, the street entrance at the center. A few benches were placed along both sides, large potted plants stood sentry between them. Tall windows encompassed the front of the lobby and captured the frenetic street scene of a busy morning in Columbia City.

Mike noticed the angry man who had been escorted out. He was standing near the exit to the street. He held a phone to his ear, listening but not speaking.

"Give me a minute," Mike said to Liz as he stepped away. Liz watched Mike approach the man. She was curious, but hung back. She watched the man put his phone away and shake the hand Mike offered.

Mike wore his hair a bit longer these days and his button-down collar, no tie, and khakis gave him the look of either a social worker or a teacher. Liz knew teachers. She had been raised by two of them.

The chamber doors opened and the attendees emerged in small groups. No one looked happy, the anxiety thick.

Many were engaged in conversations while others made their way to the exit, hurrying to get on with their mornings.

Quinn was speaking with the sandwich shop owner. The woman was holding one of Quinn's business cards. She nodded at whatever Quinn was saying, looking a little less dejected. Their conversation ended and the woman walked toward the exit.

"It could have turned to shit in there," said Quinn, glancing around the lobby as she stepped over to Liz. The women were of the same height, but that's where the similarity in appearance ended. Quinn's short, black hair was in contrast to Liz's mid-length blonde. She wore a short, flowing dress with a denim jacket, serious laced boots and huge earrings. Large, dark eyes, dramatically lined, worked in contrast with ivory skin. The ensemble would have looked ridiculous on Liz, but it worked on Quinn. Liz was in her usual: a striped oxford shirt, slacks and jacket. No jewelry, little make-up. No frills.

"It didn't escalate, thanks to you," Liz acknowledged as she surveyed the crowd. "You managed to step up at the right moment."

"I tried to give options, maybe a little perspective," answered Quinn, "like reminding the council chair that even street folks need to use a bathroom once in a while."

Liz, in her late thirties, had a few years on Quinn, the Youth Advocate. The two met during an investigation the prior year and it had been Liz who introduced Quinn to Mike.

"For a morning meeting, it drew a good-sized crowd," Liz mentioned. Quinn looked in Mike's direction, saw that he was in conversation with the man who had become so angry. Liz followed her gaze. They watched as Mike and the man parted company. The man left the building, cell phone again in hand.

"I feel for him," Quinn told Liz. "I feel for all the businesses, but attacking each other isn't going to help. And what of the punks? Many of these kids are in serious need of help. Most of them haven't learned how to meet their own needs in 'socially acceptable' ways. A lot of adults, privileged or struggling, either forget that or never realized it because their homes of origin were stable and caring."

Quinn paused for a moment, took a deep breath. "Sorry. You already know my feelings. I try not to come off like a bitch, but how many of these business owners slept on the street when they were fifteen?"

"No need to tell me," Liz responded. "You know more about the punks than most of them do anyway."

"Quinn. Good job in there," said Mike as he returned to where the women were standing. "Well said. I'm sure people appreciated it."

"Thanks," Quinn told Mike. "We attempted something similar in Seattle with some success. It helps for us to be visible on the streets. That's where the kids are."

"True. Just remember to stay safe," Mike reminded Quinn.

"Sure," Quinn replied, "but I'm concerned with the safety of the kids, too. Many of these kids hang out in busy areas because they are scared, especially the younger ones."

Liz and Mike nodded at Quinn's words. The woman knew a lot about life on the streets. She had gained her knowledge the hard way. As a teenager, Quinn had survived the streets as a gutter punk in Seattle.

"What was that about? Liz asked Mike, referring to the conversation with the man ejected from the meeting. "Do you know him?"

Mike sighed. "I do know him, but not well. I've forgotten his name. He even told me again, Harry or Harvey maybe, but hell, I don't remember. He's not a bad guy. I was surprised he responded the way he did. He didn't hear what Quinn had to say. I wanted him to know that she and her staff would try to help. Also, I told him I understood his frustration, but that yelling at his neighbors wasn't helping. He agreed."

Liz wondered if Mike was acquainted with the man through sobriety support meetings. It wasn't her business so she wouldn't ask. Respecting the man's privacy, Mike wouldn't tell her anyway.

"When people don't know what to do, they feel powerless and look to place blame," said Liz. "Cops see it all the time."

"It's a kind of a compassion fatigue," said Mike. "People want to help. It's in our nature. But the size of the problem eventually weighs a person down. You become emotionally and physically exhausted. It's not only people in the community. Professionals fall into it—cops, teachers, caregivers, social workers. That's why people who do this work have to take care of themselves. That's why I run," he said to Liz. "It's not only about physical exercise."

"That's why I box," Quinn said, nodding her agreement. "It helps keep my stress to a minimum. It's a great work out."

"Boxing, Quinn? How did you get into that?" Liz asked her with wide eyes. "I'm impressed."

"It's no big deal. I took a class at a gym. I needed to step up my work out. It was like nothing I'd done before. I just go at it with a heavy bag. The release is amazing. You should try it sometime."

"Hey, I will keep that in mind," Liz answered, thinking about punching a heavy bag but doubting it would ever happen. She was more the runner-weightlifter type. "But for right now, I need to go. Duty calls." The three walked out to the street together.

A City Hall security guard, a thin, older fellow, had directed his attention to a small group of punks. The kids were dirty, their clothes disheveled. The odor wafting from them was as unpleasant as a landfill. The smell didn't seem to bother the punks or maybe they had become used to it. Despite the rainy weather, one kid was barefoot, another wore rope sandals.

"You need to move on," the guard told them. "I said earlier that you can't hang out and beg here. You didn't listen. Now move it."

"Why?" asked one of the punks. A bandana was wrapped around his head. Matted hair blossomed out behind him. Scraggly whiskers covered his chin. He had summoned more attitude than his friends and got mouthy. The punk thrust his face forward, his hands out to his sides. "We're just sittin', we're not beggin', so what's your problem?" he inquired, challenging the guard's authority. Although the punk protested, he got to his feet just the same. His grubby friends slowly followed his lead.

Liz watched, waiting to see if the encounter would escalate. The kid continued to argue, but began heading down the block.

"Just can the chatter and keep moving," the guard told him, his arms waving in the desired direction.

"Fine, old man, we're done with this scene anyway," the kid with the attitude yelled back. "But we'll see you later, don't worry about that. This is our city too, man."

The punks turned back to look as they sauntered down the street, laughing and jeering at the guard.

Confident that the punks were leaving, the guard returned to his post near the entrance to the building. He shook his head in disgust. His eyes met Liz's for a brief moment, but nothing was said.

As they headed down the block to Liz's car, they heard the strumming of a guitar and a voice singing a tune. The music was coming from the corner where a fellow sat next to his open guitar case. He was doing a respectable rendition of Dylan's "Buckets of Rain." People waiting at the crosswalk would listen for a minute, drop a buck or a few coins into the guitar case.

Buckets of rain, buckets of tears; got all them buckets comin' out of my ears / Buckets of moonbeams in my hand / You got all the love, Honey, I can stand.

Liz looked in the guy's direction long enough to decide he wasn't a nuisance before she asked Mike, "Am I dropping you at your office?"

"No, I'm heading over to the Youth Center with Quinn. I haven't been there since she took over the place. Stay safe.

I'll see you this evening." The two shared a look, refraining from a goodbye kiss. After all, Liz was on the job.

"Let me know if you need a ride," Liz said as she waved to them, walking across the street to her car. Mike and Quinn waved to Liz then turned back to the fellow who was singing.

Close up, the singer looked younger than the voice he produced, but it was hard to tell with folks on the street. Probably in his twenties, his hair was a passel of multicolored dreadlocks that sprouted in all directions, covering his forehead. His lower face sported a scruffy beard that hid his mouth so effectively that it was evident only when he opened his lips to sing.

A variety of piercings graced the street musician's face and ears. Tattoos decorated his neck and arms. The tats that were visible appeared to be either arcane symbols or small rows of scripted writing. The tee shirt he wore was full of holes and ripped at the neck. He wore cargo pants that may have been made from fabric with a camo print, but the pattern had long ago faded away.

The feeling he put into the Dylan song made the guy seem older. He had a decent voice and although Mike wasn't a musician, he knew when someone could play. The fellow used a combination of picking and strumming the six strings, his fingering precise. He finished the tune and the folks listening nearby applauded. A few more dollars landed in the guitar case as they wandered off, one by one. The street musician nodded his head in thanks.

"Come on," Quinn said to Mike. "I'll introduce you."

Chapter Four

"Sage"

The audience had dispersed and only Quinn and Mike remained. As the fellow gathered the money from his guitar case, he noticed Mike and Quinn and offered a slight wave of his hand.

"Good morning, Sage. Very nice," Quinn told him as she added a dollar bill to the pile.

"Thanks, and thank you for this," the fellow said, as he picked up the bill. He reached over and his hand came to rest on the head of a cattle dog. The dog had neither moved nor made a sound. It may have been sleeping, but until that moment, Mike hadn't seen the pooch lying there.

"Sage, I want you to meet Mike," Quinn told the young man, with a hand on Mike's shoulder. "Mike, this is Sage."

Sage nodded in Mike's direction, as the money disappeared into a pocket. He placed the guitar in the case, securing the clasps. Sage didn't offer a hand so neither did Mike. With the dog close by it wasn't a good idea to get within a couple of steps. Instead, he said, "Hey, Sage. I enjoyed the song. You know your way around a guitar."

"Nice of you to say. Playing is more my thing than singing, but I do okay. I'd just as soon be buskin' for a few bucks than panhandlin'. At least I'm offering something for your trouble." Sage looked up at Mike, smiled. Mike was taken aback by the warm smile that emerged. Sage's eyes all but disappeared as he grinned. His dark facial hair was parted by an explosion of big, straight white teeth. "I usually begin the day with one of Bob's tunes."

Mike crouched down to Sage's level so the young man didn't have to look up. A closer look told Mike that Sage was younger than he had suspected—late teens or early twenties on the outside. Mike noticed the cattle dog was clean and well-fed. "Nice pup," Mike told him, knowing better than to hold out a hand or pet the animal. "What's its name?"

"This is Zeke," he answered, stroking the fur on the pup's back. "His full name is Ezekiel, but he's Zeke to his friends." Mike noticed the dog's lead was secured to Sage's ankle. A small, aluminum water bowl was connected to the grip end of the lead by a short, narrow chain, keeping Zeke and the bowl within a few inches of Sage's knee.

"Zeke looks like a good friend to have around," said Mike. Upon hearing his name, Zeke roused, looking up at Sage. He raised his head, ears up, eyes wide. Zeke looked at Mike and Quinn with suspicion. The big, dark eyes looked innocent enough but Mike wasn't about to trust a strange dog. Especially a cattle dog.

Quinn stepped into the conversation with a request. "I'm wondering if we could ask a favor, Sage. If you see kids hanging around, would you suggest they come see us at the Center?"

Sage was looking at his dog. He glanced up at Quinn for a moment, and then directed his gaze back to Zeke. "We stay pretty clear of the punks, Zeke and me. Try to mind our business. But if we get a chance, we'll let 'em know," he said with a shrug of his shoulders.

"You should sing at the Center sometime," mentioned Quinn with enthusiasm. "A lot of the kids are musical."

"Better to stay where there's folks walking by, depending on the time of day," he said. His point being that he would rather perform where people were around that would give him money.

Once Zeke had stirred, Sage was ready to move on. He removed Zeke's lead from his ankle and attached it to his wrist. He shook out the last few drops from the water bowl and rose to his feet.

Mike stood up along with him. "Do you ever visit Brooks House?" asked Mike, referring to the men's shelter. "Food's pretty good there. Coffee's always on." Mike was assuming Sage was over eighteen, but doubted he carried ID to prove it.

"I would, but it's hard with Zeke. I don't leave him alone. Can't take him inside," Sage told him, as if there was no need to discuss it further.

"The guys will understand. They'll help you out. Tell them Mike sent you. The guy that runs the place, Gary, is a friend of mine. He'd enjoy hearing you play some Dylan," Mike offered. "Anyway, we'll let you go. Nice to meet you, Sage."

Mike watched Sage easily toss a backpack over one shoulder, his arm through the strap. He switched his grip on Zeke's lead between his hands so that it was never loose. He carried the guitar behind him to one side, the pack to the other. He made the load look more compact than Mike would have thought possible.

"Thanks for the song, Sage," said Quinn. "And thanks for the help. Take care of yourself."

"Don't thank me for helping yet. We'll have to see," he said. "See you 'round."

Mike and Quinn watched Sage head down the street with Zeke, the cattle dog in tow.

"Interesting guy, decent musician," Mike said as they walked toward the Youth Center. "How did you meet up with him?"

"He was busking at that same corner one morning, soon after I moved here," Quinn explained. "I see him most days, in one of a few places."

Mike wondered aloud as they approached the entrance to the Youth Center. "He avoids the punks. Wasn't keen on sending them to the center. Maybe it's like he said, he keeps the dog away from them."

"Sage avoids most people," said Quinn. "He keeps to himself, him and the dog. I've asked the center staff about him. They know of him, but don't know much about him."

Chapter Five

"The Precinct"

On the way to the precinct, Liz stopped at Dutch Bros. for her usual—a skinny latte, extra hot. She had grappled with whether to resist the urge to stop for coffee—she could make a pot at the precinct, after all. In the end, she gave in to temptation.

Waiting for her coffee, listening to the music that always blared out at the drive-thru coffee spot, she thought about the City Council meeting.

As far as Liz knew, the gutter punks rarely caused problems that required police involvement. The biggest complaint was usually that they were *there.* They were in the way. They got mouthy. They were dirty. They smelled.

Liz remembered the man who had caused a scene and been escorted out. Mike had mentioned compassion fatigue. Liz wondered if Quinn could release some of the pressure by making progress with the punks. The image made Liz think of a boiler explosion. *Yes,* thought Liz, *the whole thing could potentially explode.* Maybe she was thinking like a cop, but she hoped Quinn could help.

Pulling out into traffic, Liz sipped her coffee and thought about the case she'd been involved in when she'd met Quinn Hadley the year before. It was a sordid, ugly mess and Liz had barely made it out alive.

The investigation had taken Liz deep into the homeless community, not just the folks who live on the street, but the services intended to help them. The case was solved, the culprits apprehended before she'd even had occasion to talk with Quinn. But Liz learned that circumstances are seldom as they appear. There is always a story. Some end happily and others just end.

She pulled into one of the parking spots at the Justice Center reserved for ranking officers. Coffee in one hand and her bag in the other, she made her way inside the building. She intended to check in with her teams of homicide detectives, addressing any urgent messages or situations. Captain Miller would want to hear about the City Council meeting.

As Liz approached the corridor leading to the detective's squad room, she was waved down by Officer Castillo. "Good morning, Lieutenant. Before you get busy, I wanted to catch you. You have a visitor. He told the front desk he didn't have an appointment, but hoped you'd have a few minutes."

Liz sighed, keeping her exasperation in check. She was already behind schedule after attending this morning's meeting and now, the further interruption of an unexpected visitor. It wasn't Castillo's fault. She was just the messenger, but Liz would have a discussion with the officer at the desk about assuming she had time for unscheduled visitors.

"Thanks, Castillo. Did you catch a name?"

"Sorry, I didn't. The desk will have it. They signed him in. He asked Sergeant Crane if there might be a room where he could wait for you. Crane's up to his ears so he grabbed me. I placed your visitor in the small meeting room. It's less trashy than an interview room," she reasoned, and Liz had to agree. Then Castillo went on about her business.

Liz retraced her steps and walked back to the end of the corridor. *Good. She'd have that discussion about impromptu visitors right now.* She swiped her ID pass card to open the locked door leading to the "front desk" area through which civilians entered the premises.

The public entrance to the precinct was accessible only as far as the lobby. Admittance to the secured portions of the building was permitted only after being checked in, having shown ID, and when accompanied by an officer—unless you were under arrest and brought in through the booking area.

There was a large window through which people spoke with the desk sergeant while stating the reason for their visit. Through the window Liz could see that the lobby was full of people. They sounded impatient and unhappy. Liz approached the beleaguered Sergeant Crane, but would save the discussion about visitors for a later time.

"Sorry to bother you, Crane, but Castillo said I have a visitor. Where's the ID information?" she asked.

Crane reached for a piece of paper and handed it to Liz, barely distracted from the visitor at the window.

"Here, Lieutenant. I checked his ID. He is who he says he is, at least according to his ID. No appointment, but the man said you know him. Mr. Gabriel Chapin."

Gabriel Chapin. Liz hadn't heard the name in a long time. She had hoped to never hear that name again. Liz set down her coffee, taking the signature sheet from the sergeant. Crane had returned to the business at the visitor's window without looking in Liz's direction. He was too busy to have noticed her astonishment, and for this Liz was glad.

She checked the information on the visitor's log. Chapin had arrived at the precinct thirty minutes ago, requested to see Liz, and had shown an Oregon Driver's License as proof of identification. *What the hell did Chapin want?*

Chapter Six

"Gabriel Chapin"

Castillo said Chapin was waiting in the room they referred to as the *small* meeting room, not to be confused with the *large* room, reserved for team meetings and briefings. She walked directly to her office, placing her coffee on the desk and her bag in a drawer. She sat at her desk, picked up the desk phone and punched in an extension used by the custody officers. It was answered immediately.

"Pryor. How can I help you, Lieutenant?"

"There's a visitor waiting for me in the small meeting room, Pryor," Liz told him as she signed on to the computer system. "Could you let Mr. Chapin know that I've arrived and will be with him shortly. And if Castillo didn't offer him coffee, would you mind?"

"Sure thing, Lieutenant. I'm on it," said Pryor.

Liz hung up the phone. She accessed the video camera system, directing it to a view of the room where Chapin waited. He was sitting at the table, facing the camera.

Chapin looked much the same as he had years ago. He had aged, but he was making sure it looked good. Hair shorter than Liz remembered, clean shaven. He was well-groomed. Expensive suit.

Liz turned up the audio as Pryor entered the room and delivered Liz's message. She watched Chapin turn and listen as Pryor spoke to him. She watched him decline the offer of coffee or water. Chapin didn't appear to be impatient or put out by having been kept waiting. *Good, because he's going to wait a few more minutes.*

Pulling up the Oregon State DMV, Liz entered "Chapin, Gabriel." Records indicated he held a current license in good standing with the neighbor to the south. It listed a Parkdale address, east of Portland. *How could he have been so close and she not aware of it?* The thought made her skin crawl. No wants or warrants. *That was good,* she supposed. It told her that Chapin was playing it straight or that he was as skilled as ever at hiding off the grid.

Liz was grateful for a look at Chapin before walking into that room. The preview into his legal status also helped her prepare. Liz had to level the playing field. His intent was to catch her off guard by the unannounced visit. That's the way he did things. But he was on her turf and she would use that to her advantage. The data search was mostly a delay tactic on her part, but what the hell? She could, so she did.

Taking one last sip of her now, cold coffee, Liz checked her reflection in the mirror behind her office door. She adopted her best interrogation face, left her office and headed to the meeting room. She opened the door and entered the room. She wanted to sound busy and efficient, but not hurried.

"Gabriel. Hello," she said with business-like briskness. "Sorry to have kept you waiting." Liz paused for impact. "I could have saved you time had I known you were coming."

She offered her hand, shook hands with the man, then sat opposite him at the table. Liz fought the urge to wipe her palm on her trousers, ridding herself of the feeling of his grasp.

"Liz Jordan," said Chapin. It was an odd greeting, stating her name. It was neither friendly nor unfriendly but could have been taken as either. "I expected to wait. I decided on the spur of the moment to contact you," he said, but Liz didn't believe him. "How long has it been? Since we've seen each other?"

"It has been a while," answered Liz, looking directly into the man's eyes. "How can I help you?" she asked, emphasizing the word *help,* her tone suggesting she didn't care to help Chapin with anything except out the damn door.

"How have you been?" Chapin asked, evading her question. He raised his chin, in a defiant gesture, daring Liz to think he cared, in the least, how she had been.

"I'm fine," Liz answered abruptly, not wishing to exchange pleasantries. She waited a few moments, but Chapin said nothing else. "I don't mean to rush this along, Gabriel, but if you could tell me what this is about, we might both get back to our mornings."

"I attended the City Council meeting this morning," he said, glancing down at the table between them, then back at Liz. "I was surprised, seeing you. I didn't expect to. I mean, I knew that you'd been on the force here for some time. I have an interest in the matter at hand, the problems with the street kids, the gutter punks, as they're called."

"I have little to do with the Council other than communication with the department," Liz replied. "How do you suppose I could help? I'm with the homicide division. Is this concerning a suspicious death?"

"I hope not. I really, really hope not. And you are not merely *with* the homicide division, Liz. You are a decorated officer of rank. You help run the division. That's why I'm here. I need your help. A friend is asking for your help."

"We are not friends, Gabriel. We never were," Liz answered bluntly. She hated hearing him use her name, but she tried not to show it. Besides, she had no other name with which to address *him.* She certainly wasn't going to call him *Mr. Chapin.* "If I can help you professionally, I will because that's my job. Otherwise, if you are here thinking I may do you some favor, you're mistaken."

"When you hear why I need your help, you'll want to be involved in any way you can. At least that's my prediction. Doing so will be in your own best interests," he told her, with his smug, arrogant attitude. "I'm good with predictions. For example, I would have predicted Mike Dwyer would accompany you to the City Council meeting, and I would have been correct. Still the bleeding-heart liberal, hell-bent on saving the world?"

Hearing Chapin say Mike's name angered Liz, but she wasn't going to rise to the bait. She resisted the urge to cross her arms over her chest in a display of protective body language. Instead, Liz leaned back in her chair and rested her hands on the table between them. She stared Chapin in the eye, pretending she hadn't heard Mike's name or the insult to her best friend and significant other.

"You are wasting my time. What the hell do you want?"

"It's very simple. I have a daughter, Liz. She's missing and I need you to find her."

Chapter Seven

"The Youth Center"

Mike followed Quinn into the Youth Center and looked around. A huge building, it resembled a warehouse. The entrance to the common room was staffed by a fit, twenty-something man with a dark beard and pony tail, wearing a red tee shirt printed with STAFF in capitals across the front. He acknowledged Mike and Quinn as they came in, his eyes staying on the door. His job was to take notice of everyone entering the center. He manned the door like a bouncer at a club. Other than staff, adults were not allowed in without checking with Quinn, or whoever was in charge.

The bouncer guy was carrying on a conversation with a kid whose head was topped by a five-inch Mohawk. The kid appeared to be male and may have been Asian, African-American, maybe bi-racial. Ethnicity hardly mattered nor was it his most notable feature. The kid's hair was black near his scalp, but from an inch in length to the ends, was as bright orange as the aurora of the sun. He wore a crusty leather jacket, tight jeans on a skinny frame, and black polish on most, but not all, of his fingernails. He didn't look happy, his face in a scowl.

"How's your morning going?" asked Quinn as she approached the bouncer and the kid with the Mohawk. She introduced Mike to the bouncer, a guy named John, and then she turned to the kid. "I'm Quinn, but I don't know your name," she said. Quinn didn't try the usual line of introduction, pointing out that they had not met. The kid would probably stare at her like she was stupid and still not provide a name.

"Drip," he said. "Just Drip."

"Why are you and Drip sitting out here?" she asked John.

"Drip is currently not allowed in the common room. He and I are negotiating the terms of his re-entry."

"I just wanna' lie down and crash, man. I can't get a bunk until later and the cops are sweepin' the park." Drip rubbed his eyes, looking tired. "I been up all night."

"Have you eaten?" Quinn asked Drip. He shook his head slowly, uninterested. His eyes closed and he yawned, revealing a silver stud through the middle of his tongue.

"There's food in the other room if you want it, Drip. You're welcome to get something and take it outside. Until you and John come to an agreement, that's all we can do for you." She looked at John. "Mike and I are doing a walk-through. Let me know if you need me."

Mike counted about a dozen kids in the common room, sitting on the floor or lying on benches. It was early in the day and as most teens are night owls, there was little activity. He wanted to speak with some of the kids, but no one was interested in engaging in conversation this early in the day, or with Mike, who looked like he could be some kid's father.

"Teens don't like sitting at tables, so the shallow, sturdy benches work as furniture," explained Quinn about one of the recent changes. Carpeting provided the only softness. Backpacks became pillows. Fifty-gallon garbage cans stood in each corner. The perimeter walls in the common room were dotted by electrical outlets.

"The former director had the outlets added, figuring a place to charge a phone would draw kids in off the street," she said. "The plan seems to work. The room may seem cavernous and barren, but when it's full of kids, the space fills quickly. Like this, it's easy to monitor. Besides, the kids know they're safe to hang out here during the day, waiting for a bunk where they can spend the night."

Mike followed Quinn to three bunk rooms, as they were called. One of the bunk rooms was for girls, another for boys, and the third was not gender-specific.

"The bathrooms and showers have the same three designations," Quinn said. "We try to make everyone as comfortable as possible."

There were no doors on the bunk rooms, he noticed. Bathroom and shower entrances reminded Mike of the ones in his high school. No doors there either, but designed for visual privacy. For the sake of safety, staff could hear every sound that echoed from inside.

The bunk rooms resembled the youth hostels of Europe. The accommodations were like barracks and were very different than the private bedrooms offered to families at the other emergency shelters. Mike peeked inside the room designated for boys and saw four sets of bunkbeds. The other two rooms contained the same.

"Considering the age group, the bunks and baths are closely monitored with as much sensitivity as possible. We have to be vigilant about kids victimizing each other. Being a teen can be tough under the best of conditions, but for many of the street kids, life is really brutal."

"You have twenty-four beds on any given night," remarked Mike.

"Yes, and if it too cold outside, there's space for another twenty between the common room and the classroom. Kids make up their bunks when they're assigned and take them down when they leave. If they want, they can bag their bedding for a later stay. We have extra pillows and blankets for day use, when needed."

There was a large, outdoor area surrounded by fencing and covered to protect from the constant damp of Pacific Northwest weather. Off to one side, was a small area where the kids were allowed to smoke—if they followed the rules. A basketball hoop was mounted beyond one end. Two picnic tables with attached benches were positioned on the other. The outside area was vacant of kids at the moment. The area was well-kept. No junk, no litter. Not a cigarette butt in sight.

Mike and Quinn sat at one of the picnic tables "What kind of vibe are you getting from the kids?" Mike asked.

"What I expected. Most kids hit the street because of abuse or they've been kicked out. If they are picked up and under age, they get hauled in and placed in care. For some of these kids, that's what they were running from in the first place. It becomes an endless cycle until they age out of the system. They know not to carry ID or use their own names because those are links to the life they are running from."

"That's why they're cagey," Mike replied. "Self-protection."

Quinn was quiet for a moment, thinking. "They do what they have to do. Be ready to run. Stay on the defensive. At least that's the way we saw things. You become wild, feral. You don't listen to reason. You can fall prey to predators, who con you with offers of help. It's survival mode."

Mike remained quiet. He listened as Quinn shared from her experience. "And there's always a hierarchy. The older kids are tough, street-wise, the younger ones try to emulate that toughness. It's dangerous. They don't know what to do if they get into trouble."

"It's dangerous for anyone on the street, especially kids," added Mike, shaking his head.

"That's why they find a crew, assuming safety in numbers, but the wrong crew can be bad, victimizing them further. If they're lucky, like I was," said Quinn, "they find a pack that will protect them. But the I-5 corridor is a pipeline for sex traffickers. Too often, even a loyal crew can't protect them from the spotters."

"Scary," said Mike, shaking his head.

"And for kids who identify as gay or trans, it can be really rough. They are often the least trustful because they expect to be misunderstood. For some of them, that's all they've known. We try to be gender-neutral and not make assumptions. How they identify is beside the point. If they need help, we do what we can."

Mike and Quinn headed back to the common room where a lanky kid with spiked, blue hair was sweeping benches one by one. He didn't look happy about the chore, but he was making an effort. A second skinny kid with hair in a variety of colors and lengths was following him with a carpet sweeper. They appeared in need of a meal, a bath, and a bed.

Drip was lying on his back on one of the benches against the wall, one arm over his face. The Mohawk was impossible to miss. The negotiation had ended in his favor. The two skinny kids were doing their best to clean around him. Drip didn't seem to notice. Quinn took a moment to thank the skinny kids for their effort, reminding them to get some food.

Mike followed Quinn to the front entrance. "You and the staff are doing a fine job, Quinn, but that's no surprise to me. To be honest, I'm more familiar with helping adults and families. I plan to spend some time here, work a few shifts with staff. I want a better feel for how to help these kids and that's only going to happen if I'm around them."

John still manned the front entrance and Quinn looked in his direction. "What did you work out with Drip?" she asked.

"He's agreed to empty the garbage cans every day for the next week—and no more recruiting inside the center," John answered. He looked back and forth between Quinn and Mike.

"I'm not sure I want to know, but what's he recruiting for?" she asked John.

"He was looking for small bodies to help dumpster-dive. Gross, but not as bad as it could have been. He was paying them in smokes. I keep my eyes open around Drip," he told Mike. "He's talked kids into turning tricks at parties. Drip gets his cut, but the kids barely get something to eat."

"Nice," said Mike with scalding sarcasm. "I'll be in the office. Call if you need anything."

Stepping out to the street, Mike looked forward to walking the few blocks to his office. His thoughts bounced between the City Council meeting, his new acquaintance named Sage, and a kid who went by the name of Drip.

Mike walked past closed-up storefronts where the sidewalk was old and dirty. Next to an empty bicycle rack sat two kids. They were in a frightful state. The kids were dirty. They looked hungry to the point of malnutrition, but instead of dazed and out-of-it, their expressions were hyper-vigilant.

"Hey, Mister, you got any spare change?" asked one of the kids, the bigger of the two, but not by much. The voice was young and to Mike's ear, it sounded male, but it hardly mattered.

Mike had been within a step of two of their perch when they hit him up for pocket change. He stopped, thrust both hands deep in his front pockets, and ask, "Looks like you could use more than some change. What's going on with you two?"

Instantly suspicious, the kid looked at Mike through squinted eyes, checking him out. "Just hungry, Mister, that's all. You got any change or not?" The kid spoke quickly, as if he had no time or energy to waste on Mike if he wasn't interested in giving to their panhandling effort.

"If you're hungry, there's food down the block at the Youth Center. You can rest. No one will bother you. You can clean up if you want. Have you been there before?"

The kids exchanged a look that told Mike his information was not wanted. Their eye rolls told him that they viewed his suggestion as ridiculous.

"Yeah, whatever," the speaker for the two said with disgust. "If you got no change, leave us the hell alone."

The two street kids struck him as the human equivalent of feral cats living under a dilapidated porch. Mike considered calling the cops, but knew the kids would scatter before help arrived. He could call the Youth Center. He thought of the option Quinn had offered to the business owners, to try and intervene with kids.

Mike handed the kid a five-dollar bill. The cash was loose in his front pocket. Mike knew better than to take out his wallet on the street. "Get something to eat, okay?" Mike took out one of his cards and handed it to the kid, who accepted it with disinterest. "You call me if you need anything. I work with the folks at the Youth Center. Take care."

As Mike turned to walk away, he heard mumbled *thanks*. From the corner, he waited at the crosswalk to turn left. Mike turned to look back up the street at the two kids. They were already gone.

Chapter Eight

"Sara"

Liz didn't want to hear anymore, didn't want to sit in the room with Chapin another minute, but the mention of a daughter tempered her reaction. A missing daughter. A child who may be in need of help. "You had better start at the beginning," Liz told Chapin. "Not because I want to help you, not because we're friends. If there's a child missing, the department will do whatever we can to find her."

"She's not just my daughter, Liz. She's mine and Sara's. I know you remember Sara. And I'm not interested in help from the department. It's your help I want."

Hearing the name was like a punch to the gut. *Sara.* Liz had tried not to think of her over the years, of the way things had happened, how it had turned out. Thoughts of Sara made her think of Chapin, and when she thought of him, disgust overcame her. And now, here she was, sitting across a table from him.

She wanted to get out of that room, get away from Chapin. But Liz would hear him out. She would help him if there was a child involved. But not here, not now. "I can't get into this now. I have work to do," Liz was shaking. She hated that Chapin had this effect on her and she avoided looking him in the eye. And hearing Sara's name was like a ghost had entered the room, chilling her.

"By all means, go do your job, Liz. But I'm sure you will find a way to help us. You owe Sara that much. You owe her daughter."

Chapin spoke with the same air of relaxed self-assurance. He reached into a pocket and pulled out a card, placing it on the table. “Here’s my contact information. I’ll expect to hear from you before the end of the day.”

“Give me a couple of hours,” Liz told him, picking up the card. “I’ll let you know where we can meet. Follow me to the lobby. I’m going to escort you out of the building. Don’t come back to the precinct again.”

Liz escorted Chapin to the exit. Her dislike of the man was evident on Liz’s face, but there was nothing she could do about that. At the moment, she was not concerned about appearances.

As soon as Chapin was out the door, Liz turned around, not caring to watch him walk away. She made it to her office without encountering anyone in urgent need of her attention. Liz closed the office door and sat at her desk.

Sara. She said the name to herself. Memories flooded her mind as she tried to organize her thoughts. *Sara had a child? A daughter?* According to Chapin, he and Sara had a daughter together and she was missing. But why was she missing? Had she run away? Was she abducted? How old was she?

Liz had memories of Chapin too, of the shadows in his personality. He had a charismatic side that attracted others to him, but it was countered by an ugly meanness. Liz had witnessed Chapin resort to violence to keep his fellow chumps in line. And she had seen him become physical with Sara.

On one occasion, Liz had pulled him off Sara during an argument. Chapin should have been arrested, but Sara had begged Liz to let it go. He had agreed to leave the premises and Liz made sure Chapin knew he was getting a one-time break. Liz was one of the few people ever to have put him in his place. Later, Sara had thanked Liz for intervening—but warned her that Chapin would never forget it.

Now she had work to do, investigations to supervise. Liz pushed the memories away to concentrate on what was expected of her. There was nothing Liz could do to change the past. She would clear her desk of what needed to be done, contact Chapin, and learn what she could about Sara and her daughter. Liz would help in whatever way she was able. Then the whole mess would move back into the past where it belonged.

Chapter Nine

"Memories"

It wasn't easy being a rookie cop. Everyone asked why you chose to be a police officer. Was the job frightening? Had she pulled her weapon yet? And a female rookie had it especially hard. Did people ask the same questions of male officers? Maybe, but Liz doubted it.

The first question was easy to answer: she became a cop because she wanted to help people. The way Liz saw things, sometimes "help" meant putting them in jail to protect them from themselves. She didn't want to follow her parents into teaching. There was nothing she liked doing well enough to teach it to others. She had considered law, but couldn't face three more years of school and thousands more in student debt. Besides, she'd known she was destined for law enforcement. She'd felt it in her bones. She even liked the uniform, but she hadn't yet worn it though a hot summer.

She took the job seriously, but not for the reasons most people might assume. Liz was committed to equal justice. She thought the commitment should be required of anyone in uniform. Liz figured that was why she had gravitated to Mike, her best friend from college; he was as equally committed to his own ideals of social justice.

As for the other questions, no, the job wasn't frightening—but Liz was smart enough to stay alert. This required stamina, force of will, and copious amounts of strong coffee. When asked, she would mention the importance of trusting your fellow officers, the way she was taught at the academy. And no, she had not yet pulled her weapon. Liz honestly prayed she would never have to, but she figured the day would come.

Truth be said, the hardest thing about being a female rookie was dealing with the older, male cops. Some of the old guys would condescend because she was a woman. They couldn't wrap their minds around the fact that she was as capable as they were. What she lacked in bulk and muscle could be made up in fitness and agility. But at least some of them tried to give her the benefit of the doubt.

Then there were the guys who could only talk to a woman—any woman— like they were on a date. These were the guys who assumed she enjoyed their flirting. Flirting was the polite word she used to stay out of trouble. But most of the time, it was sexual harassment, pure and simple. If Liz ever became a sergeant or even a lieutenant, she would educate her team to the reality of gender equality.

Columbia City wasn't overrun with crime, but it had its share. The city and its law-abiding citizens had been dealing with a sleazy bar owner named Killian for years. Police activity in the part of town where Killian operated occurred at an almost daily rate. The news and the papers covered it all, and usually, the calls involved the man and his operations in some way.

Everyone was sick of Killian, his shabby establishments, and the low-life chumps who worked for him. Cops had worked to build a case. They knew that he was running a variety of illegal operations—drugs, prostitution, probably firearms. They had evidence, but not enough to charge him.

After significant debate about her lack of experience, Liz was pulled off patrol to assist with the investigation. The de-

ciding factor was that she was young enough to hang around without drawing any suspicion. The cops used a contact, a young woman who worked for Killian as a cocktail server. Her name was Sara Mallory.

Liz and Sara had known each other in high school. The two had not been the best of friends, but they certainly knew one another and got on well. Liz's family was middle-class, while Sara's situation was decidedly meager. Sara had been a petite and attractive girl, but only a fair student. Kinder, more benevolent classmates considered Sara delicate and child-like and they looked out for her. A rougher group saw her as weak and an easy target. Liz was tall, strong and athletic, and even in school, she looked out for the interests of others—especially those who needed a champion. Sara had needed a champion. She brought out the best in Liz, for some reason, and Liz defended Sara, protecting her from ridicule and abuse.

While Liz eventually attended college and began a career in law enforcement, higher education had not been an option for Sara. Even if her grades had been sufficient to get into college, there was no money for education. Sara needed a job, any job. She needed the income now, not in a few years, so she held a succession of low-paying jobs. But Sara never forgot Liz's kindness and when they reconnected as adults in Columbia City, Sara continued to idolize Liz, now her cop friend, as she had when they were both kids.

Physically small in stature and rail thin, Sara still reminded Liz of a sprite out of an elf story. Now a young woman, Sara still had no talent for self-preservation, always searching for someone to look out for her. Her role as an aide to the police was the result of a crush on a detective old enough to be her father—another misguided attempt at securing a protector. If Liz was a bloodhound, Sara was a trusting puppy. But to Sara's credit, she could follow directions. And she was intensely loyal.

Sara's loyalty extended to an asshole boyfriend named Gabriel Chapin. He was calm, calculating, and fueled by self-aggrandizement. Chapin enjoyed intimidating and manipulating people, especially Sara or his thug friends. He usually employed these tactics when there was a profit to be made, but sometimes Chapin targeted people for the fun of it. He was aware that Sara was helping the cops, but he weighed the risks against their future value. Poor Sara thought it was wonderful that Chapin looked out for her and for their future. As far as Liz knew, it never dawned on Sara that she was the only one taking the risks.

The department's investigation into the Killian operation lasted a few weeks. No one was arrested because the principal targets disappeared to parts unknown, along with the money, the drugs, and the guns. It ended with no arrests and three people dead. One of the three who died was Sara.

Chapter Ten

"Distracted"

Liz's memories were interrupted by the ring of the phone. Startled, she could only stare at it for a few moments while she decided what to do. *It was just a damn phone ringing*, she chided herself. *Get a grip*. Liz hated the feeling. It was unlike her.

Before the call went to voice mail, Liz picked up the receiver. "Jordan," was the terse greeting she offered.

"Hey, it's me," said Mike on the other end. "I wasn't sure I'd catch you at your desk. I walked from the Youth Center to my office to clear my head."

"Oh, yeah, good idea," she answered without thought.

"Aren't you going to ask me why I needed to clear my head?" he asked with a laugh. "I tell you, working with adults is challenging enough, but these kids are a different ballgame. Bleak."

Liz tried to pay attention. "Well, Quinn can handle it as well as anyone," she said. She took a breath then realized too late that it made her sound impatient.

Mike paused at Liz's tone. "I must have caught you in the middle of something. What time do you think you'll finish for the day? You offered to give me a ride home. I guess I should have planned my transportation better." They both knew it wasn't Mike's lack of planning that caused the issue.

"Sorry, I was reading reports," she lied, although there were reports waiting in the system for her review. Liz looked at her calendar and realized she had a couple of meetings scheduled but nothing major on her agenda. "I'll plan to leave here at six, unless all hell breaks loose. I know I sound distracted; just trying to catch up."

Liz noticed the time. She needed to arrange a meeting with Chapin. She detested the idea of seeing him again but wanted to get it over with. Then she remembered the reason he wanted to talk with her: the missing daughter. Sara's daughter.

"I'll let you get back to it. See you at six. If you get sidelined, try to let me know," Mike requested of her. It had happened more than once, that Liz was called away at odd hours or with no regard to commitments. As a lieutenant, Liz was supposed to have more control over her schedule. At least in theory.

"Six it is. I'll be on time. I have a feeling I'll be done with this day by then." *Actually, I'd like to be done with it now*, she thought. "Tell me more about the street kids tonight. I am interested and I want to hear about it."

"No worries. See you later," Mike said, and ended the call.

Liz hung up the phone and pulled Chapin's card from her pocket. She hadn't yet bothered to look at it. It did not offer much information. His name and two phone numbers, plus an email address were listed under the name GC Investments. No company logo, no physical address.

She dialed the first of the two phone numbers listed. The call went to a voice mail, but she recognized the voice as Chapin's. "You've reached Gabriel Chapin. Please leave a message. Thank you." The greeting sounded self-important. Smug. At least to Liz's ear.

"There's a playground west of Main at Thirty-Third Street. I'll be sitting at a bench on the north side. Four o'clock." Liz decided Chapin didn't need more information. Where and when was all the information he deserved.

Liz wanted to know what Chapin had been up to. GC Investments was registered as a sole proprietorship. A simple website offered little information and didn't attempt to encourage contact. The financial details available online were limited to what was legally required. It shouted vagueness.

Data searches linked Chapin's company to a variety of investigations in Oregon and California, however, charges were never brought against Chapin or his company, apparently for lack of evidence. Details were sketchy, but they hinted at import-export infractions, fiscal concerns, and property disputes. Liz figured he had paid attention to Killian and learned from his mistakes.

Several hours passed. Liz had attempted to immerse herself in police business, but she was distracted. She made it through a quick meeting with her captain, a formidable veteran of the force named George Miller. She answered a few questions for him about the City Council meeting. A pair of homicide detectives prepping for court wanted her input; another team needed direction on a case. Liz doubted she had offered much in the way of concrete help. Her thoughts often returned to Sara, a missing girl, and a pending meeting with Chapin.

Liz gave up trying. As she closed the last file and logged out of the system, she realized it was close to four p.m. Liz noted her location as "Meeting off site" for the remainder of the day. She logged out, grabbed her coat, and left the precinct.

Chapter Eleven

"The Meeting"

Carter Park was only a few minutes away. Liz parked half a block down the street, walked up, and found the bench on the north side. The park was far enough north that it wasn't popular with the street folks. It was frequented more often by school-agers whose parents enjoyed being able to send them to the local playground because the neighborhood was safer than the ones to the south.

Liz chose the location for another reason: the bench where she sat was obscured from view by a high fence and shrubbery yet she could see approaching traffic from the other directions. She had used the spot for meetings a few times for those same reasons, and it was less likely that she'd be seen.

She glanced to the south as Chapin walked up the sidewalk bordering the playground. Liz watched him approach, the arrogant swagger still evident under the trappings of age and acceptability. Liz had once seen him move with the same confidence after breaking a man's fingers for pinching profits. She was disgusted to think that he was raising a child.

Arriving at the park bench, he sat to Liz's left, eyes straight ahead.

"I'm here," Liz said, determined to get things rolling. "Tell me about your daughter."

"Her name is Kyrie," he said. "It's spelled with a 'y' and rhymes with *leery*. Sara loved the name. She said it meant *prayer* in Latin or Greek or some ancient language."

"How old is she?"

"She's fifteen."

"How is it possible that Sara had a daughter? I never saw her; never saw any evidence of a child. I talked with Sara almost every day for weeks."

"*We* had a daughter. Kyrie is *my* daughter too. She was a year old before you crossed our paths. She lived with Sara's mother. Sara couldn't care for a child and I wasn't ready for it. Our plan, mine and Sara's, was to bring her to live with us by her third birthday." Liz heard his hesitation, almost taking it for tenderness, but the caring tone evaporated.

"After Sara died, I went ahead with the plan; it just took me a little longer. I brought our daughter to live with me before she started school." Liz remembered seeing Sara's mother a few times from a distance, but she had not met the woman. As far as Liz could recollect, Sara had never mentioned her father.

"Your card doesn't say much about GC Investments and neither does the website," Liz mentioned, trying to sound disinterested.

"I assumed you'd check up on me," he said with unbridled amusement. "But you won't find anything reminiscent of my former life. Running girls and dealing drugs for Killian was sordid, unimpressive grunt work. It required me to be too close to the action. If you must know, I manage investments now, mostly property, plus some small business concerns."

"Investments. You want me to believe you're legitimate," said Liz, "but I doubt that's true. My guess is that you're more insulated now, no longer 'close to the action' as you put it. I did some interesting reading into your business this afternoon, about allegations, disputes. You're not legit. You've just been lucky, at least so far."

Chapin responded with a laugh, but he sounded indignant. "Luck has never been a factor in my life or my pursuits. I think we both know that."

"If you are operating legally, why not go the traditional route to find Kyrie?"

"Because I'd rather not and because it's not necessary," he explained. "Why wouldn't I contact an old acquaintance for help? An acquaintance who Sara considered to be a friend?"

The arrogance was stunning, but this was how Chapin's mind worked, Liz reminded herself. "Why? Because you're lucky I'm even talking to you," Liz told him in a direct tone. "Let me be clear—the only reason I'm listening is because a child's safety may be involved."

"Oh, yes. There it is, that self-righteous attitude I remember so well." Chapin was irritated by the disrespect, but he hid his displeasure behind a smirk. "You forget that I know exactly how disastrous your decisions have been."

The gall behind Chapin's statement infuriated Liz and it was all she could do to sit there another minute. She reminded herself this was about Sara's missing daughter. Liz gave herself a few moments to get her temper in check before she said, "Just tell me about Kyrie. Start with how long she has been missing."

"Four months. A rebellious streak, I assumed, except I would hear from her once a week or so. She would text me, always from a disposable phone. That ended a month ago."

"Was this the first time she ran away?"

"Yes. Yes, it was." Liz believed him.

"Do you have any idea why she ran? Although having you as a father would be any teenage girl's dream," Liz said, enjoying the sarcasm.

Chapin grinned at the jibe, but let it pass. "All I can say is that she wasn't looking forward to a second year of high school. She had become sullen, almost morose. My admin, Richelle, may be able to shed some light regarding friends. Call the other number on my card to reach her. Kyrie didn't share that part of her life with me."

"She's fifteen. Aren't you supposed to ask?"

"I'm her father, Liz. I did ask, so don't judge me so quickly. I tried. She wasn't going to tell me anything."

"Are you sure the texts messages were from her?"

"Yes, I believe they were. They were messages she would send." Chapin's answer didn't tell Liz whether the messages were friendly, hateful, or indifferent.

"I will need a recent photo of her," said Liz. "Do you have one?"

"There are two recent ones, one taken in front of Keller Fountain in Portland. It was taken soon after she left. A selfie." He reached for his phone. The photo was the wallpaper on his home screen, the same as so many fathers of teenage daughters.

The photo showed an adolescent girl with short, spiked hair, big dark eyes, and an engineered grimace. She wore a dark hoodie under a heavy, fleece vest. The recognizable fountain was in the background. The girl resembled Sara. There was no doubt it was her child. Except for the eyes. They were Chapin's. No doubt there either.

"Send it to my phone. You have my number."

"I think she has since come to your side of the river," Chapin said as he looked through his photos. "That's why I was interested in the City Council meeting. Here's the more recent picture. It was sent the last time I heard from Kyrie."

"You might be right," said Liz, looking at the second picture. It was taken at the waterfront in Columbia City, the interstate bridge over her shoulder. The change in the young girl was alarming. She was thinner and paler, which Liz wouldn't have thought was possible. She was dirty; she looked ill with deep, dark circles under her eyes, but attempted a smirk. There was an old bruise yellowing on her chin.

"The photos will help. Are you aware of other names she may use, maybe from a favorite song or an artist?" Liz asked. "These kids rarely use their real names."

"No. I'm not," Chapin said, shaking his head. He looked intrigued. The possibility that his daughter wasn't using her real name had not occurred to him. "Richelle might have an idea."

"Okay. I'll contact your admin soon, tonight or tomorrow, so tell her to expect a call from me. Listen to me, Gabriel. Don't contact me at the precinct or call my work number. If you need to reach me, call my cell only." Liz looked at the photos as they uploaded to her phone. "And I think we'd better find her in a hurry."

Chapter Twelve

"Evening"

Liz managed to pick up dinner and arrive at Mike's office right at six p.m. She was relieved that the meeting with Chapin was done and over. Her mind was so full of thoughts from the conversation at the park about Kyrie that she hadn't realized she was actually on time. Normally, she would have congratulated herself. Leaving the job on time did not happen often, but she was too preoccupied to enjoy it.

She watched as Mike walked from the building carrying two, large binders. He stepped over to the car and got in. "Hey, thanks for the ride. I'm exhausted. I didn't accomplish much, but it still felt like a long-ass day," he said, leaning over to kiss her cheek. He reached around and placed the binders on the back seat. "Something smells great. What's for dinner?"

"Curry. Tsingtao for me, sparkling water for you," she answered. Take out from their favorite Thai restaurant was the dinner of choice about twice each week. Liz made a point of picking up beverages without alcohol for Mike along with her choices of beer or wine. It had been years since he'd had a drink and she tried to support his sobriety. She worried that it bothered him when she had a drink. Liz would often ask him, but his answer was not to worry about it.

They usually had dinner together and spent most nights at Liz's. Mike kept his place a few miles away. Things had progressed between them to a comfortable pattern, but neither was rushing to make anything permanent. Liz and Mike had known each other since they were in college in the university town of Pullman and neither wanted to cramp the other's style.

"Curry sounds good. How was your day?" Mike asked. He rested his head back, happy that Liz was driving.

"Interesting. I'll fill you in later, if we have time before we collapse," she said, wanting to change the subject from talking about her day, "but I want to hear about the Youth Center."

Liz was thinking about Quinn and the staff working with street kids. Could they have run across a girl who looked like Kyrie? *It was possible*, she thought. But hoping for a fast fix was a bad way to start an inquiry. It made Liz feel lazy and she learned that when you get lazy, you miss details. Her mind was bouncing back and forth between thinking of how to begin the search for Kyrie and the memories of the girl's mother, Sara.

Deep in thought, she didn't realize Mike was talking to her. "The boys, I said. They will be happy to see us," Mike repeated. "Where the hell were you?"

"Sorry, just reviewing some details from earlier today. I apologize for being distracted," she said. "Yeah, they'll be excited. I'll feed them first, and then we can enjoy our dinner without distraction."

The *boys* were Liz's cats, adopted as stray kittens when she was a rookie in uniform. Both felines were getting old, and were now senior citizen cats. They enjoyed napping most days, waiting for either Liz, Mike, or occasionally the neighbor downstairs to appear and feed them. Eddie, a brown, white and black calico, was named for Pearl Jam's Eddie Vedder. He'd been discovered starving in the parking lot of an ugly apartment complex where Liz was serving papers. Little Kurt, a gray-striped tabby, was found mewling in a dumpster a few months later. The rescued tabby was the namesake of Liz's other favorite grunge artist from her youth, Kurt Cobain of Nirvana.

Entering the third-floor apartment, the cats greeted them at the door, instantly put out that Liz's hands were full as she had hauled in their provisions for the evening. She placed the bags on the countertop, and then quickly poured food and water into dishes for the cats. Mike set down the binders he was carrying and stooped to pet their soft fur. Hearing Liz in the kitchen, they gave up enjoying Mike's caresses to check out their food bowl.

Liz opened a bottle of Tsingtao, took a sip, and placed the other bottles in the refrigerator. She filled a glass with ice, opened a sparkling water and poured it over the ice. "I'll be right back," she said. Taking her beer with her, she headed to change out of work clothes and lock her weapon in the bedroom safe. "What's all the paperwork?" she called out on her way to the bedroom.

"Budget reports. I'm still acquainting myself with the accounting procedures for the other shelters. No two are the same, which is curious," he answered, loud enough so Liz could hear. "Someday, I will convert them all to the same system. Mike fired up the music and tracks from Petty's *Wildflowers* soon filled the apartment.

Mike headed into the kitchen and found his way to plates and utensils, placing them on the breakfast bar with the take-out containers. He drained the glass of sparkling water, refilled it. Liz joined him at the bar wearing an old Washington State Cougars tee shirt and yoga pants that had seen better days.

"It was nice seeing Quinn this morning. Good thing she was there," Liz said, remembering the Council meeting. "Tell me about the Youth Center," she suggested, pretending to dig in. She knew she should eat, but didn't have much appetite. Mike hadn't noticed or he would have mentioned it.

"Like I said earlier, it's different with the street kids. I'm used to working with families that are dealing with temporary homelessness, men fighting demons that have kept them on the margins," he said between bites. "The street kids come with a variety of issues. Most are runaways. Quinn says most of them learn to work an angle to survive. And they span years in age. The older kids prey on the younger ones. I met a kid named Drip. Has an amazing Mohawk."

"Drip, huh? Interesting story there, I'm sure," Liz said, picking at her curry.

"His angle, this fellow Drip, is recruiting kids to turn tricks at parties, when they aren't diving in dumpsters for him." Liz stopped eating and looked over at Mike. "Sorry," he said. "Dumpsters don't make for great dinner conversation."

"No, I was thinking about young kids turning tricks to survive. That's uglier than dumpsters any day." Liz hoped Kyrie hadn't been recruited in such a way. She thought of the physical and emotional damage and the change in the girl between the two photos she had sent to her father.

Mike wanted to tell Liz about the two kids that were panhandling, but decided to let it go. It was too much to explain and he didn't want Liz to question how he'd handled it. Instead he asked, "Do you remember the guy playing guitar on the corner this morning?"

Taking a bite of curry and jasmine rice, Liz nodded that she remembered the fellow. "I do," she uttered. "He looked harmless; wasn't bothering anyone, wasn't blocking a doorway."

"No, he was okay. Quinn introduced us. He goes by Sage. Nice job with a Dylan tune. Gary would have loved it," Mike said, mentioning his friend who ran Brooks House, the men's shelter. Mike stared at his food, and then he added, "I mentioned to Sage that he can always get a meal at Brooks. He told me it's difficult with his dog, Zeke."

"Zeke. That's the dog's name?"

"It is. Pup looked to be in good shape. So, tell me what was so interesting about your day?" he asked, taking the conversation in another direction.

Liz decided that Mike's account of the street kids was a good lead in to the story of Chapin's daughter, Kyrie. She decided to start at the beginning.

Chapter Thirteen

"Kyrie"

"Do you remember an investigation I was assigned to years ago?" Liz asked, between sips of her beer. "It was soon after I joined the force. We were working to close down Killian."

"Killian, huh? That *was* a long time ago. He was a piece of work. Things didn't end as planned. You didn't take well to the outcome. It hit you hard." Listening to Mike's words she remembered it. Mike was right. The case had hit her hard. It had made her question everything about herself.

"I was pretty green at the time. Trying to prove myself and all that," said Liz, making excuses. "All that effort spent on it and we didn't make one arrest. Three people died."

Mike nodded as he remembered. "You were working closely with someone on the inside. A girl you'd known as a kid. You couldn't say much at the time, but I remember she didn't make it. Afterward, it was all over the news. I never understood how she ended up helping the cops."

"Her name was Sara. And you're right, she should never have been put in that position," Liz agreed. "She was coerced into helping a screwed-up detective named Pruitt. At one time, Sara had a thing for him. She thought helping Pruitt would work to her advantage, or maybe Pruitt convinced her of that. Thing was, Pruitt never helped anyone. He was one of those old-school, rummy cops who played every end against the middle. And Sara had a boyfriend, a guy that worked for Killian."

"I remember. We ran into him months later when we were out together. You introduced us, but I don't recall a name. He acted like the two of you were friends, but I didn't believe it. It made sense when you told me later of the connection to the girl."

"His name is Gabriel Chapin. We did not come across him that evening by chance. Chapin engineered it and I knew it at the time. He visited the precinct this morning."

"The precinct? He just showed up?" asked Mike. Caught by the surprise, Mike stopped eating and stared at Liz.

"He did. Showed up out of nowhere," Liz told him, without saying that Chapin had attended the council meeting that morning. And she didn't mention that Chapin had seen them together or that he'd mentioned Mike by name.

"This was a dangerous guy, Liz. A hood. I thought all of Killian's dregs disappeared. Why is he contacting you? I mean, you can handle him, but what the hell? How did he get inside the precinct uninvited?"

"He checked in with the desk, as any visitor would. The desk officer cleared him. He claimed to be a friend of mine. After Killian's was closed down, he disappeared. He's managed to stay under the radar."

"Unbelievable," Mike said.

"He says he's involved with legitimate investments now. A quick search linked his name with some shit but nothing that stuck," she answered. "If it comes down to a deep search of finances, I may learn more."

"What did he have to say?" Mike asked her. He seldom used a demanding tone. It told Liz he was concerned. "What did he want?"

"It turns out that he and Sara had a daughter together. She's fifteen now. Her name is Kyrie. I saw pictures of the girl, Mike. According to Chapin, the girl ran away four months ago. He wants me to find her."

"Has he filed a missing person's report?" Mike asked. "Wouldn't that be the normal thing for a parent to do?"

"Chapin was hearing from the girl once in a while. The contact stopped recently."

"What does he expect you to do, Liz? You work homicide. You run half the damned department."

"He wants me to help because I knew Sara," Liz explained, trying to sound calm and collected. "He felt at the time, and he feels now, that Sara was double-crossed, that she was sacrificed. And he's right. Pruitt could have pulled her out, but he looked the other way."

"Then help implement a missing person's search with officers who handle those cases," suggested Mike. "That's all you can do."

Liz hesitated a moment, then she said, "Maybe." She was thinking about the Youth Center. "The kids that frequent the Center, how does it work?" she asked. "Do they sign in? Are there records?"

"Not regarding individual kids," Mike answered, shaking his head. "If we ask for names or press the kids about their situations, they get spooked," he answered. "Then they don't come back. We defeat our own purpose. Services are provided on a daily basis. Everything is counted. Numbers are tallied. Are you wondering if the girl, Kyrie, is on the street?"

"I'm sure she's on the street. Unless the selfies she sent her father were nothing more than a ploy to make him believe she was. They're convincing though," she said, as she picked up her phone to show Mike the photos. "The first photo was taken in Portland, the second, here in Columbia City. The change in the girl is startling."

Mike looked at the photos of the girl on Liz's phone. "I'd say you're right, it looks like she's in town, or at least she was." Mike studied the photos for a moment longer, and then said, "She's in a bad way. Could be drugs, could be she's sick, and could be from living on the street." Mike shook his head; a sigh escaped him as he looked at the girl's picture. "We can show the photos to Quinn and her staff. Maybe someone will recognize the girl."

"That's what I'm hoping," said Liz.

They finished dinner. Cleaning up amounted to placing take-out containers in the trash and putting rinsed plates in the dishwasher. Mike took his usual spot on the floor where Eddie could nudge him for attention. The cat instigated a wrestling match with Mike's left hand. Liz curled up on the couch with her feet tucked under her. Little Kurt was nearby, purring loudly over one of Petty's mellower tunes.

"Why do you want to do this on your own? You wouldn't like it if cops working missing persons were looking into homicide cases," he reasoned, and Liz agreed he was right.

"Chapin came to me for help because I knew the girl's mother," Liz explained.

"Liz, you sound as if this is someone you respect, a friend," said Mike. "This guy is a criminal, at least he used to be. Even if he claims to be legal now, don't trust him. I understand you want to find the girl, that you knew her mother, but let the Missing Person's team handle it. Tell him that's the best way to proceed for her safety because it's true."

"Mike, listen to me," she said firmly.

"What is it?" he asked, turning to her when he heard the tone in her voice.

Little Kurt had perked up and wanted to play. Liz rubbed the cat's belly while she summoned her resolve to continue. After a moment, she looked Mike in the eye. "Just hear me out. I'll try to explain."

Chapter Fourteen

"The Day Sara Died"

"My job was to be the conduit between Sara and Pruitt. It was easy for me to stay in contact with her and I didn't attract as much attention. I funneled information to Pruitt."

"Okay. That was the plan," Mike said, following along.

"Not that it helped having a plan," said Liz. "This was Pruitt we're talking about. I was too young to know what a train wreck he was. Killian's set-up began to shake loose from the inside. We figured that before long, we could take the place by force, arrest everyone, and offer deals for information. It was starting to look like it would happen."

Mike was concerned. "What went wrong?" He didn't want to hear more, but he had to ask.

"This was an election year. The chief of police wanted to keep his job. Getting rid of Killian was the headline he needed. But Killian's guys were turning on each other, money was disappearing, and everyone was pointing fingers. It started to get risky. These were not boy scouts. Every day I wondered if this was the day Killian's crew would figure out that Sara's was helping us."

"You never told me you were that anxious," said Mike. "I wish I'd known at the time."

"I know, but it couldn't have helped. I was doing my job—that's how I looked at it. That's the deal with these investigations. The expectations are high, things get rushed, there's pressure to produce."

He nodded but didn't say a word, just waited for Liz to resume the story.

"Chapin knew that Sara was helping Pruitt. In fact, he encouraged her. He wanted Killian out of the way as much as the police did, so he didn't care that she was putting herself in danger. Sara was becoming frightened. I was worried that she couldn't hold it together."

Mike was looking Liz straight in the eye. He didn't like what he was hearing, but again, he didn't interrupt.

"Pruitt notified me that the team was planning to raid the club. The chief wanted it over, wanted the whole mess to end. It would happen within the next few days. I was not to inform Sara. Pruitt didn't think she could play it cool. She knew something was up because she kept asking me if I trusted Pruitt."

"That last evening, Sara called me. She asked me to meet her at her apartment. When I saw her, I knew something awful had happened. She was pale as death and shaking from fear. She had called Pruitt even though she was told to go through me. He told her to sit tight. She was a freaking mess and that's all she got from him. Sit tight."

"Poor kid," said Mike.

Liz nodded as she looked at Mike. "She was freaked out. Sara told me that one of Killian's boys started talking crap to Chapin at one of their hangouts, throwing around accusations about Sara—that she couldn't be trusted. There were a couple of guys listening to the exchange so Chapin wasn't going to take it lying down. The guy took a swing at Chapin. Chapin hit him in the head with a whiskey bottle. Sara said the guy went down hard and didn't get up."

"I really wanted Sara out of there, Mike," Liz said, her palms grasping the sides of her face. "I didn't get the chance. She had thrown a few things in a bag, told me that she and Chapin were leaving together. I asked her where Chapin was, where she was meeting him. Sara said he was at the club and she was heading there to find him. I told her, 'No, do not go to the club. Wait for Gabriel to come here', I said. I told her it would be safer for her, but she was scared beyond reason."

"The girl had no idea what she'd gotten into," Mike said, shaking his head.

"No, she didn't, and Pruitt was a jerk. Any other detective would have taken better care of her. Pruitt called me to tell me that the team was staging to take down Killian's club. It was going to happen that night. Again, Pruitt told me not to tell Sara what was happening, but it made no sense. I should have told him to screw himself. I knew better."

"You wanted to help her, but you wouldn't have defied a ranking officer," said Mike, "even a washout." Liz stared at Mike, knowing he was probably right. She had been too young to know better.

"By the next morning, the failed raid at Killian's was all over the news. The principal targets, including Killian himself, had gotten themselves out. Two underlings, hired muscle, were shot after firing on cops. Sara's body was found in the back of the club. She had been shot in the cross-fire."

"I remember the news stories," Mike reflected.

"It didn't take long for the news to die out, the speculation to calm down," Liz remembered. "Killian was gone so no one really cared. Weeks later, I got a call at the precinct. It was Chapin. He said that he had never made it to the club that night. He went to Sara's place and she was gone, of course, by the time he got there."

"Why did he want you to say?" asked Mike.

"He wanted to know why Sara hadn't waited there for him. According to him, that was their plan. I knew that was bullshit. Sara wouldn't have made a different decision. She was adamant about going down to the club. He said she walked into a trap and it was my fault she was dead. She trusted me, he said."

"He wanted you to blame yourself," Mike told her. "People like Chapin don't take responsibility."

"I told him that Sara went to find him, that I couldn't stop her. I said she should never have been working with Pruitt. It had been a bad idea from the beginning and he had encouraged it. He said Pruitt would regret it all, that he would get his karma."

"What happened to Pruitt?"

"Pruitt's been gone for years. He quit the job a couple of years after the Killian raid. He died soon after."

"Sounds like he did get his karma," said Mike.

Liz nodded. "Chapin told me that he knew I'd been informed of what was happening, that I should have warned Sara. I could have saved her life, he said. Years later, when the two of us ran into Gabriel, he had planned for that to happen. He wanted me to know he could find me. Apparently, he didn't have a need for me. Until this morning. Neither of them ever told me they had a daughter."

"I get it, Liz. You want to find this girl, but you can't get involved beyond what you would do for any other case. And besides, you shouldn't do this guy any favor. He doesn't deserve your help."

"You're probably right," she said, thinking of Chapin. Then Liz thought of Sara. "But I do feel some obligation to Sara. She considered me a friend. I'd like to say I helped find her kid. That's more than I did for her."

Mike nodded at what Liz had to say, but he didn't like what he was hearing. "Let's see what Quinn and the others have to say. Maybe someone has seen her."

They were interrupted when Mike's phone rang. He scrambled to remove it from his pocket, moving Eddie away in the process. Mike checked the screen and said, "It's the Youth Center. I should take the call, but I want to talk more about this. What happened to Sara was not your fault."

Liz nodded. *We may continue the conversation,* thought Liz, *but it won't ease my guilt.*

Chapter Fifteen

"The ER"

"This is Mike," he said when he answered the phone. Liz watched as he listened. Something was up. "When?" he asked. Pause. "Where are they now?" Mike listened again and nodded. He glanced at Liz. "I'm sure that's true, but I'm heading there anyway."

Mike ended the call. "That was one of the staff from the Youth Center. Two kids were badly injured. Quinn is with them at the ER."

"How badly injured?" Liz asked as Mike stood up and grabbed his jacket.

"They didn't say, but if Quinn took them to the ER, it must be bad."

"Did this happen at the Youth Center?" asked Liz.

"No," Mike answered. "It sounds like they wandered in off the street."

"I'm going with you," Liz said. "I just need to throw on jeans and a jacket."

Within a few minutes they were on the road. Mike was driving. The hospital was on the Eastside, only a few minutes away. "What did you mean when you told the caller you were heading there anyway?" Liz asked.

"Quinn asked that I be notified about what had happened," he explained. "She said I didn't need to come to the hospital. She didn't want our evening disrupted, just wanted me to know what happened."

"She's had a long day too," said Liz, relieved to be concerned with something other than Chapin, Sara, and their missing daughter.

"I don't have details about their injuries," Mike said. "All I know is that two kids were badly hurt. There may have been an accident. Quinn got them to the ER so I'm concerned one or both may be in bad shape."

Mike pulled into the south entrance with closest access to the ER. Two ambulances were parked at the area designated for emergency vehicles transporting patients. He parked as near to the facility as possible and they entered the large waiting room through a wide, automatic sliding door.

The waiting room was busy with people waiting to be seen by emergency doctors or waiting for loved ones. Medical personnel—nurses, phlebotomists, orderlies—were coming and going, crisscrossing a large corridor visible beyond the waiting area. The long, broad hallway was lined on either side with doors leading to treatment rooms.

A nurse waited at the check-in desk. She looked Mike over for a quick second, satisfied that he wasn't in need of immediate assistance.

"Can I help you?" she asked. Her name tag identified her as *C. Roberts, B.S.N.*

"I'm looking for Quinn Hadley," he answered. "She's with the Youth Center. I received a call that she's here with a couple of kids."

She looked Mike in the face, nodded. "And your name is?"

"Mike Dwyer. I'm with the Youth Center too." He didn't volunteer that he was Quinn's boss because the fact wasn't relevant, at least to Mike.

"Just a moment, please," said the nurse. She turned around and motioned to a young man wearing scrubs. He had been busy at a computer station and when he saw Nurse Roberts wave in his direction, he stood and walked over. "Would you let the woman in three know that there is someone here for her?" She turned to Mike again, and asked, "Mr. Dwyer, you said?"

"Yes."

"Tell her it's Mr. Dwyer." The young man in scrubs nodded and walked quickly down the corridor, entering a room on the left. "It may take a few minutes," the nurse told him. "She's been answering questions, trying to help."

The nurse glanced at Liz, assuming she was there to support Mike. "I'm Liz Jordan. I'm a lieutenant with the police bureau although I'm not here in a professional capacity, at least not yet," Liz explained, as she showed the nurse her shield. "Has law enforcement been called?"

Nurse Roberts glanced quickly from Liz's face to the badge, the said in a quiet voice, "Yes, there's an officer with Ms. Hadley and the patients." She pointed to a small room to her right. "You can wait for her in there."

"Thank you," said Mike. The small room the nurse had indicated had a sign near the door that read, *Admissions.* Through a large window, filtered by venetian blinds, they saw a desk with a chair behind it, two other chairs side by side, and no room for anything else. The space barely provided enough room to close the door.

Mike and Liz sat, leaving the door open, and waited. Through the window, they had a view of the check-in desk and watched as Nurse Roberts went on to other pressing matters.

A siren heralded the approach of an ambulance. Personnel wearing scrubs rushed through the lobby entrance pushing a gurney. An urgent page blasted over the intercom. The message sounded garbled, but urgent and ominous, nonetheless. They looked at each other.

"Thanks for coming with me," said Mike. He covered Liz's hand with his own.

Liz and Mike waited quite a while before Quinn appeared at the doorway to the tiny room. She was no longer wearing the dress she'd been in earlier with the denim jacket. She was in baggy, capri-length jeans and a tee shirt from an Alice in Chains concert. On her feet were tennis shoes with the laces tied loosely to slip the shoes on and off her feet. "Mike, Liz. I'm glad you're here." Her face was filled with stress and worry.

When Liz saw Quinn, instinct told her the woman needed to sit. "Quinn, please sit down," she said, insisting Quinn take her chair.

"What's happened?" asked Mike, as Quinn flopped into the chair. Liz stood at the doorway, leaning against the frame, her face toward the lobby.

"A kid staggered into the center. She was bleeding and her clothes looked like she'd been in a fight. We couldn't understand what she was telling us, but she pointed outside. Then she collapsed," Quinn told them, as if she could barely believe it herself. "One of the staff ran out and found a second kid lying just outside the door. The second kid was bleeding. They tried to make it all the way inside, but that was as far as they could go."

"How are they doing, Quinn?" Mike asked.

"They are both conscious. Elle, who made it inside and alerted us, was beat up pretty badly. Blows to the face, took a hit to the head, that's probably why she collapsed. The other kid, who goes by Pooki, suffered a stab wound to the abdomen. The injury will require surgery. They just took her down to pre-op."

Aggravated assault, thought Liz. *And they're just kids.* "What's the name of the officer who responded?" Liz asked Quinn.

"Castillo," answered Quinn. "We called 911 and the officer met us here. We were fortunate to get a young officer, and a female."

"I know Castillo. She's good with kids." Liz had just seen that particular officer that morning. It had been Castillo who had ushered Chapin into a room to wait for Liz.

"Why is it fortunate that a young, female officer responded, Quinn?" Mike asked her, but glanced over at Liz.

"Well, we needed sensitivity. The doctors treating them are being kind, but of course, they need to be thorough. We don't yet know the full extent of their injuries. Elle and Pooki are best friends. Pooki is bi-gender, meaning her gender identity encompasses male and female. Elle is trans. She identifies as female. They won't give their age, but I'm sure neither of them is eighteen. Pooki and Elle are both more comfortable with women. They've had too many bad experiences with men. I hope I haven't offended you, Mike."

"No offense taken," Mike told her. "I'm sorry we have to consider such things."

Liz nodded. "At least the kids are getting the care they need. I want to talk to Castillo, see what she knows, ask what she needs on this," said Liz. She looked at Quinn, and said, "I'll make sure not to disturb."

"Tell Castillo I'll be back with them in a few minutes," Quinn said. "Thanks, Liz."

Liz left Mike and Quinn and returned to the front desk. She spoke with Nurse Roberts in a quiet voice. "I'd like to have a word with the Officer Castillo in room three, but I don't want to ask her to leave the room."

"Go ahead and walk back, Lieutenant," Nurse Roberts told her.

Liz walked down the corridor to the room designated as treatment room, number three. She heard voices emanating from the room, one younger voice, a teenager, and another that sounded like an adult, but it wasn't Castillo.

A privacy curtain was drawn across the inside of the open doorway. Liz rapped her knuckle twice on the door and the curtain was pushed aside enough to allow Castillo's face to appear. She was surprised to see Liz, but her face also registered relief.

"Lieutenant. Are you looking for me?" Castillo asked.

"Yes. I arrived with Quinn's boss," she answered in a quiet voice. "I was with him when he got the call about what happened. As long as I'm here, I wanted to ask how the kids are doing and see if you need anything from the department."

"Give me a second, Lieutenant." Liz heard Castillo softly ask someone, "Are you okay with one of our Lieutenants coming in? She wants to say hello."

A kid uttered a very faint *yeah* in response. Castillo waved Liz into the room from the other side of the curtain. She entered the room to find a nurse inputting patient notes into a computer. Lying on the hospital bed was a thin waif of a kid. Whether it was body type or lack of nutrition was hard to tell, but the kid couldn't have weighed more than ninety pounds.

Huge, dark eyes stared at Liz as she entered. Her head rested on the pillow but she didn't look to have the strength to raise it if she had wanted. A bandage around her head was capped by dark hair protruding at the top. An intravenous drip was anchored in the bend of one elbow. The kid's face, neck, and arms featured a mass of bruises, some new and severe, others looked old and partially healed. The poor kid was a Dickens character come to life.

"Elle, this is Liz," said Castillo. "She's one of my bosses."

"Hi," the kid said, in the same faint voice.

"Hi, Elle," said Liz. She acknowledged the nurse with a nod, and then looked back to Elle. "How are you doing?"

"I'm okay," answered Elle, but the weakness in the voice said otherwise. "Where's that other lady, the one named Quinn?"

"Quinn is just down the corridor. She'll be back with you soon," Liz assured the kid.

"Elle's friend, Pooki, is being taken care of. Right, Elle?" It was Castillo who had offered the information, trying to sound positive. Liz didn't want to make assumptions. She decided it was best to nod that she understood.

"She got cut bad. The Doc's gonna stitch her up," said Elle, giving Liz her quick assessment of what had occurred."

"Well, that's good then," Liz told the kid. "That's what doctors do: they take care of folks."

The nurse reviewed data on a small screen near the head of Elle's bed, and then said to the kid, "It will be good for you to talk to the officers for a few minutes, but I will be back. I want to see if we have a bed ready. With the bump on your head, the doctor wants you to stay here with us for observation, at least for tonight."

Elle nodded in response and the nurse stepped out. "I'm glad they're taking care of you," Liz said. "You made it to the Youth Center for help. You got help for Pooki. That was good." As Elle listened to Liz's words, she raised her free arm and laid it over her eyes for a moment of privacy.

"I'm sorry this happened to you," Liz told the kid. "It makes me angry that you and Pooki were hurt. I don't like to see anyone get hurt. You know what I mean?"

"Us punks get hurt all the time," said Elle, her face now vacant of the emotion that had crept in.

They heard a quick knock on the door and Quinn stepped into the hospital room. "So, how are we doing?" she asked with concern, looking at Elle. "You met my friend Liz, huh, Elle." The kid nodded, looked at Quinn with huge eyes.

"Quinn, can you stay with Elle while I talk to Castillo?" asked Liz.

"Of course," said Quinn. "I'm not going anywhere for the time being. Mike mentioned you had photos to show me. You can find me later or call me tomorrow."

"Oh, yeah, thanks," said Liz. The photos and the search for Kyrie had slipped her mind. "I'll send them to you later. You can get back to me whenever. Don't worry about it now." Liz turned to the kid lying in the bed. "Bye, Elle," she said. "Try to get some rest."

Chapter Sixteen

"Elle and Pooki"

"Long day, Castillo," said Liz after they stepped into the corridor.

"I was about to clock out when I took the call," said Castillo, brushing back loose strands of dark hair with her hand. "It is okay, Lieutenant."

"What have you found out?" asked Liz.

"I haven't talked with the kid called Pooki. They were checking her injuries when I arrived, but Elle was helpful, more so than I expected. According to Elle, she and Pooki have been squatting in a vacant building by the railroad tracks. Two days ago, Pooki was looking through garbage cans outside a diner and a guy approached her, asked if she was hungry. She said, 'yeah, that's why I'm looking for garbage food' or something like that. The guy told Pooki she could come to his house and he would make dinner. Pooki was hungry and the guy looked all right to her, so she said okay, but that her friend, Elle would want to come with her."

"Where is the diner?"

"Not far from the park. It's an ugly little place. I had a team check it out. The garbage cans are in the back alley. No one saw anything and it was two days ago. Nothing happened there anyway."

"Except an assailant may have approached a victim there," Liz mentioned. It was an important detail, in Liz's mind.

“That’s true,” said Castillo. “The guy gave Pooki an address and told her and her friend to be there in an hour. He’d have food waiting for them. Like bait, Lieutenant. Elle and Pooki found the place. The guy had a roommate. Elle says they both seemed okay. They were nice, she said. They had dinner and the guys let them sleep there. No one bothered them. Then yesterday, the roommate starts telling the guy from the alley that Elle and Pooki were going to have to contribute something if they wanted to eat again.”

“Contribute something? Is that what they said?” asked Liz, knowing *something* meant sex acts.

“Yes, Lieutenant. The kids didn’t want to, but were going along with it. Elle said you feel pressured when you get food and a place to crash. Street kids are doing what they can to survive. They are victims, they're underage. By law, they aren’t consenting adults.”

“What happened next?” Liz asked Castillo.

“The guys got rough, especially the roommate. The beatings started yesterday. Both men were pretty drunk tonight. The roommate tried to force himself on Elle; Pooki hit him in the head with something heavy. It didn’t do much damage except it slowed him down. The other guy, the one at the diner, grabbed a knife and started ‘slashing’—that’s the word Elle used.”

“Elle was sure they were both men? I’m clarifying for ID purposes, details.”

“Yes, Elle was clear on that. She was hit in the head hard, but the blow didn’t knock her out. Pooki got in the way of the knife. She got cut and the assailant dropped the blade. The knife was on the floor and both of the guys kind of froze.

Elle grabbed the knife and told the guys to stay away. Elle grabbed a towel to put pressure on Pooki's stab wound, then she picked up Pooki off the floor, and they walked out of there. All the way to the Youth Center."

"Does Elle remember the address of the house?"

"Yes, Lieutenant. We sent a team there, but the place was empty when they arrived. They're talking to neighbors for information and searching property records to find out who owns the place. They found blood evidence supporting Elle's story."

"Okay, Castillo. I'd appreciate being kept in the loop. If your sergeant has an issue with that, have him call me. If there is anything your team needs, let me know."

"I'll be in touch, Lieutenant," said Castillo. "And you can access notes in the department system as the case progresses."

"One last thing, Castillo, while I'm here," said Liz, pulling out her phone. "Have you seen this girl?" Liz showed Castillo the two photos of Kyrie.

Castillo studied the photos for a few moments. She focused on Kyrie's face long enough that Liz thought the girl may have looked familiar to the officer, but Castillo shook her head. "No, I don't think I've seen her. Could you forward the photos to my phone? If Elle's feeling up to it, I could ask if she knows her."

"I will forward the photos, but hold off on showing them to kids. I'm unsure about the girl's situation and I don't want her to hear that we're looking for her," Liz explained, "but if officers or other adults recognize her, please let me know. And let me know when you're able to talk to Elle's friend Pooki."

Chapter Seventeen

"Perspective"

Liz found Mike sitting on a bench outside the emergency entrance. "How are the kids doing?" he asked her.

Liz glanced around the entrance, but no one was within hearing distance. "The kid called Elle is stable. She'll be admitted for observation. The docs are concerned about minor head trauma, but it could have been worse. The other kid, who goes by Pooki, is in surgery to repair the stab wound. That's all I know about her condition," she said, sitting down next to Mike. "I talked with Castillo. There's a team already working on the case."

"Good. I hope they find these guys, Liz. Preying on street kids," he said with disgust. "I realize predators are fairly common, but this is so sick." Mike looked at Liz. "You'd think I'd get to a point where nothing surprises me."

"I hope you never get to the point where nothing surprises you," Liz responded, taking Mike's hand.

"How are you doing?" Mike asked her, giving her hand a squeeze in return.

"I'm fine," Liz answered. "Do you need to talk to Quinn again? I don't mind waiting. I've kept you waiting long enough."

"No, I've already made some calls," he said. "The staff at the Youth Center has things under control for tonight. Officers have been there already. Quinn and I made a plan to cover her absence at the center tomorrow morning. I'm heading there first thing. We will have a place ready for the kids to recover there when they're discharged. We're hoping they will trust Quinn enough to rest there. Let's go home."

Mike and Liz walked to the parking lot and climbed into Mike's car. They were exhausted but on edge after the events of the evening. Liz turned to Mike as he drove out of the hospital lot and toward Liz's place. She could not see him well in the dark. Liz placed her hand on his leg, a gesture of comfort. She hoped he would get some rest. Mike responded to the gesture, placing his hand over hers.

"I'm glad you were there, at the hospital," he said. "Quinn and Castillo seem like-minded about the street kids, in a lot of ways. That will help. And they were both glad for your support."

"I didn't do much," said Liz, waving off the statement, but she agreed that Castillo had handled the situation well. At the mention of Quinn's name, she remembered the photos of Kyrie. "I need to send these photos to Quinn." She pulled out her phone and sent them along with a brief explanation, but few details. "I showed Castillo the photos of Kyrie. She didn't recognize the girl, Mike. Maybe Quinn can be of help. I asked Castillo not to show them to any of the kids yet. I need a better feel for Kyrie and her situation before that happens. Alerting her that her dad is looking for her may not be a good thing."

"Quinn and her staff will help in any way they are able. Quinn is new to Columbia City, but John or someone else may know her. But you never know. She keeps her eyes open. When are you planning to contact Chapin again?" Mike asked. The way he said *Chapin* indicated his dislike of the idea.

"I don't know when I'll talk to him. I'm going to contact his admin in the morning, a woman named Richelle. Chapin says she may be helpful, that she knows Kyrie well, knows her friends."

Liz sighed, as she looked out the car window. She thought of Elle lying injured in a hospital bed. She thought of kids living on the streets and how whether they live or die can turn on a dime. It was late. Liz wanted to leave the conversation behind. She and Mike both needed sleep, but she wanted to share her thoughts with Mike.

"After I talk with this woman, I may decide to alert the missing person's team. I just want you to know that I'm considering it. If I go that route, then I'll talk to Miller myself. He will need to know everything, Mike—about Sara, about Chapin, about how Pruitt sent her in there to die."

"You already know what I think," he told Liz. "You always remind young officers about correct procedure and chain of command."

"You're telling me I need to practice what I preach?" Liz asked Mike, as he parked on the street in front of her house.

"No. I'm asking you to see the bigger picture. Did you have a Lieutenant who stressed those practices to you when you were a young officer?"

Liz stared out the window into the night. "What's happened can't be changed. And it's not about me or my position. It's about these kids, it's about Kyrie. I stood there looking at that kid in the hospital, Mike. She doesn't deserve to be living like this, on the streets. It's changed my perspective."

Mike and Liz were exhausted. They parked and locked the car and walked up to Liz's apartment on the third floor. They greeted the cats and went to bed.

Chapter Eighteen

"Punk Dream"

Standing below a rock-encrusted cliff, Liz heard voices. She looked high up into the hazy clouds that seemed to drift down in her direction. Straining to listen, she knew that the voices belonged to street kids, gutter punks. They were yelling at her, trying in their desperation to tell her something important.

"Hey! We are here! Look at us!" they called from above. "We've always been here and you never noticed," they yelled. "We are dying and it's your fault!"

They continued to scream accusations, and then one by one, at intervals of a few seconds, the kids plunged from the rocky cliff. Each punk employed a unique style as they jumped; one completed a perfect swan dive, while another attempted a somersault. But in the end, each one plummeted toward the ground below to where Liz was standing.

Realizing the danger, Liz screamed at the punks to stop, but either they didn't care to listen or couldn't hear. Arms waving frantically, she tried to warn them. "Stop! Don't jump! Please, stop!" she yelled. Tears streaming down her cheeks, she tried to catch them, tried to divert their fall, but to no avail.

As each punk jumped from the cliff above, their body hit the ground below making the same atrocious sound. Some of the punks' faces resembled Elle with huge, scared eyes and bandaged heads, while others looked like Kyrie in the last photo she'd sent to Chapin: beaten, bruised, and ill.

Liz knelt down near a kid that fell at her feet. The kid looked straight into Liz's eyes and said, "See? We told you that us punks get hurt all the time." Then they closed their eyes. In sorrow, Liz put her head close to the kid and closed her eyes, as well. Instead of silence, Liz heard a low, monotone hum.

As Liz slowly emerged from the dream, she realized that the punk at her feet had become tiny and covered with soft fur. The low, monotone hum was Little Kurt purring near Liz's face, fast asleep.

After inhaling a quick breath, Liz turned onto her back, ignoring Little Kurt's disgruntled protests. She looked around her dark bedroom. Next to her, Mike slept soundly with his back to Liz. Eddie was curled up sleeping between them, as usual. The illuminated numbers on the bedside clock said they had slept a couple of hours. She put her hands over her face, fingers pressing into her eyes as if to wipe away the images from her dream. Her breathing came in labored gasps and the skin on her face felt damp.

Lying in the dark, Liz couldn't escape the surreal images of street punks falling to their death. She got out of bed and walked to the bathroom where a dim, low wattage light burned. Looking in the mirror over the vanity, she was reluctant to make eye contact with her own reflection. She didn't need an analyst to interpret the dream. Kids were in danger, as Sara had been in danger, and Liz felt responsible.

In the hospital room, Elle's response to Liz's anger at her injuries had been, "Us punks get hurt all the time," and the kid in the dream uttered the same line. She thought about what she had said to Mike on the way home from the hospital, about the punks and their awful situations. *Shit, now they're haunting me,* she thought. *Yes,* she told herself, *her perspective had definitely changed.*

When Liz awoke to the alarm a few short hours later, it was still very early. The bedroom door was open and the precious cats slept peacefully near her. Her thoughts went immediately to the dream that had invaded her sleep, but she shook off the images. Stumbling to the kitchen, she was greeted by a note on the breakfast bar:

Fed the kids. Coffee ready to brew. Love you XXX.

Mike had already left for the Youth Center as planned. It was not unusual that he would be up and off before she was even coherent. Liz often started her day with a note and the coffee ready for her to brew. Liz pressed the button and headed to the shower.

Ten minutes later, wrapped in a towel, she sat on her bed. She sipped freshly brewed coffee; her hands warmed by the heat radiating from the mug.

Liz looked through her bag for the business card with Chapin's contact information. His admin, Richelle, could be reached at the second phone number on the card, he had said. It was early but she wanted to make the call, nonetheless. *Get it done now, before you get to the precinct,* she thought.

She dialed the second number on the card, another five zero three area code. After three or four rings, Liz's call was answered by voice mail, but unlike the other number she had called to reach Chapin, the greeting was in a woman's voice.

"You've reached G.C. Investments. You may leave a message at the tone. Thank you." The greeting was followed by the promised buzz.

"This message is for Richelle. My name is Liz. You should have been told to expect my call. Please get back to me as soon as possible. It's about Kyrie." Liz left her number and ended the call. It had been worth a try and Liz hoped to hear from the woman soon.

She dropped the phone into her bag along with Chapin's business card. Still wrapped in the towel, Liz shivered, craving more of the hot coffee. She walked into the kitchen and refilled her coffee mug. Thirty minutes later, she was on her way to the precinct.

Chapter Nineteen

"Richelle"

By mid-morning, Liz had been at her desk for three hours. She welcomed the distraction provided by the usual tasks involving her team of homicide detectives, but the punk in the hospital bed and Sara's missing daughter consumed much of her thoughts. She took a few minutes to review Castillo's notes regarding the violent assaults suffered by Elle and her friend Pooki the previous evening.

There were new details in the notes that Liz hadn't learned by talking with Castillo at the ER. The street addresses were listed, of the diner where Pooki had scrounged for something to eat, and of the residence where the attack on the two streets kids had occurred.

The report included few forensic details from the scene, but what had been found was important. Blood belonging to Pooki had been found in the living room. The knife used in the stabbing was found in shrubbery where Elle had flung it as they stumbled away. However, no obvious clues were found at the scene to indicate the identity of the two men who supposedly had lived there. No mail, no computer, no reading material, or photos. *How is that possible?* Liz asked herself. She would hope that collected prints or DNA samples would match something in the various data bases.

The neighborhood left a lot to be desired. It was comprised of small, old, ramshackle rentals with tiny lots and converted apartment units that had long ago seen their best days. This was not a neighborhood where people who lived nearby know and look out for each other. If a knock at a neighbor's door was even answered, the occupants had seen nothing, heard nothing, and knew not a thing about two men living there.

Liz made a note to Castillo that the two addresses were not that far from each other. Maybe one or both of the assailants frequented the diner. When the injured kids were up to it, an electronic facial identification technique producing facial composites might help with IDs. Liz hoped so because the police had nothing else to go on at this point.

As Liz had closed the file notes in the system, her phone rang. She recognized the number of the incoming call as the one she had dialed to reach Chapin's admin early that morning.

"Liz Jordan," she answered, offering her last name out of habit, although she hadn't intended to.

"This is Richelle. Richelle Isaacs," the caller explained. The admin sounded businesslike, but her words were rushed, in a flurry. "I apologize for the delay in getting back to you." Liz heard a hint of an accent. It wasn't in the pronunciation, but in the way the words were delivered. *Philadelphia,* she thought. *Classy, like Grace Kelly*. Liz gauged the voice to be of a woman in her late twenties to early thirties.

Liz was about to reprimand the woman for the delay. She should know that whatever she had been busy with couldn't be as important as a missing fifteen-year-old. Before Liz could give her a piece of her mind, Richelle continued, "I wanted to clear your name and number with Mr. Chapin and I couldn't reach him until a few moments ago. He had not mentioned to me that you'd be calling." Richelle said the word *calling*, slowly with emphasis, more due to a natural habit of speech than learned pronunciation.

"Well, that's unfortunate. It would have been helpful to speak with you earlier," Liz said, but she felt like she was stating an obvious point. "Your employer asked me to look into where his daughter may be. I think time is of the essence here, Ms. Isaacs. Anything you can tell me may be of help."

"Mr. Chapin contacted you because you're with the police. He said you are a Lieutenant."

"Yes, I am," Liz told her. "But at this time, I'm asking questions unofficially."

"I understand," said Richelle, but she hesitated, as if thinking of the reasons and unspoken inferences for an unofficial inquiry.

"I want to get a feel for Kyrie and her life at home. When did you start working there? How long have you known Kyrie?"

"I've worked for Mr. Chapin for six years. Kyrie was almost nine at the time I started here. There had been a procession of nannies. We got along well, Kyrie and I. When she was between nannies again, I was asked to help with her daily care as well as my other responsibilities."

"What are your other responsibilities, Ms. Isaacs?"

"Please, call me Richelle. I function much like any other admin, managing Mr. Chapin's schedule, correspondence, messages, etc. I prioritize the demands for his attention so he can devote his time to other concerns." The woman certainly made Chapin sound like a legitimate businessman, but then she was paid to. Liz would play along.

"You must put in more hours than a typical admin, if you were also caring for your employer's child."

"As I said, I function similarly, but not entirely like most other admins. For instance, I live on the premises. It was the logical arrangement when I started caring for Kyrie. Mr. Chapin operates the business from his home office. This is also my work location."

This woman, Richelle, sounded intelligent, professional. But regardless of that, she was associated with Gabriel Chapin. *What was this woman really,* thought Liz, *some kind of paid girlfriend and caregiver for the girl?* Liz reminded herself not to let her imagination run wild. Richelle's position in Chapin's home, his business, even his bedroom, was probably immaterial to finding his missing daughter. *Or was it?*

As if she had heard Liz's thoughts, Richelle explained, "I'm involved with aspects of Mr. Chapin's business, but I have my own rooms here at the house. There is a housekeeper on staff, as well. She manages Mr. Chapin's home."

"Tell me about Kyrie," said Liz, getting back to the reason for her call. "You said there had been a few caregivers. Why was that?"

"It wasn't because of Kylie's behavior or anything along those lines. Kyrie was not a difficult child, just extremely bright, precocious even. The succession of nannies was due to Mr. Chapin's attempts to manage as a single parent. I don't think he knew how to go about finding quality care for his daughter. He didn't go through normal channels, hiring intermediaries to find a suitable nanny." Liz wondered if Chapin had hired caregivers for his young daughter out of the cocktail lounges and casinos he used to frequent. Great.

"What about Kyrie's grandmother? The child lived with her when she was very young. Was she not a resource?"

At the mention of Kyrie's grandmother, Richelle did not respond right away. Liz wondered how aware she was of Chapin's past. After a few moments, she said, "I have no information about that. You'll need to ask Mr. Chapin. My impressions about the grandmother are based on the few comments Kyrie made over the years. There was nothing significant and I don't believe Kyrie has seen the woman in a very long time."

"Is it possible that Kyrie has been in touch with her grandmother?" Liz asked.

"I wouldn't know, but I doubt it," Richelle answered. "I doubt she would know where to find her."

"Okay, I may come back to that. I'll make a note to ask Mr. Chapin," decided Liz. "Let's get back to Kyrie."

"I don't have a background caring for children, you understand. Kyrie and I became friends. We became close," explained Richelle. "She seemed to gravitate toward me. She liked hearing about my East Coast upbringing, school and the like. She was interested in my opinion. We listened to each other. She was respectful toward me. Kyrie treated me like an aunt, an older sibling or cousin. That was why I was comfortable with the responsibility for her care."

"You must have known her friends, her school activities. What can you tell me?"

"Kyrie can be quiet, introspective, but she has a lot to say when the mood strikes. She had the same small group of friends for a long time. They shared interests in music and songwriting. Kyrie has an exceptional singing voice."

"You said she *had* the same group of friends, past tense. What changed?"

"The group fell apart, disbanded, unraveled, if you will. Kyrie attended St. Magdalene's, a private academy, one of the most prestigious in the Pacific Northwest. There was some trouble at school last term, honors violations that resulted in blaming and finger pointing."

"Honors violations," repeated Liz. "Could you be more specific?"

"There were photos and messages posted on social media. Kyrie became caught up in it. As the situation evolved, it turned ugly. Kyrie was not as invested in protecting herself as some of the older, more assertive students."

Liz thought that was an odd thing to say. "What does that statement mean?"

"The older students, the ones who started posting and sharing images, had college aspirations to consider. Any hint of impropriety or scandal would derail their plans. Kyrie expected that everyone would admit to their part and suffer the same punishment. Kyrie became the scapegoat. She was suspended from school briefly and required to offer formal apologies."

"Was Mr. Chapin aware of the situation?" Liz asked. Chapin had said that Kyrie wasn't looking forward to the next year of school, but said nothing of the problems she was hearing about from Richelle.

"Yes, but his view was that the issue would resolve itself, run its course." She waited a few moments before she offered more. Liz nearly interrupted when Richelle spoke up again. "Mr. Chapin wanted it to be an opportunity, a lesson for

Kyrie." Liz heard judgment in Richelle's tone. She had disagreed.

"Kyrie's father said she hadn't run away before," said Liz, "and she's been gone four months. He said she became rebellious. Was it precipitated by these troubles or was there more to it?

"I would not use the word *rebellious,*" Richelle told Liz. "I'd say Kyrie felt stung, mistreated. The issues at school had begun to fade into the background for the most part, but she remained bitter and resentful. I can't say I blamed her. Kyrie was outraged that while all of the students involved were equally at fault, many of them were never held responsible in the slightest. It really was unfair, Lieutenant. I had suggested to Mr. Chapin that changing schools might be a good idea. He disagreed. His feeling was that Kyrie would be avoiding her problems."

"Did you suspect she'd run away?"

"No! I didn't suspect she'd run away or I'd have tried to prevent it!" she said with anger. "Please remember that I care about Kyrie." Richelle inhaled audibly, and then sighed. "I apologize for that."

"Don't apologize, Richelle. I'm sure you care about the girl. I can imagine this has been hard." Liz was expecting—hoping—to hear concern and emotion in Richelle's voice. Finally, she had.

"Kyrie had not run before, but she was pushing limits. Not checking in, not coming home by the time asked, not bringing her new friends around. The rule was that if I had not met them, she couldn't spend time with them outside of school. Kyrie had been a good student, communicative and stable. She became sad, unresponsive; spending most of her time in her room."

"Any evidence of drugs? Alcohol?"

"Not that I saw, and I think I would have picked up on the signs. After she ran, I spoke with a few of her friends—the ones she still trusted—and with many of their parents. Nothing helpful came of it. I can provide you with a list of names."

"Yes, I will want to talk to them," Liz told her. "Most people are more forthcoming when law enforcement asks the questions. You mentioned Kyrie was interested in music," said Liz.

"Yes, she is and songwriting. She has a decent voice. She writes poetry and song lyrics."

"That's good to know," said Liz, as she made a note. "I have one last question for now, Ms. Isaacs, and it's important: most kids who run choose a street name. This enables them to disconnect from their past. It also makes it harder to find them. If Kyrie has chosen a street name, what do you think she might want to be called?"

"A street name; I should have thought of that, Lieutenant. Let me see...something related to music or poetry, no doubt. My guess would be along those lines, unless she's reinvented herself further."

"Okay. That's helpful. At some point soon, I need to see Kyrie's room. Please don't remove anything or make changes until that happens."

"I will speak with Mr. Chapin about allowing it, but I'm sure it will be fine."

"Richelle, excuse me, but it better be very damn fine with *Mr. Chapin*. He asked me to find his daughter. His *missing fifteen-year-old* daughter. I think I understand your position, your function, whatever—so try to understand mine. In my professional opinion, there's no time to lose here. The changes in the girl's appearance tell us if she's still okay, she's not going to be well for long."

Liz heard a sharp intake of breath, a gasp. "I understand what you're saying, Lieutenant. Certainly. What I meant to say was I will let Mr. Chapin know. Just tell me when."

"One more thing, as long as we're being honest here, and, please I need you to be honest now. I've looking into GC Investments. I know the company has been investigated. Could Kyrie's taking off, or her staying away, have any connection to Mr. Chapin's business dealings?"

"Of course, not...," Richelle said, but Liz heard her hesitate.

"Don't make me spell it out, Richelle. I need all the information I can get to find her. And if I can bring her home, we can only hope she doesn't run again. Most of these kids do run again, have you thought of that? So, I need to know."

"Lieutenant, our business pursuits have nothing to do with Kyrie or her safety," Richelle said adamantly. "She is simply uninvolved, distanced, as any child would be. And her father would not put her well-being at risk."

"Okay, I'll believe that for the time being. I hope you realize that being straight with me will play out better for Kyrie. Before I go, is there anything else I need to know?"

"Only that Mr. Chapin would do anything to have his daughter back at home with him," said Richelle. It struck Liz that the statement spoke to Chapin's wants and wishes, but expressed no real concern for his daughter's welfare.

"Then don't make me feel like I'm begging for help. I need your cooperation to find Kyrie. I'll be in touch." Liz ended the call.

Chapin would do anything, Richelle had said, to have his daughter home; anything except be sensitive to her problems and make suitable adjustments regarding her school environment. *Chapin was as self-centered in dealing with his daughter as he had been with Sara*, Liz thought.

Chapter Twenty

"Safe Haven"

When Mike arrived at the Youth Center, the day had barely begun as if the building itself yawned and stretched. He was greeted by John, the pony-tailed bouncer who had been watching the door the previous morning. Everyone was anxious about the attacks on Elle and Pooki. It had been a long evening, but the night had passed and most of the kids were still sleeping. The two men sat over coffee in the small classroom.

"Quinn asked me to stay here last night so she could be at the hospital. We were pretty busy: nineteen kids asked for bunks," John reported. "We had a few kids we hadn't seen before, and a few we hadn't seen here in a while.

"Long night for you," said Mike.

"Word got out fast and kids showed up wanting to know what happened," John answered, his coffee mug in hand. "We had two staff and four interns here overnight. There was a lot of wide-eyed fear and speculation. We tried to be as honest as possible and calm them down at the same time. An officer named Castillo was here for quite a while."

"I've heard of Castillo," said Mike. "How did that go?"

"Better than I would have expected," answered John. "She came here from the hospital. I thought she'd be questioning the kids hard for info, but she was easy on them. Wanted them to know she'd talked with Elle, let them know she would be okay. Said they were taking care of Pooki.

Castillo seemed to have figured out that pushing too hard was not going to help."

"What have you heard from Quinn?"

"She talked with Children's Services late last night. The hospital was required to notify them that Elle and Pooki had been admitted. It's an iffy situation. The kids are minors so the law holds the state responsible for them, but they have no ID. Kids know if they don't disclose any information and no parent comes forward, you can't determine who they are. On the other hand, if they're taken into custody and officials try to find the families through missing person's reports, the kids just run again. It's happened before."

"I understand the issues." Mike thought of Liz and the task of searching for Chapin's daughter. "So, what's going to happen?"

"One of the first things Quinn put in place here was to have the youth shelter approved as a receiving facility."

"That's right, I signed off on the paperwork," said Mike, after a sip of coffee. "It sounded like a formality when Quinn and I talked about it. It's a stop gap, intended to aid the most vulnerable kids."

"Yes, that's the intent. And it didn't hurt that Castillo had been on site. Elle will be released from the hospital later today. She will be allowed to recuperate here. Elle told Castillo that this is where she wanted to go."

"Any update on Pooki's condition?"

"Her injuries are bad, according to Quinn. There's deep tissue damage and she lost a lot of blood," he said with concern, one hand adjusting the pony-tail. John's gaze moved to the common room where activity had caught his eye. He didn't want kids to overhear. "The kid isn't in the best physical shape. They're hoping to avoid infection."

Mike was angry and concerned for a young person whom he had never met. He looked John in the eye but made no response.

"There's one other detail." said John, keeping his voice low. "Elle told Castillo that when they escaped the house after the attack, they were stumbling down the street. Elle and Pooki passed by two people, adults walking the other direction. They told them were hurt, that they needed help. The folks accused them of being drugged up, told them to get lost."

The anger and concern erupted, spilling from Mike's mouth. "Shit. Are you kidding me?"

"It was dark, they wouldn't have realized the extent of the kids' injuries," John reasoned. "But a little human compassion would have saved the kids from walking the extra blocks to get here."

"No wonder these kids don't trust anyone," said Mike.

John could only nod in agreement.

Chapter Twenty-one

"Moral Support"

Liz sat in her office, elbows on her desk, her chin resting on interlocked hands. She was deciding what to do. Even when she put police procedure aside, she knew the decision wasn't hers to make. Liz needed to follow the norms of decency and common sense, and she couldn't initiate a search for a missing fifteen-year-old by herself.

Kyrie deserved the weight of the department and its resources behind the search. Liz's opinion of the girl's father was immaterial. The past was irrelevant when a young girl was missing and maybe in danger.

Her office phone rang. Liz stared at the receiver, not answering it. Her thoughts kept returning to the punk dream, with kids plunging to their death and Liz screaming for them to stop. Within seconds, the phone was silent.

Liz thought of Captain Miller, hoping to speak with him. She found his calm approach and expertise invaluable. Liz picked up the receiver of her office phone and started to punch in the numbers for her captain's extension. Indecision struck yet again and she replaced the receiver in its cradle. She picked up her cell phone and called Mike. He answered on the second ring.

"Hey. How's your morning?" he asked Liz. "Hold on for just a moment." Liz could hear Mike talking to someone, but the sound was muffled. When he returned to the call, he said, "Sorry about that. I wanted to take the call when I saw that it was you, but I'm at the Youth Center. I've stepped outside."

"How are things there?" she asked.

"Busy, but staff here is on top of things. One of the kids, the one you met last night, Elle, is coming here when she's discharged from the hospital later today."

"Sounds like a good plan," Liz said.

"Apparently, they have her working with technicians to produce likenesses of the two assailants," Mike told Liz. "Castillo said they wanted that task completed before Elle was out of the hospital."

"Good. The sooner the better. Do you think it would help or hinder if I stopped by later?" Liz asked him, wanting to visit the injured kid again. "I could say hello."

"It would be great, if you have time. As a cop, you're an exception to the 'no adult visitors' rule," he kidded. "How are you doing, anyway? I asked, but didn't give you the chance to say."

"I'm okay, I guess. I talked with Chapin's admin, Richelle. She sounds like a smart woman, too smart to be working for Chapin. In the past, he coerced underlings into abject loyalty, so it makes me wonder if Chapin has something on her. I want more information about her. This woman Richelle may have an angle, but she was helpful. She's concerned; sounds like she's close to Kyrie."

"What are you going to do, Liz? Have you decided?"

"There needs to be an integrated search for the girl, Mike. I can't do that on my own. I will tell Chapin myself that's the best way to find Kyrie. I'll advise him to work with

Missing Persons. If he tells me to screw myself, I'll file a missing person's report with the information I have."

"You know it's the right thing to do. You would regret it if you didn't stop him from using you."

"Yes, it is and you're right. I'm going to Miller as soon as possible. He needs to be aware that Chapin contacted me. And I learned a bit about Kyrie. Richelle says music is her thing. Tell me, have any of the kids mentioned a girl who likes poetry? Likes to sing? A girl with a decent voice?"

"Some kids are all about music," Mike answered. "They each have their preferences. Some are dancers. Others are into art. I'll keep my ears open. And I'll ask the staff; see what they have to say. Why don't you forward her pictures to me?"

"Just did," said Liz as she pressed *Send*. "Thanks."

"Liz, isn't Connors with Missing Persons now?"

"He is. He transferred when he made Sergeant." Kyle Connors and Liz had solved many tough cases together. She would like to see him handling the search for Kyrie, but there were no guarantees of assignments.

"That has to be encouraging. Call me after you talk to Miller. Okay?"

"I will. I'll be in touch. Love you. And thanks." She ended the call.

Once again, Liz picked up the receiver to her office phone. She dialed Miller's line before she could change her mind.

Chapter Twenty-two

"Captain Miller"

Miller's administrative assistant was a formidable woman named Clarice. She answered on the third ring, aware that it was Liz calling. It wasn't unusual for Liz to call; she reported to Miller as her commander. But Clarice's job was to protect the captain's time and control access to him and she was good at her job.

"Lieutenant, what can we do for you?" asked Clarice with a professional courtesy that said, *let's not waste time here.*

"Hi, Clarice, I'm hoping to get on his calendar. Does he have any time available today?"

"Let me see...he's due at City Hall this afternoon. How much time do you need?"

"Maybe half an hour," Liz said, but she was unsure of exactly what she wanted to say.

"Come on up, and I'll see if we can squeeze you in." *Come on up* meant to the third-floor office suites, where the brass held court. With that, Clarice was gone.

Liz hung up the phone, checked her appearance in the mirror hanging behind her office door. She smoothed her hair and ran a finger over her bottom lip. She adjusted the collar of her shirt. As she studied her reflection, Liz looked everywhere but into her own eyes.

Before last night, she hadn't shared her feelings of guilt about Sara's death with anyone. She talked with Mike and now she would tell the captain. It wasn't easy, being honest.

Just *do it,* she told herself. *You should have dealt with this shit ages ago.* Liz took the elevator up to three and walked down the corridor to Clarice's desk.

"Go right in, Lieutenant. Captain is waiting for you." Liz nodded and thanked Clarice. She opened the office door and stepped inside.

Miller was sitting at his desk, which looked remarkably organized. He was looking through reading glasses at the computer monitor, head tipped back slightly, huge hands tapping keys at break-neck speed. Now in his sixties, Miller had been with the force in Columbia City over forty years. A Vietnam veteran, he had entered the police academy upon his return from Southeast Asia.

Tall of stature and still remarkably fit, Miller had never abandoned his GI-buzz cut and clean-shaven face. Gold, wire-framed glasses accented smooth, dark brown skin that showed only the slightest indication of age around mouth and chin. He was known for having a tough, no-nonsense approach. Miller had once confided in Liz that he'd had his fair share of bullshit a long time ago.

Liz approached the desk but stood, waiting for her captain to acknowledge her presence. She would not want to interrupt nor would she take a seat unless it was offered.

"Lieutenant, please have a seat. I'll be right with you," he said, peering over the top of the lenses. Liz sat in a visitor's chair as Miller finished tapping keys, closed the file, and removed his reading glasses.

Resting his hands on the arms of his office chair, Miller took a deep breath. He directed his attention to Liz and asked, "What can I do for you, Liz?"

Where to begin? Liz asked herself, deciding to start at the beginning as she had when she told Mike the story.

"Sir, I was involved on the sidelines of an investigation years ago. The target was a club owner by the name of Killian. I'm sure you remember."

Miller looked to the ceiling as he searched his memory, and then redirected his gaze at Liz. "I do. That was a hell of a long time ago."

"It was. And it ended without arrests. The principal targets fled. Three people died."

"Yes, it was a shit show," Miller said in his deep, resonant voice, "A raid that went bad. I remember it all."

"One of the three who died was a young woman who was providing us with information. I had been acquainted with her prior to my joining the force. Her name was Sara Mallory. My role was to obtain info from Sara and relay it to the team. Sara had a boyfriend at the time. His name is Gabriel Chapin. He was working for Killian."

"The name doesn't ring a bell for me. Should it?"

"Not necessarily, but he's still in the area. He claims to be operating within the law now, although a search of records makes me wonder. There's nothing conclusive, no charges due to lack of evidence, but a lot of speculation."

"Lack of evidence doesn't mean all is above board, by any means," said Miller.

"No, Sir. It does not." Liz tried to convey a lack of concern, but her tone betrayed her. "Anyway, Mr. Chapin contacted me recently."

"Why?" asked Miller in that flat tone that suggested he didn't want to hear the answer, but had no choice.

"He disclosed to me that he and Sara had a child together. I had no idea the child existed, Sir. I knew Sara fairly well, or so I believed. She never shared with me that she was a mother. The girl is fifteen now. She ran away a few months ago. Mr. Chapin has asked that I find her."

"That's unfortunate about the girl, but you're a homicide cop. He wants Missing Persons. Excuse me, Lieutenant, but that's a simple enough solution. You're going to have to tell me why I need to know any of this."

"I'm trying to get there, Sir. Bear with me. The lead investigator on the Killian case was Frank Pruitt. Sara was his contact."

"Frank Pruitt," said Miller, repeating the name with contempt. "I could have gone the rest of my days without hearing that name ever again."

"Yes, Sir, a lot of people feel the same. Sara wasn't capable of looking out for herself. She wasn't cut out for what was expected of her. She depended on Pruitt, and on me, to keep her out of harm's way. Things didn't go as they should have."

"Of course, they didn't. It was a botched raid."

"There was more to it than that, Sir. Pruitt informed me the raid was going to happen. He told me not to share the info with Sara. He didn't say why and I didn't ask. I should have. Pruitt ordered me to keep my distance, but he didn't pull me off the assignment. Sara was at the site of the raid and died there in the crossfire. I should have been honest about the danger. I could have offered to hide her, put her in a safe house. I should have done something."

"Did you feel that way at the time?"

"I did, but I panicked. I deferred to Pruitt's judgement. It probably cost Sara her life. Afterward, I doubted my ability to make competent decisions as an officer. I considered quitting the force."

"Many young officers question their ability, especially after a case like you describe, Lieutenant. We're human beings, after all."

"Yes, Sir, but Chapin knows it went down that way. He holds Pruitt and me responsible for Sara's death. Pruitt is gone so it's down to me. Chapin asked me to find the girl because I knew her mother. He feels I owe it to Sara to find her kid. That's why he contacted me."

"And you feel responsible for this debt, as well?"

"I have always felt partly responsible for Sara's death. Finding out that she left a daughter has...reminded me of that. That's why I'm here, Sir. We both know what it's like on the street. It's brutal. A young girl will be lucky to survive."

Liz hesitated, but she knew she needed to be frank with Miller. "I've spoken with Chapin twice—first, when he showed up here at the precinct yesterday morning and again in the afternoon. At his request, I had a conversation with his administrative assistant, a woman named Richelle Isaacs. Apparently, she knows the girl well. I can't manage a search for this girl alone. She deserves a comprehensive effort."

"Yes, she does and no, you cannot do it alone," said Miller. He stood, walked over to the office door. Opening the door, he stuck his head out and Liz heard the captain tell Clarice, "Notify the Mayor's office that I'm going to be late. Then find Sergeant Connors for me."

"First, there's a child missing," began Miller as he returned to his desk and sat down. "A proper search must be implemented. The girl may want to come home, she may not. But her parent contacted a ranking law enforcement officer regarding her safety. We are obligated to pursue this whether that parent agrees with our process or not."

"I agree, Sir."

"Here's the other issue, Lieutenant. What happened years ago was a tragedy. It was a mess, to say the least. A woman lost her life. But this woman was an adult making her own choices. Nevertheless, you feel responsible to some degree. It's come back to haunt you."

Liz managed to swallow. Her mind was centered on the events Miller described. For years, she'd tried to forget about Sara and the way she died. Talking of it with Miller was as much a nightmare as when the punks had invaded her sleep. Liz felt the tension rise, but she kept her herself together, at least on the outside.

She inhaled deeply. Yes, haunted was exactly how she felt, as if a ghost from her past was there in the room with her, listening.

"What else do you need me to do, Sir?"

"Prepare a report for Connors and his team with everything you've learned about this missing girl. Then inform her father that we talked. Tell him the matter is out of your hands. And," said Miller, pointing his long, index finger at Liz for emphasis, "do both of us a favor and have no further contact with this man, Lieutenant."

"Yes, Sir," said Liz with a nod. *At least, Connors would be heading the search,* she thought. As Mike said, that was encouraging.

Miller's desk phone buzzed. He pressed the intercom button and said, "Yes, Clarice."

"Captain, Sergeant Connors is here."

"Please send him in," responded Miller. He released the intercom button as the office door opened and Connors stepped inside.

Tall, lean, and fit, Kyle Connors was dressed in street clothes with a side arm on his belt. His sergeant's shield hung from his neck on a narrow chain. He looked at Miller as he closed the office door, and said, "I was downstairs when I got your call, Sir. I came up as soon as possible."

"Have a seat, Sergeant," Miller told him, pointing to a chair.

"I'm glad you were around, Connors. Sorry to pull you in," Liz told him. She glanced down at her hands, not meeting his eyes.

Liz's presence took Connors by surprise. It was obvious that she had been meeting with the captain and they had opted to include him. The reason for that didn't concern him. Connors respected Liz. He had made sergeant because she had mentored him.

"Lieutenant, what's up?" he asked.

She looked from Connors to Miller, her outstretched hand urged Miller to begin.

"We need your team to find a missing fifteen-year-old girl, Sergeant," said Miller. He explained the basics of their situation and let Liz provide a few details about Chapin and his missing daughter.

"The captain has asked me to prepare a report for you," Liz told Connors. "I'll have it for you soon."

Chapter Twenty-three

"Insult to Injury"

Liz returned to her office and put the call into Chapin. She found the number in the list of recent calls made from her phone and pressed re-dial. When the call went to voice mail, Liz wondered if the shit head ever picked up a call or just screened them.

"This is an FYI. The search for your daughter will be handled by Missing Persons. This is the best course of action to find Kyrie and that should be the priority for all of us. You can expect to hear from a Sergeant Connors or from his team. For her sake, I hope they find Kyrie. Per my commander, the case is out of my hands. Don't contact me again."

She wasn't sure whether Chapin would share Liz's change of plan with Richelle, so Liz left a similar message for her. Officers would want to talk with Richelle. They would want to see Kyrie's room, as Liz had planned to do. In Richelle's message, Liz omitted the reference to her commanding officer and she encouraged Richelle to contact her if she thought of anything that might be useful, but Liz doubted she'd hear from the woman again.

Liz had promised to call Mike after her meeting with Miller. She reached him at the Youth Center and Mike stepped outside again, as he had done earlier. Liz explained that she had talked with Miller and that the search for Sara's daughter would be handled by Missing Persons.

"I have notes to write for Connors about what I know of Kyrie. Miller already called him in. Connors will head the missing person's case. I'm out of it."

"I'm glad to hear it, Liz. It's for the best. You don't need someone like Chapin in your life, asking for favors," Mike told her. He sounded relieved and Liz was touched by his concern. "Earlier, you said you might visit Elle. She's here and settled in. Why don't you come down here later? See the place, visit Elle, and talk with some of the kids. Then we'll go home together."

"I would like to see how Elle is doing," Liz answered. "I told her last night that I was angry she got hurt. I want her to believe that."

"I think a visit from you would be good for the kid. There's something else, Liz. Elle and Pooki tried to get help on the street last night from a couple of people they passed by. They were trying to make it here to the center. I guess the folks thought the two kids were druggies; told them to piss off. Sad."

"Shit. Talk about adding insult to injury, literally." Liz was disgusted, but knew it was true. "And we expect these kids to learn to respond appropriately."

"I didn't tell you about it to make you feel bad, but it happened. I thought you would want to know."

"I'll be in touch in a while. Love you."

"Love you too," said Mike as he ended the call.

Less than an hour and two cups of coffee later, Liz had detailed everything she knew about Kyrie Chapin. There wasn't much: conversations with her father and Richelle and contact information for each of them. Liz sent the email off to Connors. He replied, almost immediately with a text:

Rec'd the report on KC. Will be in touch if I have Qs or can give updates.

Liz texted Connors back:

Hey. Glad you're on it. Just find the girl.

Liz stayed busy catching up with tasks she had neglected earlier. She looked at the time and called Mike, who was glad to hear from her. "Are you coming down here? I'd like to show you the place. And Elle is awake."

"I would like to pay her a visit, but are you sure I should?" Liz asked. "I don't want to upset anyone."

"When did you ever worry about upsetting anyone? Hell, Liz, don't start now," he said with a laugh, but they both knew he meant it. Liz could come across like a bulldozer, but she had learned to limit the effect to law enforcement interactions. "It's not an official visit anyway and I'm approving you as a volunteer."

"Okay, if you say so. I'm about finished here anyway. I'd like to run home to change. It would be nice to look less official," she said. *And unarmed, she thought.*

"Good idea," Mike told her. "Wear your usual lie-around-at-home stuff. Just throw on your oldest, ugliest sweatshirt. You'll blend in nicely."

She got off the phone, tied up a few loose ends, and made the quick trip home. Eddie and Little Kurt scarcely acknowledged her presence, but came to investigate when they heard Liz filling their food and water bowls. She put her shield and weapon in the bedroom safe then changed into old leggings and a nondescript tee shirt.

Liz studied her reflection in the mirror by the door as she pulled her hair into a messy ponytail. She was far from the soccer-mom image, but Liz did not look anything like an investigating cop. She could live with that because that wasn't the intent of her visit to the Youth Center. Liz was going to say hello to an injured kid and because Mike had suggested it. *You look like a lonely, urban denizen heading out for a run,* she told herself. She threw on the well-worn Adidas hoodie she kept on a hook nearby and walked out the door.

Stepping inside the Youth Center, Liz was caught off guard by the amount of activity. There were groups of kids everywhere. A couple of kids were sitting on the floor in the large entry area, one playing guitar, the other on the harmonica. The performance left a lot to be desired, but the kids were giving it all they had.

A young woman approached Liz. She was wearing the bright red tee-shirt printed with the word STAFF. She reminded Liz of security personnel at festival music events.

"Are you Liz?" Liz replied that she was and the young woman pointed to a doorway. "Mike's in the common room. Go on in."

Walking further into the bowels of the building, Liz heard music playing. She could have sworn it was The Clash, and she wondered who might have chosen it. *Why would these kids want to listen to British punk rock that was popular so long ago? Because it was some of the rowdiest music ever recorded?* Liz decided she didn't care why. She was impressed that someone had good taste.

Mike was sitting on the end of a bench against the wall. He waved her over and she sat next to him, just as the guys sang along with the consuming energy of that insane drum beat.

If I go there will be trouble, and if I stay it will be double / Come on and let me know, should I stay or should I go?

Mike was deep in conversation with a kid. They were comparing singing voices with words like range, tone, and vibrato. "Hey," said Mike. "Glad you're here. What's your vote, Liz: David Bowie or Freddie Mercury?"

"Uh, well. That's hard to say. Both had great voices and both were amazing showmen."

The kid sitting next to Mike on the floor was not having it. "Nah, nah...you got to choose one!" he said adamantly, as he shook his head. "It's either Bowie or Freddy; which one?"

"I'll go with Bowie. Ziggy Stardust, Major Tom," she said.

The kid's disgust with Liz's choice showed on his face. Rolling his eyes, shaking his head, like he heard a stupid joke, he pulled himself up off the floor. He looked Liz in the eye and declared, "No way, man. No one was as total as Freddy." The kid pronounced the word *total* as TOW-TALL, and applied major emphasis. Liz noticed the dramatic, heavy black eyeliner surrounding pale blue-green eyes. "But, whatever," he said. He gave Mike a fist bump and ambled away.

"That was my new friend, Toots. We share some favorite recording artists, apparently."

"Since when do you like Freddy all that much?" Liz asked.

"Hey, give me a break. I'm trying to make connections. Anyway, come on, let's go see Elle."

Taking Liz by the hand, Mike led her to a hallway. He half-turned and said, "You look relaxed. That's good. I'm glad you decided against your cop persona."

"I'm not here as a cop. Actually, I'm only here to see the place and visit a kid." When Mike put an arm around her shoulder, she told him, "Sorry. That makes me sound uninterested. That's not the case."

"For whatever reason, I'm glad you're here," he said, as he nuzzled her ear."

A staff person wearing the required red tee shirt sat at a desk situated in the hallway across from the entrances to the bathrooms and showers. "When kids are on site, the bathrooms and showers are monitored," Mike told Liz. "There are three bunk rooms. Elle's in here."

Mike put his head into a bunk room doorway. "Hey, you have a visitor, Elle, if that's okay."

"Huh? I got a visitor?" asked a surprised, weak little voice. "Yeah, it's okay. Who is it?"

Mike and Liz entered the room to find Elle on one of the lower bunks, looking much the same as she had at the hospital the evening before: small, thin, malnourished, and with the bandage still on her head.

Effort had been put into making the kid comfortable with items not found on or around the other bunks. Elle had extra pillows at her head. A small, colorful quilt that could have been constructed for a small child was spread across the foot of the bed. A tiny folding table sat near the bunk. On the surface of the table were two bottles of water and a burner phone connected to a charger. Two large dandelions and a daisy protruded from a ceramic coffee mug.

Elle was lying on one side, a pillow scrunched up under her head. Her eyes grew round with surprise when she saw Liz. "Oh, hi," she said.

"Hi Elle," said Liz. "I don't want to bother you. I wanted to say hello. Do you remember me from the hospital?"

"Yeah, the cool, cop lady brought you in. You're a boss of cops, right?" Liz assumed the *cool, lady cop* was Castillo.

"That's right," Liz answered. "My name is Liz, remember? But I'm not here as a cop. I'm just checking to see how you're feeling. How's your head?"

"A little better," the kid said.

"I'm going to let the two of you visit," said Mike, looking at his watch. "It's close to time for your medicine, Elle. I'll be back with it in a few minutes."

Elle watched Mike turn and walk out. "He's nice. I like him," said Elle.

"Yes, he's nice," Liz said, glancing over at the doorway, as she sat on an adjacent lower bunk. "Mike and I have been friends for a long time. I like him, too." She turned her attention back to Elle. "I got hit in the head one time. It hurt so damn bad. I felt dizzy, I wanted to barf," shared Liz. "Do you feel like that?"

"Yeah, it hurts like a mf," Elle told her. "I did throw up at the hospital, but just one time."

"Mike said you've got something for the headache. Is it helping?"

"It helps, but makes me sleepy. The Doc said its good I got a hard head," Elle repeated with a sheepish smile. "They give me a pain pill one at a time. Keep 'em in the office. If they were here with my stuff, some punk would walk off with 'em."

"I guess that could happen. That's a good idea then. Is there something I can bring you? Anything you need?" asked Liz. It was a question she would ask anyone she visited who was recovering from an injury, but Liz was curious what Elle might say.

"Really? You'd get me somethin'?"

"Well, yeah, as long as it's within reason."

"Umm...I like energy drinks. I like the coconut and banana-flavored ones." Elle hesitated, as if testing the waters. "And I don't got minutes left on my phone."

"I can help with that," said Liz. She would check with Quinn about whether the energy drink would follow discharge orders. "I'll get you a re-up on your minutes, but if you want, I could make a call for you. Then you can save your minutes."

"Nah, that's okay," Elle said, with a furrowed brow, "but thanks," Elle responded to Liz's suggestion like it was crazy.

"Okay, that's cool. It was just a thought. Anything else? Something to eat?"

"Can't bring food in here. They got rules."

"That's right. I knew that," Liz said. *But the kid has to eat*, she thought. After what Elle's been through, something to tempt her might be allowed.

"French fries sound good," said Elle, in a tone that suggested conspiracy. Liz wanted to laugh. She was secretly happy that something sounded good to the kid.

"Hey, no promises, but I'll see what I can do." Liz felt drawn to this kid. She wasn't sure why. They had nothing in common. Liz thought about the folks on the street telling this hurt kid to piss off. It made her want to hit something. It didn't matter that they had nothing in common; Liz's heart ached for Elle and for her friend, Pooki.

Mike walked into the bunk room. His expression told Liz there was an issue. He had a prescription bottle in his hand.

"Here you go, kid." He gave Elle a capsule from the bottle and handed her one of the water bottles to take a sip and wash down the capsule. "Liz and I need to get going. Jimmie is just outside manning the johns, if you need something. Okay?"

Liz rose to her feet. "Get some rest, Elle. I'll stop in tomorrow. Is that soon enough?"

"Yeah," she nodded. "See ya later then." Elle hunkered down and closed her eyes.

Walking back into the hallway, Mike took Liz by the hand again. "Come into the classroom with me."

Quinn was sitting alone in the classroom, her elbows on the table, her face hidden behind interlocked fingers. Her forehead rested against outstretched thumbs. Quinn looked up when Mike and Liz entered the room.

"Quinn. You must be exhausted," said Liz.

Mike closed the door to the small room. Quinn looked at Liz. It was not exhaustion that she saw on Quinn's face. It was defeat; defeat and sorrow.

Quinn took a deep breath, and said in a quiet voice, "Pooki didn't make it. She died this afternoon."

Chapter Twenty-four

"From Bad to Worse"

Liz sat down across the table from Quinn. She rested her hand over Quinn's and said, "I'm so sorry."

"There was too much damage," Quinn told them, shaking her head. "The surgeon couldn't stop the bleeding. Pooki didn't even come out of the anesthesia."

"That poor kid," said Liz, as Mike sat next to her, placing his hand on Liz's shoulder.

"We have no idea where she's from, how long she's been on the street, or if any family members are looking for her," said Mike. "We aren't even sure of her real name."

"Yes, it completely sucks." Quinn took another deep breath, trying to control herself. She looked at Liz. "It was nice of you to visit Elle. How's she feeling?"

"I wanted to visit her. And Mike wanted to show me around the center," she told her.

Mike stepped in to answer Quinn's question. "Elle's doing okay. She had a dose of her meds. My guess is she went right to sleep."

"She said the headache is better; not as much nausea," said Liz. "She asked for an energy drink and French fries. I told her I'd ask."

Quinn made a weak attempt at a smile, and said, "She can have whatever she wants. I feel like making a few exceptions. Thanks, Liz." Quinn paused, looking from Mike to Liz. "It's going to be so hard telling Elle about Pooki. They were the best of friends. I want her to hear about it before we tell the rest of the kids."

"Yes, of course she should hear it first," said Mike. "That's the decent thing to do. I'm going to see how the staff is doing. Someone may need a break. And I need to walk around." He stood up. His hand was still on Liz's shoulder. "I'll be right out here, Quinn. Take your time." The women nodded as Mike stepped out of the room, closing the door behind him.

Liz couldn't stop thinking like a cop, the instincts kicking in. "Have you spoken with Castillo, Quinn? She needs to know about Pooki."

"The hospital informed her," said Quinn. "Castillo was getting updates on both kids' conditions on a regular basis. She was informed about Pooki and asked the hospital to withhold the information. She mentioned the department would handle any announcements."

Liz nodded. She knew the reason for the change in procedure. Pooki's case was no longer an assault. It was now a murder. The investigators were not looking for her assailant. They were looking for a killer.

"Castillo—or whoever investigates—may insist on moving Elle," said Liz. "This is a different case now. As far as we know, Elle is the only witness to what happened to her and Pooki. She needs to be protected. I don't mean to add to your shitty day. I just want you to be prepared."

"No, you're right," said Quinn. "You know more about these things than I do."

"Has Castillo circulated the images of the perps, the ones Elle helped put together?"

"I don't know about that," she told Liz.

Liz pulled her phone out. She searched for Castillo's number. "I'll find out."

"Can you let me know?" asked Quinn. "And Mike was right that staff or one of the kids may need something". She pulled herself up from the table. "Shift change is coming up. I'll deal with this better if I stay busy."

"I'll let you know what I find out. Tell Mike I'll find him soon," said Liz, as Castillo picked up.

"Lieutenant," said Castillo, answering the phone call.

"Hey, Castillo, I'm at the Youth Center. I came by to see how Elle was doing. I heard about Pooki. Where we are with circulating the images of these assholes?"

"The images have been released. I'll forward them to your phone," said Castillo. "Officially, Pooki's case is still an assault, but I'll be turning it over to a homicide team, Lieutenant. It'll be their case, of course. Elle's case will be investigated as an assault, but efforts will dove-tail because we're looking for the same two assailants. You know how it goes. I'm hoping to stay involved. I'd like to help find these SOBs."

"Good, Castillo. And I know how you feel," said Liz.

Castillo wasn't finished. "Lieutenant, I talked to Kyle. Uh...sorry, I mean Connors. He said he's heading the search for a missing girl. She's the girl in the photos you showed me last night, isn't she?"

"She is," said Liz.

"Does this involve your visitor to the precinct yesterday?"

"It does, Castillo. He's the girl's father. Why?"

"Just putting two and two together, Lieutenant. I should apologize. It's none of my business."

"Don't apologize, Castillo. You're an officer of the law. A missing girl who may be in danger *is* your business."

"Thanks, Lieutenant," said Castillo, relieved that Liz didn't give her shit for crossing a line.

"Do me a favor, will you?" asked Liz. "When Pooki's case is transferred, let me know which detective is assigned? It won't come across my desk if it lands with the other team."

"Will do, Lieutenant. I would keep you in the loop anyway. And warn Quinn that someone will need to talk to Elle again very soon."

Chapter Twenty-five

"Verses"

Liz started to open the images on her phone of the two men who had attacked Elle and stabbed Pooki. Before she could get to them, she realized she had three missed calls. Two of the calls were from Chapin's number. She would not be returning his calls. She didn't recognize the number of the third call. There was no message. Odd, but she would deal with it later.

She studied the images created from Elle's memory with the aid of a technician using an electronic facial ID program. One of the faces looked to be older, rounder, someone in his forties: light eye color, wavy, gray hair, salt-and-pepper stubble covered a scowling face. The other guy was younger, late twenties or early thirties, with short, dark hair and large, hollow dark eyes. His face was pockmarked, shaven except for a soul patch, piercings in the left ear. Neither image was familiar to Liz.

Stepping out from the classroom, Liz looked around for Mike. She saw him sitting on the same bench against the opposite wall of the common room where he had discussed rock and roll gods with the kid named Toots.

Kids were everywhere. They were sprawled on the floor, on the benches. Kids were alternately sitting, standing, milling around. They talked with each other and with red tee-shirted staff. There was music playing, something wild and frenetic that Liz didn't recognize. A group of kids was asked to take their rowdy, impromptu Hacky Sack game outside.

A boy near to where Mike was sitting appeared to be writing something on the wall. On closer inspection, Liz saw that the entire space had been sectioned into squares, about eighteen-by-eighteen inches each, resulting in dozens of patchwork squares. Some of the squares were adorned with handwritten letters or poems, others with pictures, drawings. Liz was mesmerized. As she studied the squares, she was touched by the level of feeling and emotion put into them.

"Impressive, isn't it?" said Mike. "Any kid who wants a square can have one and put whatever they choose on it—as long as it's not X rated." He looked around at the squares on the wall. "Some of the contributions have been here for a while, some are more recent."

Quinn approached from the side, placing a hand on Liz's shoulder. "You've discovered the wall. I find something new, something moving, each time I look at it."

"I don't know quite what to say. It's beautiful and sad at the same time," Liz managed to tell her. She reached out with reverence, to touch one of the squares, but decided against it. It felt intrusive. "Each square represents a street kid."

"Yes, you're right," said Quinn. "It gives each kid a small avenue for expression. It's often more than that. Sometimes it's a message board. I love it." She looked over at Mike. "You two should get out of here. It's been a brutal day and you aren't used to our roller coaster of a place at the best of times."

"We'll head out soon," said Mike. "Let us know after you talk with Elle."

"I will," she told Mike. "I don't have the heart to wake her and then hit her with bad news. She'll hear it soon enough. See you both later," she told them as she walked back to the office.

"Let's go," Mike said to Liz.

"Yeah, I know you've been here all day," Liz said, still examining the wall square by square.

A particular square had caught her eye. It was near the corner, about waist high. It was a poem, or so Liz guessed by the four-line intervals written in calligraphic letters. Liz walked closer and read the following:

Hear my words, Villain, to your mercy I'll not appeal / By granting me no solace, my spirit you hoped to steal / Distrust is my only offering, enlightened have I become / Strengthened by my suffering, your deceit has made me run.

Inflicting lies and misery, that way of life you chose / A well of sorrow ever deep, such sadness you impose / No right have you to claim my trust, that honor is denied / Forfeited so long ago, false love, so well disguised.

The square was edged in tiny characters that produced an intricate black border. Up close, Liz determined they were quarter notes. At the bottom right, just inside the border of notes, small letters spelled the signature of the poet. It was simply attributed to *Lyric.*

"Mike, have you seen this?" asked Liz with excitement.

"No. I have to admit I haven't studied every line and drawing," he said with fatigue.

"I know you're ready to go. Give just a minute to ask Quinn about this, okay? I promise it'll be quick. Do you think she's in the office?"

"Likely," he said. "She's getting ready for shift change. We'll find her."

They headed through the entry area to Quinn's office where she was meeting with three young people, all wearing the required red tees. Even with the door closed, it was apparent that they were discussing something more important than a simple shift change. Quinn likely was preparing them to deal with the onslaught of emotion they would deal with when the kids were told of Pooki's death. Liz didn't envy her the task. She was reluctant to bother them under the circumstances, but Liz would make it quick.

She knocked lightly on the office door. Quinn looked up, and then signaled to the staffer closest to the door to open it. Liz stuck her head in, and acknowledging the intrusion, said, "I'm sorry to interrupt. Mike and I are leaving, but I have a quick question for you, Quinn. May I have just a moment?"

Quinn looked tired, but interested in what Liz may want to ask. "No worries," she said. As she stood, she said to the others, "You've all met Mike, our grant administrator. This is Liz. She's with the police bureau and she's a good friend of Mike's. Please allow her run of the place when she's here and if she needs anything, make it happen. I'll be right back."

They walked with Mike back to the common room while Liz explained to Quinn, "I want to ask about a particular square." She indicated the one with the poem signed by a kid named Lyric. "Do you know anything about this? Do you have any idea when this square may have been added?"

Quinn read the poem; the intrigue evident on her face. "I've missed this one until now. It is intense," she said, when she'd finished. "Lots of the kids use composition as catharsis, we even encourage it. There's pain and hate in those few lines, but I won't judge."

Looking from Liz to Mike, Quinn sighed deeply and said, "I don't know how long it's been here, but like I said, I hadn't read it before. I haven't come across a kid who goes by the name of Lyric. Let me ask John or other staff that have been here longer. They may have some insight to offer. What's this about, Liz?"

Liz looked around, not wanting to be overheard. Fortunately, the common room had cleared out a bit. She gave Quinn a quick summary of the details regarding the missing girl named Kyrie, that the girl's mother was dead, and that her father had an ugly past.

Quinn looked from Liz to Mike. She got no impression of Mike's regard for the situation, one way or the other. Her focus returned to Liz, and Quinn said, "This is about the photos you sent. I don't recognize the girl, but I'll do whatever I can to help you, Liz. But I have to ask you: will pursuing this put staff or any of the kids in danger?"

"I doubt it," said Liz, shaking her head, "but as you and Mike always remind me, the kids are in danger already. The truth is that finding this girl is now a police matter anyway. Officers are going to be around, looking at things, talking with kids who may know her. You know Connors so it's just a matter of time. Since I'm here, may I take a photo of the square?"

"Of course, if it will help," answered Quinn, "I'll ask around. Keep me the loop." She excused herself to return to her office. Liz took a photo of Lyric's square with the camera on her phone.

Chapter Twenty-six

"Callahan's"

"Come on," Mike said to Liz, "I'll buy you a burger." Mike could always tempt Liz with Callahan's, their favorite burger joint.

They left Mike's car and took Liz's. Callahan's was a dive that had been serving draft beer and burgers in downtown Columbia City since the fifties. The place was popular with attorneys and cops because it was close to the courthouse and the downtown precinct.

Callahan's served basic tavern fare. A few years back, the neighborhood establishment updated their menu options with items like nachos, potato skins, sliders, microbrews, and premium bottled beers. You would have thought it was the end of the world, as if anything other than greasy burgers and chips was a subversive plot. In time, the crisis abated. The locals made the adjustment, got used to it, and carried on.

Finding a corner booth in the back, they ordered food before they had even sat down. Liz wanted a pint of her favorite red ale. Mike was sticking with water, not even risking the caffeine in a cola.

"After this shitty day, I just want to eat and go home to sleep," Mike told Liz. "I'm planning on an early run in the morning. You are welcome to join me."

"Maybe it would be good for me, all things considered," said Liz. She hoped she would sleep without dreaming about street kids again. They talked together about Elle and about the kid known as Pooki, who died from her injuries earlier that day.

"We know very little about Pooki," Mike said, "Some of the kids who knew her described her as a goof, that she had a crazy side. She was known to grab whatever wasn't tied down, but she would never take from another punk, they said. And she looked out for the younger kids."

Liz listened to Mike thinking about the dead punk. "No, I'm guessing Pooki was no Girl Scout, but she sure as hell didn't deserve to die that way."

"No. No, she didn't," agreed Mike.

They talked about the Youth Center. Mike said he couldn't continue to spend as much time there.

"I have three other centers to support. Paperwork, not my favorite thing, is piling up on my desk," he said with only a slight tone of complaint. "I'll make a point to stop in at the Youth Center at least once a day for the next few days, see how the staff is handling things."

"I'm visiting again tomorrow," Liz told Mike. "I promised Elle French fries and minutes for her phone. Quinn said it was okay. Actually, she said I was more than welcome to visit."

"Of course, she is." Mike responded. "She's thrilled. Having a cop on site in plain clothes, blending in, and downright concerned about the kids? Liz, a cop like you is every social worker's dream come true."

Liz took a long drink of the ale. "I don't know about that. I guess it would depend on the reason for my visit. I'll tell you what though," she said pointing to her casual leggings and tight-fitting, sweatshirt jacket. "I could get used to hanging out dressed like this. If the circumstances were different, I could enjoy it."

Mike put his forearms on the table, leaning in closer. "You're thinking that poem was written and put on the wall by Chapin's daughter?" asked Mike, but it wasn't really a question.

"It fits with what Richelle Isaacs had to say. Kyrie writes poetry. Richelle said she had a talent for it, and she's a singer and songwriter. But that poem was scathing, Mike. Either someone had a really good imagination, or they were hurt deeply to write it."

A server arrived, placing house specials on the table in front of Mike and Liz. The plastic baskets lined with greasy paper held their standard order of half-pound bacon cheeseburgers, medium rare and loaded, with sides of onion rings. Without a thought, Liz asked for a second ale and Mike was ready for a refill of iced water.

Mike and Liz looked at the burgers sitting between them on the polished, wooden tabletop. On a normal day, they would be diving in, but neither of them had much in the way of appetite. Mike looked at Liz and sighed. Liz stared at the food with disinterest. She looked at Mike and tried to smile, but there was no joy in it.

"You should eat something," Mike told Liz, pointing to the glass of ale.

"We both should," Liz answered.

"Let's split one," said Mike as he took a knife to cut one of the burgers in half. "We'll sleep better with a little food in our stomachs. We'll take the other burger home."

Liz grabbed a napkin. When she looked up, she saw Connors and Castillo standing near the entrance looking for a place to sit. They were both in street clothes although now that he was a sergeant, Connors was no longer in uniform when on duty.

The place had become busy and the only open spots were at the bar. Liz saw that they were holding hands. *Interesting,* thought Liz, wishing she hadn't noticed.

When Connors saw Liz and Mike, he whispered something to Castillo, and then Castillo looked in Liz's direction. The officers gestured with hand waves, and then walked back toward Mike and Liz's booth.

When Mike saw them, he immediately said, "Hey, Kyle. Good to see you, man," and offered Connors his hand. The officer had earned Mike's respect as a rookie cop when Connors had shown a special degree of humanity to street folks in need of compassion. Mike had appreciated his attitude at the time and never forgot it. As it turned out, Connors' respectful manner with the less fortunate had helped solve a murder.

"The place is busy," said Connors. "We were just thinking we might get take-out. When we saw you, we thought we'd say hello."

"Join us, please," said Mike. "Who's your friend, Kyle?"

"Mike Dwyer, this is Emmy Castillo. Emmy, this is Mike," he said, making introductions. "You and the Lieutenant know each other. Anyway, we don't want to intrude."

"No, no, Connors. Really, have a seat," said Liz. "It's a big booth, plenty of room. I need to talk to you anyway. Castillo, please join us," said Liz, as she moved over to provide more room.

Connors and Castillo shared a look, and then they both shrugged. Connors scooted in next to Liz while Emmy took a seat next to Mike. The server stopped over to take their order, and Connors pointed to Liz's red ale, telling the server, "We'll have two of those." He looked to Castillo to confirm.

"Sounds good to me," Castillo told the server, approving Connors' choice of brews.

"You could do us a big favor by taking this off our hands," said Liz as she pushed the second burger basket toward Connors. "We ordered too much food. Eat it while it's still hot." Connors wasted no time. He thanked Liz and took a bite out of the burger. Castillo grabbed an onion ring.

"Is Emmy your full name or is it short for something?" Mike asked.

"It's short for Emilia, spelled with an E," she answered, pronouncing it *ee-MEAL-ee-ah*.

"Beautiful name," said Mike.

"Thank you. I like the traditional spelling," she said, swallowing a bite of battered onion. "I don't speak much Spanish. I can manage only a few phases to converse with my grandfather, so I like the connection with my name."

"Sorry, Emmy, you'll always be Castillo to me," said Liz. "I can't help it. Just like *Kyle* here will always be Connors."

"Connors, you speak fluent Spanish," said Mike. "I admire that skill, speaking a second language."

Connors was embarrassed. He looked at Emmy, and said simply, "Don't."

"I have to tell it. It's a great story," Emmy told him. She turned to Mike and Liz and explained.

"When I met Kyle, he assumed Spanish was my first language. Kind of narrow thinking by him, right? But with the surname Castillo and my Latina looks, I can't fault him totally. Anyway, he tried to strike up a conversation, flirting really, in beautiful Spanish," she said with a wave of her hands for emphasis. "I picked up on a few words, but before long he lost me. I said, 'Whoa, whoa, I don't understand a word you're saying'. He apologized profusely," she said as she looked over at Connors.

Mike and Liz grinned and shook their heads, looking at Connors as he rolled his eyes. "Okay, moving on now," said Connors. "What did you want to talk to me about, Lieutenant?"

Liz pulled out her phone, showing Connors the picture of the poem from the wall at the Youth Center, and explained her theory about its authorship. "I'll send the picture to you, Connors. Makes sense, according to what Richelle Isaacs had to say about Kyrie's talent for songwriting. If we can link the poem to Kyrie, and to the person she wrote it about, it may help find her."

"I've reviewed your report and checked into Richelle Isaacs. The woman is from Rhode Island originally. She has an Oregon driver's license and I found basic paperwork and financial information, but not much about her past. It's all in the file if you want to review it, but there's not much to see. I've talked with Mr. Chapin and with Ms. Isaacs about Kyrie, and sent a team to check out her room at their home. I should hear from them soon with what they discover. Maybe something related to school, friends, hopefully, something helpful."

"Good. I'm glad you're on it," said Liz. "You talked with Chapin, huh?"

"Oh, I did," said Connors, nodding slowly. "He's not happy, but I basically told him to get over himself. Reminded him to remember what's important; that it's not about him. He'll be helpful, but the tough-guy persona is his fallback position. Richelle Isaacs was helpful; you were correct about that. I think she genuinely is concerned about the girl."

Liz nodded. She looked down at the table. "Sorry, Connors, I know better. I really should not discuss Gabriel Chapin."

"We're discussing the report you prepped for me," responded Connors with a shrug. "Besides, it's out of concern for the missing girl that you asked in the first place."

The foursome put work aside, tried to chat like normal people. Soon, the day caught up with Mike and Liz. They made their apologies, paid their dinner bill, and got up to leave.

Connors ordered two more glasses of ale from the server. "We'll be in touch, Lieutenant," he told Liz, as she and Mike prepared to leave.

"We both will," added Castillo.

"I'm visiting Elle again tomorrow," Liz mentioned to Castillo. "I promised her a couple of things."

"Nice of you, Lieutenant," Castillo said to Liz. "Care from responsible adults will help get her through this ordeal. Elle liked you, I could tell. It's hard to gauge how she'll handle the news about Pooki. She's a tough a one, but it's going to be difficult."

"I'll do what I can for her, Castillo. Have a nice evening."

Climbing into Liz's car, they headed to the Youth Center to retrieve Mike's car. While Liz drove, Mike had a minute to check his phone. "I have a text message from Quinn, Liz. It says:

Talked to E about P. Very upset but dealing with it. Back to sleep. Telling kids 1 to 1. Talk tmrw.

Chapter Twenty-seven

"Curiosity"

Mike, Liz, and the cats each slept deeply. Liz was spared another visit by the street kids in her dreams, but she thought of Pooki before she went to sleep and the kid was in her thoughts again when she woke.

Mike was up early. He'd gone for a run on the track at the high school next door, was back then gone again, all before Liz was awake. He kissed Liz goodbye and asked her to let him know how Elle was doing. Liz marveled at his ability to summon such energy so early in the day. She chastised herself for not running with Mike, as she poured another cup of coffee.

The cats had been asleep in the bedroom and were now venturing out for food. Liz explained to Eddie and Little Kurt that she would be back after work. She told herself that they had listened to her with interest before finding their favorite perches at opposite ends of the sofa, resuming their naps

Liz pulled herself together and made it to the precinct within the next hour. As she entered her office and placed her bag in the desk drawer, her phone rang. She saw on the display that it was the captain.

"Lieutenant," said Miller, "I know you just stepped in the door, but I spent last night thinking about our conversation yesterday. I'm interested in what exactly happened when Sara Mallory was killed. You weren't there, so I'll have to look down another avenue."

"Why would you be interested, Sir?" Liz asked. "Sara died in the raid. And she shouldn't have been there."

"But you weren't there," stated Miller. "You didn't kill her. Who did?"

"It was cross-fire," said Liz. "It's a tragedy, but it happens."

"Even so, the round that hit Sara was discharged from one weapon," he said with his index finger extended, although Liz couldn't see it over the phone. "That weapon was in one individual's hand," Miller said.

"I'm curious. I pulled the reports after we talked yesterday," continued the captain. "There were six officers there that day—Pruitt, his partner, Crenshaw, and a four-man tactical team. Only two of the six fired their weapons. Both of the men who died were armed, as well. Their weapons were recovered. They both fired and the officers fired back. So, of the four weapons discharged, which one fired the round that killed Sara?"

"I don't know," Liz said. "I've never thought about what happened with enough rationality to examine it that closely."

"I'm not sure anyone else has either, Lieutenant. I'd like to know why. I think answers were assumed at the time, even though some questions were never asked. And I think you've blamed yourself for so long, you've denied any other scenario."

"Is that really how you see things?" asked Liz, "Or are you trying to convince me to see them in that light?"

"Yes, that's how I see things," said Miller. "I wanted you to know I planned on doing some digging."

"All right, Sir. Whatever you think is best. Let me know if I can help," said Liz. "And Captain, I believe you're aware of the attack on the two street kids."

"Yes, I am," Miller answered. "Sad story there; I've been following the updates."

"Then you'll get the news soon enough, that one of the kids died from her injuries. The case will be transferred to homicide."

"I'm sorry to hear that, Lieutenant," said Miller with a sigh. "I'll be watching that one closely. I'm glad you let me know. And I'll be in touch if I learn anything on the other issue. We'll talk soon," said Miller, and he ended the call.

Chapter Twenty-eight

"In the Stars"

Liz began tackling her to-do list, but she kept thinking about Miller's call. Why was he so interested in looking into the circumstances of Sara's death? The precise details of how she had died had no bearing on Liz's involvement at the time. A round from the weapon of one of the officers at the scene had ended Sara's life. Liz thought it was morbid to look at it closer.

At noon, Liz left the office. She purchased a re-up of phone service compatible with Elle's phone. It wasn't very expensive, so she purchased data and text packs. The convenience store next door had banana-coconut-favored energy drinks in huge, blue cans. She grabbed two of them and returned to her car, feeling as if she was forgetting something. *French fries,* she thought, *that's it.* She pulled into the drive-thru at Burgerville and ordered a large fry with extra ketchup and two cheeseburgers.

Liz activated the blue tooth and called Quinn. "Hey, it's Liz. How are things?" she asked when Quinn picked up.

"We're all okay, as well as can be expected," Quinn told her. "Most of the kids that were here overnight are still sleeping. Normally, we would have rousted them by now. I had extra food brought over from Brooks. Comfort food, I guess. How are you?"

"I'm fine," Liz said. "I have a few things for Elle, but I don't want to bother her."

"Elle's awake. She's doing okay. Sleep helped. I'd like to think that being here, feeling safe, has contributed. Castillo's here, so that may be helping too. Castillo had a few last questions for Elle before transferring the file. And Elle has asked about you, Liz. She wanted to know if you were still coming."

"You can tell her I'm on my way," said Liz. "Quinn, I want to explain to you why I'm interested in the missing girl in the photos."

"You're a cop, she's a missing kid. That's all I need to know."

"It's more complicated than that. I didn't say much last night, but it's regarding an incident that happened a long time ago. It involved my work and people I once knew. It's something I've not forgiven myself for even though it was out of my hands. It's indirectly related to that poem on the wall and finding the girl who, I believe, wrote it."

Quinn was silent for a moment, and then Liz heard her sigh. "I don't need to know details that you probably shouldn't share anyway. Knowing you, I'm sure you will resolve this. You'll make peace with it. It's in your stars, you know."

"Oh, yeah, in my stars," Liz answered. She didn't place much stock in astrology, but she knew Quinn did, and she had insisted on preparing Liz's chart. Aside from astrology, Quinn had been reading tarot cards for years, having developed the skill as a gutter punk on the streets of Seattle. At one time, she had used her mystic abilities to support herself.

"Remember Liz, you were born under a fire sign, but your rising sign is Libra. It's about balance and fairness, even justice. That's why you're a good cop, but it impacts your personal life, too. Your moon is in Virgo, reminding you to nurture yourself. Self-care is important."

"It is," said Liz, remembered the run with Mike that she had skipped that morning. "Thanks for the reminder."

"It's not a matter of remembering; give yourself the permission to take care of yourself," Quinn told her. "Honor the choices you've been given."

Liz thought about what Quinn said. Balancing the pursuit of justice with self-care was a lot to expect. "Thanks for listening," Liz told Quinn. "I'll see you soon."

Chapter Twenty-nine

"In Mourning"

Liz drove downtown and parked as close to the Youth Center as possible. It had been good talking with Quinn and Liz was glad for the chance to talk with someone about what was on her mind. It was an indulgence she didn't take lightly. *Self-care*, she thought.

As Liz walked up the block with the items for Elle, she recognized the guy strumming a guitar and singing softly. It was the same fellow they had heard singing and playing guitar the day of the City Council meeting. Mike had been introduced to him. He told Liz that the guy's name was Sage.

When she walked past, Liz heard him singing a mournful, sad song by Tears for Fears. Liz wondered if it was in response to Pooki's death. She recognized the melancholy words and forlorn melody:

All around me are familiar faces, worn out places, worn out faces / Bright and early for their daily races, going nowhere, going nowhere / Their tears are filling up their glasses, no expression, no expression / Hide my head I want to drown my sorrow, no tomorrow, no tomorrow.

Even if Sage hadn't known the kid, he could feel the sadness of others as artists often do. He shared a moment with Liz, looking her in the eye to acknowledge her presence, but not deterring from his song. Liz dropped a buck in the open guitar case and walked on.

Liz hiked up the front steps and through the entrance into the Youth Center. Quinn was sitting near the entrance talking with a kid. A staff person was nearby, the three of them in conversation. The kid was wiping their face with their hands. It was obvious the kid had been crying. Were they tears of sadness, anger, or embarrassment? It was hard to tell with kids of that age.

Quinn looked up, and seeing that it was Liz, she said, "Hey, you can go in to see Elle. She knows you're coming. Castillo is with her."

"Thanks," said Liz. "Is everything okay?" She asked the question out of habit. Dressed for the job, Liz probably looked intimidating as hell, but it was too late now.

"Yes, we're okay. Just a rough time," she said, rubbing the kid's back with one hand.

Liz nodded and said, "It was a rough night. Let me know if I can help." She tried to sound as unthreatening as possible, and then wandered through the common room to visit Elle.

"Hello, Lieutenant," said Castillo, when Liz stepped into the bunk room. She looked from Elle to Liz and back to Elle, and said, "We're just finishing up." Castillo was in uniform, of course. She had transformed from Casual Emmy, sitting across the booth the night before, back to cop mode as Officer Castillo. Looking at Castillo's uniform, Liz hoped she looked slightly less intimidating.

Elle looked up and said, "You came back," as if she hadn't believed it would happen. Her eyes were still huge and it was evident she had been crying. She still looked like a waif, but the bandage was gone from around her head.

Liz thought the kid might have showered. Her hair was clean and she seemed refreshed physically. Elle sat semi-upright in bed, very still.

"I did come back," Liz answered, setting down the bags she carried. She held the order of French fries out to Elle, and said, "Here you go. They're still warm."

"Thanks," said Elle, as she took the fries from Liz and started to eat one, although she didn't show much energy or interest.

"If you're not hungry, don't worry about it. I can bring fresh ones later."

Elle looked at the fries, nodded slightly.

"And I brought the energy drinks you wanted. Want me to open one?" asked Liz.

"That would be good," Elle said quietly, after clearing her throat. Elle said no thanks to the cheeseburger. Liz offered one to Castillo and they ate, giving the two cops something normal to do that didn't involve talking.

Liz handed Elle the small package to upload service minutes and told her about the data and text options she had purchased. "This is great, helps me out a lot. Thanks," Elle told Liz, as she laid her head back on the pillow behind her.

"Elle, I'm sorry about Pooki," Liz told the kid. She spoke slowly, gauging Elle's response to the condolences. "I want you to remember that you did everything you could to help her." Elle looked into Liz's eyes, then back at her fries. She had managed to eat three or four at most.

She nodded, tears in her eyes. Elle looked over at Castillo, and then looked at Liz again. "Pooki would have liked you guys, and she didn't like many people."

"I know how she felt," said Liz. "I don't like many people either, only really special people. Sorry to be a bummer, Elle. I wanted you to enjoy your fries."

"The fries are good. I just eat slow right now." Liz sat down on the opposite lower bunk, next to Castillo.

"Do you want to tell Liz what you told me, Elle?" Castillo asked the kid. "What you've been thinking about?"

Elle looked at Liz, tears still in her eyes. She swallowed. "Yeah," said Elle. She began slowly, measuring her words, looking to Castillo for support.

"I'm not dumb. Those assholes, they're gonna be looking for me. So, I'm thinking about going home. But that means I gotta call my grandma. I don't know what's scarier, staying here or going home."

"Your grandma is scary?" asked Liz.

"No, my grandma's okay," she said, shaking her head. "Her old man is not," she said. "He's a jerk."

"I'm sorry to hear that," said Liz. "You know, if someone is abusive, you deserve to be protected from them."

"Yeah, I hear that. It just ain't that simple," said Elle.

Liz was a cop. It was her job to protect people. In her mind, it *was* simple. She felt the nudge of the bulldozer and took a breath, reminding herself that the situation wasn't simple. Nothing was simple in the lives of these kids.

"I can call for you, Elle," said Liz. "Or Castillo could make the call, whatever you want to do. But right now, you should rest. I know you've been going over with Castillo about what happened to you and Pooki. You're going to have to talk about it all with other cops too. Telling us everything you remember about those men is how we're going to find them."

"We've talked about that, haven't we Elle? You know that's what I think too," said Castillo. "I'll help if you need me, but you're smart enough to know that you're safer off the streets. And I have to get going," said Castillo as she stood up. "I'll check in on you when I can. And you can call me anytime now that you got a new burner." She said it with a smile and that got a smile out of Elle. "Let me talk to Liz for a moment, okay? She'll be right back."

Liz and Castillo stepped into the hallway to speak privately. "What's up?" asked Liz.

"This was my last official task," said Castillo. "There were just a few more questions. The case will be turned over to Detective Morgan. You wanted to know."

"Okay, thanks," said Liz. Reese Morgan was new and worked in the other homicide unit. Liz didn't know him well. What she did know was that he was a thorough investigator.

"Elle's prints were on the recovered knife, but we expected that because she told us she held it to get away," said Castillo. "With her permission, we took exemplars at the hospital. Between you and me, we searched, but there's no match to her prints in any of our databases. I was hoping to get some background on Elle, but so far, nothing. There was another set of prints on the knife and they aren't Pooki's. So far, we haven't found an ID, but we're looking."

"But now we know that another person handled that knife," said Liz. "And if we find a match, we'll be able to prove who that was."

"We've tracked down the owner of the house where the kids were attacked through property records. The owner is in Eastern Oregon, knew nothing, wasn't overly concerned which is a nice way of saying they couldn't have cared less.

They use a local management company who claims to have rented the property to a family, but has no current contact information."

"They have no idea who was living there? That's hard to believe," said Liz.

"This isn't exactly high-end rental property. Their position is that because the rent was paid each month, they had no reason to be concerned. No one with the management company recognized either of the men from the images."

"Thanks for the update. And I'm glad you've connected with this kid," Liz told Castillo. "At least someone has."

Castillo glanced over to the doorway to Elle's bunk room. "Talk with Elle, Lieutenant. See you later."

Chapter Thirty

"Landon"

Liz stepped back into Elle's bunk room and sat down. "Are you getting any rest or are all the kids coming in to visit all day and night?"

"They have to ask Quinn to visit me. If I don't want to talk to someone, I just say I'm gonna take a nap. Then she knows I don't want to talk to 'em."

"Sounds like a good arrangement," Liz said. They sat in silence for a minute before Liz decided to ask, "So, you want to tell me anything about why it's scary to go home?"

"It's kind of not possible for me to be *me* at home. If you call my grandma, and tell her you're calling about Elle, she won't know who that is."

"You didn't go by Elle at home."

"Uh-uh," she said, shaking her head, looking Liz in the eye. "Elle is my name now, but it's for 'L', that was my initial. Not El, as in E-l. E-l-l-e," she said, spelling it out so Liz understood the difference."

"Okay, I think I understand," Liz responded.

"Don't think you do," Elle said, shaking her head. She looked at Liz. "Not quite yet."

"I'll listen if you want to tell me. But if you don't want to, or you aren't ready, that's okay," said Liz, thinking she should back off. She remembered her father, a teacher, saying that to her when she was in high-school.

"Landon. My dead name is Landon. My grandma doesn't really get it, but she wants me to be happy, you know?

"Of course, she does," said Liz in agreement.

"She's got this guy in her life, her old man. He thinks I can be the kind of person he is. He thinks he can tell a person how to be. And if a person don't listen, you just beat it into them."

"So, this guy in your Grandma's life, he didn't like that you wanted to be Elle, instead of Landon."

"It's not a matter of what I want. I can't be Landon. I never was Landon. Landon was really messed up, unhappy. But, it ain't about the name, what you call me. This is who I am."

"What about your mom and dad, Elle? Not in the picture?"

"No. Not since I was little. Social services put me with Grandma before I even went to school."

"How long has your grandma's guy been around?"

"Since I was ten. He thought it would be fun having a kid around, but not if that kid was me. It wasn't bad until I was thirteen. I was never gonna be his ideal, you know? A counselor told me it wasn't my problem, that I had a right to be true to myself."

"What did your Grandma have to say about it? She wanted you to be happy, right?"

"Yeah, but she gotta right to be happy too. He makes her happy. I was in foster care for a while, too. That was better, but not great 'cause I had to move all the time. After two years, I took off when I was fifteen."

"That's pretty generous, to be thinking of your Grandma's happiness. How old are you now, Elle?"

"I'll be eighteen in less than a year. I can make my own decisions and no one can tell me how to live as long as I don't break no laws. I can get a job."

"You've been on the street for two years? How have you been surviving?"

"Panhandling, living in squats, checking dumpsters, hitting places like this. Some places are better than others, people are nicer." Elle grew quiet for a few seconds, thinking. "If it gets really bad, you do some dude for a place to stay or some food. Gets rough though. Scary, like I said. That's how I ended up here," she said, eyes tearing up. "That's why Pooki's dead."

"Elle, it is scary. I'm sorry you had to put yourself in scary places to survive. But listen to me about this: Pooki died because the two of you were attacked. You had the right to tell those men to back off and you had the right to leave their place when you chose. Those two men made the choice to hurt you. That's why we have to find them."

The kid continued to cry, the tears falling in silence. Without thinking, Liz stepped over and sat next to Elle. She rested her hand gently on Elle's shoulder. She patted the kid's back. Liz hoped it was comforting. Elle took a deep breath, wiped her eyes with her hands.

"I'm also sorry that you couldn't be yourself at home," Liz told her. "It shouldn't be that way."

Liz handed Elle a tissue. She took it and wiped her face. "No, it shouldn't be that way," said Elle.

"I'm going to give you some time alone now, Elle. But if you want me to call your Grandma, I'd be happy to talk with her."

"Are you leaving? I mean leaving the center?" Elle asked.

"I'll be here for a while," Liz said. "I'll let you know before I leave."

Elle sighed. She had calmed. "If I decide to go home to Grandma's, I need to go back to where Pooki and I were crashing. There's some stuff of mine there."

"We will figure that out," said Liz. "You rest."

Liz left Elle to nap. She could not believe that so many people in the kid's life had failed her so completely.

Chapter Thirty-one

"Righteous Hate"

Elle was resting. That was good. The kid needed rest to recover and deserved a break. Liz had to hope that she would make the decision to contact her grandmother, but only if Elle would be safe returning to the grandmother's home. The other priority, in Liz's mind, was to keep the kid safe until the men who had attacked her and killed Pooki were apprehended. *What an awful spot for the kid to be in,* thought Liz. Maybe an alternative will present itself.

Checking her phone, she noticed another missed call from the same number that had called her the day before. No message for a second time. It was an Oregon area code but that didn't mean much. She would remind herself to look it up, especially if they kept calling.

Curious, Liz pressed the key to "call back." The call rang three times then Liz was told that the cellular customer she had reached was not available. Probably some scam telemarketer.

Quinn was sitting on a bench in the common room. Next to her sat a guy with an impressive, bright orange Mohawk, and Liz instantly knew that he was the guy Mike told her about. Mike had mentioned the guy's name, but Liz couldn't remember what it was. The guy was studying a paper he held in his hands.

When Liz approached, he glanced up at her and Liz saw anger in his eyes. The bulldozer response could have kicked in, causing Liz to react with authority, but she needed calm control to diffuse the tension.

"Cool," said Quinn. She looked up and saw Liz. "I thought you were still here. Do you have a minute?"

"I do. What's up?" Quinn's tone and manner told Liz there was no cause for alarm and she relaxed.

"Liz, this is Drip. Drip, this is Liz," said Quinn making introductions. "She's here to visit Elle," Quinn told the kid. "She's the cop I told you about."

Drip had an angry face, but his anger was directed at the sheet of paper he was looking at, not at Quinn or Liz. "What are ya, Narc? Vice?"

"I'm not here about cop business right now," Liz told Drip. "I'm just visiting a hurt kid. I'm a homicide lieutenant. If you haven't killed anyone, you're probably safe with me."

"I've seen this guy," said Drip, as he pointed to the sheet in his hand. Liz saw that it was a print-out of the images of the men that had attacked Elle and Pooki. Drip indicated the younger of the two, the thin, dark-haired man.

"Castillo asked me to show the pictures around," Quinn told Liz. "Drip is the only one so far that's been helpful."

"Do you know this man? Do you know his name?" Liz asked Drip.

"Nah, don't know him, never even talked to the dude," said Drip. "I seen him though. Trawlin'."

"Trawling?" asked Liz.

Impatient with Liz's lack of knowledge, Drip rolled his eyes. He looked at Quinn as if to say, *please, educate this woman.*

"He was looking for kids to party with," Quinn explained. Liz knew that was a euphemism for kids to have sex with. At least Liz knew that much.

Drip continued to study the photo. "I ain't remembering where, but I stay close to the park, The Beau," he said, meaning that part of town. Drip was controlling his anger, but it resurfaced when he asked, "Cops think this is the guy killed Pook?" Drip asked the question, but didn't direct it to either Quinn or Liz specifically.

Quinn deferred to Liz with an open palm, so Liz answered him. "These are the two men we're looking for in connection with the attack on Elle and Pooki. We aren't sure yet, can't prove who did what, but we know they were both there."

"Pook was okay," said Drip in anger. His head was nodding slightly, jaw clinched, eyes squinted. "She was a cool one, could take care of herself. Elle, too."

"If you remember anything, tell Quinn. She will know how to find me," Liz said. "Or ask for a cop named Reese Morgan. He's the one that's looking for these guys."

Drip nodded, took a deep breath, but still looked at the images. "Like Reese's peanut butter. Got it." He wasn't being flip or funny by linking the detective's name with the candy bars. He used the connection to remember Reese's name, short of having a place to jot it down.

"Yes, you got it," Liz told him. "Can I ask you about something else, Drip?"

"I don't know. What's that?" he asked, without looking at Liz.

"There's a poem on the wall over there. Do you know anything about it? About the person who may have written it or put it there?" Drip looked over in the direction of the square that Liz was sure had something to do with Kyrie.

"There's poetry on that wall?" he asked, his face twisted with doubt. "No way."

Drip stood and ambled over to the square in the corner, and appeared to be reading the poem in silence. Liz and Quinn exchanged a glance and followed Drip to the wall. "Harsh," he said when he finished reading. "Somebody pissed off when they wrote that," he said. Drip turned to Liz and asked, "Why you wanna know?"

"Just wondering. You don't remember reading that before?" Liz asked.

"Shit, don't think so. Woulda' remembered this," he said, pointing at the verses. "I know hate, and that's about hate, pure and simple. Righteous hate."

"Tell me what you mean by 'righteous hate', Drip," said Quinn. "I know my version, but I want to hear yours."

Drip looked her in the eye, calculating Quinn's interest and the reason for it. He must have decided she was worth his honesty.

"I was seven, just a little dude, with two younger brothers. My folks are surviving by dealing shit. We ain't talking about no happy little family, okay? I knew what was goin' on, but I knew not to talk about it. When they got busted, my old man talks my mom into taking the whole damn rap. He convinced her that he would die in prison with a shiv in his belly, that she would be safer inside than him." Drip took a moment for himself.

"He told her he loved her," he said, resuming his tale. "He promised to take care of us until she got out. She fuckin' believed him. My mother left us to go to prison, left us with him. You know what he did then? He dumped us with my aunt, who had enough of her own kids to take care of, and split with his new girlfriend. He had three more kids before a rival put a bullet in his head. My mom got hooked on shit and died within a year of coming home. Now, you tell me my hate for that son of a bitch ain't righteous."

Quinn and Liz shook their heads with sadness, sighed with frustration, knowing no comment they could make would be enough.

"I sure as shit ain't no poet," said Drip, stepping away, wanting to get away from them, away from the story that reminded him of his past. "There're poets on the street, in the park. Better ask them."

Chapter Thirty-two

"Ty"

Liz stepped out to the street, intending to return to the precinct. She looked down the block. Brooks House, the men's shelter was a few doors down on the corner. She recalled the conversation with Quinn about self-care.

A friend of Mike's spent a lot of time at Brooks, helping out in a variety of ways. The man's name was Ty. He was a Gulf War Veteran who spent years on the street. Ty knew as much about dealing with one's past as anyone. Elements in his past, coupled with his living situation, had nearly cost Ty his freedom the previous year. He was doing well and had finally accepted help from friends, especially Mike.

She didn't know if she'd catch Ty at Brooks, or if he'd have time to talk, but even if she only had a chance to say hello to Gary, the manager, it would be worth the trip.

Walking up the stone front steps, it occurred to Liz how different Brooks was from the Youth Center and at the same time so similar. The folks hanging out at Brooks were older, but most of the problems caused by not having a home were the same as the issues faced by the punks. The older folks at Brooks had more practice at living on the street, she guessed.

She approached the office and saw Gary sitting at his desk, talking with another man. Liz wasn't sure if the other man was a client or staff, but she wouldn't interrupt for long.

"Gary, how are you?" Liz said with a wave.

Liz felt herself smile. The shelter manager had that effect on people. Gary Burgess had been working with homeless men, folks fighting addictions, and troubled veterans since the sixties. Gary was tall and thin, usually in jeans and untucked flannel. He had worn a full beard and ponytail as long as Liz had known him, probably much longer. To people providing social services in Columbia City, Gary was a legend.

"Well, Liz. It's been a long time. Is this an official visit?" Gary asked, looking over his glasses with a tentative smile.

"Not at all. I was just in the neighborhood," she answered. "Is Ty around? I was hoping to say hello."

"He is. He's in the dining room. You're welcome to go on in. Do you know the way?"

"I'll find it. Thanks, Gary."

Brooks House served hundreds of free meals every day to hungry people. At meal times, the large dining room was packed like a school cafeteria. When meals were not being served, the large room was nearly deserted unless there was a sobriety support meeting in session.

Ty was sitting at a table near the coffee urn. When he saw Liz, he stood to greet her.

"Liz. How are you?" Ty took her hand in his, placing his other palm over their joined hands. It was a gentle gesture and so like him.

He looks well, thought Liz. *Happy.* Liz was glad for him.

"I'm okay. I was hoping to have a chat. Do you have a few minutes?"

"I do. Are you here on business?" Ty asked the question with caution. Neither Gary nor Ty had mentioned what *business* Liz was in. They were keeping that knowledge under their hats. Liz knew Ty well enough to know that the last thing he wanted was anything to do with law enforcement. He had had his fill.

"No," answered Liz, shaking her head. "Actually, it's personal."

"Is Mike okay?" he asked quickly.

"Mike's fine. Busy, but fine. He doesn't know I'm here. This visit is on the spur of the moment. I hoped I might catch you."

"That you did. How about a cup?" There was always hot coffee available at Brooks. For many people without a home, a cup of hot coffee might be the best part of their day.

"That would be nice. Thanks," said Liz as she stepped over to the five-gallon urn. Liz was amazed at how drinkable shelter coffee was—hot, strong, and usually fresh because they went through so much. They sat down at the table opposite one another.

"What can I do for you?" asked Ty. To Liz's ear, the question wasn't inquisitive. Ty's gentle manner made the question come off as a genuine offer of help.

"There aren't a lot of people I would talk to about this," Liz began, "and I don't say that to butter you up."

Liz told Ty about Sara Mallory, Gabriel Chapin and their daughter, now a fifteen-year-old runaway. She gave him the background about the raid on Killian's club and how Sara died. She was honest about her part in it and how she felt some responsibility.

"I honestly tried to forget about it all," she shared with Ty. "I hadn't thought about what happened for a long time. But now I've learned there's a child involved, Ty. Knowing that has made me feel even more responsible for what happened to her mother."

"You feel guilty," said Ty.

"I do, yes," said Liz.

"Whether you're to blame or not, you still feel guilty. You ask yourself if you could have done something different to change the outcome."

Liz nodded. Sara's face, as she remembered it, filled her mind.

"There's a difference between feeling sadness that a thing happened and taking blame for it," said Ty.

Liz considered Ty's words. "I get that," she said. "I can feel sadness for something that doesn't involve me directly. That's empathy. But that's not the case here. I was a part of what happened. I was involved."

"What could you have done differently that could have changed the outcome?"

"I could have warned Sara. She trusted me."

"From what you've said, you tried. It sounds like this gal trusted a lot of people—some that she shouldn't have trusted," Ty told her, "and I certainly don't mean you, Liz. You may have been one of the better influences in this young woman's life."

"I don't know...maybe."

"The past is the past. We can't change it. The reality of what might-have-been will always be out of our reach."

"True," agreed Liz, giving Ty's words some thought. "That doesn't sound like guilt. More like regret."

"Maybe. Consider the difference: guilt, at its essence, is culpability. Responsibility—whether it's placed or proven.

Regret involves feelings of remorse, mourning. Is there unexpressed grief for this young woman? If there is, maybe that's what you're carrying around. The bottom line is that you were young, new to the job. You were following orders. I know what that's like. There is no way around it—even though we both know the damage it can leave in its wake."

"You're taking about your tours in the Gulf."

"Yep," Ty nodded as he answered. "But we're not talking about me. Listen, you were young, inexperienced. This girl died from a police round and you were wearing a badge. You knew her personally. That's a lot to process."

"You're saying I identified with the cause, the action—the force that took her life?"

"Maybe. I don't want to tell you what to do," Ty offered with concern, "but you could consider talking to somebody."

"That's what I'm doing," said Liz with half a smile.

Ty shook his head, grinned. "You know what I mean. A pro."

"Yes, I know what you mean. And I will. If I need to," Liz said as she stood up. "Thank you."

"Anytime, Liz. You take care. Let me know if you want to talk again. And say hello to Mike."

Guilt and regret: words loaded with emotional impact. But there was something else on Liz's mind. She knew why she wanted to search for Sara's daughter, wanted the girl found safe, but was there more to it? Was she was drawn to Elle because she regretted how she'd handled the events with Sara all those years ago? Was she trying to make up for her mistakes?

Quinn had reminded her of balance and self-care. How did those needs factor in? *No*, Liz told herself. Helping Elle wasn't about helping Liz. *The past aside, that is not about me. It can't be about me.* Elle needed help and Liz was resolved to do what she could for her.

Chapter Thirty-three

"The Shoe Drops"

Liz made it back to the precinct, her talk with Ty having given her a lot to consider, but she'd have to set it aside until later. Soon she was deep in the minutia of details that involved overtime hours logged by her team. They all worked hard and Liz wished the job didn't bleed over into their personal time, but she knew it happened. And the public liked knowing that crimes were solved, especially when lives were lost.

She was considering fresh coffee when she looked up to see Miller in the corridor, approaching her office doorway.

"Sir, I apologize," she stammered, caught off guard as he stopped just outside her office. "Did we have a meeting scheduled?"

Liz started to stand and Miller stopped her. "Please, keep your seat, Lieutenant," he said as he stepped inside and closed the door behind him. "May I sit?" he asked.

"Of course," she said, pointing to the visitor's chair. "Is this regarding the information you hoped to find about the Killian raid? Did you come across something?"

"No, I've learned nothing along those lines as of yet," said Miller, as he lowered himself into the chair. "I'm here about a different matter, but not unrelated to it."

Liz's interest was piqued. It wasn't unusual for Miller to surprise her with a visit, but the occasion didn't happen often enough to be commonplace. Liz started to ask what she could do for him. The captain beat her to the punch.

"Lieutenant, the Department was notified this morning that on behalf of his daughter, Gabriel Chapin is suing for the wrongful death of Sara Mallory. The suit asks that the department be held responsible and names you and the late Detective Frank Pruitt as the parties guilty of negligence that led to Ms. Mallory's death."

"What?" Liz was stunned. She felt the surprise on her face. Her eyes grew wide and her jaw dropped. "Excuse me. Suing the department? Did I hear you correctly?"

"You did. He's engaged a civil litigation attorney named Connelly. Have you heard of an attorney by that name?"

"No, I haven't," Liz answered, trying to make sense of what she was hearing.

"Not surprising. Neither had I," said Miller, shaking his head. "We don't often become involved in civil cases, at least not here on our end. No one is arrested, no one is detained, no threat of conviction. It's all about responsibility and awarded damages."

"He can do this now? After all this time, this is possible?"

"He can try and yes, it is. He's claiming that the wrongful death of the girl's mother is directly related to his daughter's issues of unhappiness. He's blaming you, claiming the violent death of the girl's mother has caused severe emotional distress. He claims this is why she's had problems, why she's run away."

Liz shook her head, not believing it. It must be a sick joke. "The son of a bitch! You mentioned seeking damages. What does he want?"

“Compensation, of course. Ostensibly, for the daughter. But I’d say Chapin wants revenge. He’s demanding a public acknowledgement. And he wants you dismissed. And it could happen.”

Liz started at Miller. She wanted to respond, but her throat had constricted. She tried to speak.

“Chapin asked me to find the girl. Then he pulls this?” Liz didn’t sound like herself, her voice stilted in disbelief. She hated hearing it.

“You told him that you weren’t going to be played, that the case would be handled properly. I’m sure he didn’t like it. This is his response, although my guess is that he was already planning the legal action. He may have pursued this lawsuit even if you had found the girl,” said Miller, shaking his head in disgust.

“He’s held me responsible for Sara’s death for years,” said Liz. “He’s likely been plotting this move for a long time. This is about me. He wants to ruin me.”

“Probably. If he wanted justice, he had years to pursue it. The lawsuit cites procedural neglect and failure to protect a civilian assisting the department. Now understand, Chapin isn’t claiming that you fired the gun that killed Sara Mallory. I’m not even sure that detail is significant to him or to his attorney, at this point.” Miller straightened his jacket as he added, almost under his breath and with annoyance, “That’s more reason to find out what happened that day.”

“But, Sir, Chapin contacted me. He requested my help and I notified you. Doesn’t that attest to my handling of things appropriately?”

Miller studied Liz before he answered. "Lieutenant, in my view, it does not. The fact that Chapin asked for your help speaks to his knowledge of how you feel, of the guilt you harbor—and of his ability to intimidate you because of it."

Liz nodded. That's all she could do.

"This is a civil case. It won't be determined by evidence beyond a reasonable doubt. A preponderance of evidence will decide that a party is either responsible or not. That's a much lower standard than convincing a unanimous jury of peers."

Liz stared at Miller. She knew this, all of it. She was stunned, nonetheless and Liz had never been on this side of a potential judgement.

"You told me yesterday that you blame yourself for Ms. Mallory's death, that you feel somewhat responsible. That makes no sense to me," said Miller, shaking his head with hands outstretches. "You weren't even there when she died."

"No, I wasn't there," Liz admitted. "You're right about that. That's not the point. The point is Sara shouldn't have been there either."

Liz wanted to say more, but Miller didn't give her a chance. "I want to know if you've mentioned any of this to anyone else. Have you discussed it?"

"Only with Mike," Liz answered. "I've talked with a few people here at the department about hearing from Chapin and about his missing daughter. Why?" Liz didn't mention Quinn or her conversation with Ty.

"I'm not concerned about Mr. Dwyer. Don't talk to anyone else about any of it."

"No, Sir," answered Liz. "I won't."

"Lieutenant, I have to place you on desk duty. I can't keep you on the street. You know the political climate as well as I. Once the news of this civil suit reaches the press, they will pursue you like dogs."

"Sir...but,"

"I do not see any alternative," Miller explained, not happy with the situation either.

"This is bullshit! Captain, I can handle the press. If you put me on a desk, Chapin gets what he wants."

Miller shook his head in disagreement. "That is not my current concern, Lieutenant. The situation has the potential to become volatile. I have to keep you out of the public eye."

"You're cutting me off at the knees! Is this your last word?"

"It is. I see no other way to handle this."

"Then I'm requesting leave, Sir. I need to get out of here for a few days. The result is the same, but at least it's on my terms."

Miller looked at Liz, studied her, thinking about her decision. He didn't look convinced and he certainly wasn't happy. "If that's how you want to handle this, I can't say I blame you. Are you sure about this?"

Liz was seething, realized she was staring at the closed office door beyond Miller's left shoulder. She nudged herself enough to look Miller in the eye and said, "Yes, Sir. I'm very sure."

"I will continue to dig into this case history. You and I need to be in contact almost daily. Will you agree?"

"That's reasonable, Sir."

The captain searched Liz's face, seeing her resolve. "Your team will report to me in your absence. Notify them by email, cc'd to me. Wrap up anything you're in the middle of, forward the rest to my desk. I sincerely hope we clear up this mess as quickly as possible."

Miller stood, extended his hand to Liz. They shook hands firmly. Miller looked Liz in the eye. "This bullshit should have been resolved years ago, Lieutenant," he said. "I'm going to get to the bottom of it. But, most of all, and I need you to hear me now. Don't do anything to make matters worse!"

He turned and left Liz's office.

Liz was numb. *A lawsuit; a civil fucking lawsuit!* She went through the motions on autopilot, finishing up what she could, as Miller had instructed, and emailed her team. She forwarded issues requiring more consideration to his desk and logged out of the system. The email to her team was short and vague on details, just that she would be out for a few days. Her detectives would wonder what in hell was going on, but that curiosity was what made them good investigators. Besides, the rumors would circulate soon enough.

She sat for a moment, looking around her small office and then retrieved her bag from the desk drawer where it was kept and placed her phone inside. Liz locked the office door and walked out of the building.

Chapter Thirty-four

"Pending Litigation"

Liz drove around town for a while, not going anywhere in particular. The numbness that overcame her in her office hadn't abated, but it was slowly enhanced by anger, shame, and embarrassment. She was angry with Chapin, ashamed that it had come to this, and embarrassed. In fourteen years as a cop, Liz had never been in this position.

Eventually Liz made her way home and parked in front of her building. The weather was decent and she found the mild temperature and pleasant breeze to be at odds with her mood. She longed for heavy rain, dark skies, and chilling wind.

She sat in the car and called Mike. It didn't take more than a few minutes to tell him that Chapin had resorted to a wrongful death lawsuit and that Liz had chosen personal leave over imposed desk duty. It could cost the city a fortune in damages, and Liz's career was on the line.

"I hate to say it, but I'm not surprised," Mike told her. He had listened as Liz spilled the details. "This is what assholes do. They blame others and seek vengeance. It's the way they're wired. It doesn't make it any less of a crock of shit."

Liz could only sigh into the phone. Mike heard her resignation, telling her, "There's nothing you can do. You can't discuss it publicly and you can't even defend yourself. You'll get through this if you make it about the kids, Liz. Make it about finding a missing girl and an injured one needs our help," he said.

"You're right," said Liz. *It's too bad that's not Chapin's focus*, she thought.

"Are you going to be alright?" Mike asked her. "Where are you anyway?"

"I'm fine." Liz assured him. "It's taking a while to sink in. I'm home. I'll see you later."

Liz stepped from her car and headed up the steps to the third-floor apartment. She unlocked the door and stepped inside. She attempted to greet Eddie and Little Kurt, but her heart wasn't in it. The cats were happy to see her, but they were mildly perturbed anyway, having their nap schedule disrupted.

Making her way to the bedroom, Liz placed her badge and service weapon in the safe. She wasn't numb anymore. She was angry, downright pissed off, and her ire was directed solely toward Gabriel Chapin.

She changed into old, comfy clothes and grabbed a beer from the fridge. By now, Miller would have spoken with the team of homicide detectives, probably told them not to contact her, but Liz expected she'd hear from most of them anyway. She would have to decide what to say to them.

Liz wondered what the official statement about the lawsuit would sound like, what details would be included, and what the response would be when the news became public. The captain had been correct, the press could be ugly. There was nothing Liz could do about it except try to keep her cool, something she struggled with under normal conditions. She could only focus on other things, as Mike had suggested. And wait.

Chapter Thirty-five

"Connors"

For the past few months, Detective Sergeant Kyle Connors had been leading a team handling missing person's reports. Before that, he had done important work with the homicide division. In Connors mind, no one deserved to be brought to justice more than someone who had taken the life of another. When he made Sergeant and the opening for a team lead came up in Missing Persons, Connors jumped at the chance to work cases that could possibly lead to finding people alive and well.

It didn't always end that way; sometimes they were found alive, but far from well. If the missing person was a child or a young person, the work could be especially gratifying—or extremely heartbreaking.

Connors was trained by the best—of this, he was sure. He had discussed with Liz, his mentor, about whether he was ready to take the Sergeant's exam. Connors wasn't sure he was far enough along in his own training to assist other officers with theirs. Liz told him, and in no uncertain terms, that he was ready. She told him that he would never stop wanting to learn. Liz was skeptical, she said, of cops who thought they knew everything. Knowing he was still teachable would make him a good example for junior officers, Liz told him.

And now, Liz was dealing with her own problems and had chosen to step away. It was all because of a bullshit lawsuit and a messed-up situation that happened years ago, when she was even younger than Emmy. The entire squad room was talking about it.

There wasn't a lot Connors could do for Liz with regard to her problems except to hope they were resolved. He told her in a text message before all this, when Miller brought him in, to take care and she had responded for him to *just find the girl.* Connors was determined to do so.

In case he had missed something, Connors re-read the notes from Liz about Kyrie. He had spoken with Chapin and with Richelle Isaacs. Chapin was seething that Liz would not be the one looking for his daughter. Connors had reminded Chapin that this was about finding Kyrie, hopefully safe and sound, and not about him being in control.

Connors instructed the man not to contact Liz regarding the case. Further, he told Chapin that he would be searching for Kyrie whether he liked it or not, lawsuit or no lawsuit, so he could shut the hell up and stay out of the way—or help find her.

He left messages for the parents of three of Kyrie's friends. He had not heard back from one of them. The two who had returned his calls had offered little in the way of help, but at least they called back.

Liz noted that Kyrie had lived with her maternal grandmother as a young child, and Chapin had reluctantly supplied Connors with her name and phone number. The woman's name was Laura Mallory and she was living in Tacoma. It was late in the evening, but she picked up on the second ring.

"This is Detective Connors with the police in Columbia City. I'm trying to reach Laura Mallory."

"This is Laura. You said police? Did you say Columbia City?"

"Yes. I was given your name and number by Gabriel Chapin."

"Gabriel? I can't imagine why he would be giving my number to the police. What has that SOB done now? What's going on?"

"Ms. Mallory, I'm calling because your granddaughter, Kyrie is missing. I need to ask you a few questions."

"What? Kyrie? She's missing, you say? Hold on, I need to sit down. I'm sorry; I just got in from work. Okay, that's better. I need to be able to think."

"Can you tell me when you last saw Kyrie?"

"Gabriel hasn't let me see Kyrie for years," the woman said. "I haven't seen my granddaughter since her tenth birthday. He stopped returning my calls a long time ago. He told me if I got in touch with Kyrie or saw her without his permission, that he would have me arrested for custodial interference. I'm surprised he even gave you my number."

"I didn't give Mr. Chapin much choice, Ma'am," Connors told her. "Have you had any contact with Kyrie?"

"Kyrie calls me once in a while. She was angry with me, at first. Her father told her I didn't want to see her. Can you imagine telling a child such a thing? I told her to call me anytime she wanted. I couldn't call her unless I was sure Kyrie would be the one to answer. When she was old enough to have her own phone that changed, of course."

"When did you last hear from her?"

"I haven't talked with her in a couple of weeks. She said her father was suspicious and it was better if she called me.

She sends photos, selfies she's taken, and text messages. Sergeant Connors, what's happened?"

"Ms. Mallory, I'm sorry to tell you, but Kyrie ran away from her father's home. She's been gone for four months. Her father was hearing from her on a regular basis until about a month ago."

"Oh my god," she said. "Four months?! I don't understand this."

"You say you talked with Kyrie, had a conversation by phone, two weeks ago?"

"Yes. She called me one morning. Kyrie said she was home from school sick. She knows I work in the afternoon and evening. I work in the kitchen at Madigan Army Hospital," she added. "Kyrie didn't sound well. I told her to rest and let me know in a couple of days how she was doing. I haven't heard back from her."

"When did you last receive a photo from her, Ma'am?" Laura told him about the last photo she had received. Connors assumed it was the same photo Kyrie had sent to her father, taken near the fountain in Portland. At that point, she still appeared to be doing okay.

"This is helpful, Ma'am, and encouraging. I want to ask you to do something for me. Could you send a text message to the number you have for Kyrie? We are sure it's a burner phone so it's difficult to trace. Don't tell her we're looking for her. I just want you to make contact. Do you understand?"

"Of course, I'll do it right now. I'll ask how she's doing."

"That would be perfect, Ma'am. Ms. Mallory, I'm going to give you my number. Can you let me know as soon as you hear from Kyrie?"

"Absolutely, Sergeant," said the girl's grandmother. "I'll do whatever you need me to do! Just find Kyrie. Please."

Chapter Thirty-six

"Decisions"

Elle was lying cozy in her bunk at the Youth Center. She had been napping on and off. When she was awake, she would start to cry, thinking about Pooki. Minutes later, she would cheer up, thinking about how nice everyone had been since she'd been hurt. Especially the lady cops. She really liked the younger one called Castillo, who told Elle to call her Emmy. She reminded Elle of her cousin, Cecilia.

Cece had always been nice to Elle, even back when Elle was still Landon. She had thought a couple of times about trying to get in touch with Cece, but she had lost track of her a long time ago.

The cop boss lady was okay too. Elle thought it was nice of her to bring her snacks. She hoped she had remembered to say thank you. She was blown away that the cop boss had helped her out with a phone. She was set for a while now. And the cop boss hadn't expected anything in return—how weird was that? In Elle's world, that was too good to be true, that's what it was.

Since the cop boss had left, Elle had been trying to decide about contacting her grandma. It made Elle anxious because she never wanted to see Malcolm again. She hated Malcolm for the way he had treated her. And when Elle thought about *why* she should consider going home, she became even more anxious. Those two assholes were out there somewhere.

If Elle wasn't careful, they would try to shut her up. They would shut her up for good before she could lead the cops to them. But Elle had already told the cops all she could—what they looked like and the address of the house. *The assholes didn't know any of that,* Elle told herself.

The kid pulled out a copy of her attackers' images, the ones the tech officer had created with Elle's help. *Yeah, they looked like the guys,* she thought. She didn't like looking at the images. Emmy said the cops found Pooki's blood at the house and found the knife where Elle thought she had tossed it. It was nice to be believed, for a change. But she was still scared.

She thought about the other photo that Emmy had asked about. She had studied the girl's face, but lied to Castillo and then to Quinn about whether she knew the girl. She felt bad about that, but not too bad. It was the way things were done on the street.

The girl in the photo was Lyric. Elle didn't know much about her except that she had run into some trouble, but then all punks had trouble, didn't they? Lyric was really smart and the girl could sing like a rock star. She was part of the crew now—not something that you take lightly. Elle wasn't gonna send trouble her way.

She hoped that Lyric was keeping her head down. Elle had texted the girl twice, but hadn't heard back. Lyric knew that Elle would not betray her. Elle had to hope she could get back to the squat in time to warn her.

Chapter Thirty-seven

"Mike"

Mike was on his way to Liz's. It was the end of a long day, Liz was already there, which was out of the ordinary. Their lives, certainly their schedules were not ordinary, at the best of times. But nothing was ordinary at the moment. Liz had been forced to step away from the job she loved because an operation she'd been involved in years ago had ended badly and a young woman died.

It wasn't Liz's fault that it happened, but she blamed herself. He wished he could help her, but didn't know what to do for her.

Mike's own job was keeping him very busy at the office right now, managing services at four emergency housing options for folks living on the streets. He had a lot on his mind. Some of the street folks were just kids, punks on the streets without parents or family members. Mike had been doing this work since many of the punks were babies, but he knew he'd never get used to the sadness.

Some of these kids had experienced more cruelty than Mike wanted to think about. He thought about Quinn, who had survived the streets as a kid, and Elle, who was recovering from a deliberate attack. Then he thought of Pooki, the kid who had died from a vicious stab wound inflicted by people who had enticed her with food and a place to stay.

Mike hadn't decided whether to tell Liz about the phone call he had received this afternoon. Hearing from Chapin wasn't totally unexpected—the shit bag had been warned about contacting Liz directly. Chapin had a lot of balls contacting Mike, especially with this lawsuit on the table, and Mike had told him so. You'd think his attorney would have advised against it. But Mike knew the type. He doubted Chapin took anyone's advice.

He should tell Liz about the call, especially because he didn't trust Chapin, but also because Liz would want to know. She would not be happy about it, and with good reason. But Mike didn't want to put more stress on Liz right now. He would tell Connors or Captain Miller about it.

Chapin wanted to meet with Mike and Mike had told him to screw himself. It wasn't going to happen, so he could forget it. He had ended the call, hoping he didn't hear from the guy again.

As he pulled out from his parking space, Mike didn't notice the sedan parked across the lot. He didn't notice there were two men in the car—or that they pulled out of the parking lot and followed him.

Chapter Thirty-eight

"Finn"

Liz was on her second beer. She hadn't thought about food and hadn't eaten since the cheeseburger she'd had with Castillo while she visited Elle. A few chunks of cheddar and a sliced apple would hold her over until she and Mike decided together about dinner. She hadn't talked with Miller again.

She was thinking about Elle contacting her grandmother, but Quinn had not called. She wondered if Drip had remembered details about the guy that attacked Elle and Pooki. But Detective Morgan was the contact for any forthcoming information on that. She could only hope to be informed of any developments.

Liz hated being out of the loop. She wanted to help, to be of service, but she was sidelined. At least, she hadn't heard from Chapin again.

When her phone rang, Liz recognized the number from two previous missed calls. The caller was trying to reach her for a third time.

"Liz Jordan," she said, answering the call.

The caller was silent for a moment, long enough for Liz to think it was a crank. Then a tentative voice asked, "Is this the cop that talked to Richelle?" The voice was that of a teenaged boy. And since he mentioned Richelle, he had to be calling about Kyrie.

"I'm one of them, yes. This is Lieutenant Jordan. Richelle spoke with Sergeant Connors, as well. Who is this?" asked

Liz. The question was followed by silence. "Hey, buddy, you called me. Do you want to tell me something?"

Liz heard a long, breathy sigh filled with tension and fear. The last thing she wanted was for this kid to hang up. *Back off,* Liz told herself. *Learn what he knows.* "Are you a friend of Kyrie's? I'm not going to cause you any trouble. We just want to know that she's okay."

"My name is Finn. Yeah, I'm a friend of Kyrie's. At least, I used to be."

"What can I do for you, Finn?"

"Well, Richelle talks to my parents now and then. They want to help Kyrie, but they don't know anything that would help. The other cop left a message on our land line. To be honest, I deleted it. Am I in trouble?"

"A police officer left a message for your parents and you deleted it. But that doesn't stop him from leaving another message. Why did you delete it?"

"Because they don't know anything," said Finn. "And they don't think I know anything. I'd like it to stay that way."

"So, you want to help, but you don't want your parents to know. Okay, your secret is safe with me, Finn. What do you want us to know?"

"Well, see...I knew Kyrie was gonna run. I knew it, but I wasn't going to stop her. I didn't blame her for running. I'd have run too."

"Why did she run? And why don't you blame her?"

"Have you ever met Kyrie's dad? He's kind of a jerk."

"I have met him, but I need more than that."

"Okay, okay. Kyrie learned something about her dad. I don't know what it was. She wouldn't tell me. But she wasn't staying there, she was getting out, she said. Kyrie said it wouldn't do any good to confide in Richelle. She said she wouldn't put Richelle in that position. And she didn't want her grandma involved either."

"You know about Kyrie's grandmother?"

"Yes, I met her a long time ago, when Kyrie and I were kids."

"Was Kyrie scared of her father, Finn?"

"No, I don't think she was scared exactly. Kyrie was angry with him; really angry."

Liz thought of the poem in the square on the wall at the Youth Center. It was filled with anger, betrayal. Drip called it righteous hate. It read like it was written to a love interest, but there were other forms of betrayal. She was sure it had been written by Kyrie and shared under the name Lyric, but she couldn't prove it. If Kyrie had written it, could it be about her father?

"Finn, have you heard from Kyrie since she ran?"

It took him a couple of moments to decide to answer, and then he said, "Yeah, once or twice. But it's been a long time. The number doesn't work anymore."

"Okay, thanks, Finn. This helps. Sergeant Connors will want to talk to you. I'll tell him what you had to say, but he may have other questions. Is there another number where he can reach you?"

"Uh...I guess. He can call me at this number. It's my cell. Could you do me a favor and tell him not to leave another message at our house?" The longer Liz was on the phone with the kid, the slower he talked, like she was dragging the words out of him.

"I can't promise, but I'll relay the request. Why don't you want your parents to know that you can offer help?"

"Kyrie was welcome at my house, but I wasn't allowed to go there, see? I went there sometimes anyway, and they don't know that. But if they thought I had anything to offer, they would have wanted me to speak up sooner. But I promised Kyrie I wouldn't say anything."

"That's why you said that you and Kyrie *used* to be friends."

"Uh-huh. She'd be pissed that I said anything. I changed my mind when I heard the cops were involved."

"And you figured we'd keep calling your folks."

"Yeah," said Finn.

"Finn, do you know if Kyrie ever went by a different name?"

"You mean like, a street name?"

"Yes, that exactly what I mean," said Liz. *So, your average, basic suburban kid knows about street names,* thought Liz. *When did the lives of adolescents go so far down the rabbit hole?*

"Nah, I don't think so," said Finn. Liz heard noises in the background. "And I gotta go. Bye."

"Sure. Thanks for calling, Finn," said Liz, as she ended the call. She wasn't sure she believed Finn about Kyrie not using a street name, but it didn't matter. Liz was sure she knew the answer.

Chapter Thirty-nine

"Collaboration"

Liz started to call Connors when Mike stepped in the door. "Hey," she said, putting off the call. It would be good to talk things over with Mike. He was a good one to bounce things off, and he may have thoughts about Finn, this friend of Kyrie's.

"He tried to call you three times, huh?" Mike said, as he settled on the living room floor with the cats. "He was persistent. He must want to help. But, then again, he wanted to head off Connors from calling his folks again."

"But Richelle Isaacs gave him my number. She must have thought he had something to offer," said Liz, "and Mike, this kid Finn, he doesn't think much of Gabriel. The kid's parents didn't let him visit there."

"They must have pegged him for a scum-bag," said Mike, thinking about the call he'd received from Chapin earlier. He came close to telling Liz about it, but decided against it. "If they thought the man was bad news, makes sense they wouldn't want their son around him. I would feel the same way."

"Finn says Kyrie was angry, really angry, with her father," Liz said. "He says that's why she ran."

"Liz, call Connors. He needs to know all this. I'm not telling you that so you'll back off. I know you're concerned about the girl, and you need something to focus on right now. But Connors needs the info. Do you trust me to make a dinner decision?"

"No, you're right. I'll try to reach him," said Liz, picking up her phone. "Of course, I trust you to decide on dinner."

Connors picked up right away. "Are you still at the precinct?" Liz asked him.

"Yes, but heading out soon. I've been looking through phone records. I've had too much coffee and my eyes are crossing."

"I have some info for you. It's info about Kyrie. You're welcome to stop by on your way home."

"Liz," interrupted Mike. "Tell Connors I'm ordering pizza. If he's hungry, I'll order enough for him too."

She started to relay the message, but Connors had heard Mike in the background. "Tell Mike thanks. Pizza sounds awesome. I'm on my way," said Connors and he ended the call.

Thirty minutes later, Connors knocked at Liz's door, carrying his contribution to the meal: a six-pack of Rogue IPA and a large Calistoga for Mike. A few minutes later, Flying Pies on Main delivered a large combo, New York-style and a side of breadsticks.

Mike and Connors each took a seat at the breakfast bar. Liz stood on the opposite side of the bar, explaining that she'd been sitting all day. The pie was huge, nearly an inch thick, and took a degree of coordination to get a slice from plate to mouth. Liz offered, but neither of the guys wanted a fork. Liz watched Connors fold a slice in half, like a taco and take a bite. *Brilliant*, she thought.

"Where's Castillo...er...I mean Emmy?" asked Liz between bites.

"She was still working when I left. We don't hang out together every evening...just most of them. She turned the Youth Center file over to Morgan in homicide. Did she tell you? They're calling it the Youth Center case because they don't have full names for either of the punks."

"Yes, she told me it would happen today. Told me Morgan had been assigned. I'm not sure I'm comfortable calling Morgan right now. You know, me being on leave."

"Lieutenant, I think Morgan would be okay with a call from you."

The statement struck Liz as curious, but she wasn't going to ask. They had other things to discuss. She could get her questions answered by Castillo.

Liz told Connors about the call from Finn, and how he suspected Kyrie ran because she was angry with her father.

"I got three numbers from Richelle Isaacs," Connors confirmed. "I heard back from two families, both with daughters that Kyrie had been in school with. The third number was to this kid, Finn and his parents, so that's one small mystery solved. But I talked with the parents, not their teen-aged children. We need to interview the kids without parents around, but I can't insist on it. Parents have the right to refuse access to their kids."

"Ask them how much they might appreciate kids talking to the cops privately if it was their kid that was missing," said Mike. Liz and Connors nodded in agreement.

"Let me see if I understand," reviewed Connors. "This kid, Finn was a close friend of Kyrie's. He doesn't like Chapin and says Kyrie was angry with her dad, angry enough to take off," said Connors. "If that's true, and her anger was expressed in the poem on the wall, then it confirms she was not only in Columbia City, but was at the Youth Center. What we need is someone at the Youth Center to admit they know her as Lyric."

"That would help, but you may get more from staff than from kids," said Liz.

"True. Now I have news. I talked with Kyrie's grandmother today," Connors told them. "Her name is Laura Mallory. She lives in Tacoma." Connors took a long pull on the bottle of brew.

"I never met Sara's mother," said Liz. "I didn't know she lived in Tacoma. Chapin told me that Kyrie lived with Sara's mother when she was very young. He shared that when I doubted that Sara had a child."

"Ms. Mallory hasn't seen the girl for five years. Chapin wouldn't allow it. Made her back off by threatening her with legal action. It would seem he likes to file lawsuits," said Connors. "Ms. Mallory tried to stay in touch. Kyrie called and texted her grandmother on a regular basis, but she was careful not to alert her father."

"What a shit bag," said Mike, shaking his head in disgust, as he tossed garbage into the can and got Connors another beer.

"Indeed," said Connors, thanking Mike for the beer. "The good news is that Ms. Mallory talked with Kyrie as recently as two weeks ago. I'm trying to pin-point the place of origin of the call more accurately, but it's nearly impossible with a pay-as-you-go phone. Area codes mean nothing. But the good news is that Ms. Mallory texted Kyrie today. I asked if she would to try to make contact, and to not let on that there was a search for her. Kyrie texted her grandmother back about an hour later. Ms. Mallory forwarded the messages to me. Take a look," he said, showing the screen of his phone to Liz.

Liz read the following:

Message to/from Kyrie below:

Hi K, haven't heard from you. How are you feeling?

Better sorry How R U Gma?

I'm fine Love you, K!

Love you too

"That's encouraging, Connors," said Liz, as she handed the phone back to him.

"Yes," said Mike. "It is. And the grandmother is sure the message was from Kyrie?"

"I asked her about that," answered Connors. "She said Kyrie uses 'Gma' in messages to her, has for a long time. Ms. Mallory uses 'K' for Kyrie."

Liz's phone alerted her to a message of her own. It was from Quinn, and it read:

Are you able to stop by in a.m.? Elle would like you to make a call for her.

Elle had made a decision about contacting her grandmother. It couldn't have been easy. Liz responded that she would be at the Youth Center at nine a.m.

Chapter Forty

"Morgan"

The following morning, Liz was sipping coffee after an early run with Mike on the quarter-mile track at the high-school. The staff at the school knew Liz and knew she was a cop. The proximity to the school made for some loud evenings, especially during football season, but Liz liked living there. In her mind, it was perfect. She and Mike had spent many Friday evenings in the fall of the year watching high school games from her small balcony.

The run that morning hadn't been completely terrible. She knew she needed the exercise. Usually when Liz was running, there was a constant mantra of *shit, shit, shit,* running through her brain, just hoping to get it over with or hope that the runner's high of endorphins would kick in. This morning, as she was running the track, Liz was telling herself that it could be worse—she could be like Quinn, at an indoor gym—boxing. *No thanks,* thought Liz.

Liz decided to put a call in to Detective Reese Morgan. She checked the time, knew it was early, but Connors had mentioned that Morgan might be receptive to hearing from her, even with the lawsuit to consider.

It wouldn't make a difference to Liz about contacting Elle's family, but she wanted to know the plan for Elle with regard to the investigation. Elle would be key to the case, Liz was certain. She would need to be available, and on top of it all, Elle's legal status was up in the air.

She knew little about Reese Morgan, but what she knew was good. He was on a homicide team supervised by another lieutenant in the department. He had spent time with the state troopers before joining the department in Columbia City. He kept to himself, didn't walk around like he was full of himself, and he wasn't a pain in anyone's ass.

Liz's assessment of the guy was clouded by the fact that she out-ranked him. Much of her opinion of Morgan was as her subordinate, not a colleague. At least Morgan was smart enough to have conducted himself appropriately around her, she figured. She had heard that Morgan had family ties to Southern California. That was all she knew of him.

She pulled up a mobile directory and punched in the number for his office phone. It took a few seconds for him to answer. Liz didn't know if the system alerted Morgan to who was calling.

"Detective Morgan," he said quickly, as he answered the call.

"Morgan, this is Liz Jordan."

"Hey, Lieutenant; how are things?" he asked. Morgan must know about the civil suit and that she was on leave, but there had been no pause or impatient sigh upon learning who was calling. To Liz's ear, his question was sincere, not just polite. Morgan had even referred to Liz's rank even though Liz had merely stated her name. She took that as a sign of respect.

"Things are okay, just waiting for the dust to clear."

"And it will, Lieutenant. Your team is not happy. Can't say I blame them. They want you back on the job."

"Nice to hear, Morgan. Listen, I don't want to take up a lot of your time. I think you should know about a little side project I have in the works. It's regarding what your team is calling the Youth Center case."

"Right," he said, pausing for a moment. "Actually, Castillo said you had been assisting the survivor of the attack, the kid who was able to provide the facial mages for our perp search. How is she doing?"

"She's recovering. It helped that she was able to stay at the center, but time is running out on that. The kid, her name is Elle, has asked me to contact her family. Morgan, she's scared and wants to get off the street. As long as we are able to maintain contact, would there be any issue with her leaving town?"

"Shit, I hope not. I don't want to be the reason a street kid chooses to stay on the street. Do you know where her family resides?"

"I don't know yet. I'm heading to talk with her soon and I'll find out. It's my belief that her grandparent is legal guardian, but Elle told me that she turns eighteen soon."

"That may be the best thing for this kid," he said, talking like he knew the score. "Can I ask you to let me know how contact goes with the family? If we need to, we'll arrange for her protection as a vulnerable witness. Knowing where Elle will be living would be classified and we can coordinate security services for the home."

"That would help. How's the hunt?" she asked Morgan.

"Slow going," he said. "We're sorting through forensics, interviewing everyone we can think of, checking databases—and there's a lot of paper to chase. We're canvassing for anyone who knows who the perps are."

"Finding someone who can ID these guys would help."

"I got a call from a kid named Drip. Said you gave him my name. Sounds like a real character, but at least he called. He's pissed off about the attack. He recognizes one of the assailants, the one who stabbed Pooki, according to your kid's statement. Doesn't have a name for him, but he's trying to remember where he saw the guy."

"Yeah, Drip," said Liz, remembering the punk's sad story.

"He sounded like he wanted to help. He said the dead kid was a friend of his. If he can't remember, then I'm hoping he sees the guy again and calls me."

"That would help, too, Morgan. I'll let you know if I learn anything you need."

"I'll talk to Elle soon, Lieutenant, probably today. She trusts you and Castillo. Is there anything special I need to know?"

"Nothing that Elle won't tell you herself, Morgan. She's pretty chill. One thing though, the less you look like a cop, the better. You know what I mean?"

"I do," he said with a laugh. "Thanks for the tip."

Liz ended the call with Morgan. Checking the time, she completed a couple of necessary domestic chores, fed Eddie and Little Kurt, and headed to the Youth Center. She figured she should arrive to visit Elle just before nine o'clock.

At the other end of the call, Morgan replaced the receiver of his office phone on the cradle. Morgan had spoken with Lieutenant Jordan before, of course, but this was the first time she had had reason to call him directly. He reviewed the details of the conversation he'd just had with Jordan and told himself he had handled it well.

Picking up his cell phone, he selected a number already listed in the favorites and placed the call. The party he was calling knew it was Morgan, answering with a curt, "Yes." As usual, Morgan heard the attitude of superiority in the voice and it irritated him. *I'm a cop, for chrissake, show a little respect,* he thought.

"Got a call from your friend," Morgan said, looking around to see if he could be overheard. Satisfied that he had a moment of privacy, he continued. "She's distracted enough by my case. I'm sure we'll stay in touch. My guess is that she'll lead us right where we want to go."

"That's what I want to hear," said the voice on the other end. "And if not, we have a contingency."

"Yes, we do. And as for my case, I have it under control, but keep your guys low if you want me to resolve it."

"Understood." Abruptly, the voice was gone.

Chapter Forty-one

"Elle's Plan"

Parking a block away was the best Liz could manage, but she didn't mind. The short walk gave her a chance to survey the neighborhood. Groups of street kids sat together sipping something, probably coffee, from paper cups. A few were eating fruit or pastry items, and others, due to the relatively early hour, appeared to be sleeping.

None of the kids were blocking doorways or creating obvious problems for folks who had somewhere to be. Liz heard music and realized Sage was at his usual spot on the corner, his open guitar case next to him, singing another mournful song for anyone who wanted to listen.

Walking into the Youth Center, Liz spotted John, the big guy with the ponytail, near the door. He was talking with a kid wrapped in a blanket. The kid looked half asleep, but was making an effort to respond to John's words. John looked up as Liz entered. He said, "Good morning," and told Liz she could find Quinn in the common area.

Liz found Quinn sitting on a bench. She was talking with another kid, also wrapped in a blanket. This kid was alert, wide-eyed, sipping a steamy cup of some hot beverage.

Quinn saw Liz and waved her over. She looked from Liz to the kid in the blanket then back to Liz.

"Hey, Liz; thanks for coming. Elle is awake. She's in her bunk room. There's staff on duty back there and they're expecting you."

Liz nodded and headed to the bunk rooms. A staff person, a young woman with a huge head of flaming, red hair and in the usual red tee, was at the desk near the bathrooms. She greeted Liz with a wave. Liz waved in return.

"Hi," said Elle, glancing up when Liz knocked on the door frame. "You're here. Cool."

She was sitting on top of the covers on her bunk, dressed for the day in a skin-tight shirt with a picture of Lady Gaga and the words *Born this Way* on the front. She wore baggy, camo-print cargo pants that ended mid-calf and a wide leather belt with a huge buckle. Her dark hair was intentionally styled to stick out all over her head and the result worked on the kid. She was wearing dark eye make-up, deep red lip color, and several earrings.

Elle looked healthy and clean, the bruises healing. She looked rested. Elle could have been any kid of that age, ready for the school day. She was writing in a small notebook. The bunk was neatly made, and there was a duffle bag packed and sitting at the foot.

"Good morning, Elle. You look great. Going to a party or something?" Liz heard Elle laugh at her joke. She realized it was the first time she's heard the kid laugh. It was music to Liz's ears.

"Nah, just feeling better. One of my crew dropped off a bag of my clothes and shit."

"That was nice of your friend to bring your things," said Liz. "We could have worked out a way to get your stuff for you."

"Uh, I don't think so, but thanks." Elle hesitated, decided whether Liz could grasp her meaning, and then she continued. "I can't just take anyone to the squat. It doesn't work like that. The crew doesn't ever tell anyone where the squat is. We gotta protect it, see?"

"Especially from a cop? I get it."

"No, it's not that. Well, maybe...yeah," Elle said, with another laugh. "But the worst are other street punks that wanna crash in. You try to be nice, let them stay there, and then your stuff goes missing, or you end up with too many loud, rowdy kids around that you can't trust. That's just trouble. You have to have a crew you can trust and we all protect our place."

"How do you decide where to squat?" Elle was unsure how to answer, so Liz tried to reassure her. "I'm just interested. I won't cause a problem for you or your crew." Liz knew how it worked from hearing Quinn's stories of life as a punk. But she wanted to hear about it from Elle.

"You find an abandoned building. There are some that are better than others. We pack up and move every few weeks."

"I understand," said Liz. I'm sorry you have to live like that, but I'm glad you had a good crew." Elle nodded, and Liz asked, "I'm ready to contact your grandma, if you want me to."

"Oh yeah, thanks. About that, I have not-so-good news about my grandma, but I have really good news too."

"Okay, tell me."

"I called my grandma last night. I thought I was gonna throw up, but I did it. My grandma says she wants to help, just like always. But her old man is still there. His name is Malcolm, and I absolutely will not be around Malcolm."

"Got it, no Malcolm," answered Liz. "I have to give you credit for making the call yourself. I'm glad to help, but sometimes it feels good later to have done stuff yourself, you know?"

"Yeah, I guess. Anyway, Malcolm's sick, had a heart attack or something, not that I care much about it. But my Grandma says my cousin has been looking for me, like forever."

Elle was rushing to explain, but slowed herself down for a moment to collect herself. "I talked to my cousin, Cece. She was actually happy to hear from me. We were both crying, man." Eyes wide and happy, Elle was beyond excited, her hands in motion. She alternated between holding them out in front of her and covering her face. "Here's the good news: I'm gonna live with Cece." Elle said the words like she was scared to believe it.

"That's so cool," said Liz, reserving judgement because she knew nothing about this cousin. "I'm happy for you, Elle."

"Yeah, me too. There is a lot to figure out. Cece says we have to do it legally, but she and Grandma are gonna make it happen." Elle cast her eyes down, her demeanor falling, as well. "I think Pook would be happy for me."

"I'm sure she would, Elle. I'm glad for you, too."

"Thanks," said Elle. "I told Cece about you. She wants to talk to you."

"Great. I'd like to talk to your cousin. Where does Cece live, Elle?"

"I thought she was up in Everett where my grandma lives, but she moved to Longview. She works at the post office there." Liz was familiar with the city of Longview. It was less than an hour up I-5 from Columbia City. Perfect. Close, but safe.

"Does Cece know what happened? Does she know about Pooki?"

"Yeah, I told her. She was crying. When I told her about Pooki, Cece was mad, really pissed. She said it was terrible what happened to us."

"Yes, it was terrible. And you know we need you to come back here to help with the case against the guys that hurt you?"

"Yeah," she said nodding. "Cece wants to drive down here soon, to take me home. Quinn told Cece I can stay here if I need to, until things are figured out."

"That's great," Liz told Elle. "Let's give your cousin a call."

Chapter Forty-two

"Cece"

Liz punched the number that Elle gave her into her phone. Within a couple of rings, the call was answered by a young woman with a pleasant voice.

"Cece Havens."

"This is Liz Jordan calling," Liz said. "Elle asks that I call you. Is this a good time?"

"Yes, of course. Hello, Ms. Jordan. I'm not working today. I took a vacation day after talking with Elle last night."

"I'm sitting here with Elle," said Liz. "Can I put you on speaker?"

"Yes, but may I talk with you privately for a minute after we talk with Elle?" asked Cece.

"Yes, no problem," Liz assured her. She pressed the speaker function. "Okay, it's both of us for now."

Elle and Cece exchanged excited greetings, even though they had spoken the evening before. Liz couldn't help but notice how friendly the cousins were to each other, how caring the older cousin sounded. *Is it possible that the tide can turn for a troubled kid this easily?* But it hadn't been easy, thought Liz. Elle had been seriously hurt and her friend had been killed. The turn of events had been prompted by tragedy.

"I'm making arrangements to have you live with me legally, Elle, for as long as you want, even after your birthday if you want," explained Cece. "That's the way it needs to be. Grandma signed the documents. I'm at the court house right now. I'll be driving down to pick you up as soon as possible, early this afternoon."

"Cool, Cece!" Elle was excited. It was natural for her thoughts to return to her friend Pooki, but Liz was glad to see her allowing herself to be happy, even if it was hard to maintain. "I got my gear. I'm ready."

"Wonderful," said Cece, "and you're feeling well enough to move?"

"I feel good," Elle said, nodding. She took a breath and grinned at Liz.

Liz grinned back, unable to help herself. She offered her raised palm to Elle and they shared a high-five.

"Great," said Cece, "I'm glad. I talked with the doctor at the hospital, the one who treated you. As soon as I have the paperwork completed for you to live with me, they will forward your records to my doctor here in town. I'm hoping to bring a copy with me, so there's no confusion. That's what I'm waiting for. You're going to need follow up care. Is that okay, Elle?"

Cece said the word *confusion* with a slight edge. Liz assumed Cece to mean that she didn't want any trouble or any argument to do with her authority. She wanted to avoid anything that could delay her efforts to help her injured cousin. Liz's impression was that Cece had dealt with legal details before and knew to have her ducks lined up. *Smart,* thought Liz.

"Yeah, it's okay," Elle told Cece. "I'll do whatever you tell me to, Cece, whatever I gotta do."

"Listen, you've done whatever you've needed to for long enough," Liz heard Cece tell her younger cousin. "Those days are over. From now on, you and I will discuss things together—unless it's something you don't want to share. You can make your own choices especially about your own body. I promise." Elle looked at Liz. The kid had tears in her eyes, and she was unable to say a word. Liz put her arm around the kid and squeezed tightly.

"Do you mind if I talk to your friend for a minute?" Cece asked Elle, referring to the police lieutenant as the street kid's friend. The moniker caught Liz off guard, but it was close to accurate.

"That's fine," answered Elle, wiping her eyes with the back of her hand. "I need to lie down anyway."

"Yes, you rest. Keep your phone on, Elle," said Cece. "I'll call when I'm on my way for you. I can hardly wait to see you."

Liz took the call off speaker and stepped into the hallway outside Elle's bunk room. The same staff person and a tall, lanky black kid were seated together at the monitoring desk. Liz had not seen the kid before that she remembered, but there were dozens of kids she'd never see, even once. Big, dark eyes and the finest, softest mustache adorned his face. His thick hair was wavy, shiny and pressed tight against his head, drawn back and tied off into an explosion of waves at the back of his head.

He wasn't wearing a red tee, but the staff person was instructing him on some paperwork related to the Youth Center. A trainee, Liz guessed. They both looked up, smiled at Liz, now a regular fixture at the Youth Center. The kid's expression told Liz he was thrilled to be there, like he'd been waiting for this opportunity.

There was a spot far enough down the hallway to speak privately and not disturb the conversation between Flaming Red and Shiny Puffy-tail. Liz smiled at them and headed down the hallway.

"Okay, it's just me. What can I do for you, Ms. Havens?"

"I just want to thank you for helping Elle. Ms. Jordan, I thought she was dead. Please believe me when I say I would have been around a long time ago, but I didn't know where she was. I tried to find her."

"I believe that, I do," Liz answered. "When was the last time you saw Elle, Cece?"

"It's been two years, Ms. Jordan, too long."

"That's a long time, alright. And please, it's Liz."

"All this happened because my cousin was given no chance, no chance at a decent life, no chance to be herself," exclaimed Cece, "because our grandmother didn't stick up for her. It shouldn't have been that way. I don't know that I can ever forgive our grandmother, but it's done now. At least Grandma called me yesterday. And I want to thank you for purchasing the phone for Elle. I'd be happy to reimburse you."

"Not necessary," said Liz. "I should mention that Elle will need to return to Columbia City. Her help with the investigation into the attack may be the best way to bring these thugs to justice."

"Yes, I know. We'll do what we have to do. I talked with the manager at the Youth Center, Quinn. She's been a big help, as well. Quinn speaks highly of you. I can't imagine that you have time to assist every street kid that comes your way, but I am so thankful you were there to help Elle."

"Please stay in touch with me," said Liz. "Let me know how she's doing. This is very selfless of you. It's a big interruption onto your life."

"No, it's not. Elle, regardless of what name we call her, has been a part of my life since the day she was born. My aunt, Elle's mom, was so happy when that beautiful baby was born. But within a year, she was strung out beyond hope. She signed Elle over to Grandma and disappeared. I was a teenager. I wasn't old enough to do anything then, but now I am. I'm single. I have a good job and great friends. I don't party because I've watched so many family members ruin their lives, even my own mother."

Cece paused for a moment. "I'm sorry for going into all that detail, Ms. Jordan, um, I mean, Liz. Again, thank you so much."

Chapter Forty-three

"Songs from the Street"

When Liz stepped back inside the bunk room, she realized Elle was resting. Liz didn't want to bother the kid. She found Quinn in the office. The youth advocate was working her way through a stack of paperwork and when she saw Liz, she dropped the file from her hand onto the desk top and stretched her arms over head.

"I need a break. Please tell me you have time for a cup of coffee."

"Sounds great. Elle is sleeping. I just talked with her cousin, Cece. She said the two of you had spoken."

"Yes, we did. She sounds nice. Definitely wants to help Elle. I'll meet her later today," said Quinn. "You know, I could use a walk to stretch my legs. Let's walk down to the Java Shack for a real Cuppa' Joe, my treat."

"My arm is sufficiently twisted," answered Liz with a laugh. "Besides, talking with Elle's family this morning was the only thing on my not-very-pressing schedule."

Liz waited while Quinn checked in with her staff, especially John, who manned the entrance. The center was quiet, the issues from earlier were settled. She said she'd be back in half of an hour or so. The two women walked out of the front door of the Youth Center, headed down the block toward the park. The Java Shack was situated directly across the park, on Beaumont.

The day was dry, almost warm. The traffic on Beaumont had lightened to the usual pace for mid-morning. Doublealmond lattes in their hands, they spotted an empty park bench across the street. Several groups of punks were sleeping in the park, keeping a low profile. Two or three of the punks who were awake and having coffee themselves, acknowledged Quinn as she and Liz walked to the bench and sat down.

From the bench facing the street, Liz and Quinn, had a clear view of the park behind them reflected in the storefront windows across the street. The visual arrangement was interesting to Liz. It would be easy to surveil the park from this spot. She would keep this in mind.

“Everything okay with your kids this morning?” asked Liz, between sips of her hot, sweet latte.

“Yes,” said Quinn. “Sometimes we need to remind them about the rules, about privacy, privacy and choices. These are kids—teens—with raging hormones.”

“I remember,” said Liz. They both looked down the block and watched as Sage, the street musician, found a spot near an empty picnic table. The cattle dog named Zeke, was close by, secured by his lead.

“It’s hard enough under the best of conditions, teaching restraint. Many street kids have not been taught about boundaries, about respect for their bodies.”

Sage had taken his guitar out of the case and was gently strumming, checking the tension of the strings for the proper tuning. He nodded in Quinn’s direction. She smiled and nodded back.

They sat quietly for a few minutes finishing their coffee, listening to the tune Sage had begun to play. The song started as a haunting instrumental, but following a few opening bars, he began to weave words into the mournful melody he strummed on the guitar. As they listened, Liz and Quinn realized that the words were familiar, full of sadness and angst, the emotion raw, casting blame and disgust.

Hear my words, Villain, to your mercy I'll not appeal / By granting me no solace, my spirit you hoped to steal.

They continued to listen, both women realizing they recognized the lines.

Distrust is my only offering, enlightened have I become / Strengthened by my suffering, your deceit has made me run.

Sage, or someone else, had set the lines from the wall at the Youth Center to music. The lines were written, or at least displayed there, by someone named Lyric. Liz was convinced that it had been written by Kyrie, and that Lyric was the name she was using on the street. And if all that were true, Sage had to know the girl.

Chapter Forty-four

"Villain's Deceit"

Liz and Quinn shared a look of surprise, edged in caution. "That's Kyrie's poem," said Liz, "written as Lyric. I just know it. We need to find out what he knows, Quinn."

As Quinn nodded and sipped her latte, her gaze returned to Sage's direction with nonchalance.

"Yes, we do," said Quinn, quietly. "There's no mistaking those lines. But I know street folks, Liz. If Sage knows anything about the girl, what would be the circumstances? Is it casual? Are they friends? He's singing what may be her lines—either with her permission or he stole them. I don't get a vibe from him that's he's aggressive or dangerous, but I've learned you never know until you know for sure. I guess I still don't trust anyone."

Liz took a deep breath and tried not to stare in Sage's direction. She didn't want to appear to be studying him.

"How should we handle this?" Liz asked Quinn, staring at her empty paper coffee cup.

Quinn had been deep in thought when she asked, "I introduced Mike to Sage, but you've not met him, have you?"

"We've not been introduced. Mike told me about Sage and Zeke, the dog. I've heard him busking though, even stopped to listen and gave him some cash. Why?"

"When you approached him on the street, you were headed to the Youth Center?

"Yes, to visit Elle. I heard him playing on the corner but didn't get very close." Liz guessed where Quinn was going.

"Sage doesn't know you're a cop. He has no reason to think you are anyone other than Liz, my friend and center volunteer. You even look the part." Liz noticed for the first time that she and Quinn were both in similar, casual clothes—tees, leggings, jackets.

"True," said Liz. "If I were asked directly, I'd have to admit to being a law enforcement officer, but I'm definitely not on duty." *Because of the lawsuit,* thought Liz. Anger welled up, but she brushed it aside. There were other things to focus on.

"Then let's try to make that work to our advantage. We're just admirers of his skill with a song, familiar with the words he was singing. We are youth advocates, by the way. That's the truth. I would have read the poem and may have concern for the kid named Lyric. I'd ask questions, if possible. Just follow my lead."

"Okay, Quinn. That should work."

"And Liz, don't take this the wrong way, but try not to act like a cop."

"Agreed," said Liz. "I'll try, but I'm not sure what that feels like."

Liz and Quinn stood and approaching the sidewalk trash receptacle, deposited their empty cups. They walked to the grassy edge of the park lawn and headed in Sage's direction at a leisurely pace. Sage was finishing a short, instrumental number just as they stepped over to where he was seated near a picnic table in the shade.

Quinn waved and greeted him with, "Hey Sage. Good seeing you."

"Hey, Sage; I'm Liz. You're very good."

"Definitely," added Quinn. "We enjoyed listening. Mind if we sit for a minute?"

"I don't mind," he told them. "And thank you, by the way, for the compliments."

Quinn and Sage both glanced at Zeke. The dog seemed to be sleeping, but Quinn and Liz wouldn't be close enough to cause concern.

"Don't let us keep you from playing," Quinn told Sage.

"Please," Liz told him. "You can go ahead. We'd love it." *Maybe he'll sing Kyrie's song again.*

"It's time for a break," he said, as he placed the guitar down next to him on his left side. Zeke was lying at his right.

Liz looked at Quinn for a moment, and then dove in with an idea. "Would you like coffee? I could grab one for you, or we can stay with the pup for you while you get it?"

The look of humored surprise on Sage's face said that he seldom had anyone offer to do him a favor, much less watch the dog. "Well, in truth a cold brewed coffee would hit the spot. I always have someone go in for me. I don't leave Zeke with strangers."

"Hey, no worries, I've got time. I'll be right back," said Liz, getting back to her feet. "Cream or sugar?"

"No, thank you," said Sage. "Black, please." He reached into a pocket for cash.

Liz nodded at Sage's request, then said to him, "Black coffee, as the java gods intended." She put her hands out in front of her that the cash was not necessary, the coffee was on her. Sage responded by smiling and placing his palms together. He bent his head forward in a slight bow, offered a thank you.

Looking at Quinn, Liz asked her, "Do you need to hurry back, Quinn, or will you wait? I shouldn't be gone more than a few minutes."

"I'll be here," answered Quinn. *Perfect, Liz. Great idea. A natural offer and it gives me a few minutes to talk to Sage alone.*

Sage and Quinn watched as Liz left them, heading back through the park and across Beaumont to the Java Shack.

Quinn turned to Sage, and asked, "I have to ask a question: that sad, mournful sing you were singing a few minutes ago, the lyrics, they remind me of somebody, but I can't place the artist. Help me out here, would you?"

"You wouldn't have heard of them," he said, stroking Zeke's back and rubbing his ears. Quinn was sure she heard the sleeping pup snore. "It's no one famous." Sage paused. He seemed to be deciding what to say next. "Actually, my sister wrote the words. She asked me to put them to music for her."

"Your sister? I'm in awe of her creativity. But the tone, the anger, they make a bold sentiment for someone young. She must be an older sister."

"No, she's younger," Sage told Quinn, with a shake of his head, "But old for her years, due to no fault of hers."

"I'm sorry to hear that. I hear it too often, you know. It was that way for me, at one time, a long time ago. Had to learn fast what shit was what, watch my own back. Depend on my crew."

"Where was this?" Sage asked her, searching her face for honesty, satisfied that he found it.

"Seattle. The university district a few years back. I had my reasons for running. Your sister, is she your blood sis or crew? Not that it matters. Crew is like blood, usually more so."

"Truth," he answered. Sage looked around the park. Quinn was worried he was feeling distrustful, would want to bolt. *Had she pushed too hard? Made it too personal?*

Sage dropped his eyes to his dog and stroked the smooth, brindled coat of fur. He looked Quinn in the eye and she was not prepared for what Sage said next.

"She's my sis from the crew. Calls herself Lyric," he said. "She's very talented, has a way with words, voice like an angel."

"Nice. I'd love to hear her sing. *I can't believe I'm hearing this,* thought Quinn, trying to keep from reacting when he mentioned Lyric by name.

"Hasn't been on the street long. We were looking out for her, me and the rest of the crew." Sage looked around the park, and then he sighed, and turned back to Quinn.

"Now there's just me, Eli and Lyric. She wants to head north, up near your stomping ground. She's got a granny says will take her in in a heartbeat." Quinn had to assume that the girl must trust Sage to have confided in him.

"That's great news for her, Sage. She's lucky. Why isn't she there?"

"She says it's risky, for her and for her granny. She refuses to bring harm to her granny. She's really scared of someone and hates them at the same time. That's why she wrote the song. It's titled *Villain's Deceit.*"

"Could I be of help to her?"

"I don't know," he answered, shaking his head. "Maybe."

Quinn pursed her lips, sighed. She nodded. "Sage, let her know that I'll do whatever I can to get her to her grandmother. I have ways of making things like that happen."

"I will. I am getting scared for her. Like I said, there used to be others. There were five of us. The kid that died a few days ago was my sis, too."

"Then you know Elle," stated Quinn. "She was with Pooki that night. You know we've been taking care of her."

Sage nodded slowly. "Yes, and she's doing okay now, but it was scary. I know that she's going to her cousin's. I'm glad for her. Elle has been on the street longer than any punk should have to be."

He looked toward Beaumont and saw Liz returning with his coffee. He and Quinn had a couple more minutes of privacy. "I was the one who dropped off her stuff at your place."

"Do me a favor, Sage," said Quinn, leaning closer. "Pooki and Elle trusted us and came to us for help when they were attacked. Please remember that. My job is to help the kids, as they choose to define it. I'll do the same for Lyric."

"You know I can't tell you where she is," he said.

"I know," answered Quinn. "But you can deliver that message."

"I'll talk to her. Can't promise how she'll react. It's her decision."

"Of course. Please ask her if she needs anything. I'll send it through you."

At this suggestion, Sage nodded, sweeping his dreads away from his face. "Are you gonna tell your friend, Black Coffee Liz, the cop?"

"You know who she is?" asked Quinn, feeling caught out. "Sorry, we didn't aim to deceive you. Liz isn't on the job right now. You don't want her to know about Lyric?"

"I don't know if it matters," he said, shaking his head, dreadlocks bouncing slowly. "Elle told me about Liz. She's some boss-lady cop. She was helping Elle."

Quinn glanced in Liz's direction. "Yeah, well, Liz isn't here today as a cop, like I said," Quinn assured him.

"No, I don't guess so," said Sage. "Never had one of the City's Finest get me coffee before."

"Sage, I'll wait to mention the news about Lyric. I want to give you a chance to talk to her first, but I have to tell them soon because they're looking for her. We both know that if she feels threatened, she may take off. Will you talk with her soon and get back to me?"

As Sage nodded to Quinn, Liz was within a few steps.

Chapter Forty-five

"Missing Evidence"

Captain Miller was at his desk early. He had been at it heavy for hours, searching through old reports submitted by officers regarding progress on each shift. He had to dig deep through years of reports stored on the department server. He used particular names and dates to narrow his searches, but progress was slow.

He found some of what he was looking for, but it hadn't been easy. It was as if the records had been stored incorrectly on purpose. *Oh, but that kind of thing never happened, now did it?* He was a cynic, however, Miller preferred the word realist.

Now, he was looking at other old reports, forensics generated at the conclusion of the investigation known as *Killian*. Miller was delving deep into what had occurred in the club that evening, deeper than anyone had in the fourteen years that had passed. The further he read, the more convinced he was that the entire operation from the beginning to the tragic end had been a train wreck.

Several of the accounts were almost identical to each other. This fact alone was curious. If Miller were a less tenacious sort, he would have missed the oddness of it. One glaring detail stood out like a sore thumb. One member of the team had reported that the "body of a female civilian was found in the office area, where she appeared to have crawled for cover" during the onslaught.

Further, a key piece of evidence was missing or had been omitted: nowhere in the file was the forensic report on the weapon that fired the shot that killed Sara Mallory. Miller could hardly believe it wasn't included in the information. He needed to obtain that report. *But where in hell could it be?*

Chapter Forty-six

"The Crew"

Liz approached, looking back and forth between Quinn and Sage for a moment, trying to gauge what she had missed, but not wanting to ask. She stepped over to Sage and handed him the large covered cup filled to the brim and a paper bag.

"There are bagels and a pack of dog biscuits for Zeke. I wanted to bring you something that would keep if you wanted to save it."

"Nice of you," he said. "I thank you and for the coffee, too." He took a long sip, wiped his mouth. Smelling treats, Zeke perked up. Sage took a biscuit from the small inner bag and offered it to the pup, who accepted it eagerly.

Quinn and Liz spent a few minutes in quiet conversation with Sage. They brought Liz up to speed about how Sage knew Elle and had known Pooki as part of the same street crew.

Liz told Sage how sorry she was about what happened to his friends. He accepted her condolences with silence, but nodded, offered Zeke another dog biscuit, sipped his coffee.

"Just unload the rest. Tell her the other part," said Sage, taking a bagel from the bag. He broke the bagel in half and placed half back in the bag, rolling down the top of the paper.

"It should come from you," said Quinn. "I think that's best."

Finishing the half bagel, Sage poured water from a container into the small water bowl he kept for Zeke. The dog lapped up the water to near the last drop, then looked Sage in the eye, sharing a telepathic message. Sage rubbed the dog's ears, and then extended the lead slightly, allowing Zeke to wander over to a shrub a few yards away. Zeke raised his leg to pee on the shrub, and then returned to sit near Sage. Sage drew the length of the lead back in. The degree of understanding between the man and his dog was uncanny.

"There are, *were* four of us," Sage began, looking into Liz's eyes. "There was me, Elle, Pooki, and Eli. Eli doesn't venture away from the squat much. I'm not going to tell you why 'cause it's his business. We just tell him it's his job to man the fort, you know? So, he feels special—which he is anyway."

One last sip and Sage had finished his coffee. He folded the paper cup exactly in half and stowed it in his pack to dispose of it properly.

"A few months ago, Elle and Pook met a gal. Young, but tough. They were talking about music and she told them she liked to write. They wanted me to meet up with her, so I did."

"She was cool, but having a rough time of it, wasn't doing well. She said she was a singer, but felt too sick to carry a tune. I was pretty sure she'd been roughed up. She claimed not, but Eli thought so too, and she finally told us the truth. She settled in with us that night and has been there ever since. She goes by Lyric. We collaborate. She wrote the lines to the song I was singing earlier."

"That's good news, Sage," said Liz, looking at Quinn. "I appreciate you telling us. So, she's okay?"

"She's okay. She's doing better than she was at first. For living in a squat, I'd say she's doing fine. Like I told Quinn, I won't take you to her. And you won't get there by following me, I guarantee it. But I will talk with her. I believe Quinn will help her, if Lyric will agree to it."

"I understand," said Liz. "It's great news just to know she's with a good crew, that she's got friends looking out for her. Can I ask a couple of other questions?"

"Yes, I guess," said Sage as he stretched out his legs, "since you were nice enough to treat us. I can take a few more minutes, and then I need to get back to playing."

"I'm assuming Lyric is a street name. Has she told you what her real name is?"

"No, and we don't ask. She'd say if she wanted to."

Liz opened the photos of Kyrie on her phone, pulled up the first of the two. It was the one Chapin said she had sent him soon after leaving home. "Is this Lyric?" she asked, showing the photo to Sage.

He confirmed that it was the girl he knew as Lyric. It didn't escape Liz that Sage had just confirmed that Lyric, a trusted part of his crew, was Kyrie. Then she showed him the other photo, the one in which Kyrie's condition seemed to have deteriorated.

"That's what she looked like the first time I met her. She resembles the other photo now; except she's chopped her hair off short. Eli helped her dye it green. He's handy with chores like that."

"Did Quinn tell you that the words to the song you were singing are inscribed on the wall at the Youth Center? The lines are amazing, unforgettable. And they were signed by an artist named Lyric? That's what brought us to you."

"No, she didn't tell me that, but it makes sense," he said, looking at Quinn. "I wouldn't have seen them. I've never been inside the center, even when I dropped off Elle's stuff. But Lyric has. She stayed a few nights there, on and off."

"Before I started working there, is my guess," said Quinn.

"It doesn't surprise me that she left a calling card," Sage told them. "Creativity will find an outlet. It has to. She's not going to be happy that you heard me singing her words," he said. "It never occurred to me not to."

"We're going to leave you to it, Sage. You've been a big help and I won't betray your trust. I want you to know that." Liz dug into her bag for a pen and a business card. "Listen, the cop that's looking for Lyric, his name is Connors. He's the best, most compassionate cop you could ask for." Liz wrote Connors' name and number on a card and handed it to Sage. "Encourage Lyric to call Connors. He will not only help her, he'll protect her."

"She's protected now," said Sage, proud of what he had been able to offer the kid. "But I'll tell her. She's got choices now. You know, I've heard of your guy, Connors. All the street folks that have been around here a while know Connors. Decent guy. Now, let me ask you a question."

"Sure," said Liz, as she stood, she and Quinn ready to leave.

"You're a cop. You come across as fair, compassionate. Why don't you deal with all this yourself?"

"Good question," said Liz. "Let's just say I'm not working right now." Liz tried to sound casual, but she could hear the tension creep into her voice. "I'm spending some time helping at the Youth Center."

Under his dreads, Sage raised his brows. He propped his chin on one closed fist, and looked at Liz.

"Huh," he said. "I do believe you've run into some shit, Coffee Lady. Sounds like you been in with a bad crew."

Chapter Forty-seven

"A message"

"Sage trusted you, Quinn. I won't contact Connors, at least for a while, but let's hope Sage convinces Kyrie to reach out for help. He is concerned about her, he even said as much."

They walked back to the Youth Center with renewed vigor. Walking along next to Liz and listening to her friend's thoughts, Quinn couldn't help but think that it might be better if Liz didn't have all the details. Quinn trusted Liz, but the bottom line was that she was a cop.

"I know there's a search for the girl, Liz. I understand the protocol. But if Kyrie doesn't want to be found, if she feels she's in danger, she'll bolt. I know this. I know the feeling. Please give Sage a few days."

"Don't worry," Liz reassured her, "Besides, I wasn't there when he shared the details. You urged Sage to trust me and I will honor that trust." *And I know where to find him if it comes to that,* thought Liz.

"But we learned that Elle knows Kyrie, knows her as Lyric," said Quinn. "She and Pooki brought her home, sought help from Sage and brought her into the crew. Elle never would have told us she knew her. But she may have told Kyrie about the search for her. Sage may be aware of it, too."

"Yes," Liz said to Quinn, "but even if that's true, he decided to trust you anyway."

Arriving back in entrance to the center, Liz told Quinn she would see her later, but added, "You handled the meeting in the park well. Really well. Only someone with your insights would have been gained that degree of trust."

Quinn stayed silent, but acknowledged Liz's comments with a slight smile. Then she touched Liz on the shoulder. "You should be here when Elle leaves with her cousin," Quinn said. "Elle would want you here and it would be good for you to meet Cece. We don't often have special days like this. Please be a part of it with us."

Liz looked at her phone and saw that she had missed a call from Mike. She must have just missed him, but wouldn't have picked up during the chat with Sage.

"I would like that. And when I talk to Mike, I'll mention it. See you later. Would you tell Elle for me that I'll be back?"

"Of course; I'll be in touch when we hear from Cece. It's exciting, you know?" And at that, Quinn turned and went inside.

Liz walked back to her car, waiting to get off the street and use Bluetooth to return Mike's call. The call went to voice mail so Liz left him a message. She quickly shared the news about Elle and her cousin, Cece, and the invite to say goodbye to the kid.

Finished with the message, she pulled into traffic and selected music. Wanting something upbeat, she selected the band Modern English from her playlist. "Melt with You" began playing. *Perfect,* she thought.

She was almost home, enjoying the tempo of the song when the alert of an incoming call displayed on the Bluetooth screen. Liz didn't recognize the number. She let the call go to voice mail, a screening practice she rarely employed as a cop on duty because most calls were too important to ignore.

Following her own greeting, she heard a voice she recognized as belonging to Gabriel Chapin. Although the son of a bitch had been told not to call her, he was defying that directive and from a number she would not familiar with. He was trying to fool her into answering.

"Since you have refused to remain discreet, the search for my daughter has been blown out of the water and out of our control. I asked you to find my daughter, Sara's daughter, and you refused my request. You left me no alternative than to consider legal recourse. Regardless of that, I don't like being cornered into decisions. You will regret forcing my hand." Click. The message ended. The threat was clear, unmistakable.

Hearing his voice unnerved Liz. Chapin had left the message soon after Liz had been in the park with Quinn, talking to Sage. It made her skin crawl. They had been discussing Kyrie. *Had they been watched? Had they been observed talking to Sage?* Liz thought about this. She thought hard about it—about how her initial reaction had been of one of fear.

Anyone who knew Chapin would cower at that message. But Liz wasn't most people. She reminded herself that she was trained to protect herself and others. Chapin had known her years ago as a rookie cop, a young kid who had a lot to learn. He didn't know the cop she had become, the strength she possessed.

Liz knew that Chapin wanted to scare her. *No more*, she told herself. Anger filled her chest. *Threaten me, you asshole?*

You made me feel for years that I had caused Sara's death. You wanted to intimidate me into handling the search for Kyrie. But it's all on you, Gabriel. Your daughter is probably missing because she can't stand the sight of you. If I have my way, Kyrie will never have to see you ever again.

Liz realized that she had pulled up in front of her home. She had been so angry, her thoughts so intense on Chapin, that she didn't remember the drive.

Chapter Forty-eight

"A Knock at the Door"

Liz climbed the two flights of steps up to her apartment and let herself in. Eddie and Little Kurt didn't react with excitement because it wasn't time to eat. They managed to respond with obligatory meows, encouraging Liz to stroke their fur.

Having had enough coffee but craving more, Liz brewed a small pot. She took her cup out to the balcony and sat looking out over the track and field next door. She closed the sliding door to keep the cats in.

The weather was decent. No rain was falling. Scattered clouds filled the sky, but it had become cooler. Sipping her coffee, she watched high schoolers run the track below. Other students sat, spread out on the grassy field, stretching as a teacher called the moves.

She had assumed correctly that Mike was in a meeting. She received a text message to that effect and that he had tried to call just to say hello. He would be at the Youth Center later and he was excited for Elle.

Liz was still angry at Chapin's message and she wanted the ire to subside. The caffeine wouldn't help, but the warmth of the beverage was comforting. She seldom had opportunity to sit outside on her little balcony during the workday. She couldn't remember having done so before.

The department needed know that she's heard from Chapin. Not only that she had heard from him, but that he had threatened her. Liz relished the last sip of her coffee and called Miller. When Clarice answered at his office, she didn't sound surprised to be hearing from Liz and put the call through to Miller.

"Liz. I'm glad to hear from you," said Miller. "So, how are you?"

Liz pictured him sitting at his desk, reading glasses perched on the bridge of his nose. She could almost see his huge left hand holding the receiver, gold wedding band accented against brown skin. She imagined him wearing a tasteful, understated tie his wife had purchased for him.

"I was doing well, Sir." Liz told Miller about the threatening message from Gabriel Chapin. "He's not happy that I confided in you about our mutual past, and that I made the search for his daughter an official one. He mentioned the lawsuit as his 'last resort.'"

"When was this?" asked Miller and he did not sound happy.

"Recently, within the past hour. I had managed to avoid his calls up to now, but he called from a different number. When I didn't pick up, he actually left a message. It's on voice mail. Dumb on his part."

"Voice mail, that's good. You have a record. I'm sure you haven't deleted the message."

"No, Sir."

"Get a hold of a department tech and have them copy that message. I want the message and a transcription in our system for the legal department. And inform Connors, if you haven't already. The search for his daughter is his case and I know he's talked with the man. Connors needs to clarify a few things with him."

"I'll call Connors right now," Liz answered, wishing she could inform Connors of what she and Quinn had learned from Sage. But she couldn't do that. Yet.

"Good. And Lieutenant?"

"Yes, Sir."

"Watch your back. We will talk again soon."

"Yes, Sir. I hope so. Good-bye."

Ending the call with Miller, Liz contacted the tech department. She talked with a technician named Renee, who was able to access Liz's mobile phone and copy the message without disrupting service.

"We do it all the time," Renee told her. The level of technology was amazing to Liz, but in truth it baffled her. Renee said the original message would remain on Liz's phone until she chose to delete it.

There was a knock at Liz's front door. It caught her off guard as she wasn't expecting anyone. She recalled Miller's advice to watch her back. Feeling paranoid, Liz thought about her personal weapon, a .357 revolver that she kept stashed in her bedroom safe, where it was safely tucked away most of the time.

The handgun was registered and she had a concealed carry permit, of course. She rarely carried the gun because she was almost always on duty. She had owned the .357 for a long time, long before she had acquired the slightly bigger, more powerful 9 mm, her department issue.

Like a scene from a shoot 'em up movie, gunmen were known to knock then step aside out of sight, wait until they assumed the resident was checking the peephole, then fire into the closed door. The plan was only effective if the thugs were sure the target was home, and had the habit of using the peephole. And Liz's car was downstairs for all to see.

Liz had a peephole in her front door but she rarely used it. Years ago, she'd had three tiny, shaded windows, five-by-five inches each, installed to the left of her entry. At first glance, they appeared ornamental, but the middle one was a one-way window. She looked out to see Connors standing at her front door.

Relieved and feeling a tad foolish, Liz opened the door.

"Hey, Connors," she said and stepped aside to let him in.

"Lieutenant; I saw your car downstairs. Hope you don't mind me dropping in. It was on the spur of the moment."

"No, no, Connors, of course I don't mind. Come in. Sit down. Bother the cats at your own risk."

Connors sat on the couch next to Little Kurt. The disgruntled tabby uttered a perturbed growl, and flew into the bedroom. Eddie, the calico was unfazed. "I wanted to see how you're doing and I have some details I think you'd want to know. And I want your take on them."

"Okay, good. I just talked to Miller, by the way. I have news for you too. You go first. Can I get you coffee?"

"No, on the coffee, but thanks. The deal is we checked phone records for Chapin and Isaacs. It appears that the photos and the last few messages weren't sent to him directly. They were sent to Richelle. We don't know if Richelle forwarded them or if someone else did. We only know they went to her phone first, then to Chapin's. Richelle is either not very bright—which isn't my impression—or she's complicit in Chapin's schemes. Or she's a victim, too. Looking into her background hasn't told us anything."

"No, it didn't and I only talked with her by phone. You interviewed the woman face to face. She seemed bright to me too, Connors, sounded like she cared about Kyrie."

"I thought so, as well," agreed Connors.

"Complicit, or involved to some degree by her own choice, doesn't seem likely. She's probably been coerced," reasoned Liz. "That would make her a victim, just the same. When I talked with her, I was well aware that she is in Chapin's employ. To what extent he expects her loyalty, and why, I can't imagine."

"I'm sure that's part of it, Lieutenant."

"Connors, Chapin is a vampire. He gets his teeth in, finds a hook and doesn't let up. I should know. But I'm done with that."

"What do you mean?"

"That's what I want to tell you," said Liz, as she reached for her phone and pulled up the message. "I got a message from him. Listen to this."

Liz listened to the message again, as she played it on speaker for Connors. It made her feel cold, but in a rigid, firm way. Ice over a pond in winter—a protective layer, impenetrable.

Connors sighed, shook his head, his cheeks red with anger. "I warned him not to contact you, that you were not involved in the investigation. I told him to stay out of the way while we find his daughter."

"It's not in his character to do what he's asked," Liz answered. "He does what he wishes. I said I was done with this. What I meant about being done is that Chapin knew me as a kid, a rookie cop. He doesn't know who I am now. I'm older, wiser and meaner when I need to be. He approached me as he knew me and that's how I reacted."

"Mike asked me if I would have handled the operation back then as I would now. I couldn't wrap my brain around it, Connors, but of course, I wouldn't. No one is the same person they were that long ago, after that much time. Especially not someone like me, that's been on the job so long."

Staring at Liz, Connors nodded. "You're right there, Lieutenant. What you say makes sense. But the man is under your skin and that's not like you. I have to tell you, it's concerning."

Liz waved off Connors' concern, and said, "I'm fine, Connors. Really, I'm better than I was, once I decided not to let him get the better of me."

"And you will stay away from him?"

"I don't want anything to do with him. I want your team to find his daughter. I'm convinced she ran away because of him."

Liz thought about Elle and Pooki and that they had known Lyric. The kids had been attacked, one killed, and the assailants were still out there. But she couldn't tell Connors about the connection. Not yet. But he might come up with questions on his own.

"I don't know how these kids survive," said Liz. "It's tough being a kid on the street. Brutal. Kyrie's missing. She's living on the street somewhere. In one picture, she looks beat up. Then the two kids were attacked, and one died. Has Morgan gained any ground with identifying the guys in that house?"

"We got an ID on one of them. An old mug shot. His team is looking for him and trying to ID the other guy." Connors pulled up the information on his phone. "The creep they ID'd is Espy, first name Roger. Ring any bells?"

Liz considered the name. Roger Espy. "No, I wish it did."

"Maybe when Morgan's team finds Espy, he can lead them to the other creep. They're both pieces of work, but Espy's buddy is the one that stabbed the kid who died, according to Elle's statement."

"Espy is the older one?"

"He is."

"He's the one that got rough first, expected the kids to put out. But you're correct that his friend grabbed the knife. What a pair."

"Yeah," answered Connors. He was thinking about something. "I got an odd message. It was left a little while ago. Guy sounded old, maybe on purpose. He mentioned me by name; wanted me to know that Lyric was okay. That was all he said."

"He used the name Lyric? Like on the poem at the Youth Center? How did he get your number, Connors?" asked Liz, knowing full well it had to be Sage that had called—or some guy that Sage asked to make the call for him. The effort wouldn't call off Connors' search for the girl so Liz had to wonder why he bothered.

"I don't know how he knew to call me or how he got my number. But he referred to her as Lyric and said she's okay. That was all I cared about. I hope it's true."

Chapter Forty-nine

"Coming Clean"

Liz met up with Mike by mid-afternoon for Elle's send off. She was greeted at the door by a red-shirted staff person and was asked to wait in the common room. Several kids were scattered around the large room, mostly hanging out, staring at their phones. A few were sleeping. One or two of the kids looked at Liz as if to say, *who the hell are you?*

Through the large office window, Liz saw a young woman talking with Quinn and Mike. Mike waved when he saw Liz. Liz waved back just as the young woman turned and looked in Liz's direction, offering a big smile. The fourth person in the office was homicide detective Reese Morgan.

The young woman had dark hair pulled into a short ponytail, without a strand out of place. Big, dark eyes, a full mouth and a nice smile, she had a build similar to Elle, and it was easy to see the familial connection. She was simply dressed in jeans and a shirt that fit snug to her tiny shape; silver hoop earrings complimented by her dark hair. Cece Havens was a mature version of her cousin.

They stepped out of the office and Cece made a bee line for Liz, her hand extended.

"Ms. Jordan, I'm so pleased to meet you. Cece Havens," she said as she shook Liz's hand. "Thank you so much for your help." Liz was five-nine and even though Cece wore high-heeled boots, Liz towered over the petite woman.

"Very nice to meet you, Ms. Havens; I see you've met everyone else," said Liz, indicating Mike and Morgan. "Is Elle ready to go?"

"Hello, Lieutenant," said Morgan, offering his hand. "Elle is ready, as far as I'm concerned. I've talked with her and with Ms. Havens. We've made plans to be in touch and they know who to contact if they have any problems."

Quinn went to find Elle and help with her things from the bunk room. Morgan turned to Liz and asked, "May I have a quick moment, Lieutenant?"

"Sure. Excuse us for just a minute, Ms. Havens. We will be quick." She and Morgan stepped a few feet away.

Reese Morgan was around Liz's age with a short, stocky build. He looked athletic, but with the fire-plug body of a weight-lifter instead of the slender, strong runner's build that Mike possessed. Reese wore short, blond hair with a trendy cut, his blue eyes hid behind wire frames. Clean shaven, like all the men on the force, he had taken Liz seriously about looking casual when he visited the Youth Center. Instead of the usual suit and tie, Reese was in jeans and an old, gray tee-shirt bearing a gym's logo.

"Good to see you, Reese. What's up?"

"Lieutenant, we've identified one of the assailants from an old mugshot. Had to dig way back and use age-progression software. He was arrested here in town almost twenty years ago. Nothing since. Name's Espy."

Liz pretended this was news to her and she hoped Reese bought it. "Good. Do you know where the shit bag is?"

"Not yet. But we will." The detective hesitated. "Lieutenant, Espy was connected to a crooked businessman here in town, named Killian. I wanted you to know."

Liz looked him in the eye, wondering if he was aware of her connection to Killian and the operation to close him down. Morgan's statement that he *just wanted her to know,* told Liz that he knew about the Killian investigation from years ago. Morgan hadn't been around long, but word traveled fast.

She decided it wasn't relevant—facts were facts. She nodded, and then asked, "Okay. No activity for twenty-years? Anywhere?"

"No Ma'am."

"Are you conferring with Connors in Missing Persons? The case he's working on is connected to Killian, too, although indirectly. Background, you know."

"Yes, we're keeping each other in the loop."

"Okay, good. Thanks for the info, Reese."

Interesting, thought Liz. The older of the two assailants had who attacked Elle and Pooki had been associated with Killian, long before Liz, Chapin, or Sara were involved. Liz would deal with that information later.

"Lieutenant, there's one other detail," said Morgan. He dropped the volume of his voice, not wanting to be overheard. "The body of the dead kid was moved to the morgue."

Liz would have expected as much. It was standard procedure. The department and the prosecutor's office would be pressing charges when the killer was apprehended. The Medical Examiner was part of the process.

"Myers would like to speak with you. He asked that I give you the message."

Well, that's just great, thought Liz. *That's all I need, a chat with Myers.* Liz hated Dr. Myers, the Chief Medical Examiner nearly as much as she hated Gabriel Chapin.

"Thanks for the message," Liz told Morgan, and then they stepped over to rejoin the others.

"I'm sorry for addressing you as Ms. Jordan when you're a police Lieutenant," Cece said to Liz. "I didn't mean any disrespect."

"None taken, besides, Elle mentioned that you work for the postal service. You have my undying respect, believe me," joked Liz.

"Yes," Cece answered, with a smile. "I've been with USPS for seven years, since college. I'm behind the scenes. Logistics. But I like it."

"You and Elle should call me Liz."

"Oh, thanks. That's sweet. Call me Cece. Ms. Havens makes me feel old."

Quinn and Elle came walking from the rear hallway. Elle looked happy, but tired, and slightly overwhelmed. But who could expect otherwise? She didn't approach anyone, hung back near Quinn who carried Elle's duffle. Elle had a bag slung over her shoulder. The two bags probably held everything the kid owned in the world.

Cece stepped over to her young cousin. They had met together for a brief time privately to become re-acquainted before Cece's meeting in the office. If it was awkward for them, they were hiding it well. Elle was a little taller than her cousin but slighter in build. Liz thought she looked so very young.

With an arm around Elle, her other hand on her cousin's arm, Cece turned to face the others. "I've waited for this day for a long time. Elle and I thank you all for your help. Right, Elle?"

Elle nodded. She looked around at all the faces. Quietly, she said, "Thank you. That's all I can think of right now." Punks hugged Elle, others offered high fives. A couple of the kids seemed to be upset at Elle's good fortune. Liz figured they were wishing it was them going home and her heart went out to them.

Elle said good-bye to the staff, then to Quinn and Mike, giving them each a hug. She shook hands with Morgan. She turned to Liz. "Hi," she said.

"Hey, yourself. How are you doing?"

Elle closed her eyes, took a breath. "I'm good. Tired, but good. Can I talk to you for a second? Just us?"

"Sure." Liz pointed to the bench against the wall. It didn't escape Liz that they sat beneath Lyric's poem.

"You know the lady cop? Not you, the young one?"

"Yes, I know Castillo," said Liz, laughing.

"Sorry, I didn't mean it like that," said Elle, quick to apologize.

"No worries. She is young, younger than me, at least. What about Castillo."

"Well, if I kind of lied to her, would I be in trouble?"

"I can't answer that because I'm not Castillo, and I don't know your reason. What did you *kind of* lie about, Elle?" Liz was distracted by the noise in the common room. She looked around, surveyed the activity, and then focused her attention on Elle.

"Castillo asked me if I knew a girl. I said I didn't. But I do. I was just scared for the girl and for me." Elle had decided to come clean about knowing Lyric. Liz was proud of her.

"If you were scared to tell the truth, scared for yourself or someone else, that's a tough call. Were either of you hurt by your lie?"

Elle thought about the question. "I don't think so. I wasn't. I don't think she was. I'm pretty sure she's okay for now, but she's really scared."

"But you're telling me now, so you changed your mind."

Elle glanced up at the poem on the wall and took a breath. She looked at Liz, motioned toward the lines of poetry on the wall, and said. "That's hers. Her name is Lyric. I know you talked to Sage about her, you and Quinn."

"Yes, we did. But thanks for telling me yourself."

"Sage will help you find her. It's for the best, but we have to do it our way."

"I hope he does, Elle. I want her to be safe. Lyric deserves that like you're going to be safe with Cece."

"Yep," said Elle looking over at her cousin.

"And Elle?"

"Yeah?"

"Don't lie to cops anymore. We have reasons for asking questions. We're not being nosy. We're trying to help and we need help, too."

"Okay, I'll try."

Sitting side by side in the shadow of her friend's poem, Elle extended her hand to Liz and they shook in agreement of their pact. Then Elle wrapped her arms around Liz and hugged her.

Chapter Fifty

"Miller's News"

A group of folks walked Cece and Elle outside. After final good-byes, the two headed down the road. It was an encouraging event for Mike—when a person from the streets, even one person, finds a home, a real home. For Quinn, it was even more significant; a gutter punk connecting with family members willing to take them in. And a punk willing to give trust a try.

Mike was headed back to his office. He said he had two meetings, neither of which he was looking forward to because they both involved begging for money. He hated having to do it, but it was the reality of the work. Mike had many skills, but kissing ass wasn't one of them.

Liz was glowing with warmth from inside after talking with Elle. It wasn't the news that Elle and Lyric were part of the same crew—Sage had confirmed that. It was the added plus that Elle had told Liz herself. The kid trusted her, and Elle's embrace was filled with authentic human connection.

Since she was dressed casually and not on the job, Liz decided to extend her feelings of warmth. She wrapped her arms around Mike and kissed him. They were near enough to the Youth Center that a few kids saw them and responded with gestures and melodic *oohhhhhs*. Drip, the punk with the famous Mohawk, yelled, "Hey man, get a room, why don't yuh?" After yelling the taunt, he raised one fist high and chortled.

Mike kissed back, but their arms fell to their sides when he started laughing. "We're not exactly modeling appropriate behavior," he said to Liz.

"Sure, we are. We're sharing a special moment after experiencing the good fortune of another," said Liz with a smile. "Watching a quick kiss and a hug between people who love each other is good for anyone's soul. Some of these kids may never have seen how adults behave when they truly care for each other."

"You may be right," said Mike, kissing Liz again. "I'll be home before six. I'll pick up food. Any requests?"

"Hey, you know," said Liz, with a thought. "I'll be home. I should cook something. It's silly to have take-out when I could throw a meal together."

"Sounds good," Mike said with a dubious expression, "Interesting...and a little scary, but good. The choice is yours. Let me know one way or the other," said Mike, then he took off for his office. He turned around as Liz walked to her car, and yelled, "I'll check the scanner for fire alarms in our neighborhood." Liz smiled, shook her head.

As they parted company, neither of them noticed the sedan that came down Beaumont Street. Or that it followed Mike back to his office.

Less than hour later, Liz was home after a stop at the grocery store. She threw chucks of grilled chicken, cans of diced tomatoes, black beans, green chilis and Texas chili spices into the slow-cooker. Fast-track chili was one of her mother's go-to meals. It always turned out delicious. You would have thought it had simmered for hours. Liz sent Mike a text. "Soup's on." In a meeting, he sent back a thumbs-up emoji.

Liz popped the cap on a Rogue Ale. It had started to drizzle outside, not enough to call it rain, but more than a mist. Liz thought to sit out on her tiny deck and enjoy the fresh, cool air.

As she started to open the sliding door, her phone rang. It was Miller calling. She was surprised to hear from him again and assumed he had a question about a current case. Beer in hand, she sat down on the couch.

"Captain, is everything okay? Is something up with my team?" she asked when she answered his call.

"All is fine in that regard. Things are moving along as we would expect. I'm calling about something else. I didn't mention it before, but I spent some time today reviewing archived records," said Miller. "You may not realize this, but most of the paperwork that was filed pertaining to the Killian operation was shit. Your account was one of the more helpful, and you'd been on the job less than a year."

"That's good to hear, Sir," Liz said, wondering what else Miller had dug up and whether she wanted to hear it. Liz sipped her ale.

"You were reporting to Crenshaw, according to the files. He was Pruitt's partner and he was present at the raid, correct?"

"Yes, officially," answered Liz, searching her memory. "I reported to Crenshaw, but Pruitt always had a say in things. Pruitt, Crenshaw and a four-man tactical team were there, from what I understand."

"But Crenshaw never submitted a report. It either doesn't exist, or it's been deleted. My gut tells me he didn't submit a report because it's not referred to nor is it listed in the summary. That's highly irregular." Liz listened, but had no idea where Miller was going with this.

"My next discovery," said Miller, "is that three of the members of the tactical team filed reports that were almost word-for-word with what Pruitt submitted. But the fourth TAC team officer, named...," Liz waited as papers rustled until the captain found the notation, "...McCleary, included information in his account that the others did not."

"McCleary. I have no recollection of a McCleary," said Liz.

"Neither do I and I can't seem to find him either," said Miller. Liz was intrigued by what Miller had to say.

"McCleary's report claims that the body of a female civilian, who we know was Sara Mallory, was found not in the back area, but in the office. He assumed she had crawled there to escape the melee once the shots started flying."

"The office area?" asked Liz, with surprise. "Killian's office was always locked. Only a few people had keys."

"Yes, I learned that from your report. You included a detailed physical description of the premises."

"Sara didn't have a key," remembered Liz, shaking her head. "Even if she had one, she wouldn't have been able to crawl back there and let herself into a locked office after she had suffered a gunshot that proved to be fatal."

"I agree. And as I wondered the other day, which weapon fired the round that killed her? And whose hand was holding it when it was aimed at Ms. Mallory and fired? I searched the entire cache of reports from inception to summary. Sara Mallory's forensic examination notes are not included."

Liz thought back to the day after Sara died. Not only was evidence of her death collected, but Liz knew full well that an autopsy had been performed. Liz put the terrible memories aside when she realized the captain was speaking. "As it turns out, I had to gain access to some very confidential files to find them. But I managed it."

"Who signed off on the forensic documents?" Liz asked Miller, "I mean, as far as the autopsy."

"You and I both know who it was, Lieutenant."

Liz knew the name of the forensic pathologist in question. It was Myers. And they were far from friends. In fact, they hated each other. Myers considered himself to be a scholar steeped in erudition. He viewed Liz and most other officers as being beneath him, intellectually and socially. Liz had an altercation with him in the morgue the day following Sara's death. They had not spoken of the incident again. Captain Miller was one of the few people who knew of it. But Liz wasn't going to waste time thinking about Myers right now.

"That's a lot to take in," answered Liz, trying to absorb what she was hearing. Where the hell did Miller find the missing documents? Liz wanted to ask, but Miller was a captain and he had his ways. As it turned out, she didn't need to ask. The information was forthcoming.

"The forensic exam notes were in a disciplinary file, of all places," said Miller. "When Pruitt put his papers in to retire, there was a fuss about how much of his pension he should be eligible to collect. He had not made many friends along the way. Pruitt was constantly under scrutiny. He was denied promotions, rate of pay increases, you name it. Personally, I don't think he deserved anything, but that's my opinion." Liz listened, but didn't comment.

"One of the pension committee reviewers was particularly zealous about research," Miller continued. "He insisted on looking into many questionable cases connected to Pruitt. He was adamant about re-opening the file into the Killian job because three people had died. The forensic data regarding Sara Mallory's death was buried in the back of that file. No one would have looked for it, unless, like me, you followed the trail from Pruitt to Sara's death and then to McCleary's report."

"And to me," said Liz.

"Yes, Lieutenant. Here's what I think: Pruitt was a crooked cop. He fudged and fiddled whenever possible. My contention is that he replaced three reports of the events with doctored ones that mirrored his own. He managed somehow to delete Crenshaw's report and any mention of your performance that day. He left your report intact because your account didn't include information about the raid because you weren't there. I have no idea how McCleary's report was missed, but thank God that it was. I was curious to begin with, but McCleary's report is what made me search for evidence of how Sara died."

"And you found out she probably died where she was found, in the locked office in the back of Killian's club," said Liz. "Probably not even during the raid."

"Yes, but what's most significant is the evidence. Sara didn't die from an officer's round or from a bullet fired by one of Killian's men that died in that raid. The bullet that killed Sara came from yet another weapon, a weapon that has never been linked to any other event. And it certainly wasn't found with her."

Liz realized she was staring into space and her jaw had dropped. "This is all hard to believe," said Liz. She ran the fingers of her free hand through her hair, stood and walked over to the sliding door to look outside.

"Yes, it is, Lieutenant," Miller responded. "I asked myself if sharing what I had discovered would cause you more stress, but my experience has been that answers often bring relief. I hope this information will serve to help you, at least in the long run."

"I'm glad you told me, Captain. Answers do help. I agree."

"Good. And Lieutenant, I'm not finished. I want to find that weapon." With that statement, Miller ended the call.

Liz walked back to the couch, and sat down. The cats had joined her in the living room. She looked at the clock, realized how late it was. *Where the hell was Mike?* He hadn't answered her messages, and that was odd.

She went into the kitchen to check that Eddie and Little Kurt's bowls had fresh food and water. She tried to eat, but wasn't interested. Liz had prepared the meal to share with Mike and he wasn't there. She left the chili on low heat, leaving items out for Mike. He would be hungry. She wondered if he had decided to attend a meeting at the last minute. *But,* thought Liz, *Mike would have let me know.*

Miller's news about Sara's death hadn't helped her appetite. *If the cops hadn't been responsible, then who was? Was it possible that Sara had ended her own life?* No, Liz didn't think so. Especially now, knowing that she had a baby daughter named Kyrie when she died.

Liz grabbed paper and pen and jotted down a list of all the players she could remember who had worked for Killian. She added Espy's name to the list even though he had been around before Liz's time. She reviewed each name and anything she remembered about them and tried to imagine who might have done such a thing. No one had reason to kill Sara and in doing so, would have come up against Chapin. Everyone knew Sara was Gabriel's girl. No one would have wanted to suffer his wrath.

When she finished, Liz texted Mike again; still no reply.

Chapter Fifty-one

"Grabbed"

Mike walked out of the office with a dozen thoughts circulating in his brain. His meetings had gone well in the end, but the effort had been exhausting. It was later in the evening than he had planned to work. He vowed to purge the day and enjoy the evening.

Across the street, a vendor was still selling bouquets of cut flowers from a cart. He could arrive at the apartment bearing an offering and thank Liz for cooking. He was starving and wondered what she had prepared.

He was looking at the flowers, making a selection, when someone tapped him on the shoulder. As he turned around, a fellow he didn't recognize was standing there.

"Aren't you Mike? From the Youth Center?"

"I am," Mike answered with reserve. "Can I help you?"

"I thought it was you. There's a punk in the alley," he said, pointing behind him. "He's not moving. I think he's in a bad way."

Mike looked at the guy. He looked like someone he should know, but he couldn't narrow it down on the spot.

He looked down the alley, and saw it was darker in that enclosed area than in the twilight settling in on the street. There were few people out and street lights were coming on.

Mike looked to the flower vendor and asked, "How long will you be here? I want this bunch, but I need a minute."

The vendor answered that he would be there another half hour. Mike was close enough to look the vendor in the eye, and hand him a twenty. "If I'm not back in five minutes, call an ambulance, and come look for me," Mike told the man. The vendor took the twenty and agreed to the five-minute deadline.

Mike turned to follow the man into the alley, looking around at his surroundings. "Where's the kid?"

"He's over there behind the dumpster," the man said, pointing. "My buddy stayed with him while I went for help."

When they got to the alley entrance, Mike saw another man, bent over near a dumpster, looking at something, but Mike couldn't see what. A sedan facing the other direction was parked at the opposite end of the alley,

The guy by the dumpster was older, bigger than the guy on the street. He looked up and before Mike could say anything, the street guy grabbed Mike from behind. Once Mike was held fast by both arms and couldn't run, the guy stepped away from the dumpster and landed a swift punch to Mike's abdomen.

The grab stunned him and the punch took Mike further by surprise. He doubled over in pain, the wind knocked out of him. Street Guy pulled Mike up to stand and Dumpster Guy pounded a vicious punch into Mike's nose. Mike felt himself fall, but he didn't care about anything except the pain in his face. He couldn't stop himself from going down anyway because his knees had given out.

Before he passed out, he heard a cattle dog barking in the fog.

Mike woke up lying on his left side. He was first aware of the pain in his face and the throb in his gut. He was able to open his eyes and when he looked around, he saw, in dim light, that he was lying on a mattress covered with a blanket. His mind drifted to dormitory life years ago, or a camping trip. Was he dreaming about college? Was he camping? Was he dreaming about camping in college?

Looking around, he gathered he was in some kind of building. Not a tent or outdoors. So much for the camping dream. The place was old, huge. He surveyed the expanse between him and the ceiling above as best he could without rolling over. He guessed the distance to be thirty or forty feet. There were exposed lengths of rusty pipe, old, long metal rafters and ceiling joists. If this was a college dorm, the place should be leveled.

He rolled over, tried to sit up and almost made it, but went back down. A voice said, "Careful. Not too fast there." Someone was with him. He started to strike out, but he wasn't able. He remembered the two men in the alley. One of them had approached him on the street and lured him into the alley. He remembered a second guy, the bigger one that hit him hard—twice—while the first guy held him. The asshole that hit him hadn't said a word, but he didn't think the voice he heard belonged to the guy that had lured him.

It occurred to Mike that this voice was soft, the words kind. Mike turned. The eyes he looked into were very light blue, surrounded by a head of hair in a variety of shades. The heavy mustache and beard were light in color. A man. Yes, he'd heard a man's voice. The man he was looking at was neither of the two from the alley. *Where was he? What had happened?*

Chapter Fifty-two

"The Squat"

Mike ran his tongue around his mouth. Dry, but he could feel that his teeth were intact. His face hurt like hell. His gut hurt when he moved.

"Here. You should drink some water," the man said. Mike watched as the man broke the seal on the plastic bottle and handed it to him. Mike drank greedily. He saw blood on his shirt, probably from the nose punch.

"Who are you? Where the hell am I?" Mike asked. His voice sounded weak, but clear, only slightly echoed in the cavernous space he explored with his eyes.

In the low light emitted by a propane lantern and a few candles, he was able to make out blankets, tattered towels, and clothing items hanging on makeshift lines. A propane stove sat on a table constructed of cinderblocks and a half-sheet of drywall, a camp-stove percolator was on one burner. Half of a case of water bottles, like the one Mike had just drained, was on the floor near the simple table. Curiously, no garbage was in sight.

Three or four thin mattresses were distributed around the floor, the sleeping bags and various other items of bedding were neatly organized. An array of books, magazines writing implements, and art supplies were all scattered around in an oddly specific fashion. The place resembled the Parisian turret of turn-of-the-century Inklings. On second thought, it looked more like a crack house that employed a housekeeper. He heard another man's voice. It came from Mike's right, somewhat behind him.

"How are you feeling?" Mike looked in the direction of the voice and saw a face he had seen before. It was Sage, the street musician. He was about twelve feet away, sitting on the floor with his back leaning against the wall. His guitar was nearby, as was Zeke, the cattle dog.

"Well, my nose hurts like hell and my gut aches," he answered looking at Sage. "Thanks for the water, though," Mike told the other man. "I would like to know where the hell I am and how I got here."

"I have ibuprofen and acetaminophen," said the guy who'd handed Mike the water. He stood a few feet away, speaking kindly and quietly. "I would suggest ibuprofen. It will help more with the swelling. But it's up to you." Sage and the second fellow ignored Mike's questions.

Mike directed his attention to the man. "I recognize Sage, but I don't know you. I'm Mike."

He man stepped to the cache of drinking water, reached for a bottle, and handed it to Mike. He picked out two, small items from a plastic crate and offered them to Mike, as well. They were bottles of over-the-counter pain relievers which looked to be in the original containers.

The man looked at Sage, and with one nod of his head indicated a message about something.

"This is Eli," Sage told Mike. "And you are in our place, otherwise known as the squat."

As the words were spoken by Sage, the man identified as Eli began singing, "Be it ever so humble, there's no-oh place like home." Eli sang with a voice as soft as the one he used to speak. Mike thought he detected a slight smile behind the whiskers.

"If you need what would be referred to as the facilities, there are buckets behind the wall over there," Sage said, pointing to an area on the other side of the huge room. "You'll find bags for the large jobs, as we say. Help yourself to paper. We put our names on rolls as they're a precious commodity. Bags are sealed and put into a bucket. Pee straight into a bucket or just go outside."

Trying to absorb the detailed instructions didn't help the ache in Mike's head. He opened the bottle labeled Advil and shook three pills onto his palm. The small, brown pills certainly looked like Advil tablets, so he popped them into his mouth and swallowed them with a big sip of water.

"Thank you," he said to Eli, holding the bottles out to the man.

"You'll need to take more in a few hours," answered Eli. "Keep them near your bed."

Mike nodded and attempted to stand. He made it to all fours, then slowly to his feet. He was more stable than he would have suspected. "If you'll excuse me, could you direct me to exactly where the facilities are? I'd hate to take a leak in the wrong place."

With Eli's help and the assistance of a flashlight, Mike made it to the improvised latrine. It was a walk of forty feet or so from the sleeping area. Eli left him alone to go about his business. Mike stepped into an empty room with no door. Pointing the flashlight beam, Mike could see the room well. Against the wall on the other side of the room were several 5-gallon buckets, all empty, of which Mike was very glad.

They all appeared to have been rinsed. A large propped-open window provided ventilation. Several half-rolls of toilet paper sat on a bench.

Returning slowly, Mike looked around to get a better grasp of the current situation, then resumed his place on the mattress with caution. Eli had taken a seat on a mattress, presumably his own. Behind the length of Eli's mattress, an improvised bench had been placed. It was loaded with sundry items including books, small boxes concealing God knows what, a lighted candle, another flashlight, and a few items of neatly folded clothing. Zeke, Sage's dog, was now sitting on the mattress next to Eli.

Mike thought of his phone. Before he panicked, thinking it had been lost or stolen, he saw it lying near where he had been sleeping. Checking the battery charge, he saw it was drained. Dead. Mike placed the phone next to the Advil bottle on the floor by the mattress.

"It was on the ground in the alley," Sage explained. "I assumed it was yours because it was clean."

"Thanks for picking it up." At this, Mike thought of another important item. With discretion, he checked to see if his wallet was in his hip pocket.

"It's there. We aren't thieves," Sage said.

"Sorry, didn't mean to offend."

Sage shook his head. "You didn't. You're entitled to check your shit."

"What time is it?" Mike asked Sage. "How long have I been here?"

"Hard to tell the exact time, no clocks and phones go dead. We sort of rely on sun-up and sunset. It's late—or early depending on your view of things. Maybe midnight. You've been here with us since about sundown."

Mike felt hunger pains in his stomach. He was surprised by it, but remembered he hadn't eaten. Liz had expected him. He didn't know if she was frantically worried about him or totally pissed off.

"If you are hungry, there are bagels left. Your cop friend, Liz bought them for us," Sage told him.

"How did you connect me to Liz?'

"It isn't important," said Sage. "I watch. I know things. It's how I stay alive."

Mike accepted half of a bagel. "Okay, now can you tell me what happened?"

"Sometime yesterday evening, Zeke and I were downtown, near Main and Beaumont. I heard a flower vendor call into an alley, 'Hey, Mister,' and he calls out, maybe three times. He saw something, turned around, and headed back to his cart of flowers and took off. Zeke started to get a certain growl in his throat, a growl I recognized. Two guys were carrying someone, trying to get him into a car parked in the alley."

"I let Zeke off his lead, something I rarely do, but it seemed called for. He went for one of the guys, had him by the arm. They dropped the guy they were carrying, who turned out to be you. The other guy, the one Zeke left alone, says 'oh, fuck this,' runs to the driver's side and gets in the car. I call Zeke off. He released the guy's arm and Zeke placed himself between you and car."

Mike looked over at Zeke, stretched out by Eli, enjoying belly strokes. He loved dogs, had owned several, but had never trusted a cattle dog. Mike's opinion of the breed had altered considerably. "I owe you my thanks. You and Zeke," Mike told him.

"The guy that Zeke got a taste of climbed in the car, clutching his arm. They drove off in a hurry. Zeke can be pretty convincing."

"But how did you get me here?" Mike asked.

"Shopping cart," said Sage, pointing to a cart that was sitting off to the side of the room. Mike had not noticed it before. It blended into the surroundings, he guessed.

"We put you in the cart. Wasn't easy. You were dead weight, but we managed. Covered you up the best I could. It took me a while to get back here. I'm always careful, watching my back. We protect our place. It isn't much, but we feel safe. We haven't had to move in a while. No one looked at us twice—a punk with another one passed out in a shopping cart? No one cares."

"I've been out the whole time?"

"You started to wake up when we got here and Eli was cleaning up your face, checking your nose. It wasn't broken, he said. You went out again." Mike looked from Sage to Eli, then back to Sage.

"Eli was a medic in the army," Sage offered.

"About a hundred lifetimes ago," added the soft-spoken Eli.

"Thanks, Eli. For taking care of me," Mike said. "Hard to believe you got me in the cart. I know how heavy dead weight is."

“I helped pull you out, got you inside, but I don’t venture out much. I haven’t left these hallowed halls in some time,” Eli told Mike, but he was looking at Sage.

“Then who helped you, Sage?”

Mike heard faint footsteps from a corner of the large room that he had not yet had the opportunity or the need to explore. There was another person in the room.

Chapter Fifty-three

"Lyric"

Turning in the direction from which the steps came, Mike saw a teen-aged girl. She stopped her advance when she knew that Mike was aware of her. She was young, small in stature. Mike could not see her well in the dim light of the room. She appeared to have short, chopped hair that looked to be a faded, greenish color, but Mike wasn't sure. Big, dark, cautious eyes, a square jaw, and a set mouth told Mike she was scared.

"You're Mike," the girl said. "I'm Kyrie. You can call me Lyric."

Mike knew that this girl was Kyrie, Chapin's daughter, the instant he saw her. He had seen the photos Liz had on her phone. "Hello, Lyric. Yes, I'm Mike. I'm glad to know you're okay. You look like you're doing better than I am right now."

Lyric walked over and sat cross-legged on the floor next to Eli. Zeke roused and chose to jump down and join the girl on the floor. Mike noticed a rug, an old mat, actually, on the floor under Eli's mattress. It amazed him how much effort had been put into making the place habitable.

"I was in the alley with Sage. I helped carry you," she said.

"I appreciate the help, but why did you bother?"

"We know some of the same people," Lyric told him.

"Who?" asked Mike.

"Elle. She and Pooki were besties. Older than me, they both knew their way around. I was not doing well when they found me. I got roughed up by an asshole that tried to rape me. He drugged me, but the moron didn't give me enough of it. Lucky for me he was so stupid."

"I'm sorry to hear that happened to you," said Mike. "It really stinks."

"Yeah," said Lyric, nodding. "They brought me here."

"Who else do we know in common?"

"Quinn," said Sage, answering for her, "Although Lyric hasn't met her yet. Quinn will always be a punk in her soul. It's like addiction, it never leaves you." Mike nodded. He knew what Sage meant. "And Black Coffee Liz," Sage said to Mike with a smile. "She bought the bagels and treats for Zeke," he explained. "We talked in the park."

Lyric and Sage shared a look, and girl looked anxious. "I didn't have much choice after they heard me singing your words," Sage told her. "I had no way of knowing you had posted the lines on the wall."

Liz does drink her coffee black, thought Mike. "As for Quinn or Liz, you can trust them both. I would trust them with my life. And I really need to let Liz know where I am," Mike said. "Does one of you have a phone I could use?"

Sage, Eli, and Lyric exchanged looks between themselves. "You should hear what Lyric has to say first. You may be safer here with us than at your office or the place where you live," said Eli.

"You've been followed," Lyric told Mike. "I recognized one of the guys in the alley, the big one, the one that hit you. They didn't see me. And I didn't know the other guy."

"How did he not see you?"

"I stay out of sight. Don't go out much."

Mike looked at Lyric and figured a quiet, lithe girl of her size could wear a hoodie and slip in and out of almost anywhere undetected.

"How do you know the guy?"

The girl hesitated, deciding how much to divulge. "I've seen him with my father."

"With your father?"

"Yes. He worked for my father, they had meetings together. That's how I knew not to trust him."

"Depending on what you decide, we'll get you home, or we will get a message to your friend Liz," said Eli.

Chapter Fifty-four

"Worry and Instinct"

It was a sleepless night. Liz dozed on the couch, sleeping for no more than a few minutes at a time. She kept waking with a start, thinking she heard Mike come in. She had put away the chili and finished cleaning up about midnight. Liz needed to stay busy. She hadn't been concerned about preserving leftovers. By two a.m. she was no longer angry, just consumed with worry and wanted Mike home.

At 6 a.m. she called Connors. It had been only twelve hours since she had expected Mike to walk in the front door, not the twenty-four that would allow for a missing person's report. But Connors knew Mike. He would know that there was no good reason for his not coming home. Connors would know, like Liz did, that Mike had been prevented from going about his evening routine. Mike was in danger. Liz was sure of that.

Connors got word out fast, and within an hour, he notified Liz that Mike's car had been located. It was parked on the street near his office. He may have parked it there himself, when he returned from the Youth Center in time for those dreaded meetings. He often parked on the street if there were no available spaces in the small lot. At this point, there was no way to tell.

"Yesterday evening," said Connors, "there was an emergency call from a street vendor. The guy was selling cut flowers off a cart near where Mike's car was parked. About 6:30 last night, give or take, he sold a bouquet of flowers to a man.

The buyer said he'd come back for his flowers, but he was going to check on someone in the alley. He told the vendor to call an ambulance and to come get him if he wasn't back in five minutes."

"That sounds like something Mike would do," Liz told Connors.

"It does," Connors agreed. "The buyer left a twenty with the flower vendor. The vendor appreciated it because it covered the cost of the flowers and then some. A few minutes passed, he closed up shop, walked over and called down the alley for the guy that gave him the twenty. He got no response. The flower vendor went a few steps closer, and saw what he thought was a group of homeless people having a row. He wanted no part of it, but at least he made the call like he said he would."

"Mike buying flowers?" said Liz, perplexed. That idea was as odd as Liz making chili. It could happen, but it was still odd.

"Don't know if it was Mike. The vendor didn't have much recall about what his customer looked like. The 911 call for an ambulance was logged. When the EMTs got there a few minutes later, no one was in the alley."

"Street folks know Mike," reasoned Liz. "Most do anyway." She knew if it was Mike that the vendor saw, had talked to, then it wasn't street folks that caused him trouble, unless it was a ruse meant to make anyone think as much. "How many 'homeless people' did this vendor think he saw?" Liz asked.

"He didn't count. His best guess was more than two, less than ten. He was beat, end of his day. At least he did what the customer asked. When it looked sketchy, he told the EMTs what he saw. They reported it to us."

"Yeah, okay. I'm just trying to eliminate looking in the wrong direction, Connors."

"Considering the proximity to his office and car plus the time the interaction allegedly occurred, I'm going to assume it was Mike until I know differently."

"Shit, Connors. I appreciate that you're taking this seriously, but we have to do something. We have to find Mike! You and I both know what this is about. It's about me and Chapin. He threatened me, remember?"

Connors inhaled loudly and exhaled with as much vigor. "Yes, I know. And I know that you'll make the best decision—to trust us to look into it," he said. It wasn't easy for Connors to continue, but it was necessary. "You need to back off. Let us handle things. We will find Mike. If Chapin is involved, we'll find out."

What Liz heard Connors saying was that if she stuck her nose into his efforts to look for Mike, it would muddy the waters. "I can't just do nothing, Connors! Let me help."

"You can't. The only thing you can do is keep your phone close by in case Mike calls."

"Fine," she said, but it was far from fine. "Then I want constant updates."

"You'll get them, now I need to go," said Connors, and he ended the call.

Liz tossed her phone on the breakfast bar. Damn it! From an official stand point, Liz's involvement could be perceived as meddling that may hinder the search to find the person most important to her in the world. Right now, she wasn't concerned with guilt, regret, or events from long ago. She was too anxious to think about mistakes in her past.

No, no, no. Screw this, Liz told herself, thinking of the message Chapin had left on her phone. He wanted to cause her worry and pain, and knew that hurting Mike would accomplish that. Chapin wouldn't do this himself. He wouldn't dirty his own hands. No need. He had thugs at his beck and call, no doubt. He would have flunkies grab Mike for him. And they might have looked like homeless folks on purpose to cast suspicion in that direction—or to gain Mike's attention.

Liz was not cleared to access case notes on the department server, but she wasn't locked out of the system. She had not thought to note the address when she'd talked with either Chapin or with Richelle. It took only a few minutes for Liz to pull up Connors' notes including Chapin's home and office address in Parkdale.

Unsure of what she would find or how she would proceed when she got there, she decided to be ready for anything. She left her department-issued weapon locked in the gun safe, removed the .357 and donned the shoulder holster. She covered the weapon with a jacket and went out the door, headed for Chapin's residence. It was almost 8 a.m. Still rush hour, but she didn't care.

Chapter Fifty-five

"Problems in the Ranks"

Morgan was walking to his car, heading into the precinct to begin his work day, when he felt the vibration of his burner phone, the one he used for private business. He looked at the screen and thought, *Damn it! What now*? These idiots were getting on his nerves. They were so incompetent, just one screw-up after another.

If he was paid a decent amount of money as a cop, he wouldn't have to do side jobs for people who made a lot of dough in ways he didn't want to hear much about. There was no way he was going to live the lifestyle he wanted on his cop's salary. Picking up a few extra K was the only way to make it happen. It was easier than most people would think.

On top of dealing with the man who was paying him for this side job, he had to clean up messes made by his goons—because, as a cop, Morgan had the resources to deal with them. The old guy, called Espy, was nothing more than a jerk, a wannabe gangster from the old days. He probably could have run a crew of hoods in his prime, but that ship sailed years ago.

Morgan doubted that even in his prime Espy had been smart enough to keep his shit under the radar. And Espy had been ID'd from an old mug shot. Morgan was trying to decide how to deal with that too. His crony, Curtiss, the younger dude, wasn't as dumb, but he was slimy, shifty—scary in a way what told Morgan to watch his back around him.

"What?" he answered, in the privacy of his vehicle. Morgan tried to sound in control. He had to keep his emotions in check with these idiots, but it was becoming increasingly difficult.

"We ran into a problem last night," said the older guy. "We had the guy in our grips, man."

"Okay, good. What's the problem?" asked Morgan.

"Out of nowhere, a homeless punk lets his mean, damn dog attack us. We had to get the hell out of there fast."

"Okay, you got a dog bite. Where's the guy?"

"You're not hearing me, man. We had to get out of there. Fast. Had to leave him there."

Morgan couldn't believe what he was hearing. "Wait a second. You're telling me that you grabbed the guy, and then left him there because you were scared off by a damn puppy?"

"Listen to me, you asshole flatfoot pig. That was no puppy. It was a death hound! You would a' shot the fuckin' dog. If I'd had a piece, I woulda' shot it."

Morgan took a breath, tried to calm himself. This was bad. It was really, fucking bad. "Where is the guy now, genius?"

"Couldn't say." In his mind's eye, Morgan could see the guy shaking his head. He could almost hear the rattle caused by having no brain within the thick skull. "We been watching his place, no sign of him. His car hasn't moved. We're staying low. There's always a buncha' you cops in that part of town, trying to look busy."

"Does the boss know?"

"Not yet. Wanted to tell you first. Whaddaya' want us to do?"

"I want you to get your stupid asses off the street before someone recognizes you. You know, I'm still trying to clean up your mess from your little play session that you couldn't keep under control, the little party where that kid got stabbed by your creepy friend? Remember?"

"Aw, shut the hell up, alright? Yeah, it got outta hand. It happens."

"This is all we need, you dumb shit! Keep your damn phone on and wait for my call. Don't inform the boss. I will tell him myself. It will be up to him how we move. If I have my way, you'll be looking for a new scam to work by the end of the day."

"Don't you threaten me! I was handling jobs in this town before you were born, you pretty little pissant cop, hiding behind your damn badge..."

Morgan punched the button to end the call. He slammed the phone into the dash of his car. He cursed himself, the morons working for the boss, and the boss himself. He was screwed and he knew it.

He calmed down enough to think. He needed to talk to the boss. Now. Morgan called the precinct, and talked with one of the detectives on his team.

"Hey, yeah, good morning. Look, I got a message I need to follow up on. We may have a lead, but I don't want to waste your time if it's nothing. Okay...yeah...I'll be in as soon as possible and I'll send you the address."

Morgan ended the call. He'd send an address, as he promised, just not the correct one. He pulled out and headed out to talk to the boss.

Chapter Fifty-six

"Someone you Love"

Liz pulled up in front of a large, brick home, set well back from the street. Like his neighbors' homes, Chapin's was situated on a large lot. There looked to be close to two acres of trees, grass and shrubbery surrounding the home. At the street end of a long, paved driveway stood a gate with a call mechanism, ensuring no one came or went that the occupant didn't authorize.

The other end of driveway reached to a three-bay garage unattached to the house. The neighborhood was old and established and Liz bet that the people who lived here chose the area for the privacy and to feel a part of a fabricated American gentry class that doesn't really exist.

She checked the address one last time, then pulled up to the gate, noted the security camera perched on the top, and pressed a button on the call box. Liz heard the distant buzz emanate from the device and waited to be acknowledged.

"Yes," answered a young woman's voice.

"Is this Richelle? I'm guessing it is. You already know it's me, Liz, because you're looking at me on a screen, no doubt. Let me in and tell your boss I'm here. We need to talk."

"Yes, it's Richelle, Lieutenant Jordan. Please wait for a moment. I'll inform Mr. Chapin you are here and see if he's available."

"Richelle, cut the crap," Liz snapped at her. "I don't give a shit if he's available or not! Either let me in now, so I can talk to your boss, or I'll ram down this gate with my car and surprise his ass. Your choice. You have five seconds."

"Ms. Jordan, please, wait a moment. I can't admit you without clearance."

"Okay, here we go, have it your way," said Liz, putting her car in reverse, ready to back up and plunge forward at top speed.

"Wait! Just wait. Don't damage the gate. I'll let you in."

"Good choice, Richelle," said Liz, putting the car back into 'Drive' as the electric gate engaged and started to open. Liz drove down the long driveway. She parked head in, which was not the norm on the job. She'd been taught to park her vehicle, pointed in the direction she would be leaving the location. But she wasn't on the job. She was beyond that now.

By the time Liz was out of her car, she was met by a young woman standing at the open front door. Liz assumed this to be Richelle Isaacs in the flesh.

"Richelle," Liz called out with sarcasm. "Nice to meet you, at last. Sorry for the attitude, huh? Where's your boss? Did you tell him I'm here?"

Richelle was tall, Liz's height, and slender. She wore a trendy haircut and color job that made her look young. She was dressed in high-end jeans that probably cost more than Liz spent on the suits she wore when on duty. The jeans were paired with a blouse made of some expensive-looking fabric and a sheer, loose sweater.

Richelle's appearance was casually business-appropriate, except for the combination of emotions on the otherwise attractive, artistically made-up face—fear, trepidation, dread, maybe some anger. Mostly, fear and dread.

"Yes, and he'll be right with you. You can wait in the living room to the left," said Richelle backing away from the doorway, trying to physically distance herself from Liz.

Entering the house, Liz surveyed her surroundings out of habit. She had looked around in much the same way coming up the driveway, and walking from her car to the front door.

"Good, Richelle. I'll wait about thirty seconds then I'll go looking for him." Liz's statement caused Richelle to freeze where she stood in the entry, her hand on the front door. She could not utter a response. She had not yet closed the front door. Richelle stood, mouth gaping. Just as she found her wits, Richelle and Liz turned, hearing footsteps approach from behind.

"Close the damn door, Richelle. What is wrong with you?" said Chapin, walking toward them from the opposite end of the long entry hall. He spoke to his admin, but his eyes were peeled on Liz. Richelle snapped out of her shock, or whatever hit her, quickly closing the door.

Liz stepped back and slightly to the left, toward the designated living room.

"Good. You're here. Let's do this," said Liz, her eyes returning Chapin's stare. She extended her left arm, inviting the man to join her in his own living room. "You'll need to come with us, Richelle. That way I can keep my eye on you."

The living room could be closed for privacy behind heavy, dark oak French doors. Liz kept an eye on Chapin and started to close one side.

"There's no need to close the doors," said Chapin. "There's no one else here, Liz—no one to hear our conversation. The housekeeper left early to do the marketing. Just relax. Can we get you a drink? You look like you could use one."

He motioned toward Richelle, when he offered the drink, indicating that she would be expected to play bartender, as if she was domestic help instead of his admin. He sat down on the plush sofa, reclined back slightly, with this left arm on the sofa back, and crossed his right knee over his left. He puffed out his chest, took a breath, as if grateful for the inconvenient interlude into his extremely busy and important schedule.

"No Gabriel, I don't want a drink," Liz said, with eerie calmness. "Where is he?"

"Where is who?" he asked, his brows arched.

"You fucking know who!" Liz screamed, no longer calm. She glanced at Richelle, who again had frozen on the spot, and said at a lower volume, "You should sit down. You're not looking so good."

Richelle quickly found a place to sit on a nearby chair, like a well-trained dog that had been instructed to sit. Her chin was tucked, in self-preservation mode; her hands gripped the arms of the chair. She stared at Liz.

"You left me a message, said that I'd regret not helping you the way you wanted, turning the search for Kyrie over to the proper team of detectives," Liz said, feeling her anger rise in her chest, up her throat. "That threatening message is now documented with the department. If anything happens to him, it's your ass, you arrogant son of a bitch!"

"Yes, yes, I left you a message in a fit of anger," said Chapin, with practiced smugness, "but that doesn't mean I have any idea what it is you're talking about at this moment. Tell me, Liz, is someone that you love missing? Like my daughter is missing?"

Liz felt her emotions approach overload, the panic and stress she had been dealing with coming to the surface. She couldn't control her reaction and being in the same room with Chapin unleashed her ire. Like a gut reaction, she spewed out her anger in Chapin's direction.

"Mike! What have you done with Mike?! Where is he?!" Liz had lost all reason. All she could think was that Mike was in danger and it was all her fault. She had to get him out of this trouble. She drew the .357 from the shoulder holster. She heard Richelle gasp with fright. Chapin tried to keep cool, appear unalarmed, unimpressed. But Liz saw his eyes grow a bit rounder and he took a slight intake of breath.

"You have about ten god damn seconds, you asshole, to tell me where he is or call off the goons that have him, and you'd better believe that I mean it. And you should hope and pray he hasn't been harmed."

Chapin said nothing. He stared at Liz with contempt. She stepped closer to where he sat on the sofa, leaned in until her gun was inches away from his chest. "Where the hell is Mike?!"

Chapter Fifty-seven

"Urban Camping"

Before going to sleep, Mike thought about what Sage and the others had to say, especially what Lyric had said about him being followed and about the man she recognized as one of her father's associates. Mike wanted to let Liz know he was okay, but he knew what she would do. She'd blast in with four barrels, not listening to anyone about any alternative plan. For the moment, the priorities were to stay hidden, stay safe, and keep the others safe, too.

Mike managed a few hours of sleep. He dreamed that he and Liz were running on the track below the apartment. The dream evolved into Mike running alone on downtown streets, screaming for Liz, but unable to find her.

It was light when Mike woke up to the smell of coffee. Eli was sitting on his mattress. When he saw that Mike was awake, he rose and asked, "How are you feeling?"

"Hey," said Mike. "I think I may survive, thanks to the three of you."

"There's coffee. Can I get you a cup?"

"I can't think of anything I'd rather have right now. Thank you, Eli."

Eli poured a cup of piping hot coffee into a metal mug and brought it to Mike. "Here you go. We have packets of sugar and sweetener. Sorry, no cream or milk."

"This is fine, thanks," said Mike, accepting the mug.

"You may want to take a dose of ibuprofen with that coffee; the caffeine will help it kick in."

Mike sipped, then said, "Good idea, but this is good for now." Mike was surprised by Eli's coffee—hot, fairly fresh, strong—and he took another sip. He was surprised by many things, actually. He was surprised to have slept at all, and by how comfortable and reasonably clean his mattress was. He had discovered that the thin mattress had been covered by a tarp, then two blankets. The blankets had been tucked in the corners with G.I. precision.

Looking around, Mike didn't see Sage or Lyric. Zeke, the dog, was gone too. Eli read his thoughts. "Sage left early. It's a weekday. He finds a corner to busk at while folks are bustling to their jobs. Lyric has Zeke out for some play time. They're safe out back this early."

Eli refilled his cup with coffee and sat down. Mike nodded. Looking into his cup, he had a thought.

"Eli, where do you get your water? I'm not asking out of concern for the coffee. The coffee's good. I'm just wondering."

"There's a hose. The city neglected to turn it off when the building was vacated. It happens sometimes. We only use it for cleaning up. Bottled water for anything we eat or drink. Zeke drinks the hose water so it's probably okay, but I don't trust it."

"You are in charge of running things around here, I guess. You take care of the squat, don't you?"

Eli shrugged. "We all have our jobs. It's basically urban camping."

"Sage mentioned you were in the military. A medic," said Mike, remembering some of the conversation from late last night.

"Yes, two tours. Army, mostly in North Africa, but some time in Yemen and Afghanistan. When you're trying to keep yourself and the guys mobile and vertical, you learn ways to make do with almost nothing. It was good training for life on the street."

The social worker in Mike wanted to ask a bevy of questions: *how old was Eli? What had happened that put him on the street? When had he served? Did he access VA benefits? What of his family?* But Mike was in no position to pry, and his assistance had not been requested. At the moment, the roles of the two men were decidedly reversed—Eli was the helper; Mike was in need of the help.

"Well, you seem to have it down," Mike said, surveying his surroundings in the morning light streaming in from a dirty window.

"It works. Sage makes most of the cash, but we all contribute. Elle and Pooki panhandled and turned some tricks now and then. I didn't like that they resorted to it, but they felt it was all they could do to help out. They ran errands for supplies, too. Now, there are only three of us."

"I talked with Elle a little bit, while she was recovering at the Youth Center. Tell me about Pooki."

"Pooki was a cool kid. Funny, would have you in stitches. With all she'd been through she still had a sense of humor. She was younger than Elle. She tried to be smart, but she could be her own worst enemy."

"Did you know where they went that day?"

"I suspected as much when Pooki came back for Elle, but I didn't know exactly what was up or where they were going. Pooki made herself available to people looking for variety. It's a way to survive for a lot of the kids. If not for Pooki, Elle wouldn't have been there, but if not for Elle, Pooki would have died there with the moron that stabbed her."

Eli reminded Mike of Ty, a friend of his going back years. Ty was a few years older than Mike and they didn't have a lot in common. Mike had not served in the Armed Forces whereas Ty was a Gulf War vet. When he met Ty, the man was living on the streets, trying to make sense of the life he had returned to after his deployments, but knowing he would never be the same. Mike had been more fortunate. At least he had always had a place to live.

Ty had learned to trust Mike and the feeling became mutual. In the beginning, Mike had been a resource for Ty when the man needed help. Mike knew that Ty had been a huge help to Liz and to Connors when law enforcement needed an ally on the streets. In all honesty, Ty's friendship became a source of support for Mike because trying to stay sober was one thing they did have in common.

Mike caught a similar vibe from Eli: gentleness. Both men exuded calmness, as if they had each reached a quiet understanding, a truce, with their deleterious pasts. He wondered if the similarities were due to personality type or aftermath of their combat experiences. Mike decided Ty would be okay with Eli. He felt like Ty would trust him and that was good enough for Mike.

Noise erupted near the entrance to the room. Zeke came running in, making a beeline for a water bowl that Mike had not seen before. Lyric was close behind the dog. She stopped when she saw Eli and Mike sitting casually, having their coffee, conversing together. She reached for a bottle or water and chugged it down. The scene would be normal for a teen and a pet, and Mike almost forgot they were homeless and squatting in an abandoned building.

"Good morning, Lyric," Mike said to the girl.

"Hi," she replied. "How are you doing?"

"Better. Eli's coffee is a cure for what ails you. Thank you again for your help yesterday."

Lyric grinned and nodded. "You're welcome. That's probably true about the coffee, but I don't like it. Tea sometimes."

Zeke solicited pats and strokes from Eli and Lyric. Then he sat down a few feet in front of Mike, his tongue hanging out of his mouth, panting. He looked at Mike, as if to say, *you needed my help in the alley and I did my job*.

Mike remained cautious of the dog, until Lyric said, "He's okay, Zeke. Say hello to Mike."

The dog moved a little closer. "He'll be fine," Lyric told Mike, taking a seat on the floor near him. As Lyric stroked the dog's fur, Mike tentatively did the same. Zeke sat patiently, letting Mike get used to him. He panted in Lyric's direction, and then turned to look at Mike, tongue still wagging.

Mike continued to pet the pup, saying calming phrases, like, "Good boy, Zeke." When Zeke had decided he'd had enough, he laid down next to Mike.

"Look at that—you've made the grade," said Eli, "but then, Zeke's a good judge of character."

"Yeah, he was last night. Scared off the assholes for us," said Lyric. "Did Eli mention your phone?"

Eli shook his head, and said, "Not yet." Mike saw that his phone was not where he's placed it. "Sage took it with him,"

Eli said. "He'll find a place to charge it. We didn't want to wake you to ask. You can trust him."

Mike wasn't completely convinced, but strangely, he was glad that Sage was charging his phone. "Great. That's nice of him." Anyway, what else was he going to say?

"With your phone charged, you can decide what you want to do," said Lyric. "But I have more to tell you."

Chapter Fifty-eight

"Lyric's Tale"

"I don't know much about my father's past or his business, but I know he's not a typical businessman. He's never been like my friends' parents. I didn't notice when I was younger. Over the last year or so, I would hear people whisper, friends' parents would act weird. I started to pay more attention to things I could overhear, conversations between my father and Richelle. I began observing my father's business associates. Sometimes I'd get a weird vibe from them. It's not only his business that's weird. His whole life is like a big secret he doesn't share with anyone. Not even with me. I suspect you know things about my father, too."

"Some," said Mike. "Not a lot."

"Your friend, Liz, knows my father. I've put pieces together—old conversations I overheard between my grandmother and my father. Elle picked up on stuff, so did Sage. They told me things that Quinn at the Youth Center said about your friend, Liz. And I know that Liz knew my mother." Lyric looked Mike in the eye and asked, "Did you know my mother? Her name was Sara."

"No, I didn't know her," Mike answered. "I never met her. But Liz has talked with me about her." Lyric nodded at the information.

"Last year, I was suspended from school for three days," she said. She waved the comment away, rolled her eyes. "It wasn't a big deal. It involved social media and stuff we shouldn't have been doing. We all knew it. We knew better.

It happens all the time nowadays, anyway. Let's just say some of my so-called friends said I was behind the whole mess. Like, sure. But it didn't matter—it was wrong and I knew it. At least I was mature enough to take my punishment, unlike some of the others. Richelle wasn't pleased, but she was cool about it. We talked through things, like always. But my Dad was, well, my dad, a jerk. 'An opportunity to learn what not to do,' he said. 'Don't be so stupid next time. Learn to not get caught.'"

Mike listened to the girl. He wasn't a parent and didn't want to pass judgement, but Chapin's response to his daughter's troubles sounded harsh—and unhelpful.

"It was pretty ugly for a while. Richelle and I wanted to look around at other schools, to give me a fresh start, new friends. My father said that wasn't an option."

"Anyway, while I was suspended from school, I was up early one morning. Actually, I was up all night writing and hadn't been to sleep yet. Two men were in my father's office with him and they were talking. Richelle wasn't there. It was too early. One of the men sounded smart, professional, like a teacher. He was business-like, respectful. I could tell that my father liked him. He said things to my father, like, 'Yes, Sir. I completely understand. Good point.' You know what I mean?"

"I think so," said Mike. "He was kissing your dad's butt."

"Uh-huh. The second guy was different. I had seen him coming and going several times. My dad talked to the man like he didn't like him, but had to deal with him, you know? He didn't sound very bright. He was older and sounded mean. He cussed a lot to make himself sound important, you know, not that he liked the sound or the feel of the words rolling off his tongue, but like he didn't know many other words. A teacher told our class, 'Profanity is a weak mind's way of expressing itself.' The older guy reminded me of that."

Mike wanted to laugh—that a kid Lyric's age would be aware of the old adage about why people resort to profanity. Then he recalled that the young girl was a poet, with the street name *Lyric,* and it made sense. She paid attention to words and expression. Not wishing to dissuade her from continuing, Mike simply nodded.

Lyric took a deep breath to continue her story, but hesitated. She looked at Eli, who encouraged her with, "Go on, Lyric. It's okay. Tell him."

"I was in the back hallway. I just sat there, listening for entertainment's sake. It wasn't the first time I had eavesdropped. I heard them mention my mother by name so I listened more closely. Then they talked about a man my father and the older guy used to work for."

"Was the name Killian?

"Yeah," she said, nodding. "And they talked about a cop, but not Liz, a guy from a long time ago. They joked about this cop. They thought he was dumb. They said he wasn't smart enough to have 'come on board', as my dad put it. They blamed him for whatever happened to their boss. They said he used my mom for something. Some job."

"Was the cop's name Pruitt?"

"Yes, I think it was. It sounds right."

"I'm surprised you remembered the names," said Mike. "Are you sure you heard them correctly?"

"I listened closely when I knew they were talking about my mom because my father rarely mentioned her." Lyric spoke with a directness that dispelled doubt. "The older guy seemed to have known her too. That made me angry. I'd not been around anyone else who had known my mom—except for my grandmother. It was important to me."

"Sorry, I don't mean to doubt you or interrupt with questions. You said they mentioned your mother."

"Yeah...," she said quietly. "The older guy called my mother a name. My dad got mad. The other guy that was there, the smart one, he intervened. It went on like that. Then the old, dumb guy, the mean one says, 'Don't beat yourself up forever. You did what you did, had your reasons at the time, remember?' My dad answered, 'She was mine, and she was sweet, but she was too naïve to stay alive.'"

Tears formed in Lyric's eyes. The last part of her story was especially painful for her. "I heard my father say, 'You're right, I had no choice. Sara was going to cause me nothing but trouble. I had to get rid of her.'"

Chapter Fifty-nine

"Paths Crossed"

Morgan parked down the block from the man's home. He was deciding how to explain to Chapin that the goons he had hired to lure his daughter out of hiding had made a monumental mess of things. They couldn't even complete a grab intended to give them leverage. He needed to put his best cop slant on the situation. Hopefully, the boss would see things his way. He usually did.

It was one thing to risk his career working with smart, savvy characters, like Gabriel Chapin, but it was another to deal with the idiots he hired for muscle. Morgan wanted the idiots out of his life.

Chapin had done some research, for which Morgan had to give him credit. In an effort to find his kid, Chapin had looked into the community of gutter punks rummaging around downtown like vagrants. He had contacted an old crony, named Espy, to search around downtown and find the girl. Chapin even let Espy bring a sidekick. But then Chapin had acted on impulse, never a good idea, in Morgan's estimation. He had contacted Lieutenant Jordan, whom he considered a hidden resource, and intimidated her into helping behind the scenes. Morgan would have advised against this, and he would have been right.

When Chapin received a message from Liz that she had chosen to *neglect her responsibility,* as he put it, and go to Captain Miller about everything, he was furious. He did not want a host of nosy cops hanging out around his home and place of business. That was his reason for using Espy and Curtiss in the first place.

Morgan knew immediately when he met these cretins that they would be more trouble than they were worth. Neither of them had an idea what they were doing. Instead of keeping patient ears to the ground and waiting at the hovel Chapin had provided them to hole up in, they got bored and lured a couple of punks in for a party. They were stupid, it got out of hand, one kid was seriously injured and the other one died.

Then Chapin expected Morgan to work magic. The man needed a discreet fix with a cop's eye and ear. First order of business was damage control, cleaning up Espy and Curtiss' screw-up. Second, was to eavesdrop on the search for his daughter. Chapin was determined to resume control of the search for his kid. His plan was to have the cops do the heavy-lifting, find her before they did, and bring the girl home—before she could contact her meddling grandmother.

Things hadn't gone according to plan, but that didn't surprise Morgan. The boss would have to see his point, that his goons were too hot and needed to get the hell out of town. Morgan had searched for a known pedophile on which he could pin the punk's murder. He had wanted this done before someone ID'd stupid, old Espy from his mugshot. Curtiss, the sick asshole, was the cutter, anyway. Street guys that looked like him were a dime a dozen.

Morgan decided that he could convince the kid that got beat up, the one that left from the Youth Center with her cousin, that he found the right guys. If she didn't concur with the story, well, he'd deal with that too. He knew where to find her.

With the first feat accomplished—the assault and murder out of their way—and the real killer safely out of reach, Morgan knew that either Liz or Quinn would lead him right to Chapin's kid. They were so thick into the punks, it was inevitable. Then he got the call about the screw-up when they tried to grab Liz's friend, Mike. Now he had to deal with this mess.

Parked on the street, Morgan started to get out of his car when he saw a vehicle coming out of Chapin's driveway. The car stopped for a moment at the curb, the driver checking both directions. Morgan stopped short of opening his driver's door to exit, pulled back, and saw that the car turned right. It headed the opposite direction down the street. It wouldn't pass by him, so Morgan wasn't at risk of being spotted.

Liz Jordan was driving that car! Morgan knew the visit hadn't been official because Jordan wasn't working, but when he thought about it, it made sense to see her here. By now, he reasoned, she had to know that her friend, Mike had had some trouble and she would have instantly blamed Chapin for it. Recovered from the ordeal, Mike had probably given his description of the thugs to officers, and every cop in Columbia City was looking for them.

Morgan would need to work fast and convince Chapin to see things his way. He waited until Liz was well out of range before he exited his car, deciding to leave it on the street. The walk-through gate was unlocked, as it often was for grounds maintenance. He trudged up the drive to Chapin's home.

Chapter Sixty

"Faces and Voices"

"Lyric...," said Mike. "I'm so sorry—that it happened at all, and that you had to hear that. No one should have to hear that."

The young girl collected herself before she spoke, wiping her face with the back of her sleeve. "Even knowing so little about my father, I never expected that. Not that he would kill my mom, the mother of his own kid! The son of a bitch killed my mother!" Lyric pursed her lips, squeezed her eyes tightly shut. "That's when I ran. I couldn't stay there."

"What about your grandmother?"

"My father was fine with dumping me on her, letting her raise me for my first few years, but he refused to let me see her. I heard him threaten her. It was awful. When I got a phone of my own, we talked once in a while and texted. She doesn't know I ran."

"Actually, she does." Mike explained to Lyric about hearing Connors tell Liz that he had talked with her grandmother. "Your grandmother, is her name Laura? Laura Mallory?"

"Yes! Is she okay?" asked Lyric with alarm.

"I'm sure she's fine," Mike assured her. "She's worried about you."

At this, they heard footsteps approaching, then a shrill whistle. Hearing the familiar sound, Zeke was awake in an instant and bounding toward it. Sage stepped into the doorway. He placed his guitar case and pack on the floor and crouched to greet his excited pup. Sage was soon on his back on the floor with Zeke, the dog too thrilled to contain himself.

After a few minutes of play, Sage sat up and took a bag from his pack. He handed the bag to Eli, who began to unload provisions. Mike saw packages of ramen, snack bars, coffee, other simple items, most likely purchased with proceeds from Sage's singing and playing effort.

Sage studied Lyric, suspecting something had upset her. "You doing okay?" he asked the girl.

The girl looked at Sage. She nodded and then answered softly. "I told Mike why I ran."

"Tough story, but its good you told him. He needs to know why we've been so cautious." Lyric nodded as Sage looked from Eli to Mike.

"Did Zeke get out?" asked Sage.

"Uh-huh, we ran around a bunch," Lyric said. "We both did. Felt good."

"I bet it did, thanks," he said to Lyric.

Sage turned to Mike, and said, "Lyric only goes outside if Zeke or myself are around. She feels safer." He had Mike's phone in his hand, and handed it to Mike. "I took your phone to find a place to charge it. I really didn't want to wake you. You've got fifty-percent now. Sorry that you can't charge it here, but we have no power. Phones are pretty secure these days. Charging is all I could do without a lock code."

"It's okay, Sage. Thanks," said Mike. He took his phone from Sage's hand, placed it next to the bed he'd been using.

"Word is out that you're missing. There was an unmarked police car parked at the Youth Center. Then Quinn and a cop dressed in plainclothes came out the front entrance together. It was Connors. I hadn't seen him without his uniform. They asked me if I had seen you."

"You know Connors?" Mike asked Sage. Then he said to Lyric, "He's the one heading the search for you. You can trust him."

"Well," said Sage. "I know who he is." At that, Mike gave him a funny look. "He's been around a while. That's what I told Liz, that everybody on the street knows Connors. And yes, I trust him. More than most cops."

"What did you tell them?" asked Mike.

"That I was half asleep when I got to my corner, sat down and started playing. I wasn't going to lie, but I wasn't going to tell them you were back here at the squat with Eli. I didn't know what you wanted to do, Mike. And I'm not going to give Lyric up. Not until she's ready. Quinn asked me where Zeke was. I said with a friend, sleeping in. All true. She came out later with coffee for me from her office. The person I expected to see, but didn't, was Liz."

Mike gave a sigh, thought to check his phone. He had text messages and two voice mails from Liz, starting at six-thirty the previous evening. There was another message from a second number he recognized as Connors' phone, left early that morning.

Then Mike looked at Lyric and Sage and had another thought. He found the photos Liz had forwarded to him, the created images of the guys who had attacked Elle and Pooki.

"I'd like to show you something," he said to Lyric. He handed the phone to her. "These photos aren't great. They're images that Elle helped put together of the guys that attacked her and Pooki. Do you recognize either of these guys?"

Lyric looked at the photos for several moments. "Oh, shit," she said. She handed the phone to Sage who studied them too. They looked at each other, then at Mike.

"These are the guys that Elle said attacked her?" asked Lyric. "The shit bags that killed Pooki?"

"They are renderings from Elle's memory, yes," Mike confirmed. "She worked with a technician to create them."

"Mike, look at those faces," begged Sage, handed the phone to Mike. "Those are the assholes that jumped you!"

"And that's the guy I recognized in the alley." Lyric was adamant. "The same one that was talking to my Dad. About my mother."

Chapter Sixty-one

"Deadly Connections"

Mike took the phone from Sage. He studied the photos of the men under suspicion of luring and attacking Elle and Pooki. He had to admit that they resembled the two guys in the alley last night. One was younger, the one who approached him on the street, then held him as this older guy beat him. They had employed a similar ruse with the kids—lure under pretense and then attack. Although Mike had been beaten unconscious, he had fared better than the kids.

He felt stupid for not noticing the resemblance. His gut told him that the guy who approached him on the street looked familiar, but he hadn't paid enough attention. He had been preoccupied, his mind on work, when the slime ball tapped him on the shoulder as he looked at flowers. Mike wasn't stupid. He knew better than to lower his level of caution on the street, but that's exactly what he had done.

"Okay, let's think about this," said Mike. "The two assholes that Elle described as the ones who attacked her and killed Pooki are the same thugs that jumped me." He turned to Lyric and said, "And you recognize one of them, having seen him with your father. And you overheard him having a conversation with your dad about your mother, and, um...," he hesitated, wanting to be as delicate as possible, "how she died."

"Yes," said Lyric. "He's the same creepy guy, I'm telling you, I'm positive. I never saw the other one before yesterday, but that dude was working for my father." Lyric's complexion grew a shade paler as she said, "My father hired these creeps to find me!"

"We don't know that, but it's possible," Mike answered.

"Yes, we do! I know that idiot was working for my dad. He was going to use Elle and Pooki to find me. You know," she said with sarcasm, "because all of us punks look the same, right? They don't have any idea how close they came. And Pook is dead because of me."

"It's not your fault, Lyric," Mike told the girl, trying to reason with her. "These are not smart, industrious guys. They lean on people for a living. You aren't responsible for what they may have done. And it doesn't explain why they targeted me."

"No, I think it kind of does," said Eli. "Lyric's dad knows your friend, Liz. If she pissed him off enough, he would go for you."

Mike thought about what the others were saying and they were probably correct. He nodded.

"Yes, you may be right. Liz knew him a long time ago, when Lyric was a baby." He turned to address Lyric. "Your dad contacted Liz. He said she owed him a favor. He wanted her to find you without an official search. Liz decided doing so would put you in more danger. She went to her captain, told him what she knew about the day your mom died. Her death wasn't Liz's fault, Lyric," said Mike, shaking his head, "but your dad made sure Liz blamed herself all these years."

"When we talked in the park," said Sage, "she wanted me to know she wasn't acting as an officer and she wasn't happy about it."

"No, she wasn't." Mike didn't go into the details of Liz's decision to take time off, the lawsuit, or the specifics of what had happened years earlier. Instead, he asked Lyric, "When you heard them talking, your father and this guy, they talked about the man they had both worked for, you heard the name Killian. And they named a cop. Pruitt."

"That's right," she said.

"And there was a second guy talking with him and your dad, but not the slimy guy from the alley."

"No. He sounded smart, like I said, and I only heard his voice. I didn't see him."

"Okay. There no way to know who that second guy was," said Mike. "But it's all connected—your dad, your mom's death, Killian, Pruitt—and Liz. And Eli is right. I'm the pawn they want to use to coerce Liz into finding you. I need to stay out of sight until these guys are caught."

"We've agreed, Eli, Lyric and me, that you're welcome to stay here for a while," Sage told him. "If I were you, I'd be changing up this game 'cause now you may have the upper hand. But it's up to you."

"How do you figure I have the upper hand?" Mike asked.

"Because no one's been able to find Lyric," Sage answered with confidence, "so, how are they gonna find you down here?"

Mike told the crew he would take them up on their offer of hospitality provided he could pay them for their trouble. Sage and Eli were reluctant, claiming an invitation to bad karma if they should profit from his misfortune. Mike was insistent. He reminded them that Sage and Lyric had saved his life and that Eli had cared for him and his injuries. Mike said that the way he saw things, they weren't profiting. Besides, no one stays in the squat without pulling their weight and contributing.

Opening his wallet, Mike found that he had sixty-eight dollars cash. He offered it to Eli, who thanked Mike and said it was more than sufficient. Eli loaned him an old shirt, and demonstrated how to pour cold water through the stained fabric of Mike's shirt to remove the blood. Then he hung Mike's shirt to dry.

While Mike's phone had a charge, he decided to send a message. He would only send one. He felt like a shit, but he sent a message to Connors instead of Liz. Mike wanted Liz to know he was okay, but it was Connors who was searching for Lyric, he reasoned. He would ask Connors to fill Liz in. The message read:

Guys that attacked kids jumped me last night. They work for Chapin. Made it out with help from friends. Lying low til guys are found. Lyric's here. She's fine. Tell Liz I'm okay & my love to the boys.

Chapter Sixty-two

"Mike's Message"

Connors got the news out that Mike was missing to anyone on the street who he thought could help. He could not launch an official search because Mike had not been missing for twenty-four hours, but he was doing what he could. They took a look at Mike's car and the effort yielded no evidence of violence. For all they knew, Mike had simply parked and left it there.

Liz wasn't answering her phone and that concerned Connors. With Mike missing, he wouldn't put a knee-jerk reaction past her. He might feel the same way if someone near and dear to him was missing and a character like Chapin was holding a grudge.

Connors found Quinn at the Youth Center and filled her in on what he knew about Mike's disappearance. Connors guessed that the scene witnessed by the flower vendor was a ploy made to look like street folks were involved. Connors' gut told him it was bullshit and Quinn agreed. But someone on the street may have seen something.

He shared with Quinn that he hadn't talked to Liz since early morning and Quinn hadn't seen her since Elle's goodbye. It went unsaid, but they both were concerned that Liz hadn't been in touch with either of them.

Connors felt his phone vibrate, alerting him to a new message. He read the message quickly, and then read it a second time. He looked at Quinn.

"What is it, Connors?" she asked. His expression told her it was important.

"Listen to this," he said as he began to read Mike's message aloud to Quinn. He watched Quinn's eyes take in the news with relief. At least they had heard from Mike. Then Connors had a thought.

"This message was sent from Mike's phone, but not necessarily from Mike," he reasoned. "Anyone with Mike's phone could have sent it."

"It's from Mike," said Quinn, "Only a very few close friends know that Mike and Liz referred to the cats as 'their boys.'"

"Yeah, true enough. He was jumped, he said, but he's safe. Somewhere," added Connors. "Mike says the guys that jumped him were the same two that Elle identified as her attackers. And that they work for Chapin. Morgan needs to know this. And wherever Mike is, Lyric, as Kyrie is known on the street, is with him."

Mike was with Lyric, thought Quinn. *That meant Sage knew where Mike was too*. The pieces were coming together and it made perfect sense to Quinn, but she kept quiet. Quinn and Connors had spoken with Sage earlier that morning. He told them he knew nothing about a missing man. So Sage was helping Mike as he'd been helping the girl.

"I'm glad to know they're both alright," she told Connors. It was a tough choice, but Quinn would keep the rest of what she knew to herself for now. It was risky, but if they moved too fast, the girl may run again.

"Absolutely, but Mike being in contact with the girl may have put them both in even more danger, if these guys do work for Chapin."

"Then you need to find them," answered Quinn, "and quickly. Before Chapin's men find them."

Connors knew Quinn was right. He needed a game plan and he was thinking about how to convey this new information to Liz and to Morgan when he got a call from Dispatch.

"Connors," he said when answered.

"Sergeant, Detective Morgan requested that you meet him at the scene of a suspicious death. Apparently, it's related to a current case of yours. He's at the home of...sorry, let me check the notes...a Gabriel Chapin. He said that you have the address. Parkdale police are on scene, as well."

"Got it, I'm on my way. Suspicious death? Do we have the ID of the deceased?"

"Yes, Sergeant. It's Mr. Chapin. He was found dead in his living room."

Chapter Sixty-three

"Guidance"

Quinn sat in her office with the door closed. The door was never closed unless she was in a meeting, but she needed privacy and quiet to think. The message Connors received from Mike was good news, but Quinn knew that Mike and Lyric were in danger. She wasn't a cop and she didn't presume to think like one. But Quinn had strengths of her own.

She was certain she could find their squat, but she didn't know much about possible places to hole up around here, not like she had in downtown Seattle. Quinn could not risk being followed. She wouldn't bring danger their way—and Sage trusted her to give him some time.

Quinn needed some guidance, the sort of guidance that she trusted. She picked up her tarot cards, held them in her hand as they absorbed her energy. She closed her eyes, and took a deep, cleaning breath to calm her spirit and open her mind.

She concentrated on the question at hand, not about finding the answer as much as how to approach the quest and whether she should even pursue it. Quinn turned the first card, and then placed it in the appropriate place, followed it with another, and then a third, continuing until the reading was complete. Quinn gathered the insight offered by the cards, knowing she was ready to proceed.

Connors arrived at Chapin's home, met at the end of the drive by a Parkdale officer. He was admitted to the scene and directed to find Morgan, who was expecting him. Inside, he spent a few minutes in conversation with Morgan and a Parkdale murder cop named Valentine. They brought Connors up to speed.

Approximately an hour ago, a passing neighbor walking a dog had been alerted to suspicious noises coming from the home at the other end of the drive. Well, actually, it had been the dog who had been alerted, pulling his owner toward the house. The fearful neighbor retreated, making a quick exit for his home on the next block to call the police. Chapin had been shot in the chest, most likely killed instantly. No weapon had been discovered at the scene. Morgan explained to Valentine that the deceased was involved in current investigations on their side of the river.

"Just what are you working on and how is this man connected?" asked Valentine. The veteran investigator's expression showed his interest along with a degree of skepticism.

"I'm with Missing Persons," Connors told Valentine. "I've been searching for Mr. Chapin's fifteen-year-old daughter. She's a runaway and we're convinced she's in Columbia City hiding among the throngs of street punks. At least she was. We have photos taken in the park downtown."

"As I told you before Connors arrived," said Morgan, "I'm looking for two assailants who attacked a couple of street punks across the river, one of whom died from their injuries."

"That's what you told us," said Valentine, "but why did that case bring you to my back yard? And why didn't you notify us?"

"I received a message that one of the assailants we're looking for, the one who has been ID's through an old mug shot, was at this address and wanted to talk to me. The guy's name is Espy and the message said he wouldn't wait long. I had no idea the place was connected to Connors' case until you told me who had been found dead. I planned on contacting your office before I approached the premises. But things got weird in a hurry."

It was Connors who spoke next. "Right before you called for me to meet you here, I received information that links this Espy guy to Chapin."

"How did you get that?" asked Morgan, with a blunt edge to the question.

"Records link both men to an old hood named Killian," said Connors. It was true, but he wasn't ready to say more.

"You two can continue to swap details at a more appropriate time, please," said Valentine, wanting to move things along. They went over the timeframe of the events, when the neighbor had walked by with the dog, and when Morgan had arrived at the scene.

"Detective Morgan," asked Valentine, "Who let you in?"

"I buzzed at the gate, but got no answer," Morgan explained, thinking fast. "The walk-through gate was open. I left my car on the street and walked up. To be honest, I was suspicious, having been told to meet a suspect, then finding no one around. I saw Chapin from the front window. The back entry was open. I did a quick search of the house. There was no one there."

"And you said things got weird in a hurry when you arrived here to meet up with this Espy character. How so?"

Morgan took a breath and looked at Connors before he answered. “I’m not sure I should say before I talk to my superiors.”

“Look here, Morgan,” said Valentine, “I’ve got a dead guy lying over here with a hole in his chest. If you saw something or have other information, you have to tell us, man. You know how these things roll. Every minute counts.”

Morgan sighed. “Did the witness with the dog mention seeing a vehicle leaving the premises?”

“No, he claims to have seen nothing like that,” replied Valentine.

“As I pulled up about to park on the street, I saw a car leaving. Lieutenant Liz Jordan was driving.”

Connors stared at Morgan in disbelief. “What are you talking about, Morgan?” he yelled. “Are you sure?”

“Of course, I’m sure, Connors!” Morgan yelled back just as loudly. “I know what I saw!”

“Pipe down or I’ll have you both escorted off my crime scene,” said Valentine with authority, his hands outstretched as if to fend off any more outbursts. “This Lieutenant Liz Jordan, she’s with your department, I take it.”

“Yes,” they answered in unison.

“Why would she be here? Is she overseeing the case?”

Connors listened with dread, while Morgan explained to Valentine that Liz had a connection to Chapin regarding an investigation that went back years. Then Connors shared that Lieutenant Jordan’s significant other, a man named Mike Dwyer had not been seen since the evening before.

This wasn’t a lie. Connors had not seen Mike—he had only received the message that he was okay. But Connors wasn't going to reveal that detail or that Chapin had recently threatened Liz.

"Alright, guys. Thanks. I need to talk to Lieutenant Jordan. Who does she report to?" asked Detective Valentine.

Chapter Sixty-four

"Another Knock at the Door"

Liz was an emotional mess when she left Chapin's home. She was operating on worry, adrenalin and little sleep. She drove straight to her apartment. When she arrived home, she returned the .357 to the gun safe, fed Eddie and Little Kurt, started a fresh pot of coffee and stepped into the shower. The piping hot water washing over her helped collect her wits. *What the hell had happened to Mike? Where was he? Was he okay?* Chapin had been no help regardless of how hard she had tried to get information from him.

Richelle was no help either, although even if she knew anything, loyalty kept her quiet. Connors had told Liz that the photos of Lyric had originated on a phone other than Chapin's. Liz had asked him about it. Chapin ignored the question and blew it off as insignificant, but Richelle didn't look pleased. She met Liz's eyes with an expression of disgust that said *I'm finished covering for this guy.*

Liz suspected that he had taken them from Richelle's phone without her knowing. Kyrie had wanted to stay in contact with Richelle, but not her father. He wasn't going to acknowledge that slap in the face.

Out of the shower and dressed, Liz remained plagued with worry. She poured coffee for herself and sat on the couch. There was not much Liz could do except wait for word about Mike. In a few hours, if he had not been found, an official search could begin. Even with the coffee in her system, she drifted off. When she stirred herself awake, she wasn't sure how long she had been out but the coffee mug was cool to the touch.

Liz realized that the alerts on her phone were turned off and that she had missed several calls from Connors. She hoped he had some news about Mike. She started to call him back, but here was a knock on her front door.

Stepping to the tiny, secret window to the side of the door, she was surprised to see Captain Miller. She opened the door to greet him.

"Captain," she said. Then Liz saw that behind Miller stood a man she didn't recognize.

"Lieutenant, may we come in?" requested Miller.

"Yes, of course, Sir. What is this?" She moved aside so the two men could enter her home and Liz was hit with sudden panic. *No, no,* she thought, *please, this cannot be about Mike.* She closed the door and turned to look each man in the eye, one at a time, searching for answers.

"Lieutenant Jordan, this is Detective Valentine with the police in Parkdale, Oregon." Liz and Valentine exchanged nods of polite acknowledgement at the introductions. "I was contacted by Detective Valentine because Gabriel Chapin was found dead in his home this morning."

"What?! Chapin's dead?" Liz asked them. She was shocked, but relieved that the visit wasn't about Mike.

"Yes, Lieutenant, it appears that he is," said Valentine. "Can you tell us where you were earlier?"

"Me? Why?"

"Because you were seen leaving his home," answered the detective.

Liz started to ask, *by whom?* But she knew it didn't matter.

"Detective Valentine has requested an interview with you with regarding Mr. Chapin's death and under the circumstances, I'm compelled to grant it," said Miller. "He's agreed to conduct the interview in our precinct and with me present."

Liz was shocked. Chapin was dead? She'd been seen leaving his place? She was to be *interviewed,* a nice way of saying *questioned,* by a detective from another department? *Shit, shit, shit!!*

"Shall we, Lieutenant?" said Miller, indicating the door.

"Let me get my jacket." Liz looked at Miller and asked, "Is there any news about Mike?"

"Not that I'm aware of," answered Miller. "But we will find out."

Chapter Sixty-five

"Questions"

The interview room at the precinct was familiar to Liz. She had been in the room many, many times, but always as the one to ask the questions or to observe one of her team as they questioned a person of interest. At this moment, the room felt alien, as though she had never been inside it before. She belonged on the other side of the table. Liz was fortunate that, due to her rank, every courtesy possible was extended. At least for now.

This was serious, but Liz was too anxious about Mike to trust her responses to be accurate and helpful. She needed to get a grip on herself. She was, after all, being questioned about a suspicious death, and she had been observed leaving the scene.

She had been sitting in the interview room alone when the door opened and Valentine, the homicide cop from Parkdale was led into the room by Captain Miller. Liz could only imagine what they may have shared with each other already, but she trusted the Captain. Miller and Valentine took seats at the table across from Liz.

"Is there any word about Mike?" Liz asked. "I could handle this shit storm a lot better if I knew he was okay."

"No, we haven't heard anything yet. I'm sorry," said Miller, shaking his head. "Listen to me, Liz. Gabriel Chapin is dead. The two of you are connected by incidents in your background. He filed a lawsuit naming you as a responsible party. It's on record with the department that he threatened you. You need to clear your head and tell us exactly what happened this morning. And you'd better start with last night."

"Yes, you're right," Liz answered, her forehead resting on outstretched fingertips. "I talked with you about six-thirty or seven. I was waiting for Mike to come home when we talked." Liz placed her hands on the table, her arms straight, and sat back in her chair. "Mike didn't come home all night. I tried to reach him several times. I didn't hear back. I finally called Connors early this morning. He couldn't do much officially at that point, but I was calling him as Mike's friend. And mine."

"It was about six this morning when you talked with Connors?"

"Yes, I think it was around six. I waited until it was light. Connors listened to what I had to say. He called back an hour later, told me that Mike's car was parked near his office. He said a call had come in yesterday evening about some odd activity that might have involved a group of street folks in the same neighborhood. He felt the circumstances warranted having Mike's car checked out and did I agree? Of course, I agreed. It didn't matter if I agreed or not—Connors didn't need my permission anyway."

Miller nodded. "Okay, Lieutenant. We're listening. Tell Detective Valentine what happened."

"I was at Chapin's home. I planned to confront him. He is behind this, I know it, Captain. There is no other explanation," said Liz, shaking her head. "The shit bag threatened me. His wanted to intimidate me. He has to control things," explained Liz, her volume rising with each point she made, accentuating the words, *threatened, intimidate, control,* making each sound especially pointed.

"Lieutenant, you need to calm down," said Valentine. "Take a minute, and then tell us what happened at Chapin's home."

"His admin, Richelle Isaacs, answered the call from the security gate."

"And she let you in, just like that?"

"No. Not at first."

"What did you tell her, Lieutenant?"

Liz was direct. She looked Valentine in the eye. "I needed to talk to him. I told her either she could let me in, or I could drive through the gate."

"You're a police Lieutenant," said Valentine. "And you threatened to barge into a private residence?"

"Captain, Mike is missing!" she exclaimed, ignoring Valentine and directing her answer to Captain Miller. "Chapin knew where he is, I was convinced of it."

"Were you armed?" asked Valentine. Miller was listening intently, but he allowed Valentine to ask his questions.

Liz didn't want to answer that question. She chewed the corner of her lip, stared daggers at the detective. "Yes. I had my back-up," said Liz.

"Did you draw it, Lieutenant?" asked Valentine, in a direct tone.

"The asshole had threatened me! He stood there and told me it sucks to have someone you love go missing! He should have told me where Mike was!"

"Did he?" asked Valentine, in the same tone.

"No, or I wouldn't have gone home, would I?" she shouted back.

Liz stopped herself, apologized to Valentine for the attitude. "Sorry, but if he had told me anything useful, I would have gone to find Mike. I pulled my gun to scare him, but he wasn't scared enough to tell me anything. He might have been shot, but I did not shoot him. I wanted to, damn it, I wanted to! But Chapin was alive when I left. My weapon hasn't been fired. Richelle was there. She will tell you that what I'm saying is true."

"And you went straight home when you left," asked Valentine.

"I did."

"Did you shower when you got home?"

Liz looked at Valentine after he asked the question. *Why would he ask that?* Then she realized that Valentine was gathering his own evidence, and not in Liz's favor.

"Yes."

"Your back-up, where is it now?" the detective asked her.

"Locked in my gun safe. In my bedroom."

The impact of Valentine's questions hit her, and Liz became agitated, her volume increased again. She looked at Miller.

"Hold on! Are they searching my place?! Did they obtain a warrant, Captain?" Liz could scarcely believe she was asking these questions.

"No," answered Miller. "At least, not yet, but it could happen. And there's nothing else you want to tell us?"

"No," answered Liz, trying to calm down. "I don't think so. I pulled my weapon because I wanted to know what happened to Mike. That's it. Look, I know the man is dead, but my unfired weapon and Richelle's statement will clear me."

"As for your weapon, yes, that's true," said Valentine. "Will you allow us to retrieve it for testing?"

"Of course. But what about Richelle?" Liz felt her stomach clench. "She wasn't shot. Was she?"

"We don't know," Valentine told Liz. "Let's hope not, but there's no trace of her at the home. Richelle Isaacs was not found in the house—alive, dead or wounded." Valentine acted as though he didn't believe that the woman had even been there, although Liz figured he was just hedging his bets.

"When the housekeeper returned from shopping" Valentine continued, "she found her place of employment in chaos, cops everywhere. She had not seen Ms. Isaacs that morning, she told us. The only person she had seen or spoken with on the premises was her employer, Mr. Chapin."

Liz learned that it was Reese Morgan who had reported seeing her leave Chapin's house. He was there, he told them, acting on a tip that he could find one of the assailants in the Youth Center case on the premises.

"Wait," said Liz. "Morgan saw me leave Chapin's home and I don't deny being there, but Morgan was there, too. Why aren't you talking with him?"

Miller and Valentine shared a look. It was Valentine who answered.

"We are. We're talking with anyone, including Morgan, who can offer anything to the time frame. Morgan was first on the scene. He discovered Chapin's body. According to Morgan, he arrived as you were leaving. We can time his arrival to a radio call he made to Parkdale police. The call was patched in soon after the neighbor with the dog called 911. We appreciated knowing there was an officer there."

"We have to acknowledge the fact that Morgan was on duty, Liz," said Miller. "He had a legitimate reason for being there. Unfortunately, you didn't."

There were details that Valentine didn't share with Liz. He didn't know what the details meant as of yet, but when he discussed them with his captain over in Parkdale, they made the decision to share the following information only with Captain Miller:

First, Gabriel Chapin's BMW was found in the garage for everyone to see, but Richelle Isaacs owned a late-model Nissan that was seen in the neighborhood frequently. Her vehicle was not parked in the usual spot behind the house, nor was it in the garage, or anywhere else on the premises.

Then, a set of tire tracks was discovered at the rear of the residence, but they did not match either Chapin's BMW or Isaacs' Nissan. *Interesting, but the vehicle that left the tracks could have been driven by anyone,* they told themselves. And all they had at this point were tracks.

Finally, when Valentine looked into the emergency call made to police that morning, he found that it was not placed by the neighbor walking the dog, as was initially assumed. When questioned again for other details, the neighbor stated that he intended to call 911, but then heard sirens. Valentine had not been able to determine who had placed that call. Yet.

Chapter Sixty-six

"Search"

Quinn studied herself in the mirror. She was dressed as her former punk self, in old jeans, a tattered hoodie, and an ancient down vest. Her short, black hair was in the wild style of a crusty, urban punk. She wore an old, but decent pair of heavy boots because on the street, if your shoes are falling apart, you do something about it. If anyone told her that she looked like the new manager at the Youth Center, her response would be 'Yeah, I hear that a lot, but that bitch is way older than me'.

In her hand she held a small knife, the blade concealed in a leather sheath. She had stolen the knife from her stepfather, who was the reason she sought refuge on the streets in the first place. Her mother's asshole husband had been grooming her for abuse for years and when he finally tried to force himself on her, she'd hit him on the side of the head with a baseball bat.

She checked the blade—it was sharp and clean, and the spring on the hinge was tight. She'd never cut anyone with the knife, but had, on occasion, made the threat. Quinn was certain that without that little knife, she probably would not have survived the street.

Thinking of looking for the squat made her think of the ugly, shitty places her crew had used to get off the streets. She thought of Misty, Liam and Howie. Although she had lost track of Misty ages ago, she still saw Liam and Howie once in a while. They were still a couple, living in Eugene, and had started a family together. Quinn thought about another friend from those days, the one that brought Liz to her in Seattle last year. Quinn shook that memory from her mind. It was too depressing

She stepped out of her tiny downtown apartment, determined to find the squat and offer help to the gutter punk known as Lyric. Having lived the life, Quinn was convinced that she needed to find the girl before the cops did. She knew the girl's frame of mind—that cops meant trouble for punks, pure and simple. Persuading Lyric to believe otherwise would be difficult.

And there were two dangerous men out there somewhere, intent on finding Lyric and returning her to her father. They had tried to grab Mike. He knew he was still in danger, that's why he was hiding. Quinn would put nothing past these creeps. They had killed Pooki and put Elle in the hospital. She figured there was no time to lose.

Quinn walked a few blocks south and headed to the park. She avoided walking fast, like she had somewhere to be. Punks had nowhere to be. She sat on a picnic table, took a sip from the bottle of water she carried clipped on her pack.

In the ER, Elle told Castillo that she and Pooki had been squatting in an abandoned building down by the railroad tracks, so it made sense to start there. Quinn watched vehicles maneuver quickly through the industrial area nestled into the lowland valley. Fruit orchards, berry fields, and canneries were built there decades ago, with irrigation systems drawing from the lake further to the west. Two or three of the canneries were still operating seasonally, but it wasn't harvest time so there was nothing happening. Most of the once-prosperous enterprises were now abandoned.

Quinn figured she would encounter a few of the old-timers, the long-displaced folks who had claimed spots under the railroad overpasses. In some ways, the street dwellers were no different than any other faction of the population: there were folks who might genuinely help you, some who could be trusted to a degree, and there were others who you never, ever wanted to turn your back on.

Chapter Sixty-seven

"Harley"

Approaching the overpass, Quinn looked around at the groups of people huddled around makeshift campfires, staying warm, cooking simple meals. Others were passing a bottle around, many were smoking. She heard the sharp, lonesome strains of a harmonica somewhere nearby and saw an excited dog or two wagging their tails.

Shit, thought, Quinn. If and when she found the squat, it would be protected by Zeke the cattle dog, as sentry. Sage had trusted the pup enough to leave him "with friends" that morning when she and Connors had asked him if he'd seen Mike. She didn't know it then, but Zeke must have been left with Mike and Lyric.

Maybe Zeke wasn't as hard to get along with as Sage had initially made out, but the last thing Quinn was going to do was bother a dog she didn't know. Better to stay clear. Everyone knew that. That's why so many street folks' best friend is their dog.

Mike had his phone. He had texted Connors. *Should I let him know I'm looking for him? What if Mike wasn't the one to see the text? How would Sage react if she came walking up?*

Quinn decided to take the chance and texted Mike:

Read your text to Connors. Tell Sage I'm looking for you.

A few minutes later, a response popped up:

Ok. Good. I'll get back to you.

Quinn put her phone way. Before she could decide on her next move, a man sitting near a fire burning in a short barrel hailed her over.

"Hey, dearie," he said, "You wouldn't have an extra smoke on you, would you?"

Quinn approached him, reaching for the pack of cigarettes she had thought to have with her for such occasions.

"Sure," she said, assuming an attitude, "and while I appreciate the benefit of the doubt, I ain't exactly a dearie." She handed the old guy a smoke, which he accepted with a nod of his head.

"Oh, now, yes you are. And I thank you kindly, dearie," he responded, as he placed a long twig in the fire waited for it to ignite, then lit his cigarette from it. He inhaled deeply, and was soon wrapped in a dose of nicotine. "I'm Harley. On account of I used to ride." Harley took another deep drag.

"I'm Hadley," she answered, giving her surname, but not indicating it as such.

"Hadley and Harley, that makes us quite a pair," he said with a chuckle. "I can offer you a cup of joe," said Harley.

"It sounds okay, but I'll pass." Harley nodded, smoked his cigarette. "But if you don't mind, can I sit here for a bit?" Quinn asked.

"Of course, you can. Take a load off, dearie."

"Thanks. I'm looking for a friend. Said he was down this way," said Quinn, looking around. "Thought I would have found him by now."

"Your friend got a car?" Harley asked.

"Hell, no," she laughed. "What do you think?"

"Just asking is all. You be careful. There's new folk down that way." Harley pointed toward one of the old cannery sites a few hundred yards away.

"Oh yeah?" said Quinn, feigning interest. She looked in the direction Harley had indicated as she took a cigarette out of the pack for herself. Quinn wasn't a smoker, but she could pretend. She hoped to keep Harley talking by offering him another, which he readily accepted.

Harley nodded. "Can't quite figure out what's happening. Don't trust 'em though."

"Why?" she asked, as she lit the smoke, preparing to make it look as if she inhaled.

"Well, for one thing, they do got a car, but there ain't much in it. They sure aren't living in it. Why hole up in an old dusty shed if you got a car to sleep in?" Street logic and Quinn agreed. She nodded at Harley's words.

"How long they been there?" she asked.

"Since this morning," he said. "Watched 'em pull up."

"Huh. How many?" asked Quinn.

"Two fellas. A man got out of the car and checked the place out. Then another guy got out of the car and went inside. Ain't seen 'em since. Pulled the car around the other side. I saw it when I was searching for bottles."

"Two guys, huh?"

"Uh-huh, and these guys don't look like folks I want to tangle with," said Harley.

"You already got enough to handle," Quinn told the old man, empathizing with his situation. On the street you tend to mind your business and never borrow trouble. "What do they look like?"

"One older guy, big fella. Younger, skinny guy. Slick. If you ask me," said Harley with a secretive tone, his hand held to one side of his mouth, "they're hiding."

Quinn listened as Harley described the two men who had attacked Elle and Pooki.

"Huh," answered Quinn, appearing to think about it. "Best to leave it."

"If you wanna take a look, I can watch for you," offered Harley.

"I don't know. Let me find my friend first. See what he thinks."

"I'll be right here—always here, dearie. Good luck finding your friend."

Chapter Sixty-eight

"The Shed"

Leaving Harley with one last cigarette for later, Quinn thanked him for the spot to hang out. She thought about what the man had to say. Folks on the street can get confused. Others are keenly observant and have a gift for detail or they wouldn't have survived the life. Quinn placed Harley with the keen observers.

There was specific danger attached to the two men whom he had described, but Harley wouldn't know that Quinn was aware of it. He had warned her about the "new folks" but asked about a car first, keeping his cards close. He wanted to know if the friend she was looking for was one of the "new folk" he'd seen earlier. She chose to believe that the old guy was worried for his own safety and wanted Quinn to be careful. Aside from it all, Quinn was curious.

It was beyond dusk and Quinn was both grateful for the cover of darkness and anxious at the added risk to her safety that the night brought with it. She left the encampment and walked back to the street and then in the direction of the abandoned shed.

The rickety structure was around ten feet by thirty. It looked to have been used for storage. Through a covered window, a faint light moved, fluttered, like a flashlight in motion. Someone was in there. Situated below the windowless door were three cinderblock steps. This one door looked to be the only way in or out.

The car Harley had seen was parked under an attached cover intended for smaller pieces of equipment. The small sedan was backed in. Effort was given to clearing the area of a dozen or so boxes and crates that were now positioned to obstruct the car from view. If Harley hadn't mentioned the vehicle, Quinn might not have noticed it.

What if this wasn't the creeps? What if they were just down-on-their-luck folks, trying to get off the street, she asked herself. No, it was the assholes. Not enough stuff in the car to be living in it, Harley was right about that. And he had described them to a tee.

She sat in the darkness a safe distance away from the shed, listening. No sound came from the shed. *I'm not a cop,* said Quinn to herself. *There's only so much I can do.* She took her phone out and called Connors, but the call went to voice mail. There was another person Quinn could ask to help.

Chapter Sixty-nine

"Call for Help"

Liz returned to her apartment a few hours later. She had agreed to have both of her weapons analyzed. She knew neither of them had been fired. Valentine allowed Miller to retrieve them himself, but the ballistic tests were run at the lab in Parkdale.

When it was determined that Liz was telling the truth, at least about her own weapons, Miller had returned the guns to her with express instructions that they be returned to the gun safe.

Valentine was satisfied that Chapin had not been killed with either of Liz's handguns, but she had been seen at his residence around the time he died. Liz was to remain available in case there were other questions for her. Miller assured Valentine of his confidence in his Lieutenant, and Liz knew it was the only reason she wasn't held.

And Liz had a few questions of her own: *who had shot Chapin in the chest? Where was Richelle Isaacs? Where was Lyric? And most importantly, where was Mike? What the hell had happened to him?* If he had been harmed, Liz would never forgive herself. And she would never give up until she found out who was to blame.

Liz's phone rang. She saw that it was Quinn and answered the call.

"I'm glad you answered. I need your help," Quinn told Liz, keeping her voice down.

"Quinn? Where are you? What's going on?"

"I'm down on the westside, near the tracks. I'm looking for Sage's squat. I want to find Lyric. Have you talked to Connors?

"Not yet. I know he's been trying to get in touch with me. I was unavailable for a while." Liz explained to Quinn that Gabriel Chapin was dead, that she'd been questioned after being seen at his home and that Richelle Isaacs was missing.

"Chapin? The missing girl's father? This is turning into a mess."

"You said you need help," Liz said. "Where are you? Are you okay?"

"Yes, I'm okay. I tried to call Connors. He didn't pick up—that's why I'm calling you. Listen, Liz. Connors received a text message from Mike earlier today. We still don't know where he is, but we know he's okay. He told Connors that he's hiding somewhere. Mike asked him to let you know he's in good hands. Then Connors got a call and took off in a hurry. It must have been about Chapin."

"Thank God," Liz managed to whisper, under her breath. Sucking in air, Liz was able to take a deep breath for the first time since late last night. She sat down, grasping at the meaning of Quinn's words. Mike was okay.

"His message said that the guys who attacked the kids jumped him last night. He said they work for Chapin," explained Quinn. "Mike said he was rescued by friends and is hiding until the jerks are found."

Relieved, Liz tried to focus on the rest of what Quinn was saying "He was jumped by the guys that assaulted the two punks? And they are connected to Chapin? I knew it. My gut knew it. It just made sense."

"Mike also mentioned Lyric," said Quinn. "She's there with him. You and I both know she's with Sage. So, Mike is there with them too."

Liz was stunned by what she was hearing, but she trusted Quinn. "Start over, tell me what's going on."

"Well, there's more to it than that. I found the jerks that hurt the kids. I know where they're hiding."

Connors sat at a table in the room the coordinating teams were using as a command center. He was piecing together information that was coming from a variety of sources—records, interviews, even from Quinn and Mike. He needed to talk with Morgan, tell him about the connection between the men Morgan was searching for regarding the punk's death, the attack on Mike, and the missing girl Connors was trying to find.

Morgan had shared with Valentine about seeing Liz at Chapin's home and he had been positive it was Liz. Connors knew Morgan had to share the information, but he wished he had been able to talk with Liz about it, find out what was going on first. And now Liz had been questioned about Chapin's death and that was not a happy circumstance.

He glanced around the large room. Connors looked around for Morgan, but wasn't seeing him. Maybe Valentine knew where he was. Morgan had taken a call and stepped out, but that was some time ago. He should have been back by now. *Where the hell was Morgan?*

Valentine stepped into the room and waved Connors down. "There's been a development."

Chapter Seventy

"Harmonies"

After too much time sitting and laying around, Mike needed to stretch his legs. He walked back and forth between the railroad tracks and the abandoned building where Sage and his friends had set up their refuge from the world.

As he walked, Mike considered his experiences over the past two days. He had been lured under false pretenses and attacked by criminals who considered it their job to kidnap him, maybe end his life. He owed that life to two gutter punks named Sage and Lyric and to Zeke, the cattle dog. His injuries had been nursed by a compassionate, knowledgeable former army medic, named Eli, holed up in an abandoned fruit processing plant.

He had offered his Good Samaritans less than seventy bucks for their help because it was all he had on him. He and Liz could easily blow that much on dinner out, but to Sage and the crew, it was a windfall. Eli had accepted the contribution with gratitude and hadn't asked for more. The juxtaposition was mind-blowing.

That afternoon, Mike listened while Sage and Lyric sang a few songs with Sage on guitar. On a couple of tunes, Eli joined in on harmonica. They began with a tune Mike wasn't familiar with, but he was honored, nonetheless. The song was simple, it's meaning unmistakable.

I am weary and spent, down so, very low / Dirty and ill, filled with sadness and woe / If this were a dream I'd wake from this hell / How can I make it in a cold, cold world? / No pillow, no blanket, no lock, no door / Where is that alley that I slept in before? / I have no comfort, no warmth, no friend / Why do I stay, in this cold, cold world?

Their voices blended beautifully. It was the first time Mike had heard Lyric sing and her voice was impressive. Mike requested a Dylan song, knowing Sage had several in his repertoire. They delivered a moving duet of "If You See Her, Say Hello" that nearly brought Mike to tears.

When they finished, Mike couldn't resist an opportunity to ask about Sage's past.

"Where did you learn to play?" Mike asked Sage. "Are you self-taught? And how did you learn so many great songs from decades before you were born?"

Sage looked down at Zeke nestled in beside him. He gently stroked the dog's soft fur. Sage glanced over at Eli, who encouraged him to answer. "I studied music for seven years, starting with piano when I was nine. My grandmother had a piano. She played, as well, and encouraged me. It was an easy transition to guitar. People often don't realize the connection, but they are both stringed instruments. The basics are the same."

"You're quite accomplished," said Mike.

"He is," added Lyric. "Sage has taught me a lot about music theory. I didn't get the theory training because I didn't play an instrument."

"But you write songs," Sage pointed out to her. "The first song we sang, 'Cold World', was written by Lyric," Sage told Mike. "I put her words to music."

"Like the one on the wall at the Youth Center," said Mike. "It's beautiful, Lyric. Poignant."

"Yeah," she said. "Thank you."

They all looked at Sage, urging him to continue his story. "I went to live with my grandparents when I was eight. My dad was gone and my mom, their daughter, had problems with drugs and alcohol. Grandmother saw music as an outlet for me. Then my grandfather died when I was thirteen, my grandmother three years later. The state said I had to live with my mom again. They said she was stable enough. I was smart enough to know that was bullshit. So, I took off."

"I'm sorry to hear that, Sage," Mike said, and he meant it.

"Thanks. And I'm sorry to tell it. My grandparents were sixties and seventies music fans—folk, rock, blues—all of it. They were big on Dylan, especially my grandfather. To hear them tell it, they had been on the fringes when they were young. Maybe that's where I get it. This was my grandfather's guitar," he said, stroking the instrument with reverence. "It was the only possession of theirs I took with me when I left."

Mike felt his phone vibrate indicating a text message:

Chapin found dead this morning. Still searching for suspects. I get that you want to hide but need to bring girl in soon.

The message was from Connors. Chapin was dead?! Mike was shocked by the news, but even as he looked at Lyric, he couldn't feel sadness. He knew Connors was trying to be patient, but he was anxious to have Lyric in custody for her own protection.

Mike waited to talk to Sage alone. Finally, Lyric stepped away to help Eli.

"I need to tell you a couple of things," Mike whispered, glancing toward the entrance, and then looked back at Sage. "There's a coordinated search going on for the two assholes that jumped me. They were already sought for questioning about Elle and Pooki's attack."

"Good," replied Sage, nodding. "I hope the cops find them."

"Me too. I hope they lock them away for a long time," said Mike.

Sage studied Mike for a moment, and then asked, "What else aren't you saying?"

"Quinn's wandering around down here. She's looking for us." Sage's expression was unreadable. "It seems that Connors shared my text with her. She wants to help."

"Help with what?" asked Sage.

"She's a youth advocate," Mike explained with a shrug. "I'd say her main motivation is to offer help to Lyric, the same way she helped Elle. I doubt she's interested in getting in your business. Or Eli's."

Sage continued to study Mike's face. He stroked his whiskers, fingered his dreads, thought about what Mike had to say. "Well, if I had to place a bet on someone finding us, it would be Quinn. Her knowledge of the street is part of her."

"It is, and like you said, the life never leaves you," said Mike. "I think you can trust her, but it's up to you. That's why I'm telling you this."

"I trust her, but if it's Lyric that Quinn is interested in helping, then it's up to Lyric to decide whether she talks with her," Sage explained, the decision made. "Same for Eli. I will explain things to him, that I trust Quinn and why, but he won't like it. He's nervous around people he doesn't know. And he doesn't know many people."

"I understand," said Mike. "I'll follow your lead. I owe you that much. But aside from Quinn, there's an active police search for the girl. Can't hold them off for too long."

Around the corner in the dark, near the entrance to the squat, Lyric was listening to Mike and Sage's conversation. The police were looking for the men who jumped Mike in the alley—and they were searching for her. She was only fifteen. They would make her go home. To her father.

Lyric was not about to let them find her. She wasn't going home no matter what. She was in a panic as she flew around the corner to confront them.

"Your friend is coming here? The cops are on their way?! They're going to make me go home! Please don't let them take me!" she pleaded with Sage. Then she turned to Mike. "I helped you! Please don't let them do this! If they take me home, I'll run again!"

"Lyric, listen," began Mike. But she was in a state. Sage started to approach her but she resisted.

"No, no! I have to get out of here before they find me!" Lyric ran over to her bed, grabbed a backpack and started stuffing things inside it. Eli had heard their voices and hurried inside, a worried look on his face.

Mike went to Lyric. He held the girl and tried to calm her.

"I'm not going home! I won't do it," she exclaimed, shaking her head in defiance.

"Lyric, listen to me. Sit down for a minute and listen," Mike begged the girl.

It was a struggle to convince her to comply, but she sat down. Mike sat next to her.

"You won't be going back to your father," he said calmly. "I'm sorry to tell you that he was killed earlier today."

"What? What are you saying?" Lyric's panic was replaced with shock. "My father's dead? What happened?"

"I don't have any other info. That's all I know. I'm sorry."

Lyric melted as the news sunk in, not from sorrow as much as the shock. She fell against Mike, letting him support her.

Chapter Seventy-one

"Surprise, Surprise"

Quinn explained to Liz what she'd learned from Harley, about two suspicious men in a shed down near the old canneries, that he described them to be the two who had attacked the kids.

"It's an abandoned storage shed and there is someone in there. They tried to hide their vehicle. If they aren't homeless, they're hiding."

Liz considered the mess she was in already. First the lawsuit, and now Chapin had been shot and she'd been seen leaving his house. She decided she didn't give a shit about any of it. None of that mattered to her. All Liz could think about was finding Mike. And Quinn had discovered where two men, most likely Espy and his friend, were hiding.

"You could be right," she told Quinn. "If these are the assholes we are looking for, we need to find Mike before they do. Tell me how to find you."

"Come west down River Road, that way you'll miss the overpass and draw less attention," Quinn directed. "Park your car near the strawberry fields and walk west, toward the tracks. There's a large sign that says Wiley Nursery. I'm near the sign, off the road."

"River Road, find the Wiley Nursery sign. Got it. And Quinn, we'll check it out, but we will alert Connors. That's it. Then we find Mike. Do you understand?"

"Yes, of course, we will."

If Quinn had found the lair where these morons were hiding, Liz decided the best move was to contact Connors and have the police take them into custody. If they weren't the two men they were looking for, they would walk away and find Mike.

Walking into her bedroom, Liz remembered promising Miller that she would keep her weapons locked up. That was the reason they were returned to her after the visit to Chapin's home. But she made that promise before she knew what had happened to Mike, before Quinn had asked for help.

Liz was a cop. If she needed to protect herself, or someone else, she would. Again, she removed the .357 from the safe. She saw the plastic cuffs and grabbed them too. The weapon was holstered and Liz knew it was loaded. She strapped it on, grabbed her jacket, and left the apartment.

Following Quinn's instructions, Liz headed west, down River Road through the light industrial area. She passed a few small outbuildings, most of them empty. Not one vehicle had come down the road in either direction. She passed the dormant fields where the strawberries grew in the spring and pulled over onto a dirt road. Liz stopped and got out of the car. She locked it and continued west on foot.

Up ahead, Liz could see a large, beat-up sign. She was too far away to read what it said, but assumed it designated the Wiley Nursery. Within a few steps, she saw that she had been correct. *Wiley Nursery, Est. 1952.* Liz saw something move toward the rear of the sign.

"Liz," she heard a voice say. It was Quinn, waving her over. She was crouched low, partially hidden by the large sign. Liz joined her behind the sign.

"That's the shed," Quinn said, pointing about a hundred yards further to the west. "There's been some activity. I was afraid they were going to take off. One of the guys came outside, walked over by the car, and then went back inside. It looked like the younger one."

Liz surveyed the area between where they hid and the shed. There were bushes to one side and an embankment across the road obscured by brush.

"Let's get closer. I want to know who's in there." She pointed to the embankment. "And just so you know, Quinn, I'm armed. I won't use it unless I need to, unless one of us is in danger. I hope it won't come to that."

Quinn nodded. She felt for her knife. It was attached to a tight leather strap around her shoulder and under one arm, much like a holster. "I have my blade. I've never had to do more than show it. I hope my good fortune continues."

They moved closer to the shed, careful to stay behind the brush in the embankment. Liz saw the movement of light inside. If it hadn't been dark out, she'd not have noticed. She heard a voice, a man's voice. Liz looked at Quinn and knew she'd heard it too. The door opened and a man stepped onto the front step. He closed the door behind him, walked down the cinderblock steps. He paused at the bottom of the steps and lit a cigarette.

In the light cast by the momentary flame of the lighter, Liz saw that it was Espy, the older of the two men sought for the attack on the kids. He wore a bandage on one arm between his wrist and elbow. This was the man who had worked for Chapin and been linked to Killian. He and his accomplice had attacked the punks, leading to Pooki's death. And they had tried to grab Mike.

Liz's plan to call Connors went out the window as soon as she saw the asshole. Fear, worry and stress had left a bitter taste in her mouth. She could hope to have a part in seeing the creeps face justice, but Liz wanted her own revenge first.

She exchanged a look with Quinn, whose eyes had been peeled on the man. They both nodded, each conveying silently, *yes, it's them.*

"When he goes back inside, we'll call Connors," said Quinn, gesturing to make up for the lack of volume.

"Screw that. These shit bags could be gone by the time a team arrived. We'd have to stop them, Quinn." Liz was rationalizing, but at this point she didn't care.

"Okay," Quinn told Liz, not that she wanted to be responsible for stopping these men, but she would trust Liz. "Tell me what to do."

Rushing the place wasn't an option. Even with Liz and another officer it would be too risky, not knowing who else was inside.

Liz looked at Quinn, and said, "We need to take them one at a time, quietly and by surprise."

Espy was enjoying his cigarette. "Come on, you son of a bitch," whispered Liz. "Move away from the shed."

They heard a rustle in the brush a dozen yards from where they hid. It sounded too big to be a bird, maybe a rabbit or a stray cat. Espy heard it, too. Liz and Quinn watched as he looked in the direction of the sound, and then walked a few paces down the road. They watched as Espy reached down and picked up a rock, then walked toward the sound's origin. He came to within twenty feet of the spot where Liz and Quinn were hiding and tossed the stone into the brush. They heard the yowl of a disturbed feral cat as it scurried away. Espy seemed to enjoy the sport. He chuckled to himself, and then continued to enjoy his cigarette.

"Maybe you can distract him," whispered Liz. "I can surprise him from behind." Quinn nodded. Liz didn't know how the plan might play out, but if Quinn was willing, so was she.

Liz glanced in the direction of the shed. There was enough distance between them that if they were quiet, they might not be heard. It was a chance they would have to take. And they wouldn't have a lot of time.

Before Liz realized what was happening, Quinn had made a move. She crawled up the embankment and stepped out of the brush onto the road.

"Hey, mister, that's my cat! What the hell you doing?" she asked the guy. Espy was caught off guard. He gaped at Quinn like she was a crazy person. The burning cigarette fell from his open mouth. *Shit!* thought Liz.

"I've been looking for him all fucking day, and you throw rocks at him!" Quinn sounded unhinged, her arms outstretched in exasperation. She moved to the center of the road, hoping the idiot would follow her lead and keep his back to Liz. Espy moved in the direction Quinn wanted. He gaped at Quinn, trying to make sense of what he was hearing, but Espy wasn't falling for it.

"Bullshit. You got no cat. Get the hell outta here, stupid punk." Espy waved his arms at Quinn as if her presence was of no consequence.

This was their chance. Liz climbed up the embankment and was on the guy instantly. She wanted him on the ground, figuring that was the only way to match his size and strength. With her full weight, he shoved him from behind, knocking him off his feet.

Holy shit, thought Liz. It felt like she had run full speed into a wall of meat. Espy went down on his hands and knees, but he got himself up on his feet. Quinn had the sense to move opposite Liz in Espy's field of vision, so he couldn't keep an eye on them both at the same time.

"What the hell is this?" he studied Liz for a moment, then said, "You're a little old for a punk, ain't yuh?" He glanced over at Quinn, then back at Liz. "This'll be fun."

Quinn looked toward the shed. There had been no motion or sound from that direction, but it was only a matter of time. One shout from Espy and they would have company.

"I'm a police officer," Liz advised him. "I'm arresting you on suspicion of aggravated assault." It was a risky move on Liz's part. She was not carrying her shield, but at the moment she didn't care. Liz pulled her jacket back enough to show Espy her sidearm.

Liz's statement and the sight of her weapon caught Espy off guard, but the tough-guy attitude returned quickly enough.

"Like hell you are," he snickered. "You two little bitches ain't no threat."

In a flash, Espy moved toward Liz and planted a backhanded blow across her face. Liz went down on one knee before she knew what happened. The smack was hard; it felt like the side of her face had exploded. She tasted blood.

Figuring the situation was going to get out of control fast, Quinn threw herself at Espy from behind with all the force she could muster. He went down on his knees and Quinn kicked him in the side. Espy grabbed Quinn's foot, pulling her onto the ground. Liz managed to land a kick to the back of his head, ramming his face into the old asphalt.

Espy's face hit the road surface with a thud and he released Quinn's foot. She scrambled away.

"Stay down!" Liz ordered, but Espy wasn't done. He tried to get to all fours, but reflex demanded he grab his injured face. He could only manage to roll onto his back.

Liz was fast. She drew the .357, but instead of taking aim for a shot, she swung the gun around hard and fast and the butt connected with the side of Espy's thick head. He stayed on the ground this time, on his back with all four limbs splayed. He moaned so Liz knew he was alive.

"Who's the little bitch now, fuckhead?" said Liz, wiping blood from her mouth. She turned to Quinn. "You okay?"

"Fine," answered Quinn, breathing hard. "I'm not the one that took a hit to the face. How's the jaw?"

"Hurts like hell, but I'm okay," Liz answered. She flexed her lower jaw with caution and carefully touched the side of her face with her fingers. "Asshole can hit. Help me get him out of the road."

Liz holstered her gun and they dragged Espy further into the dirt at the side of the pavement.

Hearing something behind them, Quinn and Liz skulked to the side of the road and turned around, looking toward the shed. They watched as someone stepped out of the door and walked down the cinder block steps. It was the skinny asshole. He was looking for Espy, but he went searching in the opposite direction, calling Espy's name. It was the break they needed.

"Quinn, keep an eye on that guy. I'm going to cuff this one. I'll be right behind you."

"Got it," Quinn answered, and took off in the same direction as the skinny guy, staying close to the brush.

Liz took plastic cuffs from her pocket and secured them around Espy's wrists, hands behind him. Then she crouched back in the cover of the brush.

She was about to get her phone out and call Connors, when a third man came out the door of the shed. It was Reese Morgan.

Liz didn't want to believe it, but there he was and this was no official visit. Morgan was in league with the creeps; he knew about the assaults on Elle and Pooki. He may have been behind the attempt to grab Mike. That meant Morgan had been working for Chapin.

Now it made sense why he had been so quick to tell Valentine about seeing Liz leave Chapin's home. He was using her to throw up a smoke screen, a diversion. *Had Morgan killed Chapin,* Liz wondered? If he had, he'd be desperate to cover his tracks and make a run for it.

Liz watched as Morgan ran to catch up with Espy's skinny partner. Liz heard them calling out to each other. They were searching for Espy. Liz wasn't sure where Quinn was, but she hoped she was out of sight.

Her mouth was still bleeding. Liz could taste the blood. Her hand ached from grasping the gun and hitting Espy in the head. Liz looked at him lying there on the ground. Espy was still, eyes closed. Liz didn't want to risk rousing the bastard, but she couldn't resist. She kicked him hard in the stomach. *That's for Elle, you son of a bitch.*

Then she went to find Quinn.

Chapter Seventy-two

"Knockout"

Quinn watched the skinny guy head for the nearest abandoned building. She followed him to the back of the old, wood-sided structure. A tall stack of wooden pallets stood near an outbuilding. She headed in that direction and crouched behind them.

Willing herself to breath silently, she listened. She could hear foot falls and breathing. The sounds were from a distance, but getting closer. So far, he had not advanced near to where she hid. Quinn heard a voice. Listening closely, she realized it was not one voice, but two.

"Where is he, you idiot?!" the second man asked, keeping his volume to a minimum, but trying to sound like the boss.

"I don't know, man! He stepped out for a smoke. I heard something funny and went to check. He's gone, man." The second man had used a louder voice, giving Quinn a better idea of where they were. She estimated about thirty yards away and to the side of the building. Quinn reached under her jacket and took the knife from its sheath.

"The other man spoke again, at the same lowered volume. "Perfect, just perfect!"

"Hey, pal! You can kiss my ass, ah-right? We were in good shape, so shut the hell up, man!" The skinny guy was angry, very angry, but he was focused on finding his friend. Quinn had to hope that gave her an advantage.

"Check this area," said the second man, as he pointed in the direction of the pallets. "And do it quietly! I'm heading around the other side of the building." Quinn could hear the skinny man shift his feet and move toward her hiding place.

She moved quickly, through the tight opening between the stacked pallets and the outbuilding. Quinn watched from the other side as the man walked around the pallets, within seconds of finding her. Quinn heard him say, "Espy? Where the hell are you?"

Quinn came around the other side of the pallets. The man's back was to Quinn. He looked thin, wiry. He was not much larger than Quinn in stature. If she used her blade on him, he would most likely be able to alert his buddy to the assault—unless she killed him. And she was less likely to place a serious wound from this angle.

Making a snap decision, Quinn placed the blade of her knife between her teeth. She tugged to loosen and remove the leather strip which she used to carry her blade close to her body. She wrapped the strap tightly around her right hand, making a fist, as she had been taught to do by her boxing instructor. Quinn put her knife in her left hand, keeping it handy. She tapped the man on the shoulder.

It took a moment for him to realize what was happening. He turned around, clearly not expecting to see a crazed punk with a knife in one hand. His eyes fixed on the knife in Quinn's left hand.

The angle was perfect and she planted a right-hand punch directly on the side of the asshole's nose. Quinn heard a crack. Unless she'd heard the sound of her own bones crunching, she'd broken the guy's nose with that punch. He grabbed his face, too stunned to retaliate.

The pain in her knuckles made Quinn want to scream a stream of swears words, but she managed to resist the impulse. She flexed her right hand and could tell the bones were intact and functioning. Before the asshole could regain his footing and defend himself, Quinn hit him again with a haymaker. She watched his eyes roll back and his legs fold beneath him. Out cold.

Quinn listened and heard the second man coming around the side of the building from the other direction. Quinn crouched silently, squeezing her right hand between her thighs. She bit her lip to keep from crying out in pain.

"Curtiss? Where the hell are you?" the man whispered loudly. He looked around for a moment or two, then to Quinn's surprise, headed back the way he had come, back to the street.

Looking at the asshole named Curtiss lying on the ground, Quinn checked her fist. She was able to move her fingers, but it hurt like hell.

Chapter Seventy-three

"Two Down"

Liz snuck around the side of the building in time to hear Morgan and the skinny guy arguing. She backtracked a few steps and took position around the corner of one of the buildings. Unsure of what she might be expected of her, Liz drew her weapon. Then she watched as Morgan ran back to the road a few minutes later. He was scurrying back in the direction of the shed.

Her first impulse was to call out to Morgan, announce herself, and hope he would see surrender as his best option. But what had happened to Quinn? Where was the other guy? She considered shooting Morgan in the back of his leg to stop him, but decided against it.

Liz heard a vehicle start up a few moments later. She peeked out as Morgan's department rig drove off and Liz went to find Quinn.

She found her near a stack of pallets with the asshole named Curtiss, on the ground knocked out. Liz looked at Quinn, who was flexing the fingers on her right hand in obvious pain.

"Sorry to take so long," Liz explained, catching her breath. "There was a third guy in the shed we hadn't figured on. It was Detective Morgan. He must be in on all of it."

Quinn was surprised, but more concerned with the pain in her knuckles.

"Nice job," Liz told Quinn, looking down at Curtiss. Taking the second pair of cuffs, she secured them on Curtiss' wrists. "This shit head isn't going anywhere either."

Liz took out her phone. Connors picked up on the first ring.

"Connors, I'm with Quinn. She couldn't reach you so she called me. She decided to venture out and look for Mike and the girl. She stumbled across where Chapin's goons, Espy and the other one, were hiding."

"Is she okay?" asked Connors. "I was a little tied up. There's been a lot going on."

"Yes, she's fine. She's been a big help," said Liz, looking at Curtiss' messed-up face. "We are down near the railroad tracks. They were hiding in an old shed by the berry fields. Espy and the other asshole are both down and secured. Listen, Connors, Morgan was here. He's in with them."

"Yeah, we know. That's why I've been busy. Where is Morgan now?"

"He took off just a few minutes ago. He's in his department vehicle. It was weird, Connors. It was like he gave up. He got in his car and drove off."

"He didn't give up. I know where he's going. He's tying up loose ends. You and Quinn sit tight. We're on our way."

Chapter Seventy-four

"Reunion"

Connors arrived with Castillo and two uniformed officers. They searched the shed, but found nothing except the sedan stashed outside. They arrested Espy and Curtiss and hauled them away. The creeps weren't in great shape, but neither was seriously hurt.

With Espy and Curtiss in custody, Connors called Mike, who told him where to find the squat.

Mike and the crew decided to wait outside. They watched as a vehicle's headlights slowly approached. The cattle dog, intent in protecting his friends, was on alert. Sage had him on his lead and did his best to allay the dog's concerns.

The car stopped and two figures emerged. Mike saw Connors first. Then he saw Liz step out of the car and run toward him. Mike moved in her direction, but made it only a step or two before Liz had him in a tight embrace.

"Mike. Oh my god, I'm so sorry. I've been so scared," she said into his ear between kisses. She placed her hands on either side of Mike's face, checking his injuries, and asked, "Are you okay?"

"I'm fine. I've been well cared for, Liz. Don't apologize. None of this is your fault." Mike saw blood and the swelling on Liz's face. He touched her jaw gingerly and asked, "What happened to you?"

"I'll explain later. I'm okay. I didn't know where you were," Liz told Mike through her tears. "Connors couldn't reach me, but I finally talked to Quinn."

A black and white pulled in behind Connors' vehicle and parked at an angle. Out stepped Officer Emmy Castillo and Quinn. Castillo walked over and stood beside Connors. They were both dressed in casual street clothes, their shields displayed in the same fashion, on chains around their necks. Quinn stood nearby.

When Liz and Mike finally let go of each other, Mike and Connors shook hands and hugged, rocking back and forth. Liz hovered, not leaving Mike's side. Connors put his hand out to Sage, who grasped it while holding onto Zeke's lead with the other.

"We spoke earlier," said Connors, introducing himself. "Thanks, man. I owe you."

"We all owe you so much, Sage," said Liz, acknowledging his help.

"I've heard your name before," Sage said to Connors, "on the street. I know your rep. This is Eli," said Sage, making the introduction. "And this," he told Connors slowly, "is Lyric."

Lyric stood next to Eli, his arm around her shoulder. Her expression was fearful and uncertain. Connors looked in Liz's direction, but it was Mike who spoke up.

"Lyric," he said, "This is Liz. She's my friend that you've heard so much about."

The two acknowledged each other cautiously. Lyric wiped her face with her sleeve. She studied Liz for a moment, and then blinked a few times. "You knew my mother," the girl stated, tears in her eyes.

Liz's grief for the girl was overwhelming. She realized that she had not prepared herself for meeting Sara's daughter. Her throat tightened. She could barely draw breath. Her eyes watered, but Liz managed to control her emotions. She was grateful for Mike's grip on her hand.

"Yes," she answered, "I knew her." There was more to say, but it wasn't the time.

Lyric stared at Liz, tears forming. "Where is Richelle? Does she know about my father?"

Liz looked at Connors, who stepped up. "Ms. Isaacs is safe and yes, she knows about your dad," Connors replied. "We will talk about that in a while. Can we go inside and sit down?" he asked Sage.

They followed Sage and Eli into the huge, old building. Lyric sat down and tears overcame her. "I need to call my grandmother," she said. "I want her to know where I am." Zeke sensed that the girl needed comfort and headed to her side as soon as Sage released the lead.

"I've talked with your grandmother several times since I began looking for you," Connors assured her. "She's on her way from Tacoma and should be here soon."

Upon hearing mention of Lyric's grandmother, tears formed in Sage's eyes, his fists raised in a sign of victory. Eli choked up, as well. The two young men were elated. Their efforts on the girl's behalf had succeeded.

Sage looked at Quinn, wiping his eyes. "I guess you found us," he said.

Quinn nodded, checking her knuckles. "It was a team effort," she said, wincing with pain.

"Thanks for your help," Connors told Quinn. "You've been busy," he said. "I was freaked out when I missed your call, but it couldn't be helped. I guess my worry was wasted."

Quinn looked at Connor, amused. "I never take worry for granted, Connors. I'm fine—but it was iffy for a while." Quinn looked from Liz to Connors. She shook her head and said, "I don't think I could be a cop."

Connors looked at Quinn's hand. It had started to swell and bruise. "The officers outside have first aid and ice packs." Quinn nodded and headed outside to find a cold compress for her knuckles.

Leaving Lyric with Castillo, Connors motioned to Mike and Liz to step away and they followed.

"We had every cop within fifty miles looking for Ms. Isaacs and her Nissan," Connors said. "The woman and her car were found at a small warehouse facility in Parkdale. It appears that she was more than an administrative assistant. Isaacs and Chapin were partners in a very lucrative enterprise. He had pulled her out of the ranks years ago."

"Like he had with Sara," said Liz.

"Yes, it probably began that way. We found her loading up cash and valuables including diamonds and other gems. That's the newly-designated currency when you don't want transactions traced. If she'd left it and come back for it later, she may have slipped by us. But she got greedy. We found Rohypnol and other date rape drugs too, which made sense because there was a significant stash of fake IDs. We also found a mass of passports of young women, probably held as insurance for their compliance. They appear to be mostly teenagers.

"They were trafficking young girls?" asked Liz.

"It appears so. It will take time to sort it all out. Richelle managed to destroy a lot of documents and storage devices before we got there. But we found the gun Richelle used to kill Chapin. Apparently, they had a disagreement after your visit this morning."

Liz stared at Connors with disbelief. "Richelle shot Chapin? Why?"

Before he could answer Liz's question, Connors' phone rang. He looked at the screen and said, "Excuse me. I need to take this."

Chapter Seventy-five

"Loose Ends"

Elle had been sleeping most of the time since arriving at Cece's. It may have been due to her recent injuries or just the relief of being off the street. The small home near Lake Sacajawea was comfortable and cozy.

She hadn't been around family for a very long time and Cece knew that Elle needed time to become reacquainted with her. She and Elle spent time talking together. Cece was happy to have Elle home with her and the kid was welcome to stay for as long as she wanted.

Cece's phone alerted her to an incoming call. She checked the time. It was late and she didn't recognize the number.

"Hello," she answered.

"Ms. Havens, this is Detective Morgan in Columbia City. I apologize for the hour. I realize it's late."

"It's fine, Detective. I'm still up. What's the matter? What can I do for you?"

"I'm sorry to inform you of this, but we have reason to believe the men who assaulted Elle have discovered your location."

"Oh, no," answered Cece. Surprise and fear crept into her voice. "How is that possible? We trusted your department to keep her safe. What are we going to do?"

"We need to move her as soon as possible," Morgan informed her.

"But she just got here," said Cece. "And I'm going with her. How soon?"

"Now, Ma'am. We're actually in your driveway. We can't spare any time."

"Alright," she answered, with a sigh. 'Elle is sleeping. I'll let you in. Give me a few minutes, okay?"

"Yes, Ma'am."

Morgan was anxious to end this whole nightmare. He had made a decent amount of cash working for Chapin, but those two idiots had almost done him in.

Morgan had arrived at Chapin's home that morning just as Liz was pulling out of the driveway. He left his car on the street and walked up to the house. Richelle and Chapin were having a hell of an argument. Morgan hid behind a huge cedar near the house and listened to Richelle scream at Chapin that things had become too risky. She insisted they needed to get out, that they had the resources to disappear. Chapin refused to go anywhere without his daughter. Richelle shouted that he needed to listen to her, for once. She tried to convince him that they would find the girl as soon as possible, and she would join them. He had had suspicions, but hearing them argue, it was clear to Morgan that their relationship had been more than business.

Then he heard the gunshot. He didn't know who had been shot until Richelle flew out of the house, jumped in her Nissan, and sped away. It was a miracle that she hadn't seen him.

Morgan went inside to find Chapin lying dead. Espy and Curtiss had been summoned by Chapin and with impeccable timing, had walked in right after Morgan. Espy was stunned at first, but got over it quickly. Curtiss just stood there with a sleazy look on his face, like he enjoyed staring at the dead man.

They heard a dog bark and looked out the front window. A nosy neighbor walking his dog was looking past the gate, up the driveway toward the house. Shit, thought Morgan. Then the man stopped. He glanced up at the house with a concerned expression, and then headed down the block. Morgan told Espy and Curtiss to get lost, find a place to keep out of sight. He would find them later.

Morgan was a police officer at the scene of a crime. Now he just had to behave like one. And he would, right after making an anonymous 911 call. He used his disposable phone for the call, waited a few minutes and called Parkdale Police on his department phone, alerting them of who he was and what he had discovered.

It had all gone well until he met up with the idiots for what Morgan hoped would be the last time. They were hiding in an abandoned shed near the railroad tracks. He paid them enough to keep quiet and was about to leave when Espy went out for a cigarette and disappeared. He and Curtiss searched for him. Then he couldn't find Curtiss either. Screw these dumbasses, Morgan thought. I'm out of here. He'd been listening to the police radio, but so far, there had been no mention of the two wanted men.

The way Morgan figured it, Richelle Isaacs was the only one who could link him to Chapin or the two dumb shits—and Morgan knew a lot about Chapin's trafficking and could implicate Richelle. She had to know that, too, although they both know he couldn't prove any of it. Morgan knew Richelle had argued with Chapin and shot him. Morgan figured she was long gone by now, hoping to save her own ass. The way Morgan saw things, neither of them would cause any problem for the other.

Morgan told himself that all he had done had been to provide private security of sorts. His role had been as the inside man with the department, mopping up the trail leading back to Chapin if things got too muddy. But that was about to change because it came down to this: the kid, Elle, could ID Espy and Curtiss as her attackers. No one knew if Jordan's friend Mike could ID the idiots or not. No one could find him. Maybe he was in a dumpster, robbed and silenced by street people.

Morgan needed to end this, get rid of Elle and her cousin, and disappear. He wasn't happy about the prospect of killing two people, but it had to happen. Morgan had enough money to get out of the country and live comfortably on some beach for a while. His career was in the shitter anyway. Like he told Cece on the phone, he couldn't spare any more time.

He walked up to the front door. He knocked to alert Cece that he was there, thinking that she would let him in. The front door opened and two uniformed officers were standing in tactical gear, weapons drawn.

"Put your hands on your head! Now!" they demanded. There were two officers in the same gear behind him. Morgan wasn't about to turn to look because he heard their boots hit the front walk.

"Wait, wait! I'm on the job, I'm a cop!" Morgan yelled to them, his hands above his head.

"We know who you are," an officer said, as he put cuffs on Morgan. "If I were you, I'd shut the hell up." Within seconds, Morgan was cuffed, checked for weapons, and sitting in the back of a black and white.

The officer in charge at the scene was named Daniels, and he was with the Longview City Police. Daniels pulled out his phone and called Connors.

"This is Daniels, Sir. Scene secured. Suspect is in custody. Your witness and her guardian are safe. Good call. He came straight here."

"Way to go, Daniels. Thanks, and thank your team." Connors ended the call from Daniels and told the others, "We got him."

Chapter Seventy-six

"Aftermath"

Connors knew that Elle was in danger. After Valentine linked Morgan to the two wanted men, Connors guessed that Morgan would head up the freeway to Longview and attempt to silence the kid.

Radio communications to Morgan were halted, except for mundane chatter, making him believe he hadn't been caught out as a dirty cop. Connors knew that his team wouldn't make it there in time. The officers in Longview had pulled off the operation without a hitch and Connors and the rest of the cops in Columbia City were in their debt.

After Connors and the others arrived at the squat, it was hours before everyone finally left and Eli and Sage were, once again, alone and in the peace of their small, borrowed corner of the world. Connors had asked them both, more than once, what they needed, wanted, longed for—but the two men insisted they were in need of nothing. It was enough for them that Pooki's killer had been caught and that Lyric was safe.

Mike and Liz returned to the squat two days later, stocked with supplies as a gesture of thanks. They found the place abandoned, empty—not a trace of Eli, Sage or Zeke, the cattle dog. Mike was not surprised, but he was still devastated.

That evening, Liz and Mike ventured out to Callahan's for burgers and brews. Connors and Castillo met them there. After four double burgers with extra cheese and bacon, fries and several ales, the subject of Reese Morgan entered the conversation.

"Were you at all suspicious, Connors? Did he ever slip up and show his hand?" asked Liz.

"I thought it odd that he was so quick to tell Valentine that he's seen you at Chapin's. But Valentine shared with Miller that it wasn't the dog-walking neighbor who called 911," said Connors. "After they got the recording of the call, they confirmed it was Morgan. Morgan saw you leave the scene and it was too damned convenient. He had to use that to throw suspicion your way."

"It's hard for me to believe that Richelle shot Chapin," said Liz. "I'm still shocked, to be honest. When did you suspect her?"

"That was Valentine, too. He figured that either Morgan or Richelle had shot Chapin. It seemed a lot more likely to be Richelle after determining they had been, not only business partners, but lovers. Her prints were found on the gun found at the Parkdale warehouse and gunshot residue was found on Richelle's clothes and hands. Faced with that evidence, she turned pale, but screamed 'lawyer' anyway. You know what they say about murder; it's usually either love or money. This time it was both."

Liz rubbed her forehead, thinking about Chapin and the visit she had paid him the morning he died.

"I knew he was a soulless SOB—but to leave me hanging for all those years, making me think Pruitt and I were responsible for Sara's death." Liz shook her head, "He played me. He was the one that killed her and wanted me to feel that I'd abandoned her. He wanted everyone to think a cop had shot her during the raid."

"Don't think about it anymore, Liz," said Mike, with Connors and Castillo nodding in agreement. "Sara's death was never your fault—then, or now. You may have been played, but so were a lot of people."

Liz looked at the faces around her, then closed her eyes, tipped her head back, and took a deep breath. "Lyric overheard everything—her father and Espy discussing her mother's murder. What a terrible thing for a kid to hear."

"It will be rough for her, but she's strong," said Mike. "She managed to stay alive on the street, knowing the value of a crew, of friends. Quinn says that's how she survived."

"Did Lyric know about her father and Richelle?" asked Liz. "Did she know how they made their money?"

It was Connors who answered. "Hard to tell. She claims she didn't know they were involved, but she's a smart girl. And I think she's dealing with the fact that her father and Richelle, the people she was closest to, were both killers. We don't have any indication that she was aware of the trafficking. Lyric seemed genuinely surprised and disgusted by the idea. But who knows?"

Chapter Seventy-seven

"No Apologies"

Myers, the chief medical examiner, had begun his career in public service at around the same time Liz had become a cop. And now, the pathologist was responsible for confirming that Pooki's death was the result of a criminal act of assault. Myers wanted to speak with Liz, but under the circumstances, she could only guess why. Knowing how Myers' brain worked, he may fabricate some question for her about Pooki's death, however, Liz suspected that Myers wanted to gloat over the fact that her past had caught up with her.

She remembered what had transpired between her and Myers in the very morgue where he was now the chief. She remembered it as if it was yesterday. If security had not been present to intervene, the outcome could have been much worse, far beyond two colleagues merely hating each other.

Liz walked into the offices of the staff at the Medical Examiner's office and approached the doorway to Myers' office. She saw the pathologist sitting at his desk. He was focused on paperwork, giving her the chance to catch him by surprise.

"You wanted to see me, Myers?" Liz asked clearly and directly, trying to keep her dislike of the man at bay.

Hearing her words, Myers looked up, meeting Liz's eye, but only for a moment. It was evident she had caught him unaware, but when he realized who it was that had approached him, he looked away as if Liz's presence was of no significance.

"Lieutenant," said Myers, as he returned the cap to the fountain pen in his hand. "A phone call from you would have sufficed."

"It's fine, Myers," Liz responded with contempt, "can we just get on with it. It's been a hell of a week. What do you want?"

"I want to check in with you about the teenager from the streets who was attacked and killed. My office was asked to confirm that her death was directly caused by the injuries she sustained." Myers appeared to check his notes. "There's no question about it, of course, and sadly, we have no way to identify her. Reports place you at the emergency room when the two teens were treated. Your visit wasn't official, but I wonder if you have anything to add."

Liz studied Myers for a moment, considering his inquiry. "I have nothing to add," she told him, shaking her head, "except that it's very sad that the kid died the way she did, but it's also sad that she was living the way she was."

Myers nodded at Liz's words, but he wasn't finished. "Also, I wanted to speak with you because in reading through the reports, I've learned that the accused killer and his accomplice are connected to the Sara Mallory case."

Liz was stunned for a moment, hearing Myers call Sara by name. He remembered her too, it seemed. *But*, thought Liz, *of course he did.*

"Yes, that's correct. It had to do with Killian and people who worked for him. Frank Pruitt was involved. So was I, but then you know that," Liz reminded Myers. "Why? After all this time, why in hell do you care?"

"Because I've learned, Lieutenant, that you knew Ms. Mallory prior to her involvement with the department." Myers' tone was beyond scolding. He was incensed, demanding an explanation. "For the life of me, I can't understand why you never told me that you had been acquainted with her, that you knew her."

"At the time, I just couldn't." Liz's words stumbled from her. "I was unable to explain it then. I'm not sure I'm any more capable now."

"You knew the woman outside of your job as a police officer. That detail was important information, considering how you conducted yourself that night, here in this very morgue."

"Listen to me, Myers. You accused me of causing Sara's death! I was already reeling with the impact of what had happened. I was young and new to the job. I don't mean that as an excuse. It sounds lame, but I really didn't know what I was doing."

"I was new to my job, as well!" shouted Myers. "I saw my role, in part, to provide sensitivity to the deceased. I still do. You were trying to pay your respects. If I'd known you better, I might have suspected other reasons for your reaction to her death. But I'm not a mind reader, Lieutenant. Not then, not now."

"I wanted to tell her I was sorry." Liz felt tears stinging her eyes as she struggled to keep her voice clear. She would not, could not cry in front of Myers. It was unfathomable. Liz turned to face the closed office door.

"But I had no authorization to allow what you were asking of me. You weren't a family member. Paying your respects wouldn't have been helpful."

"Damn it, Myers!" Liz shouted as she pounded her fist into the door." It would have been helpful to me! I needed the opportunity to do that. I needed to do it then and even more so now! Sara had a daughter, Myers, a daughter who found out how her mother died! I'm not able to tell her that I told her mother...that I told Sara...how sorry I was that she died. You took that from me!"

"You attacked me for not allowing you access to Ms. Mallory's remains! Lieutenant, you were crazed that evening. I thought you were intoxicated or worse, dealing with the hardest thing the job could have asked of you—the taking of a life."

"That wasn't what happened!" Liz yelled.

"But you refused to tell me otherwise," said Myers. "That's all you had to do. And you didn't tell me that you knew her."

"That was my business," said Liz, holding her ground. "I was doing the best I could."

"Things have come full circle, Lieutenant. Don't you think it's time that you and I resolve this animosity? Had I been aware of your feelings of responsibility for the death of someone you knew, I would have been more careful about spouting accusations. I hope you believe that."

"I have to get out of here, Myers. This is too much for me right now. I do regret being so out of control. And I regret throwing you against the wall that night. I don't blame you for shoving me back. That is all I can say right now."

Liz threw open the door to Myers' office. She headed down the corridor and out of the building. She made it to her car before her emotions overtook her. The exchange had been as close to a conversation about their differences as she and Myers would ever have. There were no apologies, but they both acknowledged mistakes.

Chapter Seventy-eight

"Grief and Mourning"

Liz spent an afternoon with Lyric and her grandmother, Laura, before the two of them headed to Laura's home in Tacoma. Lyric had decided that she no longer needed to use the street name. She wanted to be called Kyrie again, the name that her mother had given her.

Sara Mallory was buried in a cemetery north of the city. If Chapin had known or cared where Sara had been laid to rest, he had never mentioned it to his daughter. Laura and Kyrie wanted to pay their respects and they asked Liz to go with them.

They arrived at the cemetery with offerings of flowers and found Sara's grave. The small headstone was inscribed with her name, Sara Elaine Mallory, and the dates of her birth and death. She'd been twenty-three years old.

They placed the flowers on Sara's grave and Kyrie embraced her grandmother. They stood together, looking at the bouquets and the headstone. Liz stood close by. Laura asked Kyrie if she would mind if she returned to the car, that she felt chilled. Since it wasn't cool out, Liz guessed that Laura wanted to give Kyrie time alone with Liz.

Liz offered to stay with her and the girl nodded her assent. Laura kissed Kyrie's cheek and told her to take all the time she wanted. They sat together on a nearby bench. Liz wasn't sure if the girl wanted to talk or sit in silence, but she would follow Kyrie's lead.

"I wonder why my mother didn't tell you about me."

"I don't know the answer to that. My guess is that she knew you were safe and happy and that's what mattered most."

"I thought I was safe with my father, with Richelle." Kyrie paused, thinking. Liz could only imagine what thoughts had been going through the girl's head after what she had learned. "She was so nice to me, I thought Richelle cared about me."

Liz sighed. "I'm not defending her or your father, but I don't believe either of them ever intended to hurt you, Kyrie."

They sat in silence for a few minutes, taking in the peaceful surroundings until Kyrie said, "I wonder how different my life would be if my mother was here."

"There's no way for you to know. But you can imagine what it might be like, what she might be like. You'll keep her with you in your thoughts."

"I still can't believe my father...did what he did. I'll never forgive him."

"I would understand if you don't. That knowledge is a lot to live with. I'm no authority, but give yourself time. And you and your grandmother will have each other."

"Yeah," she said, but she didn't sound convinced. "Someday, I'll write about how I feel. I'd like to write another song for my mother. Not about how she died, but about her. A tribute. That might help me."

"I think it would," Liz said. She put her arm around Kyrie, her heart breaking for the girl. "That would be beautiful, Kyrie," Liz told her. "I hope you'll share it with me."

Chapter Seventy-nine

"No Regrets"

Liz had a conversation with Miller over the phone the following morning. She sat on her couch, drinking coffee, her precious cats purring nearby.

"First things first," said Miller. "We recovered the weapon Chapin used to kill Sara Mallory. It was in a safe in his home. And I have reason to believe that Chapin had Frank Pruitt in his pocket. I don't know what he was holding over Pruitt's head, but it was enough to make him alter and hide records."

"Do you think Sara might be alive today, and watching her daughter grow up if Frank had been an honest cop?"

"Maybe, but she still had Gabriel Chapin in her life and he's the one who killed her. Frank was a loser, but we can't blame him for that."

Liz said nothing. She wasn't at all sure if she believed that, but at some point, she needed to let it go.

"Also, the department legal team met with Mr. Connelly yesterday. If a civil suit is pursued on behalf of Chapin's estate, and it's not likely, it will look much different. Chapin's death and the uncovered evidence surrounding the death of Ms. Mallory have cast a different light on things. There were questionable points with regard to Frank Pruitt, but they have nothing to do with you, so you are no longer named as a responsible party."

"That's a relief, Sir. I assumed as much, but I'm glad to hear you confirm it," said Liz.

Miller was quiet for a moment, and then he said, “I’d like to know how you’re doing, Lieutenant.”

“I’m okay,” Liz said, thinking to herself that she really was doing okay. “Mike’s fine and Sara’s daughter was found safe and sound, and she’s with her grandmother. Elle is off the street and has a home. Espy and Curtiss will be punished for their crimes, and neither Richelle Isaacs or Reese Morgan will see the light of day outside of prison for a hell of a long time.”

“Oh, yes, you are right about that,” agreed Miller. “What I’m really asking about are your thoughts regarding Sara Mallory and how she died.”

“It’s all very sad,” said Liz. “I feel sadness for Sara and for her daughter; and for her mother too.”

“And Gabriel Chapin?”

“Honestly, I don’t feel sorrow for him, not at all,” Liz told Miller. “When I went to Chapin’s house the morning he died, I did threaten him. The man was shot and killed, but I won’t mourn for him.”

“And we learned that he hadn’t cleaned up his act. He was still operating illegally. He had just gone further under the radar,” said Miller. “The situation with Richelle Isaacs was a powder keg waiting for a spark. At least, the daughter wasn’t there when it blew.”

“Yes, that true.”

“And I heard you had a conversation with Dr, Myers in the M.E.’s office. That was certainly a long time coming. I was pleased to hear it.”

“I suppose it was time, Sir. All things considered.” Liz hesitated. She didn’t want to talk anymore about Myers, but there was something else she wanted to share with Miller. It was hard to begin.

"I've been talking with Ty Phillips. You remember Ty, don't you, Sir?"

"Of course, I do."

"Ty understands some of what I've been dealing with. Problems from the past, you know. Guilt, regret, grief."

"Mr. Phillips knows a lot about those subjects," said Miller.

"Yes, he does. Ty's theory is that when we keep issues from the past hidden away, they have a way of coming back and making us deal with them. Anyway, talking helps. The memories aren't all pleasant, but I think I'll be able to live with them."

"Lieutenant, if you can do that, I'd say you're doing fine."

"Thank you, Sir. So would I."

THE END

Acknowledgements

Sincere thanks are in order to a few wonderful people who helped with the writing, formatting, design of this novel. Thanks to Savannah Foley for her honest insights, to Rey at Reyzart.com for his patient endurance of my ideas on cover designs for the trilogy, and to Matt Love, my editor, for seeing me through each draft and encouraging me to write the best story possible. Finally, huge thanks to Dave Conine for tech support from start to finish, listening as I read endless passages aloud, and for not once screaming ENOUGH!

Writing this novel was an adventure, more of an adventure than I could have anticipated. Research into the lives of street kids was an eye-opener considering the challenges they overcome to survive. For more information about homeless youth, contact Covenant House or visit www.covenanthouse.org or search for programs in your area that support at-risk youth.

Turn the page to read the first chapter of

Runaway, Book One in the City Streets Trilogy.

Chapter 1 "Runaway"

When the shelter residents returned from searching for housing, work, help, whatever—they were told the girl was dead. But when asked by the investigators, no one had noticed whether she was not at breakfast, nor could they remember if the girl had been around the night before. No one noticed. It was the story of her life, as they say. No one noticed whether she was around unless it was some degenerate Fagin-like creep who saw her as a commodity. But they noticed her now, now that she was dead. The shelter where she was staying was called Avalon, a temporary shelter for street folks who needed a place to stay.

Mid-November was wet from the incessant rain and cold at night. Avalon was busy. Families with children or single women can stay at Avalon for thirty days. Then they have to move on—to permanent housing, to in-patient treatment, to transitional housing, to another shelter, back with relations or friends, or back on the street. Avalon has a dorm, one large room, known as The Suite. The space is made available for up to four women at a time. The unnoticed girl had a bed in The Suite and had been there three days before she was found dead in the alley. Mark Twain was quoted to say that the rumors of his death were greatly exaggerated. Not so with the girl. She was gone. Had the girl been able, she would have told them what happened, how it felt. She would have told them that dying was less painful than many things she had encountered in her young life. At least her death had been quick and of that she was grateful.

The first one to notice the girl in the alley was Ty. A decent sort, Ty returned from the Gulf War a different guy from the one sent. Ty never blamed anyone else for his situation. He had simply heard, seen, and smelled more than anyone should have to in this lifetime and he was haunted by what he'd been through. He tried to work, tried to relate to people, tried to quell the nightmares, but the memories defeated him and he toppled down like one of Saddam's statues. Ty was a regular at Brooks House, the men's shelter down the street. Actually, Ty was a fixture there. And because he was a decent guy and he didn't have a temper, the staff liked him.

Ty walked from the bus stop to Avalon every Sunday at five p.m. because Mike worked the Sunday evening shift. Ty looked forward to seeing Mike on Sundays. Mike treated him like a man instead of some wasted shell person. Mike didn't divert his eyes when Ty looked him in the face and he greeted him when he saw Ty approach. Days could go by on the street without that happening. Ty and Mike would have a cup of coffee and visit like old friends.

But on this Sunday, as Ty walked past the alley, he smelled it. He knew what it was. For a few seconds he was there in the smoke and the stink and the fire. He made himself approach the lump at the side of the alley entrance and saw that it was the girl. *What was her name? Had he ever heard her name?* he asked himself. He must have. Ty took in the ugly gash at the side of her head. It was just above her right ear but more to the front. Something heavy had slammed into the side of her head, cleaving skin, tissue, and part of the skull. There was a lot of blood producing the sour smell that had brought Ty to her. The blow or blows had missed her open right eye. The girl stared into hell without seeing or caring that she had arrived.

Two others came along minutes after Ty. It was Marco and Genevieve, known as the seniors. Marco spoke with an accent although he had been in the States forty years. Having never learned to read and write and with no driver's license or Social Security number, Marco was like a ghost in that he was only seen in shadows. Marco's friend, Genevieve had been married at one time with a family. She had four children with her husband and "functioned well" until the voices started to dictate how to raise those children. At some point, Gen's path crossed with Marco's. Marco didn't mind that Genevieve heard voices because she helped him keep a stash of meds handy for his back pain. The arrangement worked for Genevieve, as well. Marco kept the street predators at bay and reminded Genevieve to eat.

Marco and Gen had followed Ty from the bus stop. When they saw him enter the alley, they followed like lemmings. Ty called to Marco, "Hey man, go get Mike. Now, man, get Mike." Ty didn't consider whether Marco knew who Mike was or if he'd know where to find him. Marco and Gen had been on the streets long enough and folks on the street knew that Mike was the guy at Avalon.

The pair stopped short of approaching the girl. *Too intense, too much,* they thought. Marco's back hurt since he hadn't had a pill since mid-day. Marco ambled toward the alley entrance and yelled for someone to get Mike. Gen was looking but not really looking. *Don't do it,* she told herself. They both took cues from Ty's demeanor. Marco and Gen could tell a hard rain had fallen. The Fates told them in their souls to be reverent because a fellow traveler had met with a bad end. Death, they knew, even of a disenfranchised soul, was sacrosanct.

Marco yelled again for Mike while heading down the alley toward Avalon. Residents appeared and wandered into the alley, stopping short when they realized that Ty had discovered tragedy. Soon, the buzz filtered to the shelter. Mike came running into the alley with cell phone in hand. "Who is it, Ty? Is it bad?" he asked.

"Yeah, man. It's the girl," Ty answered, then paused before adding, "and she's dead. What's her name, Mike?"

Mike dialed 911 and waited for dispatch to pick up. "Hell, Ty, I don't remember. I'll have to check her intake card." By then an emergency dispatcher was on the line. "Yeah, this is Mike Dwyer at Avalon. We found one of our female residents lying in the back alley." Mike paused to listen to the emergency dispatcher. "No, there's no doubt." Mike listened again, said, "Yeah...I know."

Don't miss out!

Visit the website below and you can sign up to receive emails whenever Susanne Perry publishes a new book. There's no charge and no obligation.

https://books2read.com/r/B-A-TQXL-JPTMB

BOOKS 2 READ

Connecting independent readers to independent writers.

About the Author

Susanne Perry is the author of the City Streets Trilogy, a series of crime mysteries set in a fictional urban area in southwest Washington. Previous to writing novels, Perry worked with public programs serving children and families. Future writing projects include short stories, children's books, and of course, mysteries. A voracious reader of who-done-its and historical fiction, Perry resides in Arizona and Washington.

www.ingramcontent.com/pod-product-compliance
Ingram Content Group UK Ltd.
Pitfield, Milton Keynes, MK11 3LW, UK
UKHW042004190726
13854UKWH00005B/2164